The Regency Season

BLACKMAILED BRIDES

SARAH MALLORY

MILLS & BOON

Published in Great Britain 2017
By Mills & Boon, an imprint of HarperCollins*Publishers*
1 London Bridge Street, London, SE1 9GF

THE REGENCY SEASON: BLACKMAILED BRIDES © 2017
Harlequin Books S.A.

The Scarlet Gown © 2014 Sarah Mallory
Lady Beneath the Veil © 2014 Sarah Mallory

ISBN: 978-0-263-93148-8

52-1017

Our policy is to use papers that are natural, renewable and recyclable products and made from wood grown in sustainable forests.
The logging and manufacturing processes conform to the legal environmental regulations of the country of origin.

Printed and bound by
CPI Group (UK) Ltd, Croydon, CR0 4YY

THE SCARLET GOWN

The Regency Season

DANGEROUS DUKES

August 2017

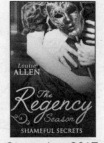

SHAMEFUL SECRETS

September 2017

BLACKMAILED BRIDES

October 2017

RUINED REPUTATIONS

November 2017

GENTLEMAN ROGUES

December 2017

PASSIONATE PROMISES

January 2018

SCANDALOUS AWAKENING

February 2018

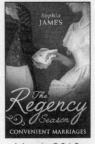

CONVENIENT MARRIAGES

March 2018

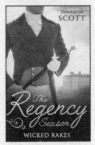

WICKED RAKES

April 2018

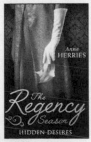

HIDDEN DESIRES

May 2018

FORBIDDEN PLEASURES

June 2018

DECADENT DUKES

July 2018

To Cecilia and David, thank you for preserving the moor that inspired a large part of this story!

Sarah Mallory was born in Bristol, and now lives in an old farmhouse on the edge of the Pennines with her husband and family. She left grammar school at sixteen to work in companies as varied as stockbrokers, marine engineers, insurance brokers, biscuit manufacturers and even a quarrying company. Her first book was published shortly after the birth of her daughter. She has published more than a dozen books under the pen-name of Melinda Hammond, winning the Reviewers' Choice Award from www.singletitles. com for Dance for a Diamond and the Historical Novel Society's Editors' Choice for Gentlemen in Question. As Sarah Mallory she is the winner of the Romantic Novelists' Association's RONA Rose® Award for 2012 and 2013 for *The Dangerous Lord Darrington* and *Beneath the Major's Scars*.

Chapter One

Mrs Killinghurst's register office was well known as the saviour of many a gently bred young lady who had fallen upon hard times and needed to earn a living. Mrs Killinghurst specialised in finding employment for such young ladies as companions, governesses or even seamstresses, depending upon their accomplishments. Her offices occupied a suite of rooms above a hatter's shop in Bond Street, and young ladies wishful of finding employment could slip along the narrow alley beside the shop and through the freshly painted doorway with its discreet brass plate.

Miss Lucy Halbrook had already made one visit to Mrs Killinghurst's establishment and now, a fortnight later, she was returning to the office, as instructed by the proprietress herself, with high hopes of obtaining the gainful employment she so desperately needed. When her father had died twelve months ago Lucy had been prepared for life to change for herself and Mama, but it was only after the funeral that Lucy discovered just how poor they really were. They had been taken in by Mrs Halbrook's invalid sister, but Lucy soon realised that although Mama had found a niche as nurse-companion to

Mrs Edgeworth, she herself was constantly harassed by Mr Edgeworth. Lucy had always thought it a little odd that the female servants in her aunt's house were all rather mature, but within days of moving in she knew the reason for it. She had so far managed to evade her uncle's lascivious attentions but she must find somewhere else to live, and soon. If she was honest with herself, she also wanted a little more independence. Her father's death had been painful, but her mother's sudden revelation that they were penniless had been even harder to bear. They had never been rich, and it was not just their poverty, but the knowledge that Mama had kept the situation from her. And what of her father, a man she had adored? To find that he was not the hero she had thought him was a severe blow. If only they had told her. After all, it was not as if she was a child. Surely they could have trusted her with the truth when she reached her majority, three years ago? She might even have been able to help. By finding employment, for example, as she was doing now.

Lucy hurried along New Bond Street, dodging between the crowds of fashionable ladies and gentlemen who were taking advantage of the mild spring weather to stroll along, giving more attention to the shop windows than to where they were going. At last she reached the hatter's and stepped quickly into the alley. It was darker than she had expected and it took her a moment to realise this was because someone was standing at the far end, blocking the light.

Her step faltered, but she pressed on. After all, Mrs Killinghurst was expecting her and she was not to be put off. She might wish she had worn a veil, but since there was no help for it, Lucy continued towards the door. The man—for it was undoubtedly a man—had apparently just emerged from Mrs Killinghurst's door, so he was either looking for work or for someone to employ. The latter, she thought as her eyes grew accustomed to the shadows and she took in at a glance his coat of blue superfine, buckskin breeches and black boots. In fact, he might well have purchased his coat from Mr Weston's hallowed portals in nearby Old Bond Street, for it fitted him perfectly with never a wrinkle to mar its elegance. His boots, too, shone with a smooth, highly polished gloss. The buckskins may well have been similarly free of creases, but Lucy had felt a frisson of something she did not quite understand when she had first observed the man and now she dared not let her eyes dwell on those muscular limbs.

Instead, she kept her head up, chin defiantly raised. She would not stare at the ground like some humble, subservient creature. Consequently she could not avoid at least one quick glance at the man's face. It was rugged rather than handsome, black-browed and with a deep cleft in his chin. There was a latent strength about him that sat oddly with his fashionable dress—clearly he was no Bond Street Beau. Whatever his status, Lucy's main concern was that he was blocking her way. His curly-brimmed hat almost brushed the roof of the alley and his broad shoulders filled the narrow space.

She observed all this in the time it took her to cover the short distance between them, and it struck her in the same instant that he was the most solid and immovable object she had ever encountered. She stopped, but refused to be intimidated and returned his direct gaze with a steady look. His grey eyes were curiously compelling and again she felt that tremor run through her. An odd, unfamiliar mixture of excitement and attraction that had her wanting to know more about this man and at the same time to turn around and run for her life.

Lucy quelled such feelings immediately. She was not the sort to run away from a problem—not that there had ever been many problems in her life until now. She realised a little sadly that her parents had protected her from the harsher realities of life. Perhaps a little too much. But all that was at an end. She must now stand up for herself and that meant not being intimidated by this solid wall of man standing in her way. She wondered if she was going to have to ask him to move, but at that moment he stepped back, pushing the door open with one hand.

Silently, Lucy sailed past him and up the stairs. She had the uncomfortable sensation that he was watching her ascent, for her spine tingled uncomfortably, but when she reached the landing and looked back there was no one below and the door was firmly shut.

An iron-haired woman was guarding the small reception room at the top of the stairs. She showed Lucy into Mrs Killinghurst's office, invited her to remove her cloak and bonnet and sit down, then she shut the door upon her. Left alone, Lucy folded her cloak neatly and laid it on a chair then carefully placed her bonnet on top. There was no mirror in the room, so she could only put her hands up to make sure her soft brown hair was still neatly confined in a knot at the back of her head. She had put on the same high-necked gown she had worn for her first interview, a plain closed robe of pewter-coloured wool, and hoped she portrayed the modest, unassuming character that an employer would be looking for.

After a few moments alone, Lucy became prey to uncertainty. She thought over her previous visit, wondering if she had perhaps mistaken the day.

No, she had been sitting on this very chair, facing

Mrs Killinghurst across the desk, exactly two weeks ago. Lucy had been encouraged by the lady's businesslike air, and once she had explained her circumstances and answered a number of searching questions, the lady had risen and disappeared through a door at the back of the room. Some personal inner sanctum, thought Lucy, for she had glimpsed the carved and gilded edge of a picture frame. This had surprised her a little, for the walls of the office and the reception room were singularly bare of ornament, and Lucy had been puzzling over this when Mrs Killinghurst had returned, saying that, yes, she did think there was a suitable position for Lucy.

'It is rather an unusual position but perfectly respectable, I assure you, and the remuneration is extremely generous, considering that it is only a temporary position. You will only be required for a short period—part of May and the whole of June. However, I need to ascertain from my client—that is—you will need to come back. Shall we say two weeks from today, at eleven o'clock?'

Lucy had agreed immediately. Another two weeks in her uncle's house would be a trial, but she would manage, somehow. The date and time of the next meeting had been repeated and confirmed, Lucy remembered, with Mrs Killinghurst promising that she would then be in a position to explain the post in detail. Lucy had thanked her and prepared to leave, but now she recalled that at that point the proprietress had shown a diffidence that had not been apparent throughout the rest of their meeting.

'Good day to you, Miss Halbrook and—my dear, should you find another post in the meantime I hope you will feel free to take it. A little note to me explaining the situation will suffice...'

Lucy had looked at her in surprise.

'I assure you, Mrs Killinghurst, I am more than content to wait two weeks, unless perhaps you think there is some doubt about my suitability for the post you have in mind?'

'Oh, no, no, I think you are eminently suitable.' Thinking back, Lucy remembered the slightly anxious timbre of the lady's voice, as if she regretted the circumstance. She had looked a little uncomfortable as she continued, 'Of course, this post is by no means guaranteed, and if something else should come up I would be failing you if I did not advise you to accept it.'

'But you do not have anything else to offer me?'

'Well, no, not at present.'

Lucy had thought it an odd way to go about business, suggesting that she should look elsewhere for employment, but she guessed it was some sort of a test of her loyalty, and she had been quick to reassure Mrs Killinghurst that she would return in two weeks' time at the agreed hour.

'And here I am,' she announced to the empty room. 'Ready and waiting to know my fate.'

The rattle of the doorknob made her jump, and she wondered if someone had been listening, for at that moment the door to the inner sanctum opened, and Mrs Killinghurst came in, smiling and apologising for keeping Lucy waiting. She went to her desk and in her haste left the door slightly ajar.

'Now then, Miss Halbrook, where were we?' She sat down, pulling a sheaf of papers towards her. 'Ah, yes. The character references I have received for you are excellent. As I mentioned when we last met, this is an unusual post. My client is looking for an accomplished young lady of gentle birth to spend some time at his house in the north.'

A movement from Lucy caused the lady to pause.

'Excuse me, ma'am, but your client is a married gentleman, I assume?'

Mrs Killinghurst shook her head.

'He is a widower, but quite respectable,' she added quickly, a little too hastily perhaps.

Lucy felt her heart sinking. She decided she must speak frankly.

'Mrs Killinghurst, is—is there anything, ah, *questionable* about this particular post?'

'Oh, no, no, nothing like that! My client assures me that a chaperone will be provided, and you will be treated with the utmost respect during your stay. You are to live at the house, as his guest. And the remuneration is extremely generous.'

She mentioned a sum that made Lucy's eyebrows fly up.

'But I do not understand. Your, ah, client wishes to *pay* me to be a guest in his house?'

'Yes.'

'But, why?'

Mrs Killinghurst began to straighten the papers on her desk.

'I believe he wishes you to be there as his hostess.'

Lucy's disappointment was searing. For the past two weeks she had been looking forward to this meeting, speculating about the 'lucrative post' that Mrs Killinghurst had in mind. A governess, perhaps, or companion to some elderly and infirm lady, or even a gentleman. The temporary nature of the post had indicated that perhaps she was being engaged to make someone's last months on this earth as comfortable as possible. Now she realised that her daydreams and speculation had been wildly inaccurate and naive. An unmarried man—even a widower— would not hire a hostess for any respectable purpose.

Thoughts of Uncle Edgeworth and his wandering hands came to her mind.

She rose, saying coldly, 'I am very sorry, Mrs Killinghurst, but this is not the kind of employment I envisaged. If you had only told me a little more about this post two weeks ago we might have saved ourselves a great deal of inconvenience.'

She had already turned to leave when she was halted by the sound of a deep, male voice behind her.

'Perhaps, Mrs Killinghurst, you would allow me to explain to the young lady?'

Lucy whipped around. Standing in the doorway to the inner sanctum was the man she had seen below.

His solid form had filled the alleyway, but here in this small office he looked even more imposing. Mrs Killinghurst rose from her seat, but she barely reached his shoulder and only emphasised the man's size. He had removed his hat to display his black hair, cut ruthlessly short, and his impassive countenance did nothing to dispel Lucy's first impression of a stern, unyielding character.

She was aware of the latent power of the man. It was apparent in every line of his body, from the rough-hewn countenance, through those broad shoulders to his feet, planted firmly, slightly apart, as if he was ready to take on the world.

Ready to pounce on her. This man was dangerous, she was convinced of it, but some tiny, treacherous part of her found that danger very attractive.

Alarmed by her own reaction Lucy stepped back, one hand behind her feeling for the door handle.

'I really do not think there is any need—'

'Oh, but there is,' he said. 'You've waited two weeks to learn about this position; it would be a pity if you were to leave now without knowing just what it entailed, don't you think?' He spoke quietly, but with a natural authority that brooked no argument and when he invited her to return to her seat, Lucy found herself complying.

He indicated to Mrs Killinghurst that she should sit down and while the lady was settling herself Lucy made a mental note that if this stranger should try to get between her and the door to the reception area she would flee, however foolish and cowardly that might appear. Thankfully, though, the gentleman contented himself with moving to one side of the room where both ladies could see him. He nodded to Mrs Killinghurst.

'Perhaps, ma'am, you would be good enough to introduce me.'

'Yes, yes, of course. Miss Halbrook, this is Lord Adversane, my client.'

He bowed to Lucy, who was surprised at the elegance with which he performed this courtesy. For such a large man he had the lithe grace of a natural athlete. She inclined her head in acknowledgement, but remained silent, waiting to hear what he had to say.

'Mrs Killinghurst has told you that I am in need of your services for my house in Yorkshire,' he began. 'Adversane is the largest estate and the most prominent house in the area. Since the death of my wife, I have lived there very quietly, but you will appreciate that this has had an adverse effect upon the neighbourhood since I am not employing so many staff, nor is the housekeeper ordering so much from the local tradesmen. I think it is time to open up the house again and invite guests—family and friends—to join me there. However, I require a hostess.'

Lucy nodded. 'I understand that, my lord, but surely there is some lady within your family who would be more than willing to fulfil that role.'

A sardonic gleam lit his eyes.

'Oh, yes, dozens of 'em!'

'Then I do not see—'

'The thing is,' he interrupted her ruthlessly, 'I have been a widower for nigh on two years now and my family and friends are all determined I should be much happier if I were to marry again. To this end they are constantly badgering me to find a wife.' He paused for a moment. 'What I am looking for, Miss Halbrook, is not only a hostess, but a fiancée.'

Lucy knew she was staring at him. She also knew that her mouth was open, but it was some moments before she could command her muscles to work so that she could close it. Lord Adversane continued as if he had said nothing out of the ordinary.

'I have invited a number of guests to stay at Adversane for the summer and I need a young woman to pose as my future wife. She must have all the accomplishments of a young lady of good family and her reputation must be above reproach. From everything Mrs Killinghurst has told me, you are perfectly suited to fulfil this role.'

'Thank you,' Lucy responded with a touch of asperity. 'Let me make sure I understand you. You wish to enact this…this charade to stop everyone, er, *badgering* you?'

'Exactly.'

'If you will forgive me for saying so, my lord, from the little I have seen of you I cannot believe that you would allow *anyone* to badger you!'

Ralph regarded the little figure before him and felt a stir of appreciation. The chit was dressed in a dowdy grey gown, demure as a nun, yet she was not afraid to voice her opinion or to meet his eyes with a challenging sparkle in her own. A smile tugged at the corners of his mouth.

'Ah, but then, you do not know my family.' This was

unanswerable, but clearly did not reassure the girl. He could tell she was seeking the words to decline gracefully and take her leave, so he added, 'I realise this is not the post you were expecting to be offered, Miss Halbrook, but I have considered my dilemma and conclude that hiring a hostess is the best solution.' How much more to tell her? He added, a shade of impatience in his voice, 'I am an educated man. I have never yet found a problem that could not be solved by logic. Believe me, there is not the least risk to your person or your good name. Indeed, it is imperative that your stay at Adversane is perfectly respectable if we are to convince everyone that the engagement is genuine. When the time comes to part I shall make sure it is understood that the decision was yours—you may be assured that those who know me will not find that at all surprising—and you will walk away with enough money to allow you to live in comfort and style for at least the next year. A handsome remuneration for less than two months' work.' He paused. 'So, Miss Halbrook, what do you say?'

Preposterous. Outrageous. Not to be considered.
These were the first words that came to Lucy's mind, but she did not utter them. Her situation, living in her uncle's house, was not comfortable. To spend six weeks as the guest of Lord Adversane, no doubt living very luxuriously, would not be a hardship, and with the money she earned she would not need to rush into another post for some time. In fact, she might even be able to invest the money—in a shop, say, or a little school—and provide herself with an income. She might even be able to travel. She forced her gaze away from those compelling grey eyes and addressed Mrs Killinghurst.

'You can assure me there is nothing untoward in this?'

'Nothing at all, Miss Halbrook. It is unusual, but you may be sure I looked into the matter thoroughly before I accepted Lord Adversane's commission. After all, I have my own reputation and that of my business to consider.' Mrs Killinghurst tapped the paper on the desk in front of her. 'The contract is drawn up, which will make everything legally binding. All that is required is your signature.'

Lucy hesitated. The offer was very tempting, and neither Mrs Killinghurst nor the advertisements she had scanned in the newspaper could offer anything else. And what choice did she have? Her uncle's attentions were becoming more persistent and it could only be a matter of time before her aunt and her mother became aware of a situation which Lucy knew would distress them greatly.

'Very well,' she said. 'I will do it.'

Ralph watched in silence as she came to the desk to sign the contract. A slight doubt shook him. Perhaps it would have been better to hire an actress to play the role he had envisaged, but the danger of being found out would be that much greater, and the matter was too important to take that risk. He would not put it past his family to investigate his supposed fiancée's background.

No, overall Mrs Killinghurst had succeeded very well. Miss Lucy Halbrook was everything he required and her breeding was impeccable, his family would find no fault there. She was not quite as tall as he had hoped, and her hair was not guinea-gold but a soft honey-brown. She also had rather more spirit than he had expected and he found himself wanting to tease her, to bring that sparkle to her eyes. He would have to be careful about that. He had been brought up to believe a gentleman should not flirt with a lady under his protection. However, he needed someone who could fulfil the role he had in mind convincingly, so she needed to be at least moderately attractive, and beneath that dowdy gown Miss Halbrook's figure looked to be good. His eyes dwelled on the rounded bottom displayed beneath the grey folds as she bent over the desk to sign her name. It might even be very good.

He quickly suppressed that line of thought. The woman was being hired for a specific purpose and that did not include dalliance, however enjoyable that might be. No, his reasons for taking her to Adversane were much more serious than that. Deadly serious.

Chapter Two

Lord Adversane insisted upon sending his luxurious carriage to carry Lucy to the north country. She had never travelled in such style, and as the elegant equipage bowled out of London she was forced to admit that there was something to be said for being betrothed to a rich man.

Two weeks had passed since that second visit to Mrs Killinghurst's registry office. Lucy had signed her contract and stepped back into New Bond Street with a thick roll of banknotes in her reticule, her new employer requesting her to buy whatever was necessary for her journey to Adversane. He had also given her the name of a very exclusive modiste and told her she might order anything she wished and have it charged to his account.

Lucy had felt compelled to question this.

'Forgive me, but if your wife is—that is, if you have been a widower for two years, will you still *have* an account?'

'Oh, my wife never bought anything from Celeste.'

Lucy had blushed hotly at the implication of his careless response, and had immediately given him back his card. He had grinned at that, giving Lucy the unsettling feeling that he was teasing her.

'Don't worry,' he said. 'There is a very good dress-maker near Adversane who will provide you with everything you need for the duration of your stay. I shall arrange for her to call on you once you are settled in.'

Recalling the incident, she wondered again if she had been wise to accept employment with a stranger and in a house so far away from everyone and everything she knew. She had looked out her uncle's copy of *The New Peerage* and learned that Ralph Adversane was the fifth baron, that he owned several properties, his principal seat being Adversane Hall, in Yorkshire. There was no mention of a wife, but she knew this edition of the Peerage was at least five years old, so presumably the marriage had taken place after that date.

Discreet enquiries of her family had brought forth very little information. Her aunt, who was an avid reader of the Court and Society pages, admitted she had *heard* of Lord Adversane, but it appeared he was an infrequent visitor to London, or at least, thought Lucy, to those circles that warranted a mention in the newspapers, even if he was well known in less respectable circles, whose ladies patronised a certain expensive modiste. She must therefore trust to Mrs Killinghurst's assurance that she made thorough enquiries into the veracity of every client who came to her.

However, just as a precaution, Lucy had kept back some of the money Lord Adversane had given her and stitched it into the hem of her cloak. It was not a lot, but sufficient to pay for her journey back to London, and knowing that she had a means of escape should she need it, she now settled back against the comfortable squabs of the travelling carriage and prepared to enjoy herself.

* * *

Lord Adversane was waiting for her when she arrived at his country seat. He was dressed very much as she had last seen him, in blue coat and buckskins, and as the coach drew up on the sweeping drive he strode across to open the door and hand her down.

'Welcome, Miss Halbrook. How was your journey?'

'Extremely entertaining.' Lucy gave a little gurgle of laughter at his look of surprise, her head still buzzing with the excitement of all the new sights and sounds she had experienced. 'I have never before been farther north than Hertfordshire, you see, so it was an adventure. Of course, I doubt I would have enjoyed it so much if it had not been undertaken in a fast and comfortable vehicle, with your servants to take care of everything for me, and overnight stops arranged at the very best coaching inns. I am very grateful to you for your solicitude, my lord.'

'I could do nothing less for my future wife.'

Lucy blushed, but quickly realised that his words were for the benefit of the servants, as was the kiss he bestowed upon her fingers. After all, if this charade was to work then everyone must believe it.

Collecting her thoughts, she stood for a moment looking up at the house. It was a very large building in the Jacobean style with stone transom and mullion windows set between diapered red brickwork. Her first impression was that it had a frowning aspect, but she put this down to the overcast day and the fact that they were standing on the drive and the house appeared to tower over them. Her eyes moved to the stone pediment above the entrance, which framed an intricately carved cartouche.

'The Adversane coat of arms,' he said, following her glance. 'The house was built for the first Baron Adversane at the time of the Restoration.'

Still buzzing with the excitement of the journey, Lucy could not resist giving voice to a mischievous thought.

'And will the shades of your illustrious ancestors approve of me?'

'I have no idea. Shall we go in?'

Chastened by his stony retort, Lucy allowed him to escort her into the house. The butler was waiting for them in the entrance passage with a line of servants, all of whom bowed or curtseyed as Lord Adversane led her past them.

'Byrne will not introduce them to you today,' he said as he took her into the Great Hall. 'You are here ostensibly as a guest, but of course they all know we are betrothed because I mentioned it to my cousin in front of the housekeeper. Come along and meet her. She is waiting in the drawing room.'

'The housekeeper?' asked Lucy, suddenly quite daunted by the grandeur of her surroundings.

'My cousin, Mrs Dean.'

There was no mistaking the impatience in his voice, and Lucy gave herself a mental shake. It was too late now for second thoughts. She must concentrate upon her new role.

Ralph swore silently, ashamed of his own ill humour. Perhaps it was understandable that he should be on edge, knowing how important it was that the girl fulfil her role to perfection, but surely he did not need to be quite so serious? He gave an inward sigh. How long had it been since anyone had teased him? Even his sisters rarely did so now. Since Helene's death they had treated him with more sympathy than he deserved. After all it was not as if he had loved his wife. He had cared for her, yes, but the strain of living with such a nervous, timid creature, of watching his every utterance, curbing every impatient remark, had taken its toll. He had forgotten what it was like to laugh…

He escorted Miss Halbrook into the drawing room where his cousin was busy filling a teapot from a spirit kettle.

'Ah, there you are, Ralph. And this must be our guest.' Ariadne carefully set down the teapot and came forwards to greet them. As she approached she fixed her rather myopic gaze upon Lucy, frowned a little then turned a puzzled look upon him. He spoke quickly, before she could voice her thoughts.

'It is indeed, Cousin.' He added quietly, 'I thought it best to tell Mrs Dean the truth, Miss Halbrook. She will introduce you to everyone as a young friend who is spending a few weeks with her, but in reality everyone will believe that you are my fiancée, is that not so, Cousin?'

He was relieved to see Ariadne's frown clear as she took Miss Halbrook's hands.

Lucy. He must get used to calling her Lucy.

'Oh, indeed. You know how quickly gossip spreads in the country, my dear. Now, before we go any further I should tell you that I am so pleased my cousin has asked me to help him with this.'

He smiled. 'I persuaded Ariadne to leave her comfortable little house in Bath and join me for the summer.'

'There is very little persuasion needed to bring me to Adversane, Cousin, and you know it.' Mrs Dean chuckled. She pulled Lucy close and kissed her cheek. 'Welcome, my dear. Ralph has indeed told me all about it, although I really do not see—but there, it will be a pleasure to have this house filled with people again.'

Lucy relaxed in the face of such a friendly welcome.

Mrs Dean led her over to a sofa and gently pushed her down onto the seat, chattering all the time.

'Now, my dear, I have prepared some tea, if you would like it. I find it very restorative after a long journey. You have come all the way from London, Ralph tells me— more than two hundred miles! You must be exhausted.'

'In which case brandy might be more appropriate,' put in Lord Adversane.

Lucy ignored him. He had snubbed her once already, so she would not risk responding to his remark.

'Tea would be very welcome, Mrs Dean, thank you.'

'Oh, do call me Ariadne, my dear. And I shall address you as Lucy, if you will allow me.'

'Gladly.' She glanced around to make sure they were alone. 'Is it safe to talk in here?'

'Perfectly, as long as we do not raise our voices.' Lord Adversane poured himself a glass of brandy from the decanter on the sideboard and took a seat opposite the sofa. He said conversationally, 'What do you want to talk about?'

'I should have thought that was obvious,' she retorted. 'We have not had the opportunity to discuss my story. We will need to agree on the particulars, if I am to be at all convincing.'

He sat back in his chair and stretched out his legs, crossing one booted foot over the other.

'It would be sensible to keep as close to the truth as possible. There is no need for false names or imaginary families. We met in London, but our betrothal has not yet been made public because you have been in mourning for your father—'

'How do you know that?'

'Mrs Killinghurst apprised me of all your details, naturally.'

'Naturally.' She eyed him with growing resentment. 'You appear to know everything about me, my lord.'

'Not *everything*, Miss Halbrook.' There was a sardonic gleam in his hard, grey eyes as they rested upon her. So he was amusing himself at her expense, yet her light-hearted comments had met with a chilly rebuff. She put up her chin.

'I know no more of you than I have been able to discover from *The Peerage*,' she told him. 'I am ill prepared for this role.'

He waved a dismissive hand. 'We have three weeks before the first house guests arrive. Time enough to get to know one another. It will be my pleasure to tell you anything you wish to know.'

His very reasonable response made Lucy grind her teeth, but she swallowed her irritation and tried to match his cool tone.

'Perhaps the first thing we need to ascertain is why my mother did not accompany me on this visit.'

'If we are keeping to the truth, then you have not told her about me. She thinks you have been employed as companion to some elderly invalid, is that not correct?'

'Well, well, yes, that is what we agreed I would tell her—'

'And it gave you the excuse to remove yourself from your uncle's unwelcome attentions.'

'I never told Mrs Killinghurst *that*,' Lucy retorted, her face flaming.

Mrs Dean gave a little tut and busied herself with the tea tray, but Lord Adversane merely shrugged.

'It is the truth, is it not? I made a few enquiries of my own before engaging you, Miss Halbrook, and what I learned of Silas Edgeworth did not lead me to think he would be able to keep his hands off a pretty young girl living beneath his roof.'

'Ralph, you are putting Miss Halbrook to the blush,' Mrs Dean reprimanded him in her gentle way. She handed Lucy a cup of tea. 'You may be sure there will be nothing like *that* going on at Adversane, my dear. My cousin may have hired you to prevent his family from importuning him, but his reasons for inviting me to act as your chaperone are to make sure that your stay here is not marred by any impropriety.' She rose. 'Now, if you will excuse me for a moment, I must go and check that your trunks have been carried upstairs and everything is as it should be.'

With a vague smile she bustled off, leaving Lucy alone with Lord Adversane. There was an uneasy silence as the door closed behind her. Lucy's glance slid to her host.

'I know,' he said, a measure of understanding softening his hard eyes. 'She tells you there will be no indecorum here, then promptly leaves us alone. I'm afraid you will have to accustom yourself to it. We are supposed to be engaged, you know.'

'Yes, of course.'

'If I have made you uncomfortable then I am sorry for it.'

His blunt apology surprised her. She put down her cup and, to cover her agitation, she raised her eyes to the fireplace. 'The overmantel is very finely carved. Grinling Gibbons?'

'Yes. My ancestor paid him the princely sum of forty pounds for it. Heaven knows what it would cost today.'

'If you could find someone skilled enough to do it,' she replied. 'My father was an artist, but of course Mrs Killinghurst will have told you. He was a great admirer of the old masters like Gibbons.'

'I am aware of that. And I knew your father.' Her brows went up and he explained. 'At Somerset House. It is the home of the Royal Society as well as the Royal Academy. We met there once or twice when I was attending lectures. My condolences for your loss.'

The words were spoken in a matter-of-fact tone, but Lucy felt the tears prickle at the back of her eyes. Rather than show any weakness she rose and went across to the window, where she stood looking out at the fine prospect, although she saw little of it, her thoughts going back to happier times.

'Papa used to take me to his studio sometimes, and encourage me to try my hand at painting.'

'There are many fine views at Adversane for you to capture.'

'I brought my sketchbook with the intention of doing just that, but as for painting—I enjoy working in oils and watercolours but I do not have Papa's gift. When I was a child I loved best to curl up in a chair and watch him at work. He had a passion for the picturesque. Vast, dramatic landscapes.' She thought of the hills and valleys she had seen on her journey. How her father would have loved them. She gave a little shrug. 'But everyone wanted portraits.'

'From the work of your father's I have seen he was very good and in demand.'

'You wonder, then, why it is I need to earn a living.' Lucy bit her lip. She had never spoken of this to anyone, but now felt a need to explain. 'He drank to excess. And gambled. I only discovered the truth after his death. With his talent, the money he earned might have paid for one or other of those vices and still allowed him to provide for his family, but together…'

'Disastrous,' he said bluntly. 'And your mother, did she—was it an arranged marriage?'

'Yes. She had a large dowry. He was a younger son, you see, and needed to marry well. Unfortunately the settlements were badly drawn up and very little was secured upon her. The money was all spent years ago.'

The room seemed to grow a little darker. The cloud outside the window had thickened and a blustery wind agitated the trees, threatening rain. She turned and came back to the sofa, throwing off her melancholy to say brightly, 'For all that they were very much in love.'

So much so that they united to keep me in ignorance of our poverty.

The swift, unbidden thought twisted like a knife in her ribs.

Ralph saw the sudden crease in her brow and the way she folded her arms across her stomach, as if to defend herself. But from what? Her parents' happiness? Not all arranged marriages ended in love, as he knew to his cost. Bitterness made him reply more curtly than he intended.

'They were very fortunate, then.' Her eyes were upon him, questioning, but he did not wish to explain himself. He looked up with relief as the door opened. 'And here is Ariadne returned. I take it the rooms are in readiness for our guest, Cousin?' He rose, glad of the opportunity to get away. This young woman unsettled him. 'If you will excuse me, I have business that requires my attention. Until dinnertime, Miss Halbrook.'

Mrs Dean escorted Lucy to her room, talking all the way. She was very knowledgeable about the house and by the time they reached the upper floor Lucy knew its history, including the improvements made by the fourth baron, Ralph's father. Lucy let the lady's chatter flow over her while she tried to take in the stunning beauty of the interior. Baroque carvings and plasterwork vied for her attention with dozens of magnificent paintings.

'And here we are in the Long Gallery,' said Mrs Dean, puffing slightly from having talked all the way up the stairs. 'The principal bedchambers lead off the corridor just along here and at the end of the gallery is the passage to the east wing, where all the guests will be accommodated.'

'I have never seen such splendid interiors,' remarked Lucy. She stopped to watch two servants carefully hanging a large painting upon the far wall, while a third stood back and directed them as to the correct alignment. 'Has Lord Adversane made a new purchase?'

'No, no, it is not new. I suppose my cousin thought it would look better here.'

Lucy regarded the painting with some surprise. It was a dark and rather nondescript view of some classical ruins, and looked out of place amongst the portraits of past barons and their wives. Mrs Dean touched her arm.

'Shall we go on?' She led the way into a dim corridor running parallel to the gallery and threw open a door at one end. 'The two main bedrooms are here. You will be occupying the mistress's bedchamber—'

'Oh, but I do not think I should!'

Lucy stopped in the doorway, but Mrs Dean urged her to enter.

'Lord Adversane thought it necessary,' she said, closing the door behind them. 'If my cousin truly intended to make you his wife then this is the apartment he would choose for you.'

Lucy's reluctance must have shown clearly on her face, for Mrs Dean smiled and patted her arm.

'You need have no fear of impropriety, my dear. Believe me, Adversane was not at all happy about putting you in his wife's room, but he knows it must be so, if his family are to believe he is serious about marrying you. There is a dressing room through that door where your maid will sleep—he has appointed one for you, of course. She has already unpacked your trunk, you see, and has probably gone off to fetch your hot water.'

Lucy made no further protest, and when Mrs Dean left her she wandered around the room, taking in her surroundings. The furniture was dark and heavy, the huge tester bed hung with faded brocade and while the walls were covered in a pretty Chinese wallpaper it was of no very recent date. In fact, there was nothing new in the room at all, and nothing to give any clue to the character of the last occupant. The brushes resting on the dressing table were Lucy's and the linen press held only the meagre supply of clothes she had brought with her. All the other drawers and cupboards were quite empty. One part of her was relieved, for she would have felt even more of an impostor if the chamber had been redolent of the late Lady Adversane. As it was, there was nothing to say this was not a guest room, albeit a very grand one.

Knowing it would be sensible to rest before the dinner hour, Lucy stretched herself on the bed, determined to go over all the questions she wished to put to her host when they met again, but within a very few minutes she was sound asleep.

She awoke when the door to her room opened and a shy, breathless voice said, 'Ooh, ma'am, I'm didn't mean to disturb you, but Mrs Green says its time I brought up your hot water and made you ready to go down to dinner—'

'That is quite all right.' Lucy sat up, stretching. 'You are to be my maid, I take it?'

'Aye, ma'am—miss.'

'And who is Mrs Green?'

'The housekeeper, miss. She sent me up.' The young girl put down the heavy jug on the wash stand and bobbed a curtsey. 'And I am Ruthie, miss, if you please.'

'Well, Ruthie, perhaps you would help me out of this gown.' Lucy slid off the bed. 'I am afraid it is sadly crumpled and not a little grubby. I have been travelling in it for days.'

'I know, miss. From London,' said Ruthie triumphantly as she unfastened Lucy's travelling dress and laid it over a chair. 'Everyone's that pleased to see you. Mrs Green says the house has been too long without a mistress.'

'Oh, but I am not—'

Lucy's involuntary exclamation had the effect of making the maid jump back, her hands clasped nervously in front of her.

'Ooh, miss, I'm that sorry, I forgot we wasn't meant to say anything!'

Lucy gazed in some dismay at the maid's woebegone face. So word had spread, just as Adversane had planned. She nodded and said gently, 'Well, do not mention it again. Now, I think I saw my green gown in the press, perhaps you will lay that out for me.'

It was her only evening gown, a plain robe of French cambric with puff sleeves and a modest neckline. Lucy thought it would look very dull against the splendid interiors of the house, but it was all she had and it would have to do.

Lucy found her new maid very willing and eager to help. Ruthie carried away Lucy's travelling gown and half-boots, promising to clean them up as good as new, then came hurrying back, determined to help Lucy to dress for dinner. Her enthusiasm was endearing, but Lucy was a little reluctant to let her do more than brush out her hair.

'Oh, but I can do it, miss,' said Ruthie, as Lucy sat before the looking glass. 'Lady Adversane's maid showed me how to dress hair in several styles. O'course that were a couple of years ago now, but I'm sure I can remember.'

Lucy glanced at the little clock. There was plenty of time to brush it all out and start again, if necessary.

'Very well, let us see what you can do,' she said, smiling. 'All I wish this evening is for you to put it up in a simple knot.'

Ruthie's face fell. 'No ringlets, miss?'

'No ringlets.'

The young maid looked a little disappointed, but she set about her task with a will.

'You were training to be a lady's maid?' asked Lucy as Ruthie concentrated on unpinning and brushing out each shining lock.

'Oh, aye, miss, I was. Lady Adversane's maid broke her arm, you see, so Mrs Green sent me up to help her.' She gave a gusty sigh. 'Oh, my lady was *so* pretty, with her golden curls and blue, blue eyes, like the china doll they keep in the nursery! It was such a pleasure to dress her. I learned such a lot from Miss Crimplesham, too— that was my lady's maid, you see—she was a tough old stick, and all the servants was a bit in awe of her, even Mrs Green, but she wasn't so bad when you got to know her, and so devoted to my lady.'

She paused to look at the honey-brown curls that cascaded over Lucy's shoulders. Lucy knew she should reprimand the maid for chattering, but she was amused by her artless talk and besides, for one accustomed to looking after herself, it was so very pleasant merely to sit quietly and have someone fuss over her.

'I was hoping that my lady would give me a reference,' Ruthie continued, beginning to gather up the heavy locks again. 'So I could become a proper lady's maid, but then of course there were that terrible accident.'

'Accident?' Lucy met her maid's eyes in the mirror. 'You mean Lady Adversane?'

'Yes, miss. She fell to her death, from Druids Rock.'

'Oh, heavens.'

Lucy had been wondering how Lady Adversane had died. She had decided she would ask Mrs Dean at some point, for she did not think she would be able to pluck up the courage to ask Lord Adversane.

She said slowly, 'How tragic. When did it happen?'

'Two years ago, on Midsummer's Eve.' Ruthie nodded, her eyes wide. 'Oh, 'twas perfectly dreadful, miss! They found her the next morning, dashed to pieces at the foot of the crag. I thought they'd all blame me, at first, for letting her go out alone, You see, I'd fallen asleep in my chair waiting for her to come up to bed.'

'I am sure it was in no way your fault,' Lucy told her.

'No, that's what Miss Crimplesham said. In fact, she was more inclined to blame herself. In a dreadful state she was, crying and saying she should've waited up for her mistress, but how could she undress her with her broken arm? No, we had a house full of guests, you see, and that night the players had come up from Ingleston to perform, and then after supper there was dancing far into the night, so it was very late before everyone went to bed. Only my lady didn't come upstairs but went off to see the sunrise, as she often did. Only this time she didn't wait to change her shoes and her thin little slippers wouldn't grip on the rock and she slipped and fell to her death.' The youthful face reflected in the mirror looked sad for a moment, then brightened. 'And now you're here, perhaps you'll keep me on as your maid, miss.' Ruthie placed the final pin into the topknot and stood back to cast a last, critical look at her handiwork. 'I'm sure I can pick it up very quickly.'

Lucy smiled. 'Have you not learned enough yet, then?'

'Oh, no, not by a long chalk. Miss Crimplesham said it would be *months* before I had learned enough to even *think* of offering myself as lady's maid. She'd started as my lady's nurse—called her "my baby", she did— and had spent years learning how to look after her, so even if Lady Adversane hadn't been dashed to pieces that night it wouldn't have done no good, for there wouldn't be time for Miss Crimplesham to teach me everything before they went away.' Lucy might have thought nothing of this artless speech, if Ruthie hadn't dropped her hairbrush and stared aghast into the mirror. 'Ooh, miss, I shouldn't've said that. No one was meant to know. My lady said it was a secret.'

Lucy held her eyes in the mirror.

'Are you saying,' she spoke slowly, carefully, 'that Lady Adversane was planning to...to *run away*?'

'Yes—no!' Ruthie's face crumpled. 'Miss Crimplesham said I wasn't to tell no one. She was that angry when she found out my lady had let it slip. Said I should be turned off if I breathed a word of it, and I haven't, miss. I haven't said nothing until today, but I got so carried away, pinning up your hair and enjoying myself so much that it just came out.' As Lucy swivelled around on the stool to face her, the girl fell to her knees, sobbing. 'Pray, don't tell the master, miss! He'll be so angry that he'll turn me off for sure. I'll be sent off without a character and I'll *never* get another position, not even as scullery maid!'

'I promise I shall not tell anyone,' Lucy assured her. She handed the maid one of her own handkerchiefs and bade her dry her eyes. It behoved her now to send the girl away, but instead she said quietly, 'It was an arranged marriage, perhaps.'

'Yes.' The muffled affirmative was followed by Ruthie blowing her nose very loudly. 'Only M-Miss Crimple-sham said her mistress was very unhappy. And once my lady had determined to run away then she had no choice but to go with her, to look after her.' Lucy's thoughts raced, and as if reading them Ruthie continued. 'My lady never loved the master—well, who could? He is so stern and cold, and when he's angry...' She shuddered. 'He frightens *me*, and I'm not a beautiful, delicate little flower like my lady was.'

'And what happened to Miss Crimplesham after the accident?'

'She went back to my lady's family. They have another daughter, you see, so she's gone to be her maid now.' Ruthie sighed. 'And I became second housemaid again. And I suppose I shall have to go back to that now.' She fixed Lucy with an imploring gaze. 'Only *pray* don't tell Mrs Green why you are displeased with me—'

'I have no intention of turning you away,' Lucy told her, patting her hands. 'From what I have seen of you so far you have the makings of an excellent lady's maid, only you will have to learn to curb that runaway tongue of yours.'

'I swear to you, miss, I haven't said a word to a soul before today—'

'Very well then, we will forget everything that has been said, if you please. Now, you had best remain here until you look a little less distressed. Then go downstairs and have your own dinner. And remember, a good lady's maid must learn to be discreet!'

'Yes, miss, thank you.' Ruthie bobbed another curtsey, then impulsively clutched at Lucy's hand and kissed it. 'I'll never open my mouth again, I promise you.'

Lucy went off, leaving the girl happily tidying her room. She doubted that such a chatterbox could ever be totally relied upon not to gossip, but that did not worry Lucy overmuch. The girl's services would suit her very well for the duration of her stay.

Lucy made her way downstairs and found the drawing room deserted. She supposed Ariadne and Lord Adversane must still be in their rooms, changing for dinner, and rather than sit and wait, she decided to explore a little. She soon found the dining room, situated on the far side of the entrance passage. The servants were there, setting the table for dinner, and when they saw her they all stopped to bow or curtsey, which made her retreat hurriedly. Another door opened on to a pretty chamber that she guessed might be the morning room, since its windows faced east. The next door she tried opened onto a room lined with bookcases. At first she thought it was the library, but then she realised it must be Lord Adversane's study, and the man himself was present. He was standing before the window but turned as he heard the door open.

'Oh.' Lucy stopped in the doorway. 'I did not mean to disturb you.' She tried a little smile. 'I was exploring...'

'Come in, Miss Halbrook. You find me examining a new acquisition.' He stepped aside to reveal a narrow table standing before the window, and on it a strange device consisting of a brass tube fixed to a mahogany base. 'My new microscope.'

'Is that what it is?' She came farther into the room. 'I have read about them, and heard of Hooke's masterful book full of the drawings he made using a microscope to enlarge the tiniest creatures, but I have never seen one.'

'Then come now and look.' He beckoned to her to approach. 'Fix your eye over the eyepiece, the mirror at the base will direct the light onto the slide. Now, tell me what you see.'

'Something quite…monstrous.' She took her eye away from the microscope and peered at the tiny object in the slide. 'Is that what I am seeing—is it a beetle's head?'

'Yes. Magnified about a hundred times.'

'But that is quite astounding.' She studied it again for a few moments.

'And there are others,' said Lord Adversane. 'Look here, this is a flea…'

Lucy was entranced as he positioned one slide after another for her to study.

'But that is quite marvellous, my lord,' she exclaimed. 'I had no idea one could see so much. Why, one might look at anything, a hair from my head, for example!'

She straightened, laughing at the thought, and found Lord Adversane standing very close. Too close. Her mouth dried, she dared not raise her eyes higher than his shirt front. Once again she had the impression of standing before a solid wall, only the slight rise and fall of the snowy linen above his immaculate waistcoat told her this was a living, breathing man. A sudden hot blush spread through her body and all coherent thought disappeared.

Ralph swallowed. Hard. He was shaken to find how much he wanted to reach out and drag the young woman before him into his arms. She had shown such enthusiasm for the microscope, had asked intelligent questions and he had been enjoying sharing his knowledge with her, so that the sudden rush of lustful thoughts that now crowded into his head was quite inexplicable. And the hectic flush on her cheeks only heightened his desire to kiss her.

The air around them was charged with danger. She remained motionless before him in a way that suggested she, too, could feel it. He was powerless to move away and stood looking down at her, wondering what she found so fascinating about his neck cloth. The distant chiming of the long-case clock in the hall broke the spell. She glanced up, a look of fearful bewilderment in her green eyes.

Hell and confound it. This should not have happened!

Ralph knew it was his duty to put her at her ease, if he could. Turning aside, he drew out his watch.

'It is getting late. Ariadne will be in the drawing room by now and I must change for dinner.'

'Yes.' Her voice was quiet. She sounded dazed. 'I beg your pardon for delaying you—'

'There is no need. I enjoyed showing you the microscope. I will look out more specimens for you, if you are interested.'

'Thank you, yes, I would very much like—that is… perhaps.' With a faint smile and a muttered 'Excuse me' she hurried away.

Ralph closed his eyes. Good Lord, what was he about, offering to show her more slides? Surely he should avoid putting them in this situation again. But it would not be the same, he argued. She had taken him by surprise. Next time he would be prepared. After all, he was not the sort to lose his head over any woman.

Chapter Three

Lucy did not go directly to the drawing room. Instead, she went back to her bedchamber and splashed her cheeks with water from the jug on the washstand. Lord Adversane had said earlier that she would have to get used to being alone with him, since they were supposed to be engaged, but just then, in the study, she had felt a profound sense of danger in his presence. She wiped her cheeks and considered the matter. He had said nothing, done nothing that could be construed as improper, yet just having him stand so close had raised her temperature and set her heart thumping in the most alarming manner.

'He is so, so *male*,' she said aloud, and almost laughed at her foolishness.

Lord Adversane had no interest in her at all, save as an employee. She must never forget that. She tidied her hair, shook out her skirts and went downstairs again to find Ariadne waiting for her in the drawing room.

'Ah, there you are, my dear. Ralph has just this minute gone up to change, so we have plenty of time to get to know one another, and I know you are anxious to be well versed in your role. I agree that it is most important if you are to convince everyone it is for real. Now, what would you like me to tell you first?'

Lucy recalled Ruthie's earlier disclosures.

'I am naturally curious to know a little more about Lady Adversane,' she explained, 'but I am loath to mention such a delicate subject to my host.'

'Oh, I quite understand, my dear. One does not want to open old wounds, and Ralph was quite devoted to her, you know.' She signalled to Lucy to sit beside her on the sofa.

'How long were they married?' asked Lucy.

'Less than twelve months.' Mrs Dean sighed. 'They met at Harrogate in the spring and were married before the year was out. I believe that as soon as he saw her, Ralph was determined to make Helene his wife.'

'So it was not an arranged marriage.' Lucy felt a little lightening of her anxiety. Perhaps Ruthie had embellished her story out of all proportion. She knew that old retainers could be very jealous of their charges, and it was very likely that Miss Crimplesham had not wished to acknowledge her mistress's affection for her new husband.

'But of course it was arranged,' said Mrs Dean. 'After a fashion. There is no doubt that the Prestons went to Harrogate in search of a husband. I wondered at the time why they did not take Helene to London. She was such a diamond that in all likelihood she could have caught a far bigger prize than a mere baron—although it is unlikely it would have been a *richer* one. But London is such a distance and Helene was never very strong. I think perhaps her parents decided she would not cope with the rigours of a season in Town. Or mayhap they were planning to take her there later, when she was a little more used to society. Only once Helene had met Ralph, she persuaded her papa to let her have her way, and it was always obvious to me that Sir James could deny her nothing.'

'So they fell in love?'

'Oh, yes, they were devoted to one another.' Mrs Dean nodded. 'And there is no doubting they were well suited, Helene so beautiful and Ralph wealthy enough to make the required settlements. I *did* think that perhaps Helene's sweet, compliant nature might—' She broke off, gazing into space for a moment before saying with a smile, 'Ralph was so gentle with her, so patient. I have no doubt that he loved her very much indeed. One only has to think that in the two years since she died he has not so much as *glanced* at another woman.' The butler entered at that moment, and she added swiftly, 'Until now, of course, my dear.'

Conversation stopped as Byrne served the ladies with a glass of wine, and when Adversane came in they talked in a desultory manner until the butler had withdrawn again. As her host took a chair on the opposite side of the fireplace, Lucy thought how well Ruthie's description of Lord Adversane suited him. Stern and cold. There was no softness in the craggy features, no yielding in his upright posture, the muscled shoulders filling the black evening coat so well that not a crease marred its sculpted form. He might have been hewn from the grey rocks she had seen on her journey to Adversane. At that moment he looked across the room and smiled at her. Immediately his face was transformed, the hard lines softened and the grey eyes warmed with amusement. She could not prevent herself from smiling back.

'So, ladies, what have you been discussing?'

'You,' said Lucy. 'Or rather, your wife.'

The warm look that had made her speak so recklessly

was immediately replaced by a black frown, yet she had no choice but to continue.

'I—I thought, for the role you have engaged me for, that I needed to know a little more about Lady Adversane.'

'Do you think anyone would dare mention her to you?'

The haughty reply should have warned her to desist, but instead she considered the question.

'They might.' She met his challenging look steadily. 'And it would certainly appear most odd if I did not evince some interest in my predecessor.'

The icy look vanished, replaced by a more disquieting gleam in his eyes.

'You are quite right, Miss Halbrook. Unless we put it about that you are marrying me for my money. In which case you need show no interest at all in me or my family.'

'Oh, dear me, no. I would not wish to feature as a fortune-hunter.' He laughed at that, and, emboldened, she continued, 'I looked in the Long Gallery on my way here tonight. I thought I might see a portrait of Lady Adversane.'

Mrs Dean fidgeted beside her, and Adversane's gaze shifted from Lucy to his cousin.

'You shall see her likeness,' he said coolly. 'But not tonight, for here is Byrne again to tell us dinner is served.'

By the time they had dined, the days of travel were beginning to catch up with Lucy, and when Mrs Dean suggested that instead of retiring to the drawing room after the meal she might like to go to bed, Lucy agreed. Ruthie was waiting in her bedchamber, taking such pains to say nothing while she helped her undress that Lucy was amused, but too exhausted to tease the girl. Once she had ascertained that Ruthie would be sleeping in the dressing room, she fell into bed and was asleep almost before her head touched the pillow.

Lucy woke very early the following morning. She had asked Ruthie to leave the window shutters open and not to pull the hangings around the bed and the sun was streaming into the room. Lucy stretched and plumped up the pillows, then she lay down again, thinking of the change in her circumstances. A maid was sleeping in the dressing room, there for the sole purpose of looking after her, and once dressed Lucy would be obliged to do very little except amuse herself. All day.

And she was being well paid for it.

With a contented smile she put her hands behind her head. She had imagined herself struggling to control a schoolroom of spoiled children, or running back and forth at the bidding of a querulous invalid, instead of which she was living the life of a rich and cossetted lady.

She slipped out of bed and walked over to the window, throwing open the casement and leaning on the sill to breathe in the fresh summer air. Her room overlooked the front of the house, where the gravelled drive snaked away between neatly scythed lawns and out through the gates. Beyond the palings lay the park, bordered by an expanse of woodlands, and beyond that she could see the craggy moors stretching away to meet the sky. How could anyone be unhappy in such surroundings?

Lucy had a sudden desire to be outside, while the dew was still on the grass. Rather than disturb her sleeping maid she dressed herself in a morning gown of primrose muslin, caught her hair back with a ribbon and, picking up her shawl, she left her room. There would be a quicker way of getting to the gardens than down the main staircase and through the Great Hall, but Lucy did not yet know it and was afraid of losing herself in the maze of unfamiliar corridors. It was still early, and although she heard the servants at work she saw no one as she made her way to the long through-passage and out of the doors that opened onto the formal gardens.

A broad terrace ended in a shallow flight of steps leading down to flower beds separated by wide gravel paths. A series of statues decorated each bed and at the far end of the gardens was a small pond and fountain. It was very beautiful and the air was already heavy with the scent of flowers, but the formal layout did not fulfil her wish to be at one with nature, so she made her way around to the front of the house, where she could stroll across the smooth grass, leaving a trail of footprints in the heavy dew.

Although it was early, a skylark trilled ecstatically somewhere above her and she thought how wonderful it would be to live here through the seasons. Immediately upon the thought came another, less welcome idea, that the late Lady Adversane had not thought so. From what Ruthie had said Helene had been very unhappy here, although Lucy suspected that it was not because of the property but its owner. As if conjured by her thoughts two horses emerged from the distant trees, galloping across the open park, their riders bent low over their necks.

Even at a distance there was no mistaking Ralph, Lord Adversane. He was riding a magnificent black hunter and was a good horse's length ahead of his companion. Man and beast were as one, flying across the turf with strong, fluid movements that made their progress look effortless. He slowed as he approached the drive, waiting for his companion to come up to him before they trotted between the stone pillars of the main entrance.

Lucy knew they must see her, a solitary figure standing in the middle of the lawns, but she determined not to scuttle away like some timid little mouse. She thought they would ride around the side of the house to the stables, and she was not a little surprised when they turned their horses onto the grass and came directly towards her.

Lord Adversane touched his hat.

'You are about early, Miss Halbrook.'

'Not as early as you, my lord.'

His brows rose a little, and she wondered if he had expected her to explain her presence. As if—and she bridled a little at the idea—as if she had no right to be there. However, he did not appear to be offended by her response and replied quite cheerfully.

'I often ride out in the morning. It is a good time to see just what is happening on my land.' He indicated the man beside him. 'This is Harold Colne, who acts as my steward here at Adversane.'

Lucy nodded. 'Mr Colne.' She shot him a quick, questioning glance. 'Acts? Is that not your main role?'

'Harry is also a lifelong friend and a business partner for some of my ventures.' Ralph grinned. 'In fact, the partnership is flourishing so much that I fear I shall soon have to find myself a new steward. However, for the present Harry manages everything here at Adversane. If you are in need of anything, you may ask him.'

'I will be delighted to help you in any way I can, Miss Halbrook.'

Mr Colne touched his hat and gave her a friendly smile. Lucy warmed to him immediately. He looked to be a similar age to Lord Adversane, but instead of short black hair he had brown curls and a kindly face that looked as if it was made for laughter.

'I have a great curiosity about this place, Mr Colne,'

she told him. 'And I shall undoubtedly seek you out, if you can spare a little time.'

'As much as you require, ma'am, although I assure you Lord Adversane knows everything there is to know about the estate.' He held out one hand to his companion. 'If you will give me your reins, my lord, I will see to the horses and leave you free to walk with Miss Halbrook.'

'What? Oh. Of course.'

Lucy kept her countenance until the steward had ridden away, then she said, her voice rich with laughter, 'I suppose you told Mr Colne I was your fiancée, Lord Adversane?'

'Not as such. It was implied, and I did not deny it.'

'Then you cannot blame him if he assumes you wish to spend time with me.'

'Of course not.'

She chuckled.

'Your expression tells me you would like to add "and very inconvenient it is, too!" Although, of course I am sure you would use much stronger language.'

Again that swift grin transformed his countenance.

'You are right, much stronger!'

'Well, I am very happy with my own company, sir, so if you have business requiring your attention, please do not feel you have to humour me.'

'No, there is nothing that cannot wait.'

Lucy dropped a curtsey.

'I vow, my lord, I do not know when I have received such a handsome compliment.'

She wondered if her impetuous remark might bring his wrath upon her, but although his eyes narrowed there was a gleam of appreciation in them.

'Vixen,' he retorted without heat.

He held out his arm to her, and she laid her fingers on

the rough woollen sleeve. She remarked as they began to stroll towards the house, 'If Mr Colne is such a good friend I wonder that you did not confide your plan to him.'

'It has been my experience that secrets are best shared as little as possible. It was necessary to take Mrs Dean into my confidence, but no one else need know of it.'

'Your reasoning is impeccable, but to deceive your friends must cause some uneasiness.'

'And are you not deceiving your family?'

She bit her lip. 'I am, in a way.' She added, firing up, 'But at least there is some truth in what I told them. I *am* employed.'

'And do I figure as your elderly invalid?'

She gave a little choke of laughter at the absurdity of the idea.

'I suppose you must be, although you are far too—' She broke off, blushing.

'Far too what? Come, Miss Halbrook. You intrigue me.'

'Healthy,' she said lamely. It had not been the adjective she had intended to use. Young. Strong. Virile. They were the words that had come to her mind, but impossible to tell him so, and she was grateful that he did not press her on the matter.

'So what *are* you doing out here so early?' he asked her.

'Communing with nature.' Her soulful response earned her a sudden, frowning look, and she abandoned her teasing. 'It is such a lovely day that I wanted to be outside. From what Mrs Dean told me yesterday I believe breakfast will not be for another hour or so yet.'

'Breakfast can be whenever you wish,' he replied. 'Did your maid dress you?'

She stopped, glancing down at her gown. 'No—why, is there something wrong?'

'Not at all. I prefer your hair like that, with a bandeau and hanging loose down your back.' He reached up and caught a lock between his fingers. 'It curls naturally?'

'Why, y-yes.' She was thrown off balance by the gesture, which seemed far too intimate. 'I usually wear it in a knot because it is more...'

'More suitable for a governess, perhaps,' he finished for her. They began to walk on. 'While you are here you will oblige me by *not* looking like a governess.'

'Very well, if that is your wish, my lord.'

'Now I have offended you.'

'Not at all.'

'You should know from the outset, Miss Halbrook, that I have no turn for soft words and compliments.'

'That is quite evident.'

Her sharp retort earned nothing but a swift, sardonic glance. Lucy knew she was fortunate; she guessed he was more than capable of delivering a brutal snub if she pushed him too far.

Lucy curbed her hasty temper. After all, it was not for her to criticise her employer. She decided to enjoy the morning stroll. Lord Adversane led her around the perimeter of the lawn and seemed disinclined to talk, but Lucy had no intention of allowing him all his own way. A gravelled spur off the main drive caught her attention and her eyes followed it to a small wicket gate set into the palings.

'Where does that lead?'

'To the moors.' Did she imagine the heartbeat's hesitation before he added, 'And Druids Rock.'

'Oh, is it far?'

'Too far to walk there now.'

She was beginning to recognise that implacable note in his voice. It told her he had no wish to continue with the conversation, but that was understandable, since Druids Rock was where his wife had met her death. Their perambulations had brought them round in a circle and she could see that they were now wending their way back towards the house. She decided to make the most of the remaining time alone with her host.

'This might be a good opportunity for me to learn something about you,' she began. 'Perhaps you should tell me...' she paused, waving one airy hand '...the sort of things a fiancée would want to know.'

'The state of my fortune, perhaps?'

'That is the sort of thing my parents would want to know,' she corrected him. 'No, tell me about *you*.'

'I am thirty years of age. I inherited Adversane some nine years ago and it has been my principal home ever since. I have other estates, of course, and a house in London that I use when the House is sitting or to attend lectures and experiments at the Royal Society—what have I said to amuse you, Miss Halbrook?'

'Nothing, only I am at a loss to see what would have brought us together.'

'I appreciate art—you will admit that we have that in common, madam.'

'But that is such a wide-ranging subject that I am not at all sure we would enjoy the same artists,' she countered, unwilling to concede anything just yet.

He shrugged. 'I enjoy riding—'

'Ah, then we do have a common interest.'

'You ride, then?'

'It was amongst the accomplishments I listed for Mrs Killinghurst.'

'But do you ride *well*?'

'That you will have to judge for yourself.' She sighed. 'It is not something I was able to do very often in London.'

'There are plenty of horses in the stables that my sisters use when they are at Adversane. We shall ride out this afternoon. That is—you have a riding habit?'

'Yes, an old one. I wore it to travel here.'

'Very well, then.' They had reached the garden door, and he opened it and stood back for her to precede him. 'I have business with Colne to attend to, but it should be finished by four. I will send for you to come to the stables as soon as I am free.'

Her brows went up. 'Send for me? Perhaps I will not be able to respond to your...your *summons*, my lord. I may have found another occupation by then.'

Ralph heard the frosty note in her voice. What cause had she to complain? If he wanted to *summon* her he would do so, by heaven. She was, after all, only an employee. He gave a shrug and responded, equally coldly.

'I have already said you will get no fine speeches from me, Miss Halbrook.'

'Then you will understand if I respond in kind, Lord Adversane!'

Her spirited retort surprised him, but he did not resent it. In fact, he rather liked it and raised her fingers to his lips.

'I shall be delighted if you do so, ma'am.'

He strode off then, but not before he had seen the look of shock on her face. He felt a smile growing inside him. He was beginning to enjoy his encounters with Miss Lucy Halbrook!

Lucy's boots were sodden from walking on the grass, and she went upstairs to change them before making her way to the breakfast room. She did not know what to make of her host. He was blunt to the point of rudeness, showed no inclination for polite conversation, yet that kiss upon her fingers was as gallant as any she had ever received. It had shaken her, along with the disturbing glint she had more than once seen in his eyes. She could believe he was autocratic and impatient, but she did not think him cruel. However, she was not really engaged to him, merely an actor, hired for a few weeks. Perhaps she might feel differently about Lord Adversane if she was his wife, and in his power.

Over breakfast it was agreed that Mrs Dean would take Lucy for a gentle drive into Ingleston.

'It is but three miles away and a very useful place to buy little things like stockings and gloves and ribbons,' Mrs Dean explained. 'We can also call upon Mrs Sutton, the dressmaker—'

'No need,' said Adversane, coming in at that moment. 'I have arranged for Mrs Sutton to call here tomorrow.'

Mrs Dean stared at him. 'Oh, have you, Ralph? Well, then…I suppose we need not see her today…'

Lucy chuckled. She was now on very good terms with Mrs Dean and did not scruple to tease her.

'Ariadne is deeply shocked,' she murmured. 'She does not know whether to attribute your actions to consideration for my comfort or to an arrogant high-handedness.'

The widow protested and cast an anxious glance at Adversane, but he merely looked amused.

'And which of those would you choose, Miss Halbrook?'

She met his gaze, quite fearless with Mrs Dean present and the width of the breakfast table between them.

'Oh, I think the latter, my lord.'

'Baggage,' he said, grinning at her.

Lucy was inordinately pleased with his reaction, but thought it best not to say any more. Instead, she gave her attention to the bread and butter on her plate, which was all she required to break her fast. As she finished drinking her coffee she asked Ariadne how long she thought they would be out.

'Oh, not long, my dear. We shall drive around the town, that you may see it, and then if you wish we shall stroll along the High Street and look at the shops. There are not that many, and we may well be back by two o'clock or soon after.'

'Oh, that is excellent,' said Lucy. She rose. 'I shall fetch my coat and bonnet and meet you in the hall, Ariadne.'

As she passed Adversane's chair he reached back and caught her wrist.

'Four o'clock, Miss Halbrook, do not forget.'

The touch of his cool fingers brought the heat rising in Lucy's cheeks. His grip was loose, casual, the sort of informal gesture that might occur between good friends, but her heart missed a beat and now it was hammering far too heavily, preventing her from thinking clearly. Thankfully, Adversane did not notice her confusion, for he was explaining to his cousin that he had invited Lucy to ride out with him.

'Oh, perhaps then, my dear, we should put off our drive to another day,' suggested Ariadne.

'There is not the least need for that,' cried Lucy, struggling to recover her composure. 'I am not one of those lacklustre females who is prostrate after the slightest exertion!'

She had spoken in jest, but an uneasy silence fell over

the breakfast room. Ariadne looked taken aback and the air was taut as a bowstring. Adversane released her, his chair scraped back and without a word he strode out of the breakfast room.

'What is it, Ariadne? What did I say?'

Mrs Dean dabbed at her lips with her napkin.

'Lady Adversane was not very strong,' she said quietly. 'At least, she could walk well enough when it suited her, but she would often take to her room for the rest of the day after the most gentle exercise, pleading exhaustion. You were not to know, of course.' She rose and came round the table to Lucy, taking her arm. 'Come along, my dear, we'll go upstairs to fetch our things and be away.'

Ariadne was right, of course. Lucy had spoken in all innocence, but she could not forget the effect of her words. She did not mention it again to Mrs Dean, but later, when she changed into her riding habit and went out to the stables, she knew she would have to say something to Lord Adversane.

He was waiting for her at the stable yard, holding the reins of his black hunter while the groom walked a pretty bay mare up and down. When Lucy appeared, the groom brought the bay to her immediately and directed her to the mounting block. As soon as she was in the saddle Adversane handed his reins to the groom and came close to check the girth and stirrup.

She said quietly, as the groom moved away, 'My Lord, what I said at breakfast—I must apologise, I did not know...about your wife.'

'I am aware of that, Miss Halbrook.'

'I did not intend any offence.'

'None was taken.' He gave the girth a final pat and stood back. 'Shall we go?'

Discussion ended, she thought sadly. He had withdrawn from her again.

It was a long time since Lucy had last ridden, and for the first ten minutes she gave her attention to staying in the saddle and controlling the bay's playful antics as they trotted out of the gates. Adversane waited only to assure himself that she was comfortable before he set off at a canter across the park. Lucy followed, and when he gave the black hunter his head she experienced a surge of delight as she set the mare galloping in pursuit. She forgot their earlier constraint and when at last her companion slowed the pace she came alongside and said with heartfelt gratitude, *'Thank* you, my lord! I do not know when I have enjoyed myself more!'

'Really? But you ride very well, you must have learned that somewhere.'

'Yes, on friends' ponies and for a short time when Papa had funds enough for me to have a horse of my own, but we only ever rode on the lanes or rough pasture. To be able to gallop—really *gallop* across the park like that—it was…it was exhilarating!'

'I am pleased, then, Miss Halbrook, and happy for you to ride Brandy whenever you wish. You do not need to refer to me. Send a message to the stables when you want to ride out and Greg, my groom, will arrange for someone to accompany you.'

'Was Brandy your wife's horse?'

For a moment she thought he had not heard her.

'No,' he said at last. 'Helene had a grey. Beautiful to look at, but no spirit at all. Now, which way would you like to go?'

She accepted that he did not wish to talk more about his wife and looked about her before answering his question. 'I am not sure...which is your land?'

'All of it.' He glanced up at the sun. 'There is time to ride as far as the Home Wood and around the southern perimeter, if you wish.'

'Oh, yes, please—I feel as if I could ride for ever!'

Lord Adversane grinned, putting his severe expression to flight, and Lucy wondered if it was just such a look that had made his first wife fall in love with him.

The idea surprised and embarrassed her. Her hands clenched on the reins and the mare snatched at the bit, unsettled. She gave her attention to quietening the horse and by the time she brought the bay alongside the black hunter again she had regained her equilibrium. They left the park and soon found themselves on a high ridge, with the moors climbing even higher on one side, while a vista of wooded hills and steeply sided valleys opened out before them.

Lucy was enchanted and eager to know more about the country—she asked him the name of the thick wood in the distance, and what river it was that tumbled through the valley, and did he really own everything as far as the eye could see? She was relieved that he did not appear to be offended by the questions that tumbled from her lips. He responded with patience and good humour, even expanding his answers and offering more information when he realised that she was genuinely interested.

Ralph found himself looking closely at this slight figure riding beside him. Her faded habit only enhanced the peach bloom in her cheeks and the sparkle in her green eyes. He usually went out alone, or with Harry, but riding with Lucy Halbrook, seeing his world afresh through her eager eyes, was surprisingly enjoyable.

As they continued their ride he told her about the family members she would meet at the forthcoming house party. She listened to him intently, her head a little on one side as if trying to commit it all to memory. It was with something very like regret that Ralph noticed the sun's shadow had moved on and he told her they should turn for home.

'Will we have time to visit the moors today?'

'I'm afraid not.' He saw the disappointment in her face and added, 'The moors are so extensive they deserve at least a day to themselves. However, we can ride back across the fields, and there will be a few dry stone walls to jump, if you are able.'

Immediately, the absurd chit was smiling at him as if he had offered her a casket of jewels.

'Oh, yes, please, only…perhaps you can find a couple of *tiny* walls for me to jump first, since I am so horribly out of practice!'

Laughing, Ralph set off across country, choosing a route that would not overtax the mare or her rider. He soon realised that he needn't have worried. Lucy was a natural horsewoman. She rode beside him, jumping everything fearlessly and with such delight that he wished the return journey was twice as long. All too soon they were back in the park with the house just visible on the far skyline and in between a vast expanse of green, springy turf. He reined in his horse.

'You appear to be at home upon Brandy now, Miss Halbrook. Would you like to lead the way to the stables?' He saw the speculation in her eyes, the quick glance she threw towards his own mount. 'Don't worry about Jupiter. He will be happy enough to follow in your wake.'

'I was thinking rather that we might race for the gates.'

His brows went up.

'Oho, are you so confident of your ability, madam?'

'Yes, if you will give me a head start.'

He regarded her with a slight frown. Sheer foolishness, of course. Childish, too. It would be reckless in the extreme to hurtle at breakneck speed across the park. One stumble could mean disaster. He opened his mouth to say so, but found himself subject to such a hopeful gaze that he could not utter the words. Instead, he pointed to a single tree standing alone some distance away.

'I'll give you to the oak.'

She needed no second bidding. He watched her careering away from him and found himself enjoying the view. She had almost outgrown the faded habit, for it clung to her figure, accentuating the tiny waist and the delectable roundness of her buttocks, seated so firmly in the saddle. She rode well, and he imagined her in his bed, thought how satisfying it would be to rouse that same passion and spirit in her by covering her soft, pliant body with kisses.

The image enthralled him and it was Jupiter's fretful protest that made him realise Lucy had reached the oak. With a word he gave the hunter his freedom and Jupiter leapt forward. He was soon in his stride and catching up with the smaller bay. Ralph leaned low, urging his horse on while keeping his eyes upon Lucy's shapely figure, trying to prevent his imagination from picturing what he would like to do when he caught up with her.

Jupiter stumbled and Ralph held him up, steadying him with a word. They were on the bay's heels now, the hunter's longer stride giving him the advantage. Sensing a victory, the black lengthened his neck and strained to come up with the bay. Ralph was so close now he could almost reach out and touch Lucy's back. The open gates were looming. She would check soon, and he would shoot past. But Lucy did not slow—she pushed Brandy on and they raced through the narrow entrance side by side, with only inches to spare.

Lucy was laughing as they brought both horses to a stand on the lawn. Glancing back, Ralph could see where they had ridden by the deep gouges the hooves had made in the turf. Old Amos would ring a peal over him for this. He had been head gardener for decades, and Ralph could almost hear him, demanding in outraged accents to know just what my lord was about, behaving like a schoolboy.

And looking into Lucy's smiling eyes, Ralph realised that was just how he felt, like a schoolboy ripe for a spree, rather than a man bent upon a plan of action that was no laughing matter.

Sobered by the thought of the dangerous game he had in mind, Ralph began to walk Jupiter towards the stables. Lucy brought the bay alongside.

'I am afraid your groundsman will be most unhappy with us, sir.'

He knew she was looking up at him, but he thought it best not to meet her eyes. She had an uncanny power to disconcert him. When they reached the stable yard, the grooms ran out to take the horses. Ralph jumped down and walked around to Lucy, holding out his arms to lift her down. It was a duty, he told himself. It was what any man would do for the woman he intended to marry and therefore it was necessary for him to do so, to convince his staff that all this was real.

She was light as a feather and her waist was so tiny his hands almost spanned it. Ralph needed all his iron will to stop himself from holding her a moment longer than was necessary. In fact, so eager was he to ensure Lucy could not misunderstand his intentions he released her a little too soon and she stumbled, off balance. Immediately, his arms were around her, even as her own hands clutched at his riding jacket. The flush on her cheeks deepened, and he was shaken to the core by a strong desire to kiss the cherry-red lips that had parted so invitingly. The grooms had walked the horses into the stables, there was no one to see them. Why should he not lower his head and take advantage of the situation?

The way his body hardened immediately at the thought caught him off guard. He had to conjure every ounce of resolve to prevent himself from giving in to it. He tried to summon up a reasonable response, but could only find anger—at himself for his weakness and at Lucy for tempting him. With rigid control, he brought his hands back and put them over hers, pulling her fingers from his lapels.

He said coldly, 'Please do not throw yourself at me, Miss Halbrook. That might be how one conducts oneself in your world, but at Adversane we expect a little more decorum.'

Her face flamed, those green eyes lost their shy smile and darkened with hurt and bewilderment. Damnation, why had he not cut his tongue out before allowing himself to utter such words? She had put out her hands to steady herself, he knew that, but he had been thrown off balance by the hunger that had slammed through him when she was in his arms. He had not known such strength of feeling since the heady days of his youth and, unnerved, he had attacked her cruelly, coldly, in a manner designed to depress any pretensions she might have.

These were the thoughts of an instant. He felt as if time had stopped, but it could only have been a moment.

He said quickly, 'I should not have spoken so. It was unforgivable—'

But she was already backing away from him, her cheeks now white as chalk, and her hands raised before her, as if to ward him off.

'No, no, you are quite right. I beg your pardon.'

Her voice was little more than a thread. She turned and hurried away, head high. He should go after her, tell her it was not her fault, that the blame was all his, but he did not move. What could he say? That he had lost control? That he had suddenly been overwhelmed with the desire to ravish her? She was an employee, here for a purpose. If she thought him in any way attracted to her it would compromise her position. She would be unable to play her part for fear of the consequences. All his planning would come to naught.

Ralph watched her walk through the arched entrance and out of sight. Only then did he move, striding into the stables, stripping off his coat as he went. He made his way to Jupiter's stall and tossed his coat over the partition. He would rub down the horse himself, brush the black coat until it shone and then he would put his head under the pump in the yard. After that he thought he might just be able to face meeting Lucy Halbrook at the dinner table.

Chapter Four

'I will not cry.'

Lucy kept repeating the words to herself as she made her way back to her room. She kept her head up, teeth firmly biting into her lip to offset the bitter shame and revulsion that brought hot, angry tears to clog her throat and prickle behind her eyes.

They had been getting on so well, it had been the most perfect outing until Adversane had lifted her down and she had lost her balance. She had been exhilarated, in love with the whole world, and when she had put her hands against his chest to steady herself she had had no thought other than to laugh and apologise for being a little giddy.

Then she had looked up into his slate-grey eyes and her world had fallen apart. Her foolishly heightened sense had thought that he had taken her in his arms instead of trying to hold her upright, and she had imagined *such* a look that it had turned her bones to water. Instead of being able to stand up straight, she had been in even greater danger of falling over and had clutched at his coat like a drowning man might cling to a wooden spar. In her silly, dizzy brain she had thought herself a princess about to be kissed by her fairy-tale prince. That, of course, was pure foolishness. No one, absolutely no one, would ever think of the saturnine Lord Adversane as a prince.

'At least he is not a rake,' she muttered as she ran up the grand staircase. 'You were standing there, looking up at him, positively *inviting* him to seduce you. Thankfully he is too much of a gentleman for that.'

She flinched as she remembered his reprimand, but it was justified. In fact, she would be very fortunate if he did not pack her off back to London immediately.

She went down to the drawing room before dinner in a state of nervous apprehension. When Ariadne asked her if she had enjoyed her ride, she answered yes, but hurriedly changed the subject, and when Lord Adversane came in she retired to a chair by the window and hoped that if she kept very still he would not notice her.

It seemed to work. Apart from an infinitesimal bow Lord Adversane ignored her until dinner was announced, when he gave his arm to his cousin. Lucy was left to follow on as best she might. Thankfully, Mrs Dean was never short of small talk at the dinner table. She chattered on, rarely requiring a response, while Byrne kept the wineglasses filled and oversaw the elaborate ritual of bringing in and removing a bewildering array of delectable foods. Lucy was too unhappy to be hungry and ate almost nothing from the dishes immediately before her. She was pushing a little pile of rice about her plate when Byrne appeared at her elbow with a silver tray.

He said quietly, 'His lordship recommends the salmon in wine, miss, and begs that you will try it.'

Lucy glanced along the table. Lord Adversane was watching her, unsmiling, but when he caught her eye he gave a little nod of encouragement. She allowed the butler to spoon a little of the salmon and the sauce onto her plate. It was indeed delicious and she directed another look towards her host, hoping to convey her gratitude. Her tentative smile was received with another small but definite nod. Whether it was that, or the effects of the food, she suddenly felt a little better.

When dinner was over the ladies moved to the drawing room. Having boasted earlier of her stamina, Lucy did not feel she could retire before Lord Adversane joined them. Mrs Dean settled herself on one of the satin-covered sofas but Lucy could not sit still. To disguise her restlessness she pretended to study the room. There was plenty to occupy her: the walls were covered with old masters and the ornate carving of the overmantel was worthy of close attention. Adversane did not linger over his brandy and soon came in. He made no attempt to engage Lucy in conversation and took a seat near his cousin, politely inviting her to tell him about her day. Ariadne needed no second bidding and launched into a long and convoluted description of her activities.

It was a balmy evening, and the long windows were thrown wide, allowing the desultory birdsong to drift in on the warm air. Lucy slipped out onto the terrace. The sun was dipping but was still some way from the horizon and she could feel its heat reflecting from the stone walls of the house. The earlier breeze had dropped away and a peaceful stillness had settled over the gardens spread out before her, the statuary and flowerbeds leading the eye on to the trees in the distance and, beyond them, the faint misty edge of the high moors. Lucy drank in the scene, trying to store every detail in her memory. She suspected such summer evenings were rare in the north and she wanted to remember this one.

It was very quiet in the drawing room and she wondered perhaps if Lord Adversane had had enough of his cousin's inconsequential chatter and retired. She stepped back into the room, and gave a little start when she realised that it was Mrs Dean who was missing. Her host was standing by the empty fireplace.

'You are very quiet this evening, Miss Halbrook.'

She sat down and folded her hands in her lap. She must take this opportunity to say what was on her mind.

'I was wondering, my lord, if you wished me to leave. If I go now there is still time for you to find someone else.'

'Do you wish to go?'

She shook her head. 'My circumstances have not changed. I am still in need of employment.'

'And I am still in need of a fiancée. It seems logical, therefore, that we should continue.' He paused. 'You are smiling, Miss Halbrook. Have I said something to amuse you?'

'You make it all sound so simple. A mere business arrangement.'

'Which is what it is.'

She looked down at her hands.

'But this afternoon, in the stable yard—'

'A little misunderstanding,' he interposed. 'Brought on by the excitement of the ride. It will not be allowed to happen again.'

'No, my lord?'

'You sound sceptical.'

'I am, a little.' She continued, with some difficulty, 'I know—I have been told—that when a man and a woman are thrown into a situation, when they are alone together…'

She blushed, not knowing how to go on.

'I understand you,' he said quietly, 'but you have nothing of that nature to fear. Let us speak plainly, madam.

I have no designs upon your virtue and no intention of seducing you.'

His blunt words should have been reassuring, but she was contrary enough to feel slighted by them. She kept her eyes lowered and heard him exhale, almost like a sigh.

'Believe me, Miss Halbrook, you will be quite safe here. I can assure you that even strong passions can be assuaged with hard work and exercise. And if not... Well, for a man at least there are establishments that cater for his needs.' Lucy bent her head even more to hide her burning cheeks. He continued after an infinitesimal pause, 'But perhaps that is a little too much plain speaking, and a subject not suited to a young lady's ears.'

'Not at all. I value your honesty, sir.'

She had not raised her head and now she heard his soft footsteps approaching. She looked up to find him standing over her.

'And I value yours. You are a sensible young woman, which is what I require in my hostess. A simple business transaction, Miss Halbrook. Can you manage that?'

She did not answer immediately. It should be easy, he made it sound so reasonable. Yet some instinct urged caution. She stifled it. If Lord Adversane could approach this in a logical fashion, then she could, too. After taking a few deep breaths she straightened her shoulders.

'Yes, my lord, I can.'

A simple business transaction.

The words echoed around Lucy's head when she lay in her bed through the dark reaches of the night. She could do this. The remuneration was worth a little sacrifice, surely. And if she was honest, the only sacrifice was that she should not allow herself to flirt with Lord

Adversane. He roused in her a girlish spirit that had no place in her life now. When he was near she wanted to tease him, to make him laugh and drive away the sombre look that too often haunted his eyes. But his sorrow was none of her concern and she must be careful not to compromise herself.

'I must not be alone with him, that is all,' she told herself.

Surely that was no very arduous task when he had even brought in Ariadne to act as chaperone. All she had to do was to live like a lady in this beautiful house for another few weeks and she would walk away with more money than she could earn in a year. She turned over and cradled her cheek in her hand, finally falling asleep while engaged in the delightful task of thinking just what she might do with such a sum.

Lucy awoke to another brilliantly sunny day. Her spirits were equally bright. For a while, yesterday, she had thought she would be leaving all this luxury behind. Instead, she had a delectable prospect ahead of her. A visit from the dressmaker.

'Byrne, where is Lord Adversane?'

Miss Halbrook's enquiry echoed around the stone walls of the Great Hall. If the butler noted her flushed cheeks or the martial light in her eye he showed no sign of it and calmly informed her that she would find his lordship with Mr Colne.

It took Lucy a little time to find the steward's office for she had not before entered the service wing of the house, but the delay did nothing to cool her temper. She knocked briefly and walked in without waiting for a response.

Lord Adversane and Mr Colne were standing by a large table, studying a plan of the estate.

'I would like to speak to you, my lord,' she said without preamble.

He raised his brows.

'Can it not wait?' One look at her face gave him his answer. He turned to Mr Colne. 'Harry, will you go on to the stables and have the horses saddled? I will join you in five minutes.' As the door closed behind the steward he leaned back against the table. 'Very well, Miss Halbrook, what is it you want to say to me?'

'It concerns the dressmaker.'

He glanced at the clock. 'Has she not arrived?'

'Oh, yes, she is here, my lord. She informs me that you have given her instructions—precise instructions—on the gowns she is to provide, down to the very colours and fabrics to be used.'

'What of it?'

'What—?' She stared at him. 'It is usual, my lord, for ladies to make their own decisions on what they wear.'

'Do you not like the colours?'

'That is not the point—'

'And are the gowns too unfashionable for you?'

'Not at all, but—'

'Then I really do not see the problem.'

Lucy drew in a long and angry breath.

'The *problem*,' she said, with great emphasis, 'is that I have no choice. I am to be measured and pinned and fitted like a—like a doll!'

'Surely not.' He picked up his hat and gloves from a side table. 'I have no doubt Mrs Sutton will ask your opinion on trimmings and beads and so forth.'

'Minor details!'

'But it must suffice.'

He began to move towards the door and she stepped in front of him.

'What you do not understand—'

'What *you* do not understand,' he interrupted her curtly, 'is that this discussion is ended.'

She glared at him. 'When I accused you of high-handedness yesterday, my lord, I did not think it would go so far!'

He fixed her with a steely gaze and addressed her in an equally chilling voice.

'Miss Halbrook, remember that I am paying you very well for your time here. If I wish you to wear certain colours and styles of gown while you are under my roof then you will do so. Do I make myself clear?'

He was towering over her, as unyielding as granite. The cleft in his chin was more deeply defined than ever and there was no softness about him, not even in the grey wool of his riding jacket. He would not give in; she knew that from the implacable look in his eyes, but she would not look away, and as their gazes remained locked together she found other sensations replacing her anger.

Such as curiosity. What it would be like to kiss that firm mouth, to have his arms around her, to force him to bend to the will of her own passion...

Shocked and a little frightened by her thoughts, Lucy stepped back and dragged her eyes away from that disturbing gaze. There must be no repeat of yesterday. He must not think she was trying in any way to entice him. Better to summon up the resentment that had brought her here in the first place.

'You have made yourself very clear, my lord.'

She ground out the words, staring at the floor, but he put his fingers under her chin and obliged her to look at him again.

He said softly, 'I am not an ogre, Miss Halbrook. I have my reasons for this, believe me.' He held her eyes for a moment longer before releasing her. He went to the door and opened it. 'Now go back upstairs and continue being—ah—fitted and pinned. You are going to have more new clothes than you can count. When this is over you may take them all away with you. Most women would be delighted with the prospect.'

She found she was trembling. Despising her own weakness, Lucy dragged together her pride and managed to say with creditable calm, 'I am not most women, my lord.'

'No.' His mouth twisted into a wry smile as she stalked out of the room. 'No, you are not, Miss Halbrook.'

Lucy went back to the morning room where Mrs Dean and the dressmaker were engaged in discussing fabric samples and looking through the portfolio of drawings that Mrs Sutton had brought with her. She was shaken by her encounter with Lord Adversane, and a little chastened, too. He was, after all, her employer, and quite within his rights to dictate what she should wear. A little spirit flared to argue that it would have been better if he had explained all this at the outset, but it was a very tiny spark and soon died.

She gave herself up to the task of looking at the various designs and samples of fabrics. She soon discovered—as she had known all along, if only she had thought about it—that she did indeed have a degree of freedom in the choice of ribbons and trimmings to be added to each gown. By the end of the session her head was spinning with all the talk of closed robes, morning and day dresses, walking dresses and evening gowns, as well as the pelisses, cloaks and shawls required to go with them.

Also—a last-minute addition that Lord Adversane had ordered in a note, delivered hotfoot to the dressmaker yesterday evening—a riding habit.

Although she knew she had no real choice, Lucy nodded and approved all the samples and sketches put before her. They were without exception elegant creations, not overly burdened with frills and ribbons, which suited her very well. As the dressmaker and her assistant began packing away the drifts of muslin, samples of fine wool, worsted and sarcenet, Lucy spotted a large square of red silk. She picked it up.

'What is this?'

Mrs Sutton looked around and gave a little tut of exasperation.

'Heavens, miss, as if I should forget that!' She pulled out the sheaf of loose papers again and selected a coloured drawing, which she handed to Lucy. 'Lord Adversane was most insistent that you should have this gown.'

Lucy gazed at the impossibly slender figure in the painting. She was swathed in red silk, the high waistline and low neck leaving little to the imagination.

'It is shown exactly as his lordship directed,' said Mrs Sutton, waiting anxiously for Lucy's reaction. 'Even to the diamond set of earrings, necklace and bracelet.'

'Scarlet and diamonds.' Lucy pictured herself in such a gown, the jewels sparkling in the candlelight, her skirts floating about her as she danced around the ballroom. 'Very striking but…it is not suitable for an unmarried lady. What say you, Ariadne?' She handed the picture to Mrs Dean, who stared at it in silence. 'Ariadne?'

The widow gave a little start.

'Oh, I do not…' She tailed off again, her troubled glance fixed upon the drawing.

'It is far too grand for me to wear,' Lucy continued. 'If we were in London, perhaps, but here in the country, what use can I have for such a creation?'

'Unless Adversane means to invite the neighbourhood,' murmured Ariadne.

Lucy frowned. 'Why should he do that?'

Ariadne made a visible effort to pull herself together, saying robustly, 'I suppose he thought you must have it. Who knows what invitations you might receive? And everyone wears such colours these days. You will not always want to be wearing those pale muslins, now will you? And I recognise the diamonds. They are a family heirloom. As Ralph's fiancée I have no doubt he will wish you to wear them.'

'Yes, of course.' Lucy dismissed her doubts, relieved by Mrs Dean's approval of the scarlet gown. To appear in public so beautifully apparelled was every girl's dream. And what did it matter that it was all a sham, a charade? It would be a wonderful memory for her to take away with her.

When the dressmaker had departed Ariadne carried Lucy off to the shrubbery, declaring that one needed to clear one's head after being bombarded with so much detail.

'I must confess,' she added, as they strolled arm in arm along the gravelled paths, 'when you went off so angrily I thought I should be sending Mrs Sutton away and ordering the carriage to take you back to London forthwith.'

Lucy's free hand fluttered.

'It was foolish of me to allow such a little thing to make me angry. I assure you, I never had any intention of leaving over such a matter.'

'Oh, no, my dear, I was not thinking of *your* intentions. I thought Ralph might order you to go. I thought he would call a halt to this whole business—not that that would be a bad thing.' She muttered these last words almost to herself and when she found Lucy's considering gaze upon her she coloured and said, as if in apology, 'My cousin is not used to having his will crossed.'

'I am well aware of that. Autocratic to the point of tyranny!'

'But he is not a bad man, Lucy. It is just that... You should understand, my dear, that he was the only surviving male child, and much loved. Although he was brought up on strict principles he was allowed to go his own way from an early age. I suppose you might say he was too much indulged—'

'I should,' put in Lucy emphatically.

'But he was not rebellious, you see, so his sainted parents never needed to curb him. They had him late in life, too, which I think made them a little more inclined to spoil him, and then, of course, they were carried off within weeks of each other by a vicious bout of influenza, and he inherited the title soon after he was one-and-twenty. From being a carefree young man he suddenly found himself with half a dozen estates and hundreds of people dependent upon him. And things were not so comfortable as they are now. The old lord had spent so much on improvements to Adversane that the finances were severely stretched when Ralph took over. He has had to struggle to rebuild the family fortunes. He needed a steady nerve and a firm hand on the reins to bring it back to prosperity. He demanded that everything should be done his way and it has worked. The fortune is restored.'

'But he rules his household with a will of iron,' objected Lucy.

'All the Cottinghams are strong-willed, my dear, and

as the heir and only son, Ralph's will has never been opposed. Is it any wonder that he has grown used to his
own way? That was why his marriage to Helene was so
fortuitous. She was all compliance and perfectly suited
to his temperament.'

'Perfectly suited to make him even more despotic,'
declared Lucy. 'The poor lady must have been wholly
downtrodden.'

Ariadne quickly disclaimed.

'He never bullied her, I am quite certain of it. But then,
Helene was so very sweet-natured, I doubt she ever gave
him cause to be angry.'

'Well,' said Lucy, thinking of the small sum she had
sewn into the hem of her travelling cloak, 'Lord Adversane may be as autocratic and demanding as he wishes,
but I shall not allow him to bully *me*, and so I shall tell
him!'

However, Lucy had no opportunity to tell Lord Adversane anything that evening, for when she joined Mrs
Dean in the drawing room before dinner she learned that
their host had gone off to visit friends and would not be
back for two days. The news left her feeling a little dis-
consolate and she gave a little huff of exasperation.

'And how am I supposed to learn everything I need
to know if he is not here?'

'My dear, no one will expect you to know everything
about Ralph,' replied Mrs Dean, looking amused. 'In
fact, I doubt anyone could do that.'

'I beg your pardon, Ariadne, it is just that… Well, I
had worked myself up to challenge him about his high-
handed ways and now I feel a little…cheated.'

'You *enjoy* confronting him?'

Her shocked expression made Lucy smile.

'I like matters out in the open wherever possible.'

She thought of her uncle's unwanted attentions and felt a little guilty that she had not brought that out into the open, but it would have caused too much distress to her mother and her aunt. Lucy had every reason to be discreet in that case. Lord Adversane, however, was another matter entirely. She added a little pugnaciously, 'If that means confronting your cousin, I will not shirk from it.'

'Then perhaps it is as well Ralph is away, or we should see the sparks fly,' retorted Mrs Dean, chuckling. 'Never mind, my dear, there is plenty for us to do. You can help me with the arrangements for the forthcoming house party. The guests have already been invited, of course—Ralph has seen to that—but there are the rooms to be allocated, furniture to be arranged, menus to be planned.'

'And just who is invited, Ariadne?'

'Well, there are Ralph's two sisters and their husbands,' said Mrs Dean, counting them off on her fingers. 'Adam Cottingham—Ralph's cousin and heir—and his wife, or course. And Sir James and Lady Preston.'

'Do you mean the late Lady Adversane's parents? But surely they will not wish to come to Adversane—'

'Oh, yes, they will! They are even bringing their daughter Charlotte with them.'

'But—do they know, about me?'

'Oh, lord, yes. Ralph told them himself when he invited them to come and stay.'

'And they still accepted his invitation?'

'Yes. I doubt they hesitated for a moment.' She patted Lucy's arm. 'I do not think I am speaking out of turn if I tell you that the Prestons virtually *threw* Helene at Adversane. They wanted her to marry well. Lady Preston would have preferred a higher title, perhaps, but the Cottinghams are an old family. Their line goes back to the Conqueror. And besides that, Ralph's wealth made him a very acceptable *parti.*'

Lucy frowned. 'But surely they will not be comfortable staying here, knowing what happened two years ago.'

'As to that, they must feel it, of course, as we all do, but life must go on. Ralph's sisters are already pressing him to marry again, which is why he has installed you here. And I hear even Lord Preston has been hinting that young Charlotte could fill her sister's shoes.'

'But that is monstrous.'

'It is hard-headed sense,' replied Ariadne drily. 'Preston will naturally want to maintain his connection with Adversane, if he can.'

Byrne came in to tell them that dinner awaited them and no more was said that evening about the house guests, but Lucy thought she understood a little better now just why Adversane had hired her.

The following days were spent in preparations for the forthcoming house party. Ariadne took Lucy on a tour of the east wing, preparatory to allocating the guest rooms. There was also a trip to Ingleston to buy additional gloves and slippers to go with all her new clothes. It was like being caught up in a very pleasant whirlwind, thought Lucy. She loved being busy and happily threw herself into all the arrangements. She discussed menus with the housekeeper and accepted the gardener's invitation to show her around the gardens and select the flowers she would require for the house. Lucy discovered that the staff was eager and willing to help, and once she had accustomed herself to the thought that she was regarded as the next Lady Adversane she found she could work very well with them all. It was impossible for Lucy not to enjoy herself, but at the back of her mind was the realisation that this would not last. At some point she would have to leave Adversane.

She pondered the idea as she sat at her open bedroom window, where the night air was scented with summer flowers.

'And when that day comes I shall go with many happy memories,' she told herself, smiling up at the sliver of moon suspended in the clear sky. 'Until then, I shall continue to enjoy every minute of my stay here!'

Lord Adversane returned the following afternoon. His arrival coincided with the first delivery from the dressmaker. He walked into the morning room to find Lucy and his cousin surrounded by a chaotic jumble of gowns and boxes and tissue paper.

'Ralph, my dear, you are back!' Ariadne smiled at him and waved a hand at the disorder. 'Mrs Sutton and her assistants must have been sewing night and day to have so many things finished already.'

'Evidently,' he murmured. 'I trust the gowns are to Miss Halbrook's satisfaction?'

Lucy had been feeling a little shy and not sure how to greet him after their last confrontation, but the challenging look in his eye roused her spirit.

'They are indeed,' she replied. 'I have yet to try them on, but the styles and colours cannot be faulted. You have impeccable taste, my lord.'

'Handsomely said, madam.' He grinned at her, then cast a faintly bewildered glance about the room. 'I am definitely *de trop* here, so I will go away and change out of all my dirt.'

'Oh, dear, how remiss of me,' cried Ariadne, 'Have you been travelling all day, Cousin? Shall I ring for refreshments?'

'No need,' he said, going back to the door. 'I shall ask Byrne to send something up to me. I shall see you at dinner.'

'My lord!' Lucy called him back. As he turned she held up two of the new creations, saying innocently, 'I have these new evening gowns now, sir. The white drawn-thread muslin with a twisted pink sash, or the cream sprigged muslin. Which would you like me to wear tonight?'

'I have not the least—' He broke off, his eyes narrowing. 'I see. You have not forgiven me for my high-handedness in dictating what should be made, is that it?'

'He who pays the piper may call the tune, my lord.'

He met her limpid gaze with a hard stare.

'But one would hope, Miss Halbrook, that the piper knows how to play. I have provided your wardrobe, madam, I leave it to you to present yourself to best advantage.'

He closed the door behind him with a decided snap.

Ariadne gave a little tut of reproof. 'Lucy, my dear, I really do not think you are wise to tease Ralph in that manner.'

'No?' A smile tugged at the corners of Lucy's mouth. 'I think it is high time someone teased your cousin. In my opinion he has had his own way for far too long!'

Lucy might well want to tease her host, but she was also eager to wear one of her new gowns, and the look of relief upon Mrs Dean's countenance when she presented herself in the drawing room before dinner caused Lucy to chuckle.

'You see I have behaved myself and chosen the cream muslin. The embroidery on the shawl Mrs Sutton sent with it exactly matches the pink sash.' She gave a twirl.

'Does it not look very well? And Ruthie found a matching ribbon for my hair, too. I hope his lordship will be pleased.'

'He is.'

The deep voice made her turn quickly to the door. Adversane had come in and was walking towards her. His dark evening coat contrasted with the white waistcoat and knee breeches, and his black hair gleamed like polished jet in the soft light of the summer evening. Lucy found herself thinking how attractive he was. That made her laugh inwardly, for no one could call Lord Adversane's craggy face handsome. Strong, yes. Striking, even. Yet the impression persisted and she quickly sat down on the sofa next to Ariadne, conscious that she was blushing.

Ralph raised his quizzing glass to look at her. He did not need it, and the gesture was more to cover his own confusion. He had entered the room in time to see her spin around, the skirts of her gown lifting away from a pair of extremely neat ankles and her honey-brown curls bouncing joyously about her head. Once again he had been surprised by the way she roused his desire.

She was no beauty, certainly not a diamond as his wife had been, but he had never seriously expected to find anyone to equal Helene. Yet there was a vivacity about Lucy Halbrook, and he found himself wondering if that liveliness would translate itself to passion if he was to take her in his arms.

Impossible. She was a lady, not a courtesan, and he had never dallied with gently bred ladies—not even Helene, although he had known from the start that he would marry her. Ruthlessly, he suppressed all improper thoughts and when he spoke his tone was at its most neutral.

'My compliments, Miss Halbrook. You look very well tonight.'

'Any tributes are due to Mrs Sutton and to my maid, sir, the one for providing the gown and the other for arranging my hair.'

She answered calmly enough and the becoming flush on her cheeks was dying away. He was relieved. It formed no part of his plan to become entangled with his employee. He helped himself to wine from the decanter on the side table and addressed his cousin.

'I have had a letter from Caroline. She and Wetherell are coming on the nineteenth.'

'Was there ever any doubt?' Ariadne turned to Lucy to explain. 'Lady Wetherell is Ralph's sister and eight years older than he. She is very eager to meet you, Lucy, but I should warn you that Caroline can be a little forthright—'

'She is damned interfering,' he said brutally.

'A family trait, perhaps,' murmured Lucy.

His eyes narrowed. The minx was teasing him again, but he acknowledged the justice of her remark with the flicker of a smile while Ariadne continued, unheeding.

'You may recall, Lucy, I told you that Ralph's sister Margaret is also coming. She is only four years older than Ralph but equally...'

'Interfering?'

Ralph laughed. 'There you have it, Miss Halbrook. Perhaps now you see why I need a fiancée to protect me?'

'Your sisters are concerned for the succession,' put in Ariadne.

'They need not be. I have an heir.'

'Adam Cottingham? He is merely a cousin.'

'He bears the family name. That is sufficient.'

'But they would prefer to continue the direct line, Ralph—'

His cousin's persistence hit a nerve. He had heard all these arguments before.

'Enough,' he said impatiently. 'I have married once for the sake of an heir. I do not intend to do so again. I shall never take another wife.' He rose quickly before anyone could respond. 'Shall we go in to dinner?'

Lucy accompanied Lord Adversane into the dining room, her fingers resting lightly on his sleeve. She could feel the tense muscles, strong as steel beneath the expensive Bath coating. He was angry, and she had some sympathy with him. His wife had been dead for but two years and he was being nagged to marry again. He must have loved her very much.

In an effort to divert his mind she asked him about his trip. He told her that he had been in Leeds, discussing the prospect of a steam railway. She dragged from her memory whatever she had learned of steam power in order to ask questions that would not result in his dismissing her as a fool. She succeeded very well, and the conversation continued during dinner. Lucy included Ariadne where she could, but although Mrs Dean professed herself interested, she was content to allow the discussion to continue around her while she concentrated upon her meal.

'Steam power has a lot to offer,' concluded Lord Adversane, when the covers had been removed and they were sitting back in their chairs, choosing from the dishes of sweetmeats left on the table. 'It has even more potential than the canals, I think, and we will be able to move huge quantities of goods to and from the new manufactories.'

'And will it mean the demise of the horse?' asked Lucy.

'Good God, no. Or, at least, not for a long time.' He

pushed a dish of sugared almonds towards her. 'Which reminds me. Did I see your new riding habit amongst all those new clothes delivered today?'

'Why, yes, sir.'

The high-waisted style was very different from her old habit, and the soft dove-blue linen not nearly so hard-wearing as the olive-green velvet, but, she thought wryly, the future Lady Adversane did not need to worry about such practicalities.

'Good,' remarked her host. 'Then perhaps you would like to ride out with me tomorrow. Greg tells me you have not been near the stables since that first ride.'

Lucy hoped her face did not show her embarrassment at the memory.

'No, I did not like to presume.'

'It is no presumption, madam. Brandy needs exercising and you may as well do that as the stable hands. You may order the mare to be saddled whenever you wish, and Greg will find someone to accompany you.'

'Th-thank you, my lord.'

'So? Are you free tomorrow? It will have to be after breakfast. Colne and I have business before that, but I should be free soon after ten.'

Mrs Dean gave a little cluck of admiration.

'You are so industrious, Ralph, to be conducting your business so early.'

'If I do not then the day is lost.' He looked again at Lucy, who met his enquiring glance with a smile.

'I shall be ready, my lord.'

Lucy was already in the stable yard and mounted upon the bay mare when Lord Adversane appeared the following morning.

'I wanted to accustom myself to this new habit,' she

told him as she waited for him to mount up. 'The skirts are much wider than my old dress. I hope Brandy will not take exception to them if they billow out.'

'She is used to it, having carried my sisters often enough.'

They trotted out of the yard and as soon as they reached the park Lord Adversane suggested they should gallop the fidgets out of their mounts. The exercise did much to dispel any lingering constraint Lucy felt, and her companion also seemed more relaxed. When they left the park he took her through the little village of Adversane, where she noted with approval the general neatness. All the buildings were in good repair and it did not surprise her to learn that most of the property belonged to the estate. They met the parson on his way to the church, whose square tower was visible beyond a double row of cottages. They drew rein, introductions were performed and the reverend gentleman smiled up at Lucy.

'So this is your second week here, Miss Halbrook.'

'It is.'

Her eyes flickered towards Adversane, who said easily, 'I was away last Sunday, Mr Hopkins, and Miss Halbrook was reluctant to attend church alone.'

Lucy cast him a grateful glance. It was almost true. Mrs Dean had cavilled at taking her into the church and, as she put it, continuing the pretence of the betrothal in such a holy place.

'We will wait until Adversane is here to escort you,' Ariadne had said. 'The Lord's wrath will come down upon his head then. Not that he will care much for that!'

Mr Hopkins was directing a sympathetic look towards Lucy and saying gently, 'Ah, yes, quite understandable, in the circumstances. You were afraid everyone would be gawping at you, Miss Halbrook. And they would be, too, I'm afraid. Perhaps you would like to come and see the church now? It has some quite wonderful examples of Gothic architecture. And I doubt if there will be anyone there at present—'

'Thank you, Mr Hopkins, but next Sunday will have to do for that. We must get on.'

'Ah, of course, of course.' The parson nodded and stepped back. 'And there is plenty of time for all the arrangements, my lord. You need only to send word when you wish me to come to discuss everything with you.'

Lucy knew not what to say and left it to Adversane to mutter a few words before they rode off.

'He meant the arrangements for the wedding, I suppose,' she said, when they were safely out of earshot.

'Of course.' His hard gaze flickered over her. 'Feeling guilty?'

'Yes, a little,' she admitted.

'Don't be. Our betrothal has given the locals something to talk about, and when it ends they will have even more to gossip over. A little harmless diversion, nothing more.'

'I suppose you are right, my lord.'

'I think it is time that we abandoned the formality, at least in public.'

'I beg your pardon?'

'You cannot keep calling me "my lord". I have a name, you know.'

Lucy felt the tell-tale colour rising up again.

'I do know,' she managed, 'but—'

'No buts, Lucy. There, I have used your name, now you must call me Ralph. Come, try it.'

She felt uncomfortably hot.

'I—that is, surely we only need to do so when other people are near—'

'And how unnatural do you think that would sound? We need to practise.'

'Of course. R-Ralph.'

He grinned. 'Very demure, my dear, but you look woefully conscious.'

'That is because I am,' she snapped.

'Which proves my point,' he replied in a voice of reason that made her grind her teeth.

Observing her frustration, he merely laughed and adjured her to keep up as he trotted out of the village.

It was impossible to remain at odds. There was too much to see, too many questions to ask. The hours flew by and Lucy was almost disappointed when Adversane said they must turn for home.

'We are on the far side of Ingleston,' he told her. 'It will take us an hour to ride back through the town, longer if we skirt around it. Which would you prefer?'

'The longer route, if you please.' Lucy recalled her meeting with the parson and had no wish to be stared at and pointed out as the future Lady Adversane.

They kept to the lanes and picked up the road again at the toll just west of Ingleston. Lucy recognised it as the road she had travelled when Mrs Dean had taken her to the town. She recalled there was a narrow, steep-sided valley ahead, where the highway ran alongside the river. It had felt very confined in the closed carriage, with nothing but the green hillside rising steep and stark on each side, and Lucy was looking forward to seeing it from horseback. She turned to her companion to tell him so and found that his attention was fixed upon something ahead, high up on the hills. Following his gaze, she saw the moors rising above the trees, culminating in a ragged edifice of stone on the skyline.

'Is that Druids Rock, my lord?'

'Yes.'

She stared up at the rocky outcrop. The sun had moved behind it, and the stone looked black and forbidding against the blue sky.

'Your cousin told me that the old track to Adversane ran past there, before this carriageway was built.'

'That is so.'

'And can one still ride that way?'

'Yes, but we will keep to the road.'

She said no more. His wife had died at Druids Rock and it must be very painful to have such a constant and visible reminder of the tragedy. She longed to offer him some comfort, at least to tell him she understood, but he had urged Jupiter into a fast trot, and quite clearly did not wish to discuss the matter any further.

By the time they arrived back at Adversane Hall Lucy felt that she had achieved a comfortable understanding with her host. Glancing up at the clock above the stable entrance, she wondered aloud if there would be time for her to bathe before dinner.

'I have not ridden so far in a very long time,' she explained.

'You had probably forgotten, then, how dusty one can get.'

'And sore,' she added, laughing. 'I have a lowering suspicion that this unaccustomed exercise will leave my joints aching most horribly!'

'I shall tell Byrne to put dinner back an hour and have Mrs Green send up hot water for you.' He helped her dismount and led her towards a small door at the back of the stable yard. 'This is a quicker way,' he explained. 'A path leads directly from here to a side door of the house, which opens onto what we call the side hall, and from there we can ascend via a secondary staircase to the main bedchambers. It is much more convenient than appearing in all one's dirt at the front door.'

'I guessed there must be a way,' she told him as she stepped into the house. 'Only I had not yet found it. Does it lead to the guest wing, too?'

'No. They have their own staircase, over there.' He pointed across the side hall to a panelled corridor, where Lucy could see another flight of stairs rising at the far end. 'My guests have perfect freedom to come and go as they wish.'

There was something in his tone that made her look up quickly, but his face was a stony mask. She began to make her way up the oak staircase, conscious of his heavy tread behind her.

'How useful to have one's own staircase,' she remarked, to break the uneasy silence. 'Was it perhaps the original way to the upper floor? Mrs Dean did say that the grand staircase was added when the house was remodelled in the last century.'

She knew her nerves were making her chatter, but when her companion did not reply she continued, glancing at the dark and rather obscure landscapes on the wall. 'And of course it gives you somewhere to hang paintings that are not required elsewhere...'

Her words trailed away as they reached the top of the stairs, and her wandering gaze fixed upon the large portrait hanging directly in front of her. But it was not its gilded frame, gleaming in the sunlight, nor the fresh, vibrant colours that made her stop and stare. It was the subject. She was looking at a painting of herself in the scarlet gown.

Chapter Five

'My wife.'

It did not need Adversane's curt words to tell her that. Only for an instant had Lucy thought she was looking at herself. A second, longer glance showed that the woman in the picture had golden curls piled up on her head, and eyes that were a deep, vivid blue.

'I had forgotten it was here.'

She dragged her eyes away from the painting to look at him.

'Forgotten?' she repeated, shocked. 'How could you forget?'

His shoulders lifted, the faintest shrug.

'My cousin had it moved from the Long Gallery the day you arrived. She thought it would upset you. Personally I would not have done so. You were bound to see it at some time.'

She found her gaze drawn back to the painting.

'She is wearing the gown I saw in Mrs Sutton's sketch.'

'Yes.'

'And the diamonds.' She swallowed. 'My hair is a little darker but…there is a striking resemblance between us.'

'Is there?'

Anger replaced her initial astonishment.

'Come now, my lord. Please do not insult my intelligence by saying you have not noticed it.' She had a sudden flash of memory: the open door in Mrs Killinghurst's office, the gilded picture frame on the wall of the inner sanctum. 'Did you deliberately set out to find someone who looked like your wife?'

'Pray, madam, do not be making more of this than there is.'

He indicated that they should move on, but Lucy remained in front of the portrait. He had not denied the allegation, so she could only surmise that his reasons for hiring her were not quite as straightforward as he had said.

'And your choice of gowns for me—are they all the same as those worn by your wife? Every one?'

'If they are it need not concern you.'

'My lord, it *does* concern me.'

'Well, it should not.' He frowned. 'I have already explained what is required of you. I can assure you there is nothing improper in it.'

'I am very glad to hear it!'

'So, does it matter what you wear?'

'No-o...'

'Then pray do not concern yourself further. Instead, enjoy living in luxury for a few weeks!' With that, he turned and strode off, leaving her to make her own way to her bedchamber.

Damn the woman, must she question everything?

Ralph stormed into his room, tearing off his neck cloth as he went. He had enjoyed their morning ride, much more than he had expected. Lucy Halbrook was spirited and intelligent and for a few hours he had put aside his cares and given himself up to pleasure. So successful had it been that he'd completely forgotten Ariadne had moved the painting and he'd been unprepared to see Helene staring down at him, large as life, from the top of the stairs. He had looked up and seen the portrait when he put his foot on the first tread, but by that time it was too late. Lucy was already before him, and all he could do was to try and think what on earth he would say to her when she saw the painting.

He was not surprised at her look of astonishment. Even Ariadne had questioned why he had hired someone who looked so much like Helene to play his fiancée. Lucy had seen the resemblance immediately and had turned to him, a question in her eyes. Green eyes, he recalled, and they changed with her moods. They looked like a stormy sea when she was angry and today, when she was exhilarated from the ride, they shone clear and bright as moss. Nothing like Helene's blue eyes, which he had once thought so alluring.

He gave his head a little shake to dispel the unwelcome thoughts that came crowding in. Kibble's voice intruded and Ralph looked up to see his valet coming out of the dressing room.

'I have prepared a bath for your lordship.'

'Thank you. Go down and tell Mrs Green to send up water to Miss Halbrook's room, if you please.' When Kibble hesitated he said curtly, 'Damn it, man, I can undress myself, you know!'

Not visibly moved, Kibble gave a stately little bow and retired. Going into the dressing room, where scented steam was gently rising from a hip bath, Ralph threw off his clothes and lowered himself into the water.

Kibble knew him well enough not to be offended by his rough tone, but what of Lucy? He had spoken harshly to her on several occasions now. A slight smile tugged at his mouth. She appeared quite capable of standing up to him, but that last look she had given him nagged at his conscience. If he told her everything, would she understand?

He could not risk it. He had known the woman barely two weeks, it would not make sense to trust her with such a dangerous secret. Safer to keep his own counsel. Much more logical.

He heard a movement in the bedchamber, and Kibble appeared in the dressing room doorway.

'A bath is even now being carried up to Miss Halbrook's room, my lord.'

Ralph was immediately distracted by the image of Lucy undressing and stepping into the warm water. There was a golden sheen to the skin of her neck and shoulders. Did that extend, he wondered, to the rest of her body...?

Kibble spoke again, in a voice with just a hint of rebuke. 'Mrs Green hopes there will be enough hot water, since she did not anticipate anyone other than your lordship requiring a bath today.'

Ralph sat up with an oath, not so much angry with his valet as with himself for not being able to dispel the thought of Lucy Halbrook.

Finding his master's wrathful eye turned towards him, Kibble unbent sufficiently to add, 'With so few guests in the house, Monsieur deemed it wasteful to light the new range in the kitchen and has been cooking on the old open range—it has a much smaller water cistern, my lord.'

'I know precisely what the difference is,' barked Ralph. 'You may tell Monsieur that since I pay him an extortionate wage to run my kitchens, I can afford to use that new range whatever the number of guests in residence, do you understand?'

'Yes, my lord.'

'Very well.' Ralph nodded towards the pail of hot water standing on the hearthstone. 'Miss Halbrook can have that to top up her supply.'

'Won't you be needing it, my lord?'

'No, I won't.' The vision of Lucy bathing was still tantalising Ralph. Great heavens, what was wrong with him? 'In fact, you had best pour in the rest of the cold water before you go.'

Lucy rubbed herself dry, her skin and spirits glowing. To be able to call up a bath at a moment's notice was luxury indeed and she could forgive her employer a great deal for that.

She could not forgive him everything, however, and the idea that she had been brought here to imitate his dead wife made her decidedly uneasy.

She left the chaos of the bath, buckets and towels in the dressing room and went into her bedchamber, where Ruthie had laid out a selection of gowns upon the bed. They were all new, and had all arrived that day. Lucy was tempted to wear the French cambric that she had brought with her, but she knew enough of her employer by now to be sure that if she did so, he would order her back upstairs to change.

In the end she chose a simple round gown of green silk over a white chemise. Ruthie dressed her hair in loose curls, caught up in a bandeau of matching ribbon, along with a pair of satin slippers dyed the same colour as her gown.

Looking at herself in the mirror, Lucy wondered if Helene had worn a gown like this, but of course she already knew the answer to that. Lucy derived some small, very small, satisfaction from the fact that however well the gown might have looked with guinea-gold curls, it could not have enhanced cornflower-blue eyes as it did green ones. Dismissing the thought as unworthy, Lucy placed a fine Norwich shawl about her shoulders and set off for the drawing room.

As she descended the main stairs she heard voices in the hall. One, which she recognised as Lord Adversane's, came floating up to her.

'Adam. What the devil brings you here?'

Adam. Lucy searched her mind and remembered that Adam Cottingham was Adversane's cousin and heir. A cheerful male voice now made itself heard.

'Don't sound so surprised, Cos. I came to take pot luck with you, as I have done often and often.'

'Aye, but not since the accident.' She heard Ralph hesitate over the last word. 'I thought you had vowed not to come here again.'

'No, well…the past is over and done. Time to let it rest, eh? We should not allow it to cause a rift in the family.'

'I was not aware that it had done so.'

'Well, there you are, then. And here I am. I take it you can spare a dinner for me, Cousin?'

Lucy continued to descend, smiling a little at Adversane's rather guarded response.

'Of course, it will be a pleasure to have you stay.'

'Thank you. So, Ralph, you old devil. What is this I have heard about a betrothal? Judith tells me you wrote to say you have installed your fiancée— *Good God*!'

This last exclamation was occasioned by Lucy's appearance in the Great Hall. She found herself being stared at by a fair-haired stranger. He picked up his eyeglass the better to study her and said sharply, 'Ralph, what the devil—?'

Lucy was tempted to run away from such astonished

scrutiny, but Lord Adversane was already approaching and holding out his hand to her.

'My dear, this boorish fellow is my cousin. He has come to join us for dinner.' He pulled her fingers onto his sleeve, giving them a little squeeze as he performed the introduction.

Mr Cottingham dropped his eyeglass and made her an elegant bow.

'Delighted, Miss Halbrook.'

Lucy's throat dried as she responded. Suddenly, she felt very ill prepared. Now that she had met one of Adversane's relatives in the flesh she was very nervous at the thought of being caught out. When Ralph smiled and patted her fingers she realised that she was clutching his arm rather tightly.

'Let us go to the drawing room,' he suggested. 'I expect Mrs Dean is waiting there for us.'

The short walk across the hall gave Lucy time to collect herself, and once Ariadne had greeted their guest, expressed her surprise at his arrival and assured him that there was plenty of time for him to change before dinner, she was able to sit down and join in the conversation with reasonable calm.

'Such a long time since I have seen you, Adam,' said Mrs Dean, fluttering back to her seat. 'I suppose there is no surprise about that. After all, we used to meet here at Adversane regularly, but of course all that changed when...' She trailed off, looking self-conscious.

'When Helene died,' said Ralph bluntly. 'I am aware that I have not entertained since then.'

'Indeed, Cousin, you have become something of a recluse,' declared Mrs Dean, recovering. 'But thankfully all that is ended now.' She turned back to Mr Cottingham. 'And will you stay overnight, Adam? I can have a room prepared in a trice.'

'No, no, I will not put you to that trouble. The long evening will give me time to get home before dark.'

'Do you live nearby, sir?' asked Lucy.

'At Delphenden, about fifteen miles hence. I am on my way home after visiting friends in Skipton and thought, since I was passing—'

'That is hardly passing,' Ralph broke in. 'You have come a good deal out of your way to get here.'

Adam laughed. 'True, but your letter intrigued me and I wanted to know more—and to meet your future bride, of course.'

He turned to Lucy as he said this, but although his words were uttered with a smile Lucy thought the look in his eyes was more speculative than welcoming.

'There is very little more to know,' Ralph responded calmly. 'Miss Halbrook and I met in London and she has done me the signal honour of agreeing to become my wife.'

'No, no, Ralph, you will not fob me off like that,' cried Adam, laughing. 'What a fellow you are for keeping things close! I am determined to know all about this engagement.'

'And so you shall.' Ralph smiled. 'There is nothing secret about it.'

'No, no, I never— That is...' Adam coloured. 'I was not suggesting there was anything... The news came as something of a surprise, that is all.'

'Miss Halbrook's father died twelve months ago and she has only recently come out of mourning. That is why we have made no announcement yet.'

Ralph's tone indicated that this explained everything.

Lucy was well aware that it did not and was relieved when Mrs Dean asked Mr Cottingham about his wife.

'How is dear Judith, Adam?'

'She is well, thank you.'

'Oh, that is good. I vow I have not seen her since the last house party here at Adversane—and how are the children?' She turned to Lucy. 'Adam has two fine boys, my dear. I suppose they are both at school now, are they not?'

'Yes, Charlie joined his brother last term...'

The conversation turned to family matters and Lucy felt she could relax, at least for a while, although she was aware of Adam Cottingham's thoughtful gaze frequently coming to rest upon her. She was not surprised, therefore, when he turned his attention towards her once more but by that time she was more prepared to answer his questions, adhering to Ralph's advice that they should tell the truth wherever possible.

When Mr Cottingham went off to change for dinner, Lucy sank back in her chair and closed her eyes.

'Good heavens, I feel completely exhausted!'

'You did very well, my dear,' Ariadne told her. 'Although I thought it a little impolite of Adam to ask you quite so many questions.'

'He is my heir,' Ralph reminded her. 'He has more of an interest in the matter than anyone else.'

Lucy sat up again. 'Do you think he suspects the engagement is a sham?'

Ralph's brows went up. 'Why should he?'

'It was the way he kept looking at me.' Lucy hesitated. 'I think he noticed my resemblance to the late Lady Adversane.'

'She has seen the portrait, Cousin,' said Ralph in response to Mrs Dean's gasp of mortification.

'And it is hardly surprising if he did notice, since all the clothes I have to wear are identical to Lady Adversane's.' Lucy lifted her chin and met his eyes defiantly. 'What is it you are not telling me, my lord?'

'There is nothing that need concern you,' said Ralph dismissively. 'However, I do think the portrait should be reinstated in the Long Gallery.'

Mrs Dean looked at Lucy. 'As long as that will not upset you, my dear?'

Lucy shook her head. 'I think it would cause a great deal more comment if you do not put it back.'

'I agree.' Ralph rose. 'Now if you will excuse me, since we will have to wait for my cousin before we can eat, I shall use the time to attend to a little more business.'

He went out, leaving the two ladies to sit in silence.

'Did you know?' said Lucy at last. 'Did he tell you he hired me because I look like his wife?'

Ariadne shook her head, her kindly eyes shadowed with anxiety.

'At first I thought it was merely a coincidence. Then, when Mrs Sutton brought the sketches for your gowns—I asked Ralph what he meant by it, but he merely brushed it aside.'

'I wonder what game he is playing?'

'Oh, surely nothing more than he has already told you,' Ariadne was quick to reply.

'I am sure it is,' said Lucy, adding bitterly, 'No doubt he thinks I am not to be trusted with his secrets!'

'I think it is merely that he misses Helene a great deal more than he is prepared to admit.'

Lucy had already considered that idea and found it did not please her.

Mrs Dean sighed. 'Adversane prides himself upon his logical mind, you see. He says every problem can be solved by the application of logic, so to find him grieving so much for his late wife is quite touching, is it not?'

'It is also a little embarrassing,' replied Lucy tartly. 'Everyone will think he is marrying me because I look like Helene. They will pity me, which I shall dislike intensely.'

'Yes, but he is not going to marry you,' Ariadne reminded her, brightening. 'So it does not really matter, does it?'

Lucy could not disagree with this reasoning, but she knew, deep down, that it did matter to her, although she had no idea why it should.

Lucy enjoyed Adam Cottingham's company at dinner. He was an entertaining guest, witty and knowledgeable, and although she thought his manner a little insincere she was grateful to him for making sure she was not left out when the conversation turned to family matters.

'You will meet Adversane's sisters, of course, when they come here for the house party,' he said as they helped themselves to sweetmeats once the covers had been removed. 'Fearsome ladies, both of 'em.'

'No, Adam, you know that is not so,' protested Mrs Dean, laughing. 'You are not to be frightening Lucy out of her wits.'

'Of course not, but it is as well to be forewarned.' Adam grinned at Lucy. 'They can be very outspoken, but you will do very well as long as you stand up to them.'

'Now you have terrified me,' she replied, chuckling.

'You need not fear,' said Adam. 'I shall be here to protect you.'

The look that accompanied these words was surprisingly intense. Lucy suspected he was trying to flirt with her and was at a loss to know how to respond. However,

Adam's attention switched to Lord Adversane when he announced that he had invited the Ingleston Players to entertain his guests on Midsummer's Eve.

'The devil you have!' exclaimed Adam.

The room was filled with a sudden tension that Lucy did not understand. Adversane's dark brows rose a fraction as he regarded his heir.

'Do you have any objections to them coming?'

'No, of course not. It is a tradition that goes back generations...'

'Precisely. They were very sorry not to be performing here last year.'

'Who are these players?' asked Lucy. 'Are we to have theatricals?'

'Yes, indeed,' Ariadne responded. 'Ingleston has its very own troupe of thespians who perform plays at certain times of the year, such as Easter and Christmas time.'

'They have been performing here every Midsummer's Eve for as long as I can remember,' put in Lord Adversane. 'Last year was the exception.'

Midsummer's Eve. Lucy felt a little chill run down her spine. So Lady Adversane had died on the night of the performance. No wonder he had not wanted them to play there last year. Surely their appearance would bring back unwelcome memories? She glanced across at her host. There was no telling what he was thinking from that stern, inscrutable countenance.

An uncomfortable silence began to fill the room, and Lucy was thankful when Ariadne stepped into the breach.

'And when shall you and Judith be coming to stay, Adam?'

'Three weeks' time, Cousin. On the nineteenth.'

'Oh?' Ariadne sounded surprised. 'But that is when the other guests are expected.'

'Adversane suggested it.'

'Yes,' said Ralph shortly. 'There will be no need for you to arrive weeks in advance this year.'

Adam turned to Lucy to explain.

'In the past we spent a deal of time at Adversane, it was almost a second home. My wife was a great help to Lady Adversane, especially with all the arrangements for the summer house party. We would spend weeks here so that Judith could assist her, but of course Cousin Ariadne is taking care of everything this year, and she has you to support her, Miss Halbrook.'

'Precisely.'

An awkward silence followed Adversane's curt response. Mrs Dean rose and quietly invited Lucy to come with her to the drawing room. She said nothing as they crossed the hall, but immediately they were alone in the drawing room she burst out with unwonted spirit, 'If Judith Cottingham did anything to help anyone I should be surprised. Whenever I've seen her here at Adversane she has either spent her time lying down in her room, or wandering about the garden, looking forlorn.'

Lucy blinked at her.

'Why, Ariadne, I have never heard you speak in such a forthright manner before.'

'No, well, usually I am prepared to give anyone the benefit of the doubt, but to hear Adam talking in that fashion—!' Her pursed lips and frowning expression told Lucy just what she thought. She continued scathingly, 'Judith Cottingham is a poor little dab of a woman with a perpetual air of gloom about her. And I did not think Helene was ever that fond of her. In fact, I think she resented her interference, because she told me once that she could not prevent Adam and his wife from coming here so often because they were Ralph's nearest relatives.

Heavens, to listen to Adam you would think Judith was essential to the running of Adversane!'

'Mayhap Mr Cottingham is very much in love with his wife. I believe such affection can blind one to a partner's faults.'

Her companion gave a most unladylike snort. 'The only person Adam Cottingham is in love with is himself! His father was a wastrel, you know. Quite profligate, but thankfully he went to his grave before he lost everything. However, although Adam managed to keep the house at Delphenden, there was never enough money—at least not to keep Adam in the manner he wished. Even his marriage did not bring him the fortune he expected, so Ralph set up an annuity for him. Not that Adam was ever grateful. It is my belief that he envies Ralph his fortune and his lands, although I doubt he appreciates just how hard Ralph has worked to make Adversane so prosperous.

'Adam positively *haunted* the place while Helene was alive, for the house was always full of visitors and that gave him the opportunity to shine, which there is no doubt he does in company. But since the accident I believe he has not been near the house, when you would have thought he would be here to support his cousin in his grief. As Ralph's heir I think he should have done more to help him over the past two years, rather than to stay away. To my mind it shows a sad lack of family loyalty—but there, it is not my place to say so, and Ralph has not encouraged visitors for the past two years. He was in great danger of becoming a recluse, you know, which would have been a very bad thing for the family, so we must be grateful that he is holding the summer house party again this year and I shall say no more about Adam's behaviour.'

Lucy was inclined to think Mrs Dean a little harsh

in her judgement of Mr Cottingham. Despite his propensity for flirting, as the evening progressed Lucy decided that he was a very friendly, cheerful gentleman and a complete contrast to his cousin, whose unsmiling countenance and taciturn manner were even more marked than usual.

Lucy found only Mrs Dean in the breakfast room the following morning, Lord Adversane having already gone off to Ingleston on business with Harold Colne. Her thoughts turned to the forthcoming house party.

'Is there anything you would like me to do, ma'am?' she asked.

'I rather thought we might go over the arrangements together later today,' said Ariadne. 'I have several urgent letters that I must write this morning so Byrne can have them taken to catch the mail. I am sorry, my dear—'

'No, no, that suits me very well,' replied Lucy. 'It is such a lovely morning that I thought I might walk to Druids Rock.'

'Alone?'

'Of course, alone. It is Adversane land, I believe, so surely it is safe enough.'

'Well, yes, my dear, of course it is *safe*, as long as one does not ascend the rock itself—but I have always thought it such a forbidding place, especially since Helene's accident...such tragic memories.'

'It holds no such memories for me, although I admit I was reluctant to ask Adv—Ralph to take me for that very reason.'

'If you will only wait until later I will come with you—'

Lucy chuckled. It had not taken her long to discover

that while Ariadne liked to busy herself around the house, her idea of exercise was a gentle stroll in the shrubbery.

'No, no, ma'am, I would not dream of troubling you,' she said now. 'Besides, it promises to be very hot later, and we would be better employed indoors than walking in the midday sun. No, I shall go this instant and thoroughly enjoy myself.'

Shortly after, attired in her sensible boots and carrying a shawl in case the breeze should be fresher on the moor, she made her way out of doors, pausing only to ask directions from one of the footmen, explaining with a twinkle that she did not wish to lose her way and put the staff to the trouble of finding her.

'Nay, ma'am, that's not likely, for Hobart's Moor ain't large and the path is well marked.'

'I believe the lane leading from the wicket gate will take me there,' she prompted him.

'Aye, ma'am, that it will. Follow the lane through the trees and that'll bring you to Hobart's Bridge. Cross that and you'll be on t'moor. There's a good track then that brings you round to Druids Rock.'

Armed with this information, and the footman's assurance that she could not miss her way, Lucy set off. The gate was in fact wide enough for a horse and she guessed the path through the trees had originally been intended as a ride. However, the undergrowth now encroached upon it and the trees grew unchecked, their branches almost meeting overhead. She was glad of her shawl for the morning shade was cool. The trees ended where the ride joined an ancient track that curved away around the belt of woodland in one direction and in the other it stretched out before her, winding down across a picturesque stone bridge and cutting through the distant moors.

She walked on and crossed what she guessed to be

Hobart's Bridge, pausing to look over the side at the fast-flowing little stream that tumbled over its rocky bed. Lucy followed the track, striding out briskly beneath the cloudless blue vault of sky. The path ran around a natural ridge in the moor, the land falling away to gorse bushes and the stream on one side while rugged slopes covered with rough grass and heather rose up on the other.

As the path wound onwards the views of Adversane were left behind and the dramatic landscape of hills and steep-sided valleys unfolded before her. She stopped several times, taking in the view and thinking how much her father would have loved to paint such scenery. She had captured some of it in her own sketchbook, but everywhere she looked there was another vista. So many views, she knew she would not be able to sketch them all before the house party was over and her employment at Adversane was ended.

She rounded a bend to find the ground ahead rising steeply and suddenly there was Druids Rock soaring above her. There could be no mistaking it, for it towered over the path at this point, dark and brooding, even in the sunshine. The old track ran to the south of the rock and continued down into the wooded valley below, which she guessed was the way to Ingleston, but Lucy chose a narrow path winding up through the heather. As she drew closer to Druids Rock she could see it was not one solid piece but a jumble of huge stones, pushed together as if by some giant hand. The southern face reared up like a cliff, but the northern side swept upwards in a gentle slope, easily ascended. Lucy did not hesitate. She walked up to the top of the ramp and stood there, revelling in the feel of the fresh breeze on her skin. It was like standing on top of the world.

Behind her, the natural rise of the moors blocked her

view of the track and only the chimneys of Adversane were visible. Looking south, with the sheer drop at her feet, the valley opened up and beyond the belt of trees directly below her she could see the town of Ingleston nestling between the hills. Leading from it was the white ribbon of road that she had ridden with Ralph yesterday.

Lucy sat down on the edge of the rock, enjoying the peace and solitude. Below her, a few wagons and horses were moving silently along the road while the surrounding land below the moors looked green and well-tended, a network of tidy walls and neat farmsteads. Most of it, she knew, belonged to Adversane. Ralph. It was a good spot from which to see the extent of his domain, but she understood why he did not come here, if his wife had fallen from this very rock. Glancing down, she remembered Ruthie's incautious words. Helene had come here in her evening dress. Had she really been so unhappy that she—?

No. She would not speculate. That would be a despicable thing to do. She scrambled to her feet and left her high perch. She would go back to the house and ask Mrs Dean what exactly had happened. She regained the track and set off back the way she had come. She had not gone far when she heard the thunder of hooves. Looking around, she saw the dark figure of Adversane cantering towards her. Lucy stopped and waited while he brought his horse to a plunging halt beside her.

'Was it you, on top of the rock?'

He barked out the words, a thunderous scowl blackening his countenance.

'Yes.' She fought down the urge to shrink away or apologise. 'It was such a lovely morning I wanted to explore.'

'Explore! Don't you know how dangerous those rocks can be?'

She replied calmly, 'I am sure in the wet they are extremely treacherous, but the ground is dry, and my shoes are not at all slippery.' She twitched aside her skirts to show him the sturdy half-boots she was wearing.

He glared down at her, and Lucy waited for the furious tirade that she felt sure he wanted to utter. After a moment's taut silence she said quietly, 'I am very sorry if I alarmed you.'

She thought she might have imagined his growl as her apology robbed him of the excuse to harangue her. He jumped down and by tacit consent they began to walk, with Jupiter following behind them.

'I saw someone on the rocks and thought it was you. I came up to make sure you were safe.'

'That was very considerate, sir, when I know you do not normally use this track. Is that because of what happened to your wife here?'

He threw a swift, hard glance at her.

'Who told you? What have you heard about that?'

'My maid said Lady Adversane fell to her death from the rock.' She added quickly, 'Please do not blame Ruthie. If she had not told me I should have asked Mrs Dean.'

'I am surprised you were not told I'd killed her.'

Lucy stopped in her tracks. He gave a harsh laugh.

'Oh, not literally. I was at the house when she fell, but it was known she was not happy.'

'You mean they think she killed herself.' Lucy's parents had often deplored her blunt speaking and she glanced a little uncertainly at Lord Adversane, but he did not appear shocked so she continued. 'Would she have done such a thing?'

'*I* do not think so, but—'

Lucy put out her hand to him. 'If she did take her own life, you must not blame yourself, sir.'

He was looking down at her fingers where they rested

on his sleeve. Gently, she withdrew them. It had been an impulsive gesture, but he was, after all, almost a stranger. They began to walk on again and despite a little awkwardness Lucy did not want to let the moment pass.

'Will you tell me?' she asked him. 'Will you explain what happened the night she died?' When he did not reply immediately she added, 'I beg your pardon. I have no right to ask—'

'But you want to know, don't you? If I will not speak of it then you will find out from someone else.'

She could not lie.

'Yes.'

'Then it is best you hear it from me. Helene walked here a great deal. Her father, Sir James, is—calls himself—a druid. Have you heard of The Ancient Order of the Druids, Miss Halbrook? Not so ancient, in fact. They were founded about five-and-twenty years ago by a man named Hurle and they are an offshoot of an older order, which Hurle considered too profane. They have their own beliefs and rituals, many based on nature and astrology. And of course they believe there is a link with the ancient standing stones.' His lip curled. 'There are no such stones at Adversane, but we do have Druids Rock. The name of the place goes back generations. No one seems to know why it was called thus, but certainly there have been no druidic rituals here in my lifetime, or my father's. When Preston learned that Druids Rock was on my land he was even more eager for me to become his son-in-law. Even before the marriage had taken place he began to come to Adversane regularly to visit the rock. As did Helene during that last spring and summer when we were living at Adversane. She even went there in the dark, ostensibly to watch the sunrise.'

'Ostensibly? You did not believe it?' Lucy closed her

lips. That was not the sort of thing one asked a man about his wife.

'I did not question her beliefs,' he said shortly. 'But I did insist that she never went there unaccompanied. She agreed always to take her maid with her, and I was content with that.' A faint, derisive smile curled his lip. 'The locals fear the place is haunted by fairies and hobgoblins, but I never heard that they injured anyone. If she wanted to get up before dawn to go there I would not forbid it.

'That is what she is thought to have been doing on Midsummer's Eve. It is thought to be the reason she was still wearing her evening gown.'

'Why did you not come with her?'

'I have no time for superstition, Miss Halbrook.'

'But what about romance?' Those dark brows rose and she blushed. 'Some would think it romantic to watch the dawn together.'

'That would be as nonsensical as my wife's druidical beliefs.' His hard look challenged Lucy to contradict him, and when she said nothing he continued. 'She was not missed until just before breakfast time, when her maid realised she had not gone to bed. I organised search parties, but it did not take long to find her. Druids Rock was the first place we looked.'

'How dreadful for you.'

'Not only for me, but for everyone who was staying at Adversane.'

'And yet, you have invited the same people to join you here again?'

'Yes.'

'And you have invited the players to come in, just as they did the night she—the night Helene died.'

'The Midsummer's Eve play is a tradition, Miss Halbrook. It goes back generations, far beyond the tragedy of my wife's death. It is not logical that it should cease because of one tragic event.'

'But surely—'

He stopped her, saying impatiently, 'Enough of this. We will talk of something else, if you please, or continue in silence.'

She chose silence, and Ralph found himself regretting it. She might infuriate him with her incessant questions but she was only voicing what others would think. It was as well that he had the answers ready. He acknowledged to himself that he had been misled by her appearance. In Mrs Killinghurst's office, she had looked positively drab in the enveloping grey gown and quite demure. If he had known she would show such spirit he would never have employed her. A faint smile began inside him. He should be honest with himself. He *did* know, from that very first encounter in the alley.

He had deliberately positioned himself at the door of Mrs Killinghurst's office so that he could observe the candidate for this post and he had seen Miss Lucy Halbrook walking towards him. He had noted the slight hesitation as she found her way blocked, then the way her head had come up as she approached him, determined not to be intimidated.

Yes, he knew from that first moment that she was not one to accept his demands without question. He should have told Mrs Killinghurst to send her away, to find someone more biddable. Even as the thought formed he realised that after Lucy Halbrook, anyone else would seem very dull indeed.

Lucy hardly noticed the continuing silence. Her mind was too full of what she had heard to make idle conversation. Lord Adversane was lost in his own thoughts and did not appear to object so she occupied herself with studying her surroundings, the rough grass and darker patches of heather, the view of the distant hills. Everything was new and interesting. Suddenly a swathe of white caught her eye, a shifting, snowy carpet nestling in a wide, flat depression a short distance from their path.

'Oh, how pretty. What is it?'

'Cotton grass.' He strode across to the dip and picked a handful of the fluffy, nodding heads. 'It grows on boggy ground. It can be used to stuff pillows, though it is not as good as goosedown.'

'It looks very fine,' she observed.

'It is. Feel it.'

The breath caught in her throat as he brushed the white heads against her cheek. The touch was gentle, as light as thistledown, but it sent a thrill running through her body. She became shockingly aware of the man standing beside her. She wanted to reach out and touch him, to connect herself to his rugged strength. It was an immense struggle to compose herself and respond calmly.

'It, um, it is as soft as silk.'

He held her eyes for a moment, a look she could not interpret in his own, then he turned away.

'Unfortunately the strands are too short to be spun into thread.'

A faint disappointment flickered through her as he cast aside the grasses and began to walk on.

Did you expect him to present them to you like some lovesick swain?

With a mental shrug, she fell into step beside him again, walking on in silence until they had crossed Hobart's Bridge and were approaching the belt of trees that separated the moors from Adversane Hall.

'Does that way lead to the Hall, too?' she asked, pointing to the old track where it disappeared around the trees.

'Yes. It leads to the main gates, but it will be quicker if we go through the old ride.'

'Is that what it is called? I came out that way,' said Lucy. 'I suppose Lady Adversane rode through it when she went to Druids Rock.'

'No, my wife was a nervous rider and preferred to walk. I never come this way.'

She looked up at the overhanging branches.

'And you have not had many guests since the accident, so consequently it is much overgrown.'

'You are right. The only people to use it now are the servants, if they are walking to Ingleston.'

'But it is such a delightful route, my lord. It seems such a shame that one cannot ride this way any more.'

'It is a loss I can bear.'

They had reached the gate leading into the grounds of the house. Ralph was about to open it, but Lucy was before him, lifting the latch and walking through, as if declaring her independence. He found himself smiling as he watched her. She was a strange mix, quiet and a little shy, yet not afraid to challenge him, and not at all cowed by his sharp retorts. He had not spoken to anyone of Helene's death for so long that it had been a relief to talk of it, so much so that he had had to stop himself from confiding his suspicions. But he could not do that, he was playing far too dangerous a game to involve anyone else. If he was wrong then innocent names would be mired by suspicion. It was his plan and he would share it with no one. He alone would take the credit for it. Or the blame.

Ralph guided Jupiter through the gate and closed it

firmly behind him. Lucy was waiting for him. The wind had sprung up and she was busy trying to untangle her shawl.

'Here, let me.' He dropped Jupiter's reins so that he could use both hands to take the shawl and drape it around her shoulders.

'Thank you. There are rainclouds on the horizon. I am glad we are back in time to avoid a soaking.'

She was laughing, completely unaware of how pretty she looked, her windswept curls rioting around her bare head and her skin glowing from the fresh air.

Kiss her.

She was knotting the ends of her shawl, oblivious of his hands hovering over her shoulders. He snatched his hands away as she turned her head to address him.

'What say you, my lord, will it last? Shall we be confined indoors by the inclement weather?'

She was peeping up at him through her lashes and he felt his blood stirring. It was unconsciously done, he would swear to it, but by God that look was damned inviting! With a silent oath he tore his eyes away from her. She was here for a purpose and he would not allow himself to be distracted.

'There is rain on the way, certainly.' He picked up Jupiter's reins. 'You can see the house from here, so there is no reason for me to come farther with you.'

Without another word, he threw himself into the saddle and dug his heels into the horse's flanks. Soon they were flying across the park, and he had to concentrate to keep the big hunter steady. As Jupiter settled into his stride Ralph found the unwelcome feelings were receding. It was the novelty of having a young woman in the house, that was all.

Since Helene's death he had thrown himself into his

work on the estate and shunned female society. He saw now that it had been a mistake. If he had not been so reclusive he would not now find himself so desirous of Lucy Halbrook's company, and he would not be so quickly aroused when they were together. After all, she was no beauty. It was her resemblance to Helene that had persuaded him to employ her, but the longer she was here the less he could see any similarity. Damnation, had he been mistaken? No, Adam had seen the likeness, he was certain of that.

'She will have to do,' he muttered as he bent low over Jupiter's glossy black neck. 'Only another couple of weeks and it will be finished. She will leave Adversane and I need never see her again. All I require of Lucy Halbrook until then is that she plays her part.'

Chapter Six

'Well, was there ever anyone so rude?'

Lucy watched Ralph gallop off across the park. She had thought they were getting on well. They had talked quite freely during their walk, which had gone a long way to allowing her to put aside some of her own reserve, but now he had rebuffed her. Lucy tried to be angry, but honesty compelled her to admit that she was more wounded by his abrupt departure.

'But why should he walk you back?' she asked herself as she turned her steps towards the house. 'If he was truly your fiancé it would be a different matter. You would have every excuse to feel aggrieved. As it is, he is paying you very well and that should be sufficient. Surely you do not want to spend more time with such a difficult man.'

She thought back to what he had told her about his late wife. Ariadne thought them a devoted couple, but Lucy was sceptical. Ralph himself had admitted Helene was not happy and she had detected no sign of affection in his manner when he talked about his wife. She stopped and uttered her thoughts to the open air.

'But if that is the case, why does he want me to look like Helene?'

She fixed her eyes on the darkening sky, as if the black clouds might give her an answer. The only response was a fat raindrop that splashed on her nose. She hurried on, reaching the house just as the heavens opened.

The heavy rain continued for the rest of the day, making the sky so dark that when Lucy went down to the drawing room before dinner she found that Ariadne had ordered the candles to be lit.

'These summer storms are so depressing,' said Mrs Dean, staring despondently at the rain cascading down the windows.

'Best to be thankful there is no thunder and lightning,' remarked Ralph, walking in at that moment. 'That sends even the most sensible females into a panic.'

Lucy, still smarting from the way he had left her that morning, bridled immediately.

'Not all females, my lord.'

He raised his brows, looking at her as if her comment was not worthy of a response. She watched him sit down beside his cousin and engage her in conversation.

Good. She was glad and did not wish to talk to him when he was determined to be so disagreeable. She had to admit that he was being perfectly civil to Ariadne, but whenever he was obliged to acknowledge Lucy he did so with such brevity that it bordered on curt. Byrne came in to announce dinner and Lucy hung back. With only the briefest hesitation Ralph offered his arm to his cousin.

It was what Lucy had intended, what she wanted, yet following them across the hall she felt decidedly alone. The rain did not help, for it made the Great Hall cold and gloomy, and when they reached the dining room she was glad to find that an abundance of candles burned brightly, giving the room a cosy glow that offset the sound of the rain pattering against the window. Mrs Dean remarked that they would need to ensure they had a good supply of candles for the forthcoming house party.

'Colne sent off an order for another twelve dozen only yesterday,' replied Ralph. 'Which reminds me, have you made up the guest rooms yet?'

'Lucy and I allocated the rooms today. There is a little furniture to be moved, but apart from that nothing need be done now. We shall make up the beds the day before your guests arrive.'

He nodded. 'And when does Mrs Sutton anticipate the rest of your gowns will be ready, Lucy?'

'She has promised them next week, my lord.'

He did not respond immediately, but when Byrne followed the servants out of the room he said, 'I thought we were agreed that you would call me by my name?'

'I beg your pardon, my—Ralph. It slipped my mind.'

'Then pray do not let it happen again.'

Ariadne shook her head at him.

'Fie upon you, Cousin, how can you expect Lucy to address you informally when you are acting so cold and… and *lordly* this evening?'

'I am paying her to do so.'

And very handsomely, Lucy acknowledged silently. However, it did not mean that she would be browbeaten. She remarked, as the servants returned with more dishes, 'Ralph cannot help being *cold and lordly*, ma'am. It is all he knows.'

With Byrne filling the wineglasses and the footmen in attendance, only the narrowing of Adversane's eyes told Lucy that her comment had hit home.

The dinner was excellent, as always, but Lucy felt a tension in the air. Perhaps it was the weather. It was very close in the dining room, but the driving rain made it impossible to open the windows.

Ariadne did not seem to notice, but whenever Lucy looked at Ralph, he appeared to be frowning and distracted. He contributed little to the conversation and by the time the covers were removed Lucy was so incensed by his conduct that she barely waited for the door to close behind the servants before asking him bluntly what he meant by his boorish behaviour.

Those black brows flew up.

'I beg your pardon, ma'am?'

Ariadne fluttered a warning hand at Lucy, but she ignored it.

'You have barely said two words together during dinner,' she retorted. 'If there is something pressing upon your mind then do please share it with us. Otherwise it would be courteous to give us at least a little of your attention.'

'If there are matters *pressing upon my mind*, madam, they are my business, and not for general discussion.'

'Dinner is a social occasion,' she retorted. 'My father always said if you cannot talk about a problem then it should be left outside the dining room. He considered family dinners to be most important.'

'When he was sober enough to attend them!'

He saw her flinch as if he had struck her, and it did not need Ariadne's outraged gasp to tell him he was at fault.

'Lucy—Miss Halbrook, I beg your pardon, I—'

She held up a hand to silence him. Slowly, she rose to her feet.

'If you will excuse me, Ariadne, I think I shall retire.'

'My dear!' Mrs Dean put out her hand, then let it fall and looked instead to her cousin. 'Ralph, how could you say such a thing? You must apologise.'

'I have done so, Cousin.'

'It is unnecessary, I assure you,' said Lucy in freezing accents.

Keeping her head high, she left the room. She closed the door behind her with exaggerated care, determined to keep her anger in check. To her annoyance she could feel the hot tears coursing down her cheeks. She dashed them away but more followed. The through-passage was empty but she could see shadows moving in the Great Hall and hesitated, unwilling to allow the servants to witness her distress.

She heard the dining room door open and a hasty tread upon the boards behind her. Heedless of decorum, she turned and raced through the passage, heading for the gardens.

'Lucy!'

She wrenched open the garden door and flew across the terrace, heedless of the drenching rain. The only light came from the house windows, illuminating the terrace with a pale gleam but leaving the rest of the gardens in darkness. Without thinking Lucy plunged down the shallow steps into the blackness. She had reached the bottom step when Ralph caught up with her, catching her arm and forcing her to stop. She kept her back to him, rigidly upright, anger burning through every limb.

'Forgive me.'

She shook her head, unable to trust her voice, but thankful that the rain had washed away all evidence of her tears. She would not allow him to think she was so weak.

'Lucy, you are right, I have had something on my mind. I have been distracted, ever since our meeting at Druids Rock this morning, but it is not something I could share with you in company.'

'That does not give you the right to throw my father's weakness in my face.'

'I know, but I was taken aback by your reproof.' An unsteady laugh escaped him. 'No one has dared to admonish me at my own dinner table before.'

'More's the pity. Now leave me alone!'

She shook off his hand, only to find herself caught by the shoulders and whirled about so violently that if he had not maintained his hold she would have fallen.

'Damn you, woman, you shall not leave me like this!'

'Like what, my lord?'

'Will you not at least be open with me?'

The injustice of his words made her swell with indignation.

'It seems to me, my lord, that it is *you* who will not be open with *me*! You bring me here, make me masquerade as your wife yet you will not tell me *why*. I abhor these secrets, sir!'

She glared up at him, trying to see his face, but the darkness was too deep. She could see only his outline and the gleam of his rain-soaked hair. Then she could not even see that, for he swooped down, enveloping her in darkness as his lips met hers. The shock of it was like a lightning bolt. Her limbs trembled and she leaned against him, clutching at his wet coat as she reeled under the shocking pleasure of his kiss.

But only for a moment. Then she was fighting, some unreasonable panic telling her that she must get away from him or risk destruction. He raised his head, but he was still holding her arms and she began to struggle.

'Let me go!'

'Lucy, I beg your pardon. I should never—'

Anger swelled within her as she tried to shake off his hold. He was her employer; he owed her his protection, yet he was betraying her trust—just as her uncle had done—by attempting to ravish her as soon as she was under his roof. And had her father not betrayed her, also, by keeping his gambling a secret instead of sharing it with her, allowing her to help him?

Her sense of injustice grew. She tried again to break free but he held her firm, and she said furiously, 'Do you think to impose your will upon me by this ruthless seduction?'

His hands fell from her shoulders and she took the opportunity to turn and flee to the safety of her room, where she relieved her anger and distress in a hearty bout of tears.

The rain had gone by the morning and the sun was shining in a clear sky, but the prospect did little to raise Lucy's spirits. She had not slept well; the night had brought counsel and she knew what she must do. Quietly, she rose from her bed, heavy-eyed and depressed. It was still early and she could hear Ruthie snoring noisily in the dressing room, so she went to the linen press and brought out the grey wool robe she had worn for her interviews with Mrs Killinghurst. She needed no maid to help her into it, and she could dress her own hair, too, catching her curls back from her face with a black ribbon. A glance in her glass confirmed her sober, even severe appearance. Squaring her shoulders, she quietly left her room.

She found Lord Adversane in the Great Hall.

'Good morning, my lord. I wonder if you could spare me a few moments, alone?'

When he turned to face her she thought he looked a little haggard, and there were dark shadows under his eyes, as if he, too, had not slept well. His searching gaze swept over her but with a silent nod he led the way to his study.

He closed the door and invited her to sit down.

'Thank you, my lord, I would rather stand.'

He walked over to the large mahogany desk and turned to face her, leaning on its edge and folding his arms across his chest.

'That, and your funereal garb, tells me this is important.'

'Yes. I am resigning my position here.'

'Indeed?' One word, uttered quietly. No emotion, no surprise. Lucy found it difficult to keep still while he subjected her to a long, long look. 'Is that because of my behaviour yesterday?'

'In part, yes.'

'For which I have apologised, and I will beg your pardon again, here and now. My behaviour was unforgivable and I give you my word it shall not happen again. Will you believe that?'

Her eyes slid to the floor.

'It makes no difference.'

'You still wish to leave Adversane.'

'Yes. Today.'

He pushed himself upright.

'Strange. I had not thought you the sort to give up at the first hurdle.'

'I am not giving up,' she replied indignantly. 'I do not believe I am the right person for this post.'

'Adam Cottingham found no fault with you.'

'He saw me for only a few hours. In a longer period he would realise that it was a sham.'

'And why should he do that?'

'Because our characters are not suited.'

'I fail to see that it matters.'

She looked at him rather helplessly.

'How are we going to convince everyone that we are betrothed?'

He was looking at her, something she could not read in his eyes.

'It is like marriage, madam. We shall have to work at it.'

'My lord, I *cannot* pretend to be your fiancée.'

'May I ask why not?'

She blushed. 'I do not feel for you any of the…the warmer feelings that are necessary to make everyone believe that I—that we—'

'Really? That was not the impression I had last night. I thought your feelings for me were very warm indeed.'

'They are, sir,' she retorted, goaded. 'I dislike you, intensely!'

'That is not important. As long as we are polite to one another people will assume it is a marriage of convenience. You are here to meet my neighbours and relatives, your chaperone has been taken ill at the last moment and Ariadne has kindly stepped in. Come, Miss Halbrook, is it so very onerous a task? I thought we were agreed the settlement I am prepared to make will more than make up for any gossip that may arise when you jilt me.'

'The gossip does not worry me but being caught out in this charade does. I should find it very difficult to hide my true feelings.' Lucy raised her head, determined to be brutally honest. 'I find you rude and overbearing, my lord. In fact I find you totally abhorrent!'

Her declaration did not appear to disconcert him in the least.

'Then you will just have to act a little, Miss Halbrook.' He laughed at her stunned silence and stepped towards her, reaching for her hand. 'You have spirit, Lucy Halbrook. I like that, although sometimes I find it hard to accept your home truths about my character. My temper is cross, as you know to your cost, but I have apologised, and I will try to curb it for the next few weeks. You have my word on that, if you will but reconsider.'

His thumb caressed the inside of her wrist, causing an extraordinary reaction. Her pulse was jumping erratically, his touch awakening an inexplicable longing from somewhere deep inside her. She was aware of a pleasant languor spreading through her body and it was difficult to think clearly. However, she had to try.

'It is not just your temper, sir. You took advantage of me.' The memory of it sent the hot blood pounding through her body again, enhanced this time by the continued assault upon her wits caused by the light-as-a-feather touch of his circling thumb.

'A kiss,' he said shortly. 'A brief sensory exploration, brought on because our senses were heightened by the ongoing disagreement. It could happen to any two people caught in those circumstances. We have my cousin here as your chaperone and as long as we are civil to one another it will not occur again.'

It all sounded so reasonable, thought Lucy, yet they were being civil now, and her senses were still heightened. He was standing very close, surrounding her with his strong masculine presence. His broad-shouldered torso blocked out the light, the grey riding coat reminding her of the shadowed cliff-like face of Druids Rock. He smelled of soap and clean linen. She could almost taste the faint hint of citrus and spices that clung to his skin, feel the strength emanating from his powerful form. Her eyes were on a level with the diamond pin nestled deep in the folds of his neck cloth, and she fixed her gaze upon it, trying to cling to some semblance of reality and stop herself stepping closer, inviting him to enfold her in his arms and repeat the embrace they had shared in the rain. She heard the soft rasp of his breath as he exhaled.

'We can do better than this, Lucy.' His voice was low and soft, melting the last of her resistance. 'Say you will stay. It is only for two more weeks, and we need only give the appearance of being happy together when we are in company. If I am boorish, then I give you leave to upbraid me as much as you wish.'

She looked up at that, grasping at a mischievous thought to put an end to her languor.

'Do you mean you will accept my strictures meekly, my lord?'

He was smiling down at her and the warm look in his grey eyes set her pulse jumping again.

'I never promise the impossible. We shall battle most royally, I fear.'

To her surprise, Lucy did not find the thought daunting. She was aware of a tiny frisson of disappointment when he changed his grip on her hand and stopped caressing her wrist.

'So, cry *pax* with me, Lucy?'

No. Impossible. There can be no peace between us. Even just standing here I can feel it.

'Very well.'

'And you will stay and be friends?'

Friends. Lucy found the idea very tempting. Despite all she had said to the contrary she would dearly like to be friends with this man, to have him trust her.

No! The danger is too great. Go. Now.

'Yes. But I shall not allow you to bully me.'

Amusement gleamed in his eyes.

'Then it should prove a very eventful two weeks.'

He lifted her hand to his lips before releasing her. Lucy

trembled inwardly as the gesture sent more shockwaves racing through her body. She did not think Ralph had noticed, for he had turned to his desk and was sorting through the papers.

He said, over his shoulder, 'Very well. If that is all, I have work to do before breakfast. You can go upstairs and change out of that abominable gown!'

No relief, no word of thanks—Lucy felt a gurgle of laughter bubbling up inside her as he resumed his usual autocratic tone. It would indeed be an eventful two weeks!

Having cleared the air, Lucy threw herself into life at Adversane. Ariadne was glad of her help with the arrangements for the house party, and Lucy cultivated the acquaintance of Amos, the aged gardener who promised her enough fresh flowers to fill the house. She also made a friend of Greg, Ralph's groom, who accompanied her on her daily rides.

Of Ralph himself she saw very little. He accompanied her and Ariadne to church on Sunday, but after that he spent most of his time with Harold Colne or on the estate, going out before breakfast and joining the ladies only in time for dinner each evening. When Ariadne jokingly remarked that he was neglecting them he said they would see more than enough of him when the guests arrived.

Lucy discovered that she missed his company. She began to take more care over her appearance when she prepared for dinner each evening. Ruthie proved herself a proficient *coiffeuse*, and Lucy was happy to sit still while the maid arranged her hair, chattering merrily all the while.

However, after her first incautious speech, Ruthie never mentioned her late mistress, and Lucy was increasingly curious to find out more about the woman whose place she was supposed to be filling. A casual remark to Mrs Green brought forth the information that Lady Adversane had been eager to learn how to run the household to his lordship's satisfaction.

'Not that the master wanted her to pander to him,' remarked the housekeeper, smiling at the memory. 'Quite nonplussed he was, whenever he found she put his comfort before her own. Told her she was mistress now, and must order things the way she wanted. He even gave her leave to have her bedchamber redecorated in any style she wished, but she wouldn't change a thing. To my mind I think she would have preferred to live in the London house, but she would not say so. Never one to make a fuss. But that was my lady's way.' She sighed and shook her head. 'A saint, she was, always looking to everyone else's happiness.'

Lucy found herself stopping in the Long Gallery to look at the portrait of Helene, now back in its original position. She tried to read her expression, to discern if she was happy or miserable, but the painted face merely stared down at her, a faint, wistful smile lifting her mouth. She wished she had the courage to ask Ralph about his wife, but even though she thought they had achieved an excellent understanding they only met at dinner or in the drawing room with Mrs Dean present, and Lucy did not feel she could mention it in company.

Mrs Sutton arrived towards the end of the following week, bringing with her all the remaining outfits, save the scarlet gown. She explained that she had had to send to London for the silk. However, she had brought so many other gowns and pelisses that Lucy was in no way disappointed. After trying them all on, she left the dressmaker and her assistant in the morning room, making the final adjustments while she went off to the stables. She had sent word earlier that she wanted to ride out and she found Brandy saddled and waiting for her. A young stable hand called Robin helped her to mount and explained that Mr Greg had gone off to Ingleston with Lord Adversane.

'So I'm to come with you today, miss,' he ended with a grin.

Brandy was fresh, and as soon as they entered the park Lucy gave him his head and enjoyed a gallop. It was only when she reached the trees and slowed up that she realised the young groom was quite some distance away. She stopped and waited for him to catch up with her. He was looking a little red in the face, and she laughed.

'I did not mean to leave you so far behind.'

'Nay, miss, that were my fault. Fair took me by surprise, you did, setting off so fast. I weren't expecting you to be such a good rider.'

He looked at her with new respect in his cheerful, open countenance, and as they turned and walked on Lucy could not resist asking if he had accompanied Lady Adversane on her rides.

'Aye, miss, for she wouldn't ride out alone. Wouldn't travel anywhere on her own, and that's a fact. Very nervy she was, which didn't suit my lord. Neck or nothing, he is. Bruising rider.'

'Yes, he is.' Lucy knew she should not ask, but Robin was a friendly lad, and there was no harm in her questions, surely. 'How did they get on, riding out together?'

'They didn't, miss. My lady was frightened of all his lordship's cattle, especially Jupiter. Horses knows, see, they can smell that sort of thing. The master said at first that my lady would have to get used to 'em, but it was no good, and after a few weeks he asked Sir James to send

over the grey my lady had always ridden.' He wrinkled
his nose. 'Overfed old mare, no pace at all. Mr Greg said
he'd never expected to see such a slug in the master's stables, and 'twas no wonder my lord never rode out with
his lady.' He stopped, flushing. 'I beg yer pardon, miss.
I should not be saying this to you.'

Guiltily aware that she had encouraged his confi-
dences, Lucy hastened to reassure Robin that she would
not repeat it to anyone. She knew she should put all
thoughts of Lady Adversane out of her mind, but Lucy
was beginning to feel a little sorry for her, if she did not
share her husband's love of horses. She could well imagine Ralph's impatience, but surely he could have curbed
it and indulged his wife in a gentle ride around the park
occasionally? She shook her head. It was not her concern.
She would only be here for another two weeks. After that
nothing at Adversane would be her concern at all.

Lying in her bed, Lucy stared into the enveloping
darkness.

'You would think,' she said aloud, 'that after spending the day helping Ariadne arrange all the guestrooms
I would be exhausted. So why am I now wide awake?'

She clasped her hands behind her head. Perhaps working in the house had brought it home to her that Ralph's
family would be arriving soon. She had grown very comfortable at Adversane with only her host and his cousin
for company, but she would have to be on her guard once
their guests arrived. She sighed, realising how happy she
had been for the past week, but it could not continue.
She had been employed for a reason, and she must play
her part. Lucy blinked. The inky blackness around her
was almost total, only relieved by the bluish square of
the window. Silently, she slipped out of bed and padded

across the room. After wrestling for a moment with the catches, she threw both casements wide.

Balmy night air flooded in, bringing with it the heavy fragrance of the newly scythed lawns and the faint, tantalising hint of roses from the flower garden. Lucy curled up on the window seat and rested her arms on the sill, leaning out to catch the cool air on her face. With a sigh, she dropped her chin on her arms and gazed across the drive to the park beyond. She felt the heavy weight of the single plait of her hair slide over her shoulder to dangle into nothingness. The darkness was not so thick out of doors, for although there was no moon the clear sky was sprinkled with stars.

"Well, Rapunzel, what are you doing out of bed at this hour?'

Lucy jumped and looked down to see a figure standing beneath her window. His face was little more than a pale blur in the darkness, but the deep voice was instantly recognisable.

'One might ask the same of you, Lord Adversane,' she retorted. 'And *what* did you call me?'

'It is from a German folk tale. Rapunzel is a maiden who is locked in a high tower and the only way her lover can reach her is to climb up her hair.'

Lucy laughed. 'That sounds very painful. Besides, my hair is far too short for that.' However, she still flicked the braid back over her shoulder, out of sight. 'I might ask you what you are doing beneath my window.'

'Jupiter lost a shoe on the way back from Halifax this afternoon. I have been to the stables to check up on him.'

'No serious damage, I hope?'

'No, Greg will take him to the smith in the morning. I am more concerned at why I should find you at your window in the middle of the night.'

'I could not sleep.'

'Are you anxious about anything? Can I help?'

His response was unexpected and surprised her into replying more freely than she had intended.

'No, thank you, sir. I have no idea why I am awake, I have been busy all day and in truth I should be very sleepy, but I am not. So I am star-gazing.'

'A good night for it. The moon will make an appearance tomorrow.' He paused. 'If you are truly awake...'

'I am.' A sudden sense of anticipation made the breath catch in her throat.

'We could take my telescope onto the roof and you could look at the stars properly.'

'Oh, I should dearly like to—' She stopped, aware of just what he was suggesting. Why, it must be nearly midnight. Regretfully she shook her head. 'That is, no, my lord. Thank you, but I cannot keep you from your rest.'

He ignored her objection.

'Put on a wrap and be ready. I will come for you. And do not light a candle, you need to keep your eyes accustomed to the dark!'

This is madness, thought Lucy as she stood by the door, listening. As soon as she heard a soft tread in the passage outside her room she opened the door a fraction and peeped out. The darkness there was leavened by a small lanthorn that gave out sufficient dim light for her to see Lord Adversane, still wearing his evening dress. Nervously, one hand went to her neck as if to assure herself that the enveloping wrap covered her from chin to toe.

'Good, you are here,' he murmured. 'Come along then. The staircase is at the far end of the east wing.'

I should not be doing this, she thought even as she stepped out of her room. Her wrap looked ghostly pale in the dim light, and she began to feel a little nervous until her fingers were taken in a firm, warm grasp.

'It will be easier if I hold on to you,' he whispered. 'Follow me.'

He led her through the gallery and into the east wing, where a long corridor brought them to a door.

'My workshop,' Adversane told her. 'There are stairs to the roof in the far corner.'

She followed him into the room. He placed the lanthorn down on a table, and Lucy looked around her. A large cupboard filled one wall. She had seen something similar once before—a cabinet of curiosities, it was called, and it could be filled with all sorts of odd things, from antiquities to rare books and stuffed animals, whatever caught the owner's interest. How she would love to come and explore here in daylight! Reluctantly, she turned away and spotted a large circular stone on the table by the lanthorn. She picked it up, turning it so that the feeble rays of the lamp showed her that it was formed like a coiled snake.

'That is a fossil,' he said, coming up. 'An ammonite, sometimes called a serpent stone. It is the petrified remains of a creature that lived in the very distant past.'

'Oh, I have heard of these,' cried Lucy. 'Is this not evidence of the flood, as it is told in the Bible?'

'Some might believe that.'

'But you do not?'

'I think this might be evidence of much older life forms.'

'Really? But I thought someone—a clergyman—had calculated the exact age of the earth.'

'I am a product of the Enlightenment, Miss Halbrook. I believe in logic and need to be convinced by reasoned argument and experiment. There are a great many theories on the origins and age of the earth, and much work yet to be done to prove them.'

'But surely not everything can be explained by reason and logic, my lord.'

'Not yet, perhaps, but one day. The Royal Society's own motto is "Nullius in verba" which means "take no man's word for it". A good maxim, I think.' He picked up the lanthorn and held it out to her. 'Time is going on. We must take the telescope up to the roof. Can you light the way?'

He ushered her across the room to a door that opened onto a flight of stairs. Indicating that she should precede him with the lamp, he shouldered the large brass instrument and followed her. The stairs were steep and narrow, and it was as much as Lucy could do to hold up her skirts and keep the light steady. At last she reached the top and opened the door to find herself upon the roof. Outside the starlight was faint, but bright enough to make the lamp unnecessary. It was possible to make out a flat walkway around the perimeter of the building, and Lucy was relieved to note that it was edged by a sturdy stone balustrade.

Ralph stepped in front of her and strode off, leaving Lucy to follow as best she might. They soon reached a small platform, where Lord Adversane set the telescope upon its tripod and began to angle it towards the sky. She put down the lamp and watched him.

'Mercury and Venus are only visible at twilight,' he said, turning back to her. 'But there is a good view of Saturn tonight, and I shall be able to show you the major constellations.'

'I know some,' she said, looking upwards. 'There, that is Ursa Major, is it not, leading to the North Star? Papa taught me that. He said if I knew which way was

north I would always be able to find my way home.' She
laughed. 'Not that I have ever needed to do so. As I told
you, my lord, this is the farthest from London I have
ever travelled.'

'And would you like to travel more, Miss Halbrook?'

'Oh, yes. When the war is over I would love to go to
the Continent, especially Naples and Rome.'

'To do the grand tour, perhaps?'

'Oh, no, I shall not have that much money, but what
you are paying me for being here will be a good start to
my savings—' She broke off, suddenly conscious of her
situation, alone in the dark with her employer. Alone in
the dark with Ralph Cottingham, fifth Baron Adversane.
She thought back to his explanation of their encounter
in the rain-soaked garden. It had sounded very reasonable at the time, but no amount of reasoning could dispel
her unease. She said briskly, 'But that is all for the future and I should not be wasting your time with it. Now,
let me see, what other patterns can I recognise? That is
Ursa Minor, is it not?'

'That's right. And there, the brighter stars that make
an elongated letter "W", is Cassiopeia....'

He continued to describe the night sky, standing behind her and directing her eyes up to the heavens. He
pointed out Draco, Hercules and Cygnis, as well as the
bright star Arcturus in the constellation of Bootes, the
herdsman. Lucy tried to concentrate, but when he laid one
hand casually on her shoulder it took all her resolution to
stand still. It was a relief when he finished his brief tour
of the skies and invited her to look through the telescope.

'But the stars are not much clearer,' she exclaimed,
a laugh in her voice. 'I fear you have misled me, Lord
Adversane.'

'That is because they are so distant. Now, look at

Saturn.' He turned her around and stood behind her, pointing over her shoulder. 'Look, there it is. Follow my finger, do you see it? A bright spot in the south.'

'Yes, yes, I do.'

'Now.' He realigned the telescope and beckoned her over. 'Now, what do you see?'

She peered through the lens and caught her breath in a gasp.

'But it is beautiful,' she breathed. 'I can see it so clearly, and it has hoops around it—' She straightened and moved away from the telescope to stare once more at the night sky. 'It is quite marvellous, my lord.'

He laughed and, clearly encouraged by her eagerness to learn, pointed out even more constellations to her.

'But this is not the best time of year for stargazing,' he told her. 'Once the darker nights are here you have more opportunity to see the planets and track them across the heavens.'

They stood in silence, gazing up. Lucy felt a strange contentment and was emboldened to ask, 'Did Lady Adversane share your enthusiasm, sir?'

She felt him drawing away from her, even before he moved.

'No,' he said shortly. 'I brought her here once or twice, but she found it tedious and very cold. We have done enough for tonight. Come along.'

Putting a hand under her arm, he took her back to the stairs, scooping up the lanthorn as they went.

'What about your telescope?'

'I shall come back for it later. For now I must get you indoors.'

The easy camaraderie they had shared was quite gone, and Lucy knew she had caused the change by asking him about his late wife. Silently, they descended to his

workshop, where Lucy thanked him politely for showing her the stars.

'I only hope you have not caught a chill in that flimsy
wrap.'

'Not at all. The night is very warm.'

He put down the lamp.

'Let me feel your hands.' He reached out and took
them in his own warm grasp. 'You are cold.'

'No, no, I assure you it is only my fingers.'

Lucy stared at his hands. Her throat dried, a voice inside was screaming that she should pull away, and she
knew she was standing far too close for safety. The darkness swirled around them, edging her closer still, like
a solid hand on her back. How easy it would be to lean
into him, to rest her cheek on the smooth silk of his
waistcoat and feel the hard chest beneath. Perhaps she
might even hear the thud of his heart. The very thought
sent her own skittering around like a frightened bird and
when Ralph released her hands and reached for her, she
quickly moved away.

'I—I must get back.'

'Of course.'

She tried to avoid any further contact, but as soon as
they stepped into the dark corridor he put out his hand and
hers slid into it, as if of its own accord. The silence of the
house pressed in around them, the only sound the faint
rustle of their moving. When they reached Lucy's room
Adversane stopped, standing between her and the door.

'It will soon be dawn. I hope you will sleep now, Miss
Halbrook.'

'I am sure I shall.'

*I don't want to sleep. I want to stay awake and live again
everything that I have seen and experienced with you!*

She was shaken by the sudden thought and could only

hope she had not spoken aloud. She forced herself to release his hand. He nodded.

'Very well, I shall leave you now.' His fingers grazed her cheek. 'Goodnight, Rapunzel.'

Lucy slipped into her room and closed the door. She leaned against it, listening for the sound of his footsteps moving away, the soft thud of his door closing. Her heart was singing with happiness. Quite foolish, of course, but she could not help it.

She smiled and whispered, 'Goodnight, my lord.'

Chapter Seven

Ralph's sisters and their husbands arrived the following afternoon, a day early, while Lucy and Ariadne were on a shopping trip to Ingleston.

'Perhaps it is not such a bad thing,' remarked Mrs Dean, when Byrne informed them that their guests were in the drawing room with Lord Adversane. 'You have not had time to get into a panic.'

Lucy tried to smile. She could not forget Adam Cottingham's remark that Ralph's sisters were fearsome ladies. However, there was no going back, for Mrs Dean had taken her arm and was marching her towards the drawing room.

The next ten minutes passed in a flurry of introductions and exclamations. Lucy was presented to Lord and Lady Wetherell and Sir Timothy and Lady Finch. The ladies had the same rather hawk-like features as their brother, but their smiles were warm, and however fearsome they might be, she took comfort from the fact both Sir Timothy and Lord Wetherell had the genial, well-fed look of contented spouses.

'Enough of this formality,' declared Lady Wetherell, coming forward and kissing Lucy on the cheek. 'You

must call me Caroline, my dear, and my sister is Meg—
or Margaret, which is what I call her when she has an-
noyed me! Now, Miss Lucy Halbrook, let me look at you.
What persuaded you to agree to marry my brother? Did
he bully you into it?'

Lucy blinked at such a direct question and could only
be thankful when Ralph answered for her.

'My dear Caroline, how do you expect her to respond
to such a question?' He came forward and took Lucy's
hand. 'I admit I had to work hard to persuade her to accept my offer, but I don't think I bullied you, did I, my
dear?'

He was smiling down at her, the mischievous glint
in his eyes inviting her to enjoy their shared secret. She
found herself relaxing.

I can do this.

'No more than usual, my lord.'

'Bravo,' cried Lady Finch, putting her sister aside so
that she, too, could greet Lucy with a kiss. 'You must
never be afraid to stand up to Ralph, my dear. His last
wife was too complaisant for her own good.'

Lucy froze. The room fell silent, and Sir Timothy
murmured a quiet remonstrance to his wife, who looked
around her, brows raised in surprise.

'What have I said that isn't common knowledge?' She
turned back to Lucy. 'You will learn that we like plain
speaking in this family.'

'But not if it embarrasses Miss Halbrook,' retorted
Ralph.

'Quite right,' agreed Caroline. 'Sit down, Meg, and
give Miss Halbrook time to grow accustomed to us.'

'And how are the children?' asked Ariadne, as if to
deflect attention from Lucy.

'Oh, they are all healthy and ripe for a spree,' replied

Sir Timothy cheerfully. 'We sent the boys off to stay with Caroline's three young scamps.'

'That's good,' said Ralph. 'They can ruin Wetherell's coverts and leave my birds in peace.'

Mrs Dean shook her head at him. 'Fie, Ralph, you know you love them all dearly.'

'How many children do you have?' asked Lucy.

'Two fine young boys,' replied Sir Timothy, pushing out his chest a little.

'And Caro has two girls and a boy,' declared Margaret. 'Delightfully noisy and boisterous, thank heaven.'

'Yes, they are, which is why we thought it would be quite unfair to subject Ralph's future wife to such lively children until she was better acquainted with the rest of us.' Caroline laughed. 'They might well have scared her off!'

An hour later, when Mrs Dean suggested that they should all retire to change for dinner, Lucy's head was reeling. She liked Caroline and Margaret very much and she enjoyed their lively banter, but it had not taken her long to realise that they were as strong-willed as their brother. She was about to follow them out of the room, but Ralph caught her hand and held her back.

'Pray do not pay too much heed to my sisters,' he said. 'Do not let their chatter worry you.'

'It doesn't. I find them very entertaining.' She chuckled. 'Although I now understand completely why you want me here.'

'You do?' His swift, frowning look unsettled her, but it was gone in a moment. 'Of course. You did not believe me, then, when I said I need protection?'

'Having met your sisters, I think we may both need protection if they discover they have been deceived.'

He pulled her hand onto his arm. 'Then let me escort you upstairs to add credence to our story.'

She walked with him across the hall and up the grand staircase, but when they reached the Long Gallery she deemed it time to protest.

'Apart from a few servants in the hall, no one has seen us, my lord.'

'Ralph,' he reminded her. 'And someone may come upon us at any time. We need practice, to make sure we always look at ease together.'

She gave a little tut.

'I mean, *Ralph*, that everyone is in their room. We have no audience, sir.'

She freed her arm, but he caught her hand and held on to it as they entered the inner corridor leading to her bed-chamber. With no windows on this passage the light was dim, and Lucy felt her pulse quickening. She stopped.

'I do not think we need to continue this any further, my lord.'

'No?'

His softly spoken response made her heart flutter alarmingly, and she stepped away, only to find her back against the wall. She was dismayed to hear how unsteady her voice was when she replied to him.

'There is no one here to impress with our charade.'

'But as I said, we need to practise. It is really quite logical.'

His free hand cupped her cheek, quite gently, but the shock of it held her motionless. She was unable to drag her gaze away from his face. Even in the dim light she noted how his eyes had darkened. He was lowering his head, he was going to kiss her and instead of making any effort to escape she ran her tongue over her lips, as if in preparation.

Then his mouth was on hers. A gentle touch, nothing like the tumultuous kiss they had shared in the rain. She closed her eyes and a tremor ran through her, like a sigh for something long desired. Her lips parted under his gentle insistence, she felt his tongue invading, exploring, and a slow burn of excitement began deep inside, heating her blood. When he raised his head she almost groaned with disappointment. Her eyes flickered open and stared up at him, too dazed to move.

His face was immobile, dark as stone in the deep shadow. He looked at her for a long, long moment. She cleared her throat, forcing herself to speak.

'Ralph—'

His hand was still cupping her face, and now he caressed her bottom lip with his thumb. Without thinking, she caught it between her teeth. Something flared in his eyes, something primeval, triumphant. She released him immediately, and he laughed softly as he drew away from her.

'I was wrong. You need no practice.'

As he turned away she forced out a few more words.

'I—I don't understand.'

He stopped and looked back.

'No, you wouldn't.' He spoke almost sadly, before adding in his usual brusque tone, 'Tell Ariadne she is not to let you out of her sight!'

'Damn, damn, damn!'

Ralph kicked the door closed behind him as he entered his room. He had made great efforts to keep away from Lucy Halbrook and allow her to forget that kiss in the garden. Not that he could forget it, for that encounter had shaken him badly. She unsettled him, which was why he had ripped up at her and then, knowing that his remark about her father had hurt her, he had wanted to make amends, only to find himself making a bad situation worse by taking her in his arms. Since then he had done his best to act with perfect decorum—apart from that midnight madness when he had taken her up onto the roof. His mind was diverted by the thought. She had been so delightful with the starlight shining in her eyes, and it had been a struggle not to succumb to temptation and kiss her, but he had behaved perfectly rationally.

Ralph told himself he wanted her at Adversane because he needed her to play her part in the forthcoming house party, but the truth was he wanted her to stay for her own sake, because he found her company stimulating. The more he saw of Lucy the more he wanted her. He tried to fight it. During the day he busied himself with his work and he had made sure they only met when Ariadne was present in the evenings, but today he had again broken his own rule and allowed himself to be alone with her.

And look at the result. His body was still tense with desire, and when he closed his eyes all he could see was her face upturned to his, those lustrous green eyes dark and inviting, the tip of her tongue flickering over those full, red lips.

By heaven, how he wanted her!

He absolved Lucy of all intent to seduce him. She was too innocent, completely unaware of her power over him. But for all that he found her presence intoxicating. A ragged laugh escaped him. If his sisters could see him behaving in this idiotic way they would have no difficulty believing the engagement was real.

Ralph frowned. He was growing fond of Lucy and did not want to hurt her by raising hopes he had no intention of fulfilling. He had already decided he could not marry again. He would never risk making another woman as unhappy as Helene had been.

'You are being foolishly conceited if you think she would even consider you as a husband,' he muttered to his reflection as he struggled with the knot of his neck cloth. 'She has already told you she does not even like you!'

And the way she responded to your kiss? The demon in his head would not be silenced. *How do you explain that?*

'Pure animal instinct. She had no idea of what she was doing. Hell and confound it, where *is* Kibble?' He tugged savagely at the bell-pull to summon his valet.

The restless mood would not leave him, and he strode to the window, leaning an arm on the frame and dropping his head against it. One thing was certain: when Lucy Halbrook did eventually find a suitor who pleased her, he would be a very, very lucky man.

Lucy kept one hand on the wall as she made her way back to her bedchamber. Her knees felt far too weak to support her, and her body still pulsed with an energy she did not understand. Ruthie bustled in from the dressing room, too excited with her own news to notice her mistress's pallor.

'Ooh, miss, I'm to sit with the ladies' maids at dinner tonight. Imagine! Mrs Green says when the other guests arrive tomorrow, us ladies' maids will have to have a table to ourselves. Was there ever anything like it?'

'No, never.' Lucy tried to be glad for her maid. 'Help me out of this gown, Ruthie, then I think I shall lie down for a little while before I change for dinner.'

'Yes, miss. Oh, and Mr Kibble passed on a message from his lordship. He says you are to wear the blue silk tonight, miss, with the silver stars.'

'Yes, yes.' Lucy stepped out of her robe and waved her maid away. 'Hang that up, Ruthie, then come back in half an hour.'

Lucy crawled onto her bed and curled up, hugging herself. *Such* feelings she had experienced when he had kissed her. Such emotions had welled up. When she had first raised the idea of finding employment, her mother had warned her of the dangers that lurked in a gentleman's household. She had told her how persuasive men could be, had explained something of the dangerous charms of a seducer, but Lucy had pictured then a leering, lecherous man like her Uncle Edgeworth. Mama had not told her that she must also beware of the treacherous longings of her own body.

The mere memory of Ralph's kiss made her writhe and hug herself even tighter. How would she be able to face him, to be in the same room with him, without wanting to touch him? She knew she would stare longingly at his mouth, desperate for him to kiss her again.

All too soon Ruthie returned with a jug of hot water. Lucy managed to wash with tolerable calm, and she allowed her maid to help her into the high-waisted evening gown of midnight-blue embroidered with silver thread. As the skirts shimmered into place Lucy was reminded of standing on the roof with Ralph, gazing up at the blue-black vault of the night sky. She had felt such happiness then, with his hand resting upon her shoulder and his deep voice murmuring in her ear as he talked to her about the stars.

'Miss, miss? Will you sit down, miss, so that I can dress your hair?'

Lucy gave herself a mental shake and sank down on the stool before her mirror. She watched patiently as

Ruthie caught her hair up in a blue ribbon and nestled little silver stars amongst her curls. She frowned.

'I remember being fitted for the gown, but I cannot recall Mrs Sutton supplying the hair ornaments.'

'No, miss, they belonged to Lady Adversane. It seems the master has kept them all this time. Fancy that!'

Lucy stared in the mirror and a cold chill of reality began to trickle through her veins.

'And this gown, Ruthie. Do you remember Lady Adversane wearing one similar?'

'Of course, miss. She said she chose the midnight-blue to match her eyes.' Ruthie gave a gay little laugh. 'She was that beautiful, but of course the stars didn't show up quite so well against her gold curls as they will in your darker ones.'

If Ruthie meant this as a comfort it fell far short. Lucy stared at her reflection and felt something inside turning to stone. Ralph wanted her to look like Helene. It was his late wife he had imagined he was kissing earlier. He did not want her at all, merely someone who looked enough like Helene to arouse him.

Lucy sank her teeth into her bottom lip to stop it from trembling. She wanted to sweep her arm across the dressing table, to send the pots and brushes and the rest of those exquisite little silver ornaments flying across the room. Instead, she folded her hands in her lap. This was what she was being paid for—to recreate the image of a dead woman.

The murmur of voices when she went downstairs to the drawing room told Lucy she was not the first, but that was what she had planned. She had deliberately left it as late as she dared to put in an appearance. As she entered the room a silence fell. Lord Wetherell raised his

looking glass to stare at her. Sir Timothy goggled, and
Margaret exclaimed, in her frank way, 'Good God, she
is just like Helene!'

'Do you think so?' murmured Ralph, coming towards
her. 'I do not see it.'

He was smiling, and Lucy forced herself to smile back.
She had no wish now to gaze at him adoringly, to think of
his kiss. When he would have taken her hand, she moved
away slightly and made her own way into the room. Caroline patted the seat beside her and smiled invitingly.

'Everyone wears these styles and colours, Margaret.
Leave the girl alone.'

But Lucy saw the speculative glance Caroline threw
at her brother.

Lucy discovered that playing a role was much easier
than being herself. She existed only as Ralph's fiancée;
quiet, complaisant and totally without emotion. When
Ralph escorted her in to dinner and asked her if she was
all right, she smiled sweetly and told him she was very
well. Conversation ebbed and flowed around her. After
dinner the ladies retired to the drawing room, where Lucy
recited without a blush the story she and Ralph had concocted about how and where they had met.

'So it was love at first sight,' said Margaret.

'Not exactly.'

'Well, I must say I was surprised to learn that Ralph
had found himself another bride,' remarked Caroline. 'I
thought Helene's death had put him off marriage for ever.'

'Did he…? Did he love her very much?' Lucy thought
it quite reasonable that a fiancée might ask the question
of Ralph's sisters.

'I never thought so,' replied Caroline frankly. 'She was

exquisitely beautiful, of course, but when one got past that she had very little else to recommend her.'

'My dear, she was the sweetest girl,' protested Ariadne.

'Yes, the sweetest little nodcock.'

'Well, I think we have only ourselves to blame that he married her,' said Margaret, coming to sit on the other side of Lucy. 'We urged Ralph to marry, and to please us he went to Harrogate, looking for a wife. Preston hurled the gel at his head and with her beauty it is hardly surprising that Ralph should fall head over heels in love and offer for her.'

'And she bored him within a month of the ceremony,' declared Caroline. 'Whereas you, my dear...' She turned and caught Lucy's hands. 'You have intelligence and a sharp wit, if I am not mistaken, that will keep a man interested for a lifetime.'

Shocked out of her role, Lucy blushed.

'How can you say so when you hardly know me?'

'I knew it as soon as we met. You have a ready sense of the ridiculous and although you are no chatterbox, what you do say shows you have an active and enquiring mind.'

'But many men do not want an intelligent wife, Caro,' said Margaret. 'The very thought frightens them.'

'Not Lucy,' cried her sister, smiling, 'Who could be frightened of her?'

Lucy laughed and disclaimed. How she would have liked to make real friends of these women, but it could not be. When the time came for her to jilt Ralph they would despise her, she knew it.

'Let us have some music!' cried Margaret, jumping up and going to the piano. 'Do you play, Lucy?'

'A little, but not that well.'

'Then we are all evenly matched. Come along, there is some music here somewhere...'

* * *

When the gentlemen came in some time later they found all four ladies gathered about the piano, singing folk songs. Margaret immediately called across the room to them.

'Ralph, your fiancée has the sweetest voice. Do come and join her in a duet.'

Lucy forgot to be complaisant and said hurriedly, 'Oh, no, I couldn't—'

'Do you mean to say you and Ralph have not sung together yet?' Caroline caught Lucy's hand to stop her running away. 'Fie upon you, brother, isn't it Shakespeare who says music is the food of love? Come and sing with her. Margaret shall play for you.'

There was no avoiding it. The sisters shepherded Lucy into place beside Ralph, music was thrust into their hands, and Margaret began to play, while the others took their seats in eager expectation. A lively version of 'Cherry Ripe' was followed by 'Early One Morning'. They were familiar songs, and Lucy soon lost her nervousness and enjoyed herself, her voice blending with Ralph's powerful tenor to produce a wonderful sound that rang around the room. When they had finished their audience clapped enthusiastically.

'Do you know, that was really rather splendid,' declared Sir Timothy, beaming at them. 'I think we shall enjoy some wonderful musical evenings here at Adversane in the future.'

'There is a lovely duet from *The Magic Flute* here somewhere,' cried Caroline, pulling more music from a cupboard. 'It would suit you both beautifully—'

'Not tonight,' said Ralph firmly. He signalled to his brothers-in-law to come forward. 'We have performed, and now it is your turn to join your ladies.'

Lucy had enjoyed herself far too much. The way Ralph had smiled at her had made her pulse race again, disastrous for her peace of mind. She went over to sit next to Ariadne on the sofa. It was only large enough for two and Ariadne's ample frame took up most of the space, so she would be able to enjoy the singing without being distracted by Ralph's disturbing presence.

However, when the couples had agreed who would sing, and Caroline had replaced her sister at the piano, Ralph came across and perched himself upon the arm of the sofa beside her. Lucy kept her gaze fixed rigidly on the piano, but she was very much aware of his thigh so close to her shoulder. He leaned back and rested his arm on the back of the sofa, his fingers playing with the curls at the nape of her neck.

It was all very nonchalant, if a little daring, for a gentleman to lounge in such a manner so close to a lady, but at an informal house party, and when the lady in question was his fiancée, Lucy knew no one would object.

She sat upright, removing her curls from his reach, but her skin still tingled at the knowledge that his fingers were so close and, even more disturbingly, she was very aware that no more than a few inches and a thin covering of kersey separated her from that long, muscular thigh.

Her mind was in turmoil. She had no idea what was sung, or even how long it went on. Part of her wanted it to be over so that Ralph would get up and move away. Another part of her, a much more invidious part, wanted it to go on for ever so that she might lean back again and feel those strong, lean fingers playing with her curls, perhaps even caressing the back of her neck.

The singing ended. Ralph eased himself off the arm of the sofa and walked over to congratulate the performers. Lucy told herself she was delighted, relieved. Margaret returned to the piano to play a sonata and the others disposed themselves gracefully around the room. It was a warm evening, and Sir Timothy threw open the long windows and stepped outside. It was growing dark, and a servant entered with a taper to light the candles. Lord Wetherell invited his lady to accompany him onto the terrace and watch the bats. For the first time Lucy saw Caroline show signs of nerves.

'Bats—horrid creatures! They swoop upon one so silently.'

'But I shall be there to protect you,' murmured her husband, holding out an imperious hand. 'Come along, Caro.'

They wandered out. Ariadne went off to tidy away the music and Lucy was left alone on the sofa. Ralph sat down beside her.

'No, please do not go.' He put his hand on her arm as she went to get up. 'I enjoyed singing with you.'

'Did Helene sing?' The question was out before she could stop it.

'Of course. She was most accomplished.'

He removed his hand and her skin felt cold where his fingers had rested. Lucy suddenly felt very depressed. One could not compete with a dead love. Compete? The very idea was ludicrous. She was an employee, little more than a servant. Ralph would never think of her as anything else.

'I should retire.'

'But it is early yet.'

'I am very sleepy.'

She rose, and Ralph followed her to the door.

'I will escort you—'

'No, please—' She turned, knowing tears were not

far away. 'I would prefer to be alone. Please remain with your family.'

He raised her hand to his lips, and the now-familiar heat shot through her veins. She said, to distract herself, 'We have more guests arriving tomorrow. I will need to have my wits about me for that.'

'You managed very well tonight.'

She glanced down. The skirts of her midnight-blue silk looked black in the dim light. Mourning colours for a dead wife. She raised her head, forcing a smile.

'I am doing what you employed me for, my lord.'

He did not correct her, and she went out, closing the door quietly behind her.

'Ralph, where is Lucy?' Margaret called across the room as she closed the lid of the piano.

He had no idea how long he had been standing at the door. Long enough to imagine Lucy crossing the hall and climbing the stairs, her silken skirts whispering about her and the little silver stars in her hair twinkling in the light of her bedroom candle.

'She has gone to bed.' He added lightly, 'No doubt you have tired her out with your endless questions.'

'Pho, we have been unusually restrained,' Meg retorted, coming across the room and taking his arm. 'There are so many questions we *could* have asked. Such as, why have you chosen a woman who looks so much like your late wife?'

'She would not have been able to answer that.'

'No, but you can.' She squeezed his arm. 'Well, Ralph?'

'She is nothing like Helene.' He saw Margaret's cynical smile and shrugged. 'Very well, there is a passing likeness.'

'Helene is gone, Ralph. You cannot bring her back.'

Margaret was the sister nearest to him in age and temperament. He was not used to seeing sympathy in her eyes, but it was there as she murmured the quiet words.

'I have no wish to bring her back,' he muttered. 'I just want—' He stopped. This was his burden, and he would not share it. Instead, he smiled at his sister. 'I want you and Caro to look after Lucy. This house party will be something of a trial for her.'

Chapter Eight

Lucy rose early the following morning. After a night's repose nothing seemed quite so bad and she decided to go out. She dressed quickly, but when she went downstairs she found that Margaret and Caroline were before her.

'Ah, so you are going out walking, too,' Caroline greeted her cheerfully when she met them in the hall. 'We are going to Druids Rock. Will you join us?'

The prospect of congenial company was too tempting. The three ladies went off together, the sisters setting a brisk pace, which suited Lucy very well.

'This is a favourite walk of ours,' said Caroline as they headed for the wicket gate on the far side of the lawn.

'Really? Even after the accident?'

'Well, that was very sad, of course,' said Margaret. 'We always spare a thought for Helene when we go this way, but we enjoy the walk, and the views from Druids Rock are spectacular.'

'Besides,' said Caroline, 'I am sure many dreadful things have happened there in the past. The Druids, you see.' She lowered her voice and said with relish, 'Dark deeds, sacrifices and satanic rituals!'

'Hush, Caro, you know that is all nonsense. Pay no

heed to my sister, Lucy. She has a penchant for horrid mysteries and Gothic tales.'

'But you must admit it does add a touch of excitement,' said Caroline. 'Oh! What has happened here?'

They were approaching the gate into the old ride, and Lucy looked up with some surprise. The trees had been cut back, allowing the sunlight to pour onto the path.

'It has been opened up,' cried Caroline. 'And about time, too. Now we shall be able to ride this way again. This must be for you, Lucy. Ralph told us you are a bruising rider.'

Lucy blushed and shook her head, wishing he did indeed care enough to do such a thing for her.

'And the undergrowth has been cut back so we can walk three abreast,' declared Margaret, linking arms with her companions. 'It is quite shocking how overgrown it had become in the past couple of years. Since Helene did not ride much this path was rarely used, but after the accident Ralph closed the gate and never came this way any more.'

'Accident!' Caroline gave a snort. 'Everyone knows she killed herself.' When Margaret protested she waved her hand. 'It is best that Lucy knows the truth, Meg, if she is going to live here. It was recorded as an accident, of course, but Helene must have been very distressed to go out without changing her gown.'

'You think she was distraught?' asked Lucy, curiosity overcoming her reluctance to discuss the matter.

Margaret looked at Caroline.

'We think she and Ralph had quarrelled that day,' she said. 'Or rather, that he had upbraided *her*, for she was such a soft little thing she never argued with anyone. There was a brittle quality to her at the play that evening, and Ralph was looking decidedly grim. At the end of the night we all thought Helene had gone to bed. Of course with so many people in the house it was all noise and confusion, and it wasn't until the following morning we discovered she had gone out.'

'It was quite dreadful when her body was brought back to the house,' added Caroline. She gave a shudder. 'I have never seen Ralph so pale. And later, after dinner, he had the most terrible row with Adam.'

'Adam Cottingham,' queried Lucy. 'His heir?'

'Yes. We were all gathered in the drawing room, and Adam had clearly been imbibing far too freely, for suddenly he burst out, "You are to blame. You pushed her to this, you cold devil. If she had not married you she would still be alive!" And Ralph never said a word. He just stood there, that closed look on his face—you know the one, Sis—until Adam stormed out of the room.'

'That is right,' nodded Margaret. 'And Ralph said, in the quiet way he has, "He is right." And then not another word upon it.'

'So he blames himself for her death,' muttered Lucy.

'Yes, but he should not,' declared Caroline. 'No one could have been more kind or forbearing, and you will know by now that that is *not* Ralph's nature. He went out of his way to look after his wife. Helene was very mild-mannered and kind to a fault, but she had no *spirit*. She crumbled at the first hint of disapprobation.'

'Caro—'

'It's the truth, Meg. Oh, everyone loved Helene and I believe she was determined to be a good wife, but she was unhappy. Ralph did his best, as soon as he realised what a nervous little thing she was he did everything in his power to set her at her ease. We never heard him raise his voice to her, did we, Meg?'

'No, he was most forbearing.'

'It's my belief she was unstable,' remarked Caroline, considering the matter. 'She would burst into tears at the slightest provocation. I found her extremely tiresome, and I only saw her occasionally. How Ralph kept his temper with her I do not know!'

'Caroline!'

'Well, Meg, it is most unfair that Ralph should be blamed because she jumped off the rock.'

'No one blames him,' said her sister. 'But he blames himself and has been punishing himself quite dreadfully. He even declared that he would never marry again, and I am thankful that he has thought better of that decision! We are so glad that he has brought you to Adversane, Lucy, and that he is hosting another house party. It is a sign that he is getting over it at last!'

'Is he?' Lucy tried to smile, but all she could think of was the portrait of Helene in the scarlet gown, and all those dresses he had insisted she should wear.

They walked on in silence, over the pretty bridge and onto the moors. The sun was climbing and by the time they reached Druids Rock it had burned off any remaining mist from the valley. They scrambled up onto the rock and the two sisters pointed out various landmarks to Lucy: the paddock where Greg had taught them to ride, the old ruin on the hill where they had played hide and seek and the neat property on the edge of Ingleston where Ralph's steward lived.

'Harry Colne is Ralph's oldest friend,' said Margaret. 'They used to go everywhere together as boys, fishing, hunting, riding—and here, of course. This was always one of their favourite places.'

'And ours, too,' said Caroline. 'This was our castle, or a pirate ship, or whatever we wanted it to be.' She laughed. 'Do you remember, Meg, when the boys were climbing the south face and Ralph fell and broke his collarbone?'

'Lord, yes. Papa was so angry. Said it served him right for being careless. Oh, it was not that he didn't love us,' she added, catching sight of Lucy's startled face. 'As soon as Ralph was well enough he brought him here and taught him the correct way to scale the rock.'

'That was Papa's way,' explained Caroline. 'He was kind, but not a great one for displays of affection. Ralph is very like him—even more so, in fact, because once he inherited the title he had such responsibilities on his shoulders that he became quite serious and lost his sense of fun...which perhaps explains why Helene found him so difficult to live with.'

Silence followed her words, broken only by the sighing of the wind, until Margaret jumped to her feet.

'Breakfast!' she declared, making her way off the rock. 'Then we must prepare for the arrival of the Prestons, and Adam and his wife.' When they were on the track again she took Lucy's arm, saying cheerfully, 'We are so very glad you are here, Lucy. We really could not like the thought of our cousin inheriting Adversane.'

'Oh?' said Lucy. 'I met him earlier this week. He seemed a very pleasant gentleman.'

'Oh, he is pleasant enough,' said Caroline. 'And very charming, if you like that sort of thing, yet he is not the man to fill Ralph's shoes. But now that Ralph is going to marry you,' she ended sunnily, 'we need no longer worry about that. Come, let us get back for breakfast. There is nothing like a good walk to sharpen the appetite!'

'I'd forgotten what a noisy family I have.'

Ralph entered the breakfast room to find everyone

gathered there and he hardly expected to be heard above the clatter of dishes and cheerful voices.

'Good morning, Ralph.' Margaret waved her fork at him. 'Will you join us? There are still some eggs and ham left, I think, and the most delicious pie, if Timothy has not taken the last piece.'

'Thank you. I broke my fast at Ling Cottage,' Ralph said, smiling at the merry scene.

'And how is Harry, and Francesca, his lovely wife? Will they be joining us for dinner?' Caroline turned to Lucy. 'Harry is more like family than Ralph's steward, but he is very busy with his own life and can rarely be persuaded to dine here.'

'Well, you will be pleased to know I have, er, *persuaded* them to come along tonight,' Ralph informed them.

His eyes rested on Lucy, noting the colour in her cheeks. He had seen her going off with his sisters that morning, and thought how much better she looked for the exercise. So much brighter than last night, when the sadness in her eyes had unsettled him. 'I came to ask Miss Halbrook if she would spare me a few moments when she has broken her fast.' All the female eyes turned on him, full of rampant curiosity. He felt obliged to add, 'There has been a delivery for her.'

'For me?'

She looked quite delightful, with the colour mounting to her cheek and her eyes wide with astonishment.

'A surprise,' declared Caroline. 'Do wait a moment, Lucy my dear, and we will all come with you.'

Ralph frowned.

'You will not!'

'Is it a secret, Ralph?' Lucy's eyes were upon him, green and luminous with shy anticipation.

'No, of course not.'

'Would it embarrass her if we came along?'

Margaret's blunt question made him scowl.

'It should not do so, but I pray Lucy will not hesitate to say if she has had enough of your company for one day!'

Lucy chuckled at that, a soft, melodious sound that he found immensely satisfying.

'Of course I should,' she said. 'But I have no objection to them coming with me to see this mysterious delivery.'

Ralph was relieved when the gentlemen declared themselves happy to remain and finish their breakfast, but all the ladies rose as one to follow him to the hall. He wished now he had said nothing until Lucy was alone, but he was impatient for her to see what he had bought for her.

A large packing case rested on the floor next to the table in the centre of the hall. Lucy reached in and lifted out a brown paper parcel. Shaking off the packing straw, she placed the parcel on the table. Ralph unfolded his pocket knife and handed it to her.

'You may need this.'

He stood back as the ladies gathered around the table, their excited chatter reminding him of family birthdays long ago, when the house had been alive with laughter. Lucy cut the string and turned to give him back the knife, glancing up at him a little uncertainly. If it had been Caro or Margaret they would have had the paper ripped off by now. He gave her a little smile and nod of encouragement. Carefully, she pulled the paper aside to reveal a square rosewood box, inlaid with mother of pearl. As she lifted the lid he heard her gasp.

'A paint box!' cried Margaret. 'How delightful—look, Caro, it even has little bowls to mix the colours.' She laughed. 'And we had to manage with oyster shells! What a lovely gift, Ralph.'

'I know Lucy brought only her sketchbook to Adversane,' he explained.

'I have never had anything like this,' she murmured, gently pulling open a drawer and revealing ranks of coloured paint blocks. She turned to face him. 'It is very thoughtful of you, Ralph. Thank you.'

'You will be able to take it with you.' He held her eyes. 'Wherever you travel.'

Lucy felt her heart skip a beat at his words. This was nothing to do with Helene. It was a gift for her, something of her own to keep.

'I shall treasure it always.'

'Well, that is no way to thank your fiancé,' cried Margaret, laughing. 'You must kiss him, Lucy.'

A blush stole up her body. She felt it burning her neck and then her whole face was aflame. She saw that a dull flush had also crept into Ralph's cheeks. He said softly, 'Well, Lucy?'

Everyone was watching. Lucy met Ralph's eyes. There was a smile in them, but a challenge, too, and she could not resist it. She stepped closer and placed her hands on his lapels, standing on tiptoe as she reached up to kiss his cheek. His hands came up to cover hers, he moved his head and captured her lips with his mouth.

Sparks flew. Cannon roared. She closed her eyes, wanting the kiss to go on for ever, but she could hear his sisters laughing and clapping, and even more disturbing was Ariadne's gasp and muttered protests. Lucy dropped back on her heels, blushing furiously. Ralph cleared his throat.

'Shall I carry the box up to your room?'

'No, no, I can manage.'

'Very well.' He released her hands. 'I must go and see Colne.'

She saw his brows contract as he heard his sisters giggling, and he bent a frowning look upon them.

'I hope you are satisfied, ladies,' he barked, then turned on his heel and strode off, shouting to Byrne to come and clear away the mess.

Chapter Nine

The final guests, Adam Cottingham and his wife and the Prestons, arrived later that day. Lucy was pleased she had already met Ralph's cousin, for she could then give more attention to his wife when the couple were shown into the drawing room. Judith Cottingham was a colourless little woman with a habit of looking to her husband after her every utterance. Her brown hair had lost any glow it might once have had and there were no roses in her cheeks. Lucy thought she looked distinctly unhappy, and put aside her own nerves in an attempt to make her smile. She did not succeed, and was relieved when Caroline drew her away.

'Do not trouble yourself with Judith Cottingham,' Caro murmured when they had moved off. 'She is such a timid little thing, and has no conversation at all.'

'She seems very dependent upon Mr Cottingham.'

Caroline flicked a glance over her shoulder.

'He is her sole delight—if you can call it delight.'

Lucy wanted to ask her what she meant but was distracted by the arrival of the last of the house guests, Sir James and Lady Preston and their daughter, Charlotte. The parents were an ill-assorted pair. Sir James was a solid gentleman with sharp eyes while his wife was a much paler creature, tall and very slim. Lucy thought she must have been pretty as a girl, but her beauty had faded to the palest pastel colours. However, Lucy's eyes were drawn to the daughter. She would have recognised Charlotte as Helene's sister even if the butler had not announced her name. She looked very much like a younger version of the portrait of Lady Adversane—the same golden hair, the same willowy figure, but she had much more animation in her countenance and had not yet outgrown the schoolgirl habit of giggling when a gentleman addressed her. Lucy observed it now, when Ralph greeted the newcomers and smiled at Charlotte, but it did not stop her feeling a little stab of something that she recognised as jealousy. What need had he to hire her when Charlotte was bidding fair to be Helene's equal?

No time to think of that. Ralph was talking to the Prestons, holding out his hand and inviting her to join them. Lucy approached nervously. She had dressed with care for this occasion, choosing a fine cream muslin gown that was so universally fashionable no one could say it was a copy of the late Lady Adversane's. She had also dressed her hair differently, drawing it all back save for a fringe of curls, and the rest cascading in ringlets from a topknot. Ralph had given her a long look when she had appeared, but he had made no comment. Now she hoped that any resemblance to Helene was so minor it would be overlooked. Certainly Sir James and Lady Preston greeted her in a kindly manner, although she found herself blushing when Sir James declared with what she thought forced joviality that he was delighted to meet Adversane's fiancée.

'It is not yet official,' replied Ralph calmly. 'There is no announcement. Nothing is drawn up.'

'No, of course, of course.' Lady Preston fluttered her fan and gave a smile that didn't quite reach her faded blue eyes. 'You wanted to inform the family first, is that not so, my lord? So thoughtful of you. Hasn't he always been a most thoughtful brother-in-law, Charlotte?'

Charlotte responded with a giggle, but Ralph was already leading Lucy away, calling to Byrne to bring more refreshments for his guests.

'There,' he said quietly, when he had drawn her aside. 'Your ordeal is at an end.'

She glanced up at him.

'How did you know I was nervous?'

'What fiancée would not be in such a situation?'

'Oh, dear, I hope it did not show too much.'

'Only to me.' He squeezed her hand. 'There is only one more couple expected today and that is Harry, whom you know, and his wife, Francesca. They are driving over from Ling Cottage to join us this evening.'

'Then he has no excuse to be late,' said Caroline, overhearing. 'If he takes the shortest way.'

Lucy frowned, trying to picture the route.

'That would be past Druids Rock, would it not?' Even as she spoke she was aware that the very name had brought conversation around them to an end. 'Oh, I beg your pardon, I did not intend...'

Sir James approached, smiling.

'Pray do not think you should not speak of that place in front of us,' he told her kindly. 'We are quite accustomed to having lost dear Helene there, and the rock has far greater significance to the world. It is not a place to be shunned.'

'Ah, the druids,' said Caroline and earned a scowl from her brother.

'No, no, my boy, do not frown her down,' said Sir

James. 'Lady Wetherell is quite right, even though I do not think she takes it seriously.' The smile he directed at Caroline was full of smug superiority. 'Despite Adversane's dependence upon empiricism and new discoveries, there is a great deal the ancients can teach us.'

'There is no evidence that Druids Rock was ever used by any ancient order,' retorted Ralph.

'No written evidence, perhaps,' replied Sir James, unabashed. 'However, when one has studied the ancients as I have done, one can sense their presence. I shall be visiting Druids Rock to watch the sunrise at the summer solstice.'

'As a guest you are, of course, free to go where you please,' said Ralph.

'Well, I shall remain in my bed, soundly asleep!' Lady Preston gave a tinkling laugh and turned the conversation to safer channels.

More refreshments appeared; wine and ratafia, and tea for those who, according to Lord Wetherell, preferred to corrupt their insides with the pernicious brew. His wife threw him a saucy look as she drew Lucy away from Ralph and carried her off to where Ariadne was pouring tea.

'You can relax now, my dear,' she said when they had collected their cups and withdrawn to an empty sofa.

'You sound just like your brother.' Lucy laughed. 'I admit I was a little nervous to meet Sir James and Lady Preston. I was afraid they would resent my presence.'

'If they do it is because they wanted Ralph to offer for Charlotte.' Caroline noted Lucy's look of disbelief and nodded. 'She may only be seventeen, but Sir James would like to maintain his links with Adversane.'

'That is what Mrs Dean told me.' Lucy sighed. 'There is a financial incentive, I am sure.'

'Yes, but not just that. Sir James would like to invite his friends to Druids Rock.' She smiled. 'Oh, we may think it a fine joke, but Sir James was one of the founder members of The Ancient Order of the Druids and he would very much like to hold a druidical ceremony at the rock. Ralph will not countenance it, although I know Helene tried to persuade him on her father's behalf. Sir James wrote again to Ralph last summer and asked if he might bring a party to celebrate the summer solstice at Druids Rock.'

'Celebrate?' Lucy's eyes widened. 'At the place where his daughter had died only twelve months before?'

'I know. It sounds very callous, doesn't it? Ralph flatly refused, of course.'

Another thought was forming in Lucy's head. She said slowly, 'Do you think that is why Helene went there—to see the sun rise?'

'Possibly, although she had gone there with her father a few days earlier to see the sunrise at the solstice. Midsummer, or St John's Eve, is a very different celebration and nothing to do with Sir James and his druids. Bonfires are lit all along the valley, and Ralph always sends a side of beef to the village, that they may feast in style. And, of course, there are the theatricals at Adversane.'

Caroline looked up, smiling, as other guests approached and the conversation moved on.

The party broke up soon afterwards and everyone went off to change for dinner. When Lucy went up to her room she found the Long Gallery deserted and she took the opportunity to look at the portrait of Helene again. She looked very wistful, but had she really been so unhappy?

'She is very beautiful, isn't she?'

Lucy jumped. She had been so absorbed in her own thoughts that she had not heard Adam Cottingham approach. Now she looked round to find him standing at her shoulder.

'I think she looks a little sad,' she remarked.

'She was.'

'You knew her, did you not, Mr Cottingham?' Lucy hesitated. 'Was she not happy here?'

He stared at the painting.

'No, she was not,' he said at last. 'Perhaps—but I should not say this to you.'

'Oh, please,' she said earnestly, 'please tell me what you think. I would much rather things were out in the open.' She thought sadly of her father, of his absences and her mother's unexplained tears. 'One cannot deal with difficulties if they are unknown.'

'Very true, Miss Halbrook.' He looked back at the portrait. 'My cousin is not an easy man to live with. He can be... How should I put it? Tyrannical.'

'Oh, surely not,' said Lucy impulsively. 'I know he can be a little abrupt, but surely—'

'She was very fragile, you see. Far too meek and quiet to hold her own against Adversane.' His glance flickered to Lucy. 'You have the look of her.'

She blushed and disclaimed, 'It is a mere fancy, sir.'

'Perhaps.' He smiled. Lucy did not know what to say, but her silence went unnoticed for Adam continued, as if he was speaking to himself. 'Everyone loved her for her kind heart, but she was too complaisant, submissive, even. She needed to be worshipped, like a goddess. Ralph never understood that. He was impatient with her. In the end I do not think she could stand it any more.'

A sudden chill ran through Lucy.

'No. He is not a tyrant, truly.' She thought of the paint box. 'He can be very kind.'

'Kind enough, I grant you, when one adheres to his wishes.' He added quickly, 'Forgive me, I should not have said that. I have not seen Ralph for some time. He may well have changed, mellowed. Yes, of course. It must be so, if he has won your regard, Miss Halbrook.'

She did not know what to say but nothing was necessary. Adam gave a sad little smile, bowed and left her.

'I'm to dress you in the blue silk again tonight, miss, with the silver stars in your hair,' said Ruthie. 'Lord Adversane's orders.'

Kind enough, when one adheres to his wishes.

Lucy desperately wanted to put it to the test, to tell Ruthie to take the beautiful gown away and bring her another, but something held her back. Her eyes went to the paint box resting on top of the chest of drawers. By that one act of kindness Ralph had bought her loyalty, at least for a little longer.

Her maid had just put the finishing touches to Lucy's hair when there was a knock at the door. Lucy remained at her dressing table while Ruthie went to answer it. Her heart began to thud against her ribs when she heard Ralph's deep voice announcing that he had come to escort Miss Halbrook downstairs.

Lucy rose and took a last look at herself in the mirror. The sun of the past few weeks had bleached her hair, making her resemblance to Helene even more marked. Why was he doing this? Why was he putting her through this ordeal?

A simple business transaction.

The words came back to her. She had agreed to it, but

had she quite understood what was involved? Resolutely, Lucy turned towards the door.

'I am ready, my lord.'

Ralph had not come into her room but was waiting for her in the passage. His figure loomed large in the narrow corridor, a shadowy form with only the snowy linen at his neck and the frills at his wrists standing out, almost glowing in the dim light. He did not move as she went out to meet him, but subjected her to a hard stare. She felt a flicker of annoyance and put up her chin.

'Well, my lord, do I look sufficiently like your dead wife?'

Nerves and unease added a sharp note to her voice, and she expected a blistering retort, but as she drew closer she was surprised to see an odd little smile playing about the corners of his mouth.

'It is strange, Miss Halbrook, but when I look at you I no longer see the resemblance.'

'Well, you may be sure your sisters saw it when I came down to dinner yesterday in this very gown.'

'You are not wearing it for their benefit.' He held out his arm. 'Come along, Miss Halbrook, or we shall be late.'

That implacable note was back in his voice. She knew it would be futile to question him further and silently accompanied him down to the drawing room. The buzz of voices she could hear through the door suggested that the other guests were already gathered. As they entered, Lucy's apprehensive gaze went immediately to Sir James and Lady Preston. Sir James merely smiled but his wife, more astute where matters of fashion were concerned, gave Lucy a long, unsmiling stare.

'Ah, here is our host.' Lord Wetherell greeted them

cheerfully. 'I was just describing the very superior brandy
you have in your cellars, was I not, Cottingham—Cottingham?'

'What? Oh, yes, yes.' Adam crossed the room to address Lucy. 'My wife is longing to become better acquainted with you, Miss Halbrook. Let me take you over
to her.'

Lucy's fingers closed on Ralph's sleeve, as if she did
not want to leave his side. Quite irrational, she told herself crossly, and hoped no one would notice. Save Ralph,
of course. He could not fail to feel her clutching his arm.
However, Sir James had addressed a question to him, and
he merely gave her hand a pat before moving away from
her. Adam led Lucy across to sit beside his wife, and he
pulled up a chair to join them.

Unlike their earlier meeting, Judith Cottingham now
exerted herself to be friendly. Gratified and relieved to be
away from Lady Preston's disapproving presence, Lucy
responded in the same vein. The conversation covered a
wide range of subjects but it was interspersed with questions. It was only natural, she thought, that they should
want to know about her family and how she had met
Ralph.

She answered as best she could, keeping to the history she and Ralph had agreed upon, but she could not
be sorry when he interrupted them, laying one hand on
her bare shoulder.

'I am sorry to carry you away, my dear, but Harry has
arrived and you have yet to meet his wife.'

His touch was very light but it sent a tingle of excitement running through her, heating her blood and rous-
ing an ache of longing deep within. Lucy quickly stifled
it, reminding herself it was all a charade to convince his
houseguests.

* * *

'Thank heaven for that,' she murmured as they moved away. 'I had not realised until they began asking me questions that there are so many gaps in the story we devised!'

'I thought you were looking harassed. We need to find some time alone to make sure our stories match. Slip away and join me in my study in... Let us meet on the half-hour. That will give us time to discuss the matter and be back here well before the dinner hour.'

His tone was matter-of-fact and the suggestion was most definitely a sensible one, but the sad truth was that Lucy did not feel in the least sensible when she thought of being alone with him. She might tell herself that she struggled even to be friends with Ralph, but his presence disturbed her in a way she did not understand. Once again she had to push aside her distracting thoughts as he led her across the room to make the final introduction of the evening.

Francesca Colne was as cheerful and friendly as her husband, and Lucy was soon at her ease.

'Lord Adversane says you live in London,' said Mrs Colne. 'This must be very different for you.'

'It is, but I am enjoying it very much,' replied Lucy.

'And have you settled in well, Miss Halbrook?' Harry asked her. 'You never did come to ask me all your questions about the house.'

She returned his smile. 'Lord Adversane answered most of them for me. And his sisters have been very good, too.' Her glance flickered over Ralph. 'They told me a little about you and Adversane when you were boys.'

'Then that is something you can tell me.' Francesca laughed.

'I think it is best forgotten,' Ralph growled, but the smile in his eyes gave the lie to his menacing frown.

Harry grinned.

'Dear heaven, what on earth have they been telling you, Miss Halbrook?'

'Nothing so very bad,' she admitted with a chuckle. 'The worst I heard is that Lord Adversane broke his collarbone.'

Harry laughed. 'Yes, on Druids Rock! We were competing to see who could scale the cliff face the quickest. Ralph was in the lead but then he missed his footing and fell. However, the injury saved him from the beating that *I* received.'

'Good gracious,' exclaimed Francesca. 'And did that stop you from doing such a foolhardy thing in future?'

'Of course not. In fact, old Lord Adversane, Ralph's father, was the first to encourage us to go back and try again, but this time under supervision. We climbed the rock many times after that without mishap.' He shook his head, smiling at the memory. 'Ralph and I were a couple of tearaways when we were boys and often found ourselves in the most outrageous scrapes!'

'Oh?' Lucy cast a laughing glance at Mrs Colne. 'I am sure we should like to hear all about them.'

Ralph shook his head and after warning Harry not to sully the ladies' ears with such nonsense he went off, leaving Mr Colne to entertain them. They were soon joined by Sir Timothy, and shortly after Lucy moved away. A glance at the ormulu clock on the mantelpiece showed her that there was some time before she needed to slip away. She noted that Ralph had already disappeared and she went over to sit with his sisters, who were engaged in a lively discussion with Judith Cottingham on the benefits of education for women. When the clock's delicate chimes signalled the half-hour she excused herself and slipped out of the drawing room.

Lord Adversane's study was situated at the far side of the entrance passage, just beyond the dining room. A few words with Ralph were all that was needed to make sure he did not contradict anything she had said to Adam and Judith Cottingham. There would be no need for her to stay more than a couple of minutes. She was so engrossed in her own thoughts that it was not until she reached the study door that she heard voices from within. She recognised Harold Colne's voice, which was raised enough for his words to carry out to her with disastrous clarity.

'I cannot remain quiet any longer, Ralph. I thought at first I was mistaken but tonight, seeing her in that gown— What are you playing at, man? And what in heaven's name possessed you to offer for a girl who is the living image of Helene?'

Lucy jumped away from the door. There was no mistaking Mr Colne's disapproval. If Harry, who was Ralph's oldest friend, was uneasy about his motives, then something must surely be wrong. She retired to the Great Hall, thankful that it was for the moment deserted.

What should she do? She could pretend she had not heard Harry's remarks, but that would not allay her own fears, which had resurfaced, stronger than ever. She put her hands to her cheeks. Had she been deceiving herself simply because she wanted to live in luxury for a few weeks, ignoring her principles because of the largess that would be hers once she had completed her contract? It was a lowering thought and crowding in close behind it came another. If Ralph had hired her merely to play his hostess then surely there was no need for her to look like Helene. She wrapped her arms about herself. Unless he was still in love with his wife's memory.

She heard a rapid footstep, and Mr Colne appeared.

He was looking troubled, but the frown vanished when he saw her.

She said quickly, 'May I have a word with you, sir, before you return to the drawing room?' She rushed on, knowing if she hesitated she would lose confidence. 'Has—has Lord Adversane told you why I am here—the *real* reason I am here?'

He frowned for a moment, then came across the hall to her.

'Yes,' he said quietly. 'Ralph has taken me into his confidence.'

'Then you know we are not engaged. That I have been hired to play a role.'

'I do.'

She searched his face.

'You know him so much better than I, Mr Colne. Tell me truthfully, do you think I should cry off now from the agreement? Adversane explained it to me, you see. He told me that he needed everyone to think he had chosen another wife, to stop them all from pestering him. I quite see that such a situation would be very uncomfortable, but is this really the solution?'

She twisted her hands together while she waited anxiously for his answer.

He said carefully, 'What does your conscience tell you?'

Lucy put her hands to her temples, saying distractedly, 'I am no longer sure! I had convinced myself there was no impropriety, but now I am here... Do you think it is very wrong, Mr Colne?'

His cheerful countenance was clouded, and he did not answer immediately.

'Miss Halbrook, Ralph has not been himself since

Helene's death. He is haunted by the event. If this helps him to come to terms with it, then, no, it is not wrong.'

'Thank you, I am relieved to hear you say so.'

'But—'

'Yes, Mr Colne?'

He shook his head.

'It does not matter. Are you on your way to the drawing room? Shall I escort you?'

'Thank you, but I came out to find Lord Adversane.'

'Then I will take you to him.' He escorted her towards the study but as they neared the door he stopped. 'If you are in any doubt, Miss Halbrook, if you should wish to withdraw from this pretence at any time or if you need assistance, please remember that you can come to me.'

'Why, thank you, Mr Colne, but if, as you say, this is helping Lord—Ralph, then I am happy to continue with it.'

'If you are sure you want to continue. I would not like you to get hurt.'

'I am quite sure, sir.'

He gave her a searching look, as if to assure himself that she was sincere, then with a nod and a smile he knocked upon the study door and ushered her inside.

Ralph was waiting for her, his impassive countenance giving nothing away.

'So,' he said as the door closed upon them. 'What have you been saying to my cousin that I need to know?'

She looked at him blankly for a moment. Harry Colne's last words were still echoing in her head. Did Harry expect her to lose her heart to her employer?

This is merely a business arrangement. Nothing more. Concentrate, Lucy!

'It seems so trivial now, but Mrs Cottingham asked

where *precisely* we had first met. I did not think they would be convinced if I said we had met at the house of a mutual friend.' She coloured a little. 'Our social spheres are very different.'

'So what did you tell her?'

'That we had met at Somerset House. I remembered you said you had met my father there, and I went with him sometimes, so it is perfectly reasonable to suppose our paths might have crossed.'

'An excellent answer.' He came a little closer. 'And did you tell them it was love at first sight?'

'Of course not! I, um, I hinted that I had an interest in astronomy.'

He laughed at that.

'Now that *is* dangerous ground! Your knowledge of the stars is limited to the few constellations we saw the other night.'

'I know, but I had to say *something*,' she confessed. A sudden, mischievous smile tugged at her lips. 'Thankfully Mr and Mrs Cottingham know even less, so I was quite safe.'

'Let us hope so.'

'It was not a lie,' she told him. 'I really did find the stars interesting, and Saturn was truly magnificent. I only wish we could have seen more of the planets.'

He smiled. 'Have you seen the orrery in the library? It is in the bay window at the far end, and easily missed if one is not looking for it. You should acquaint yourself with that, if you wish to see the way the planets orbit the sun.'

'Thank you. Perhaps I will.' For a moment she wondered if there was any point, since she would be leaving Adversane once the house party was over. She quickly brushed aside the depressing thought and said brightly,

'After all, the stars will be the same wherever I am, won't they?'

There was an infinitesimal pause before he replied.

'Quite.' He glanced at the clock. 'We had best be getting back to our guests. If there is nothing else?'

'No, nothing.'

'Then we shall say we met at Somerset House and after that I sought you out. Agreed?'

'Agreed, my lord.'

'Ralph.'

'Ralph.'

'Good.' He took her arm and led her out of the room. 'You had best remain vague about any other details.'

'How am I to do that if I am asked a direct question?'

'You need merely blush. You look adorable when you blush.'

He uttered the words as they crossed the Great Hall, and in such an indifferent tone that it took a few moments for Lucy to realise what he had said. By that time they were entering the drawing room, and Lucy had no idea whether she looked adorable, but she knew she was certainly blushing.

At dinner Lucy was placed between Mr Cottingham and Sir Timothy Finch. Ralph's brother-in-law enjoyed his food and Adam seemed preoccupied, so Lucy was spared too much conversation. Instead, she took the opportunity to study the other guests. It was a lively and informal occasion, although Lucy noted that Judith Cottingham, who was sitting opposite, had reverted to her quiet demeanour and said very little. Looking further along the table, Lucy observed a little stiffness between Sir James Preston and his host, but it was clear that the man was eager to bring his daughter to Ralph's attention. Lucy thought perhaps he might have been wiser not to include Charlotte so much in his conversation, since every time he did so, she responded with a giggle that only exposed her immaturity.

'So now you have had time to settle in, how do you like Adversane?'

Sir Timothy's question caught Lucy off guard.

'Lord Adversane is very, um—'

'I meant the house,' he interrupted her, laughing. 'I have no doubt you are pleased with its master, since you are going to marry him. But you live in town, I believe. You must find life here very different.'

She flushed a little at her error, but his friendly manner put her at her ease and she managed to smile back at him.

'I had many homes but all of them much closer to London, and you are correct—they were very different to Adversane,' she returned. 'My father was an artist, you see.'

'Yes, Ralph told me. A case of opposites attracting each other, what? Ralph being more interested in mechanical objects than art,' he added when he observed her blank look.

'Now, Tim, do not be too hard on my brother,' cried Margaret, overhearing. 'Ralph is interested in many things, and has a real thirst for knowledge.'

'He wants to explain all the mysteries of the world,' put in Sir James from across the table. He gave a sad little shake of his head, indicating that he did not agree with this philosophy.

'Adversane merely likes to know why things happen, rather than to accept them blindly,' said Harry. 'Surely that is a very reasonable view.'

'Ah, but my lord will learn that not everything can be explained by man,' replied Sir James.

Lucy glanced towards the head of the table. Ralph was

in conversation with Lady Preston but he looked up at Sir James's final statement.

'Did I hear my name?'

'I was saying, my boy, that logic and reason cannot be applied to all life's mysteries. Take Druids Rock, for instance.'

'No mystery there,' Ralph replied. 'The latest papers on the subject are very convincing. Hutton puts forward a logical argument for the way that rocks are formed.'

'But not how they come to be piled up. That is the work of a great deity.'

Ralph shook his head. 'I fear we must be content to disagree on that, Sir James.'

'I can only hope, my boy, that age will teach you wisdom,' said Sir James.

'Why, I hope so, too, sir.'

'And *I* hope Miss Halbrook will not be discouraged by all this talk of logic and cold reason,' declared Lady Preston in repressive accents.

Ralph's eyes rested on Lucy and a faint smile played about the corners of his mouth.

'Oh, I think Miss Halbrook understands me pretty well.'

Lucy's cheeks began to burn, and she was glad when Margaret turned the subject and everyone's attention moved away from her. She was happy to let the conversation ebb and flow around her, quietly hoping to avoid drawing attention to herself. However, when the ladies retired she found Lady Preston at her side.

'I am glad to see Adversane has put off his mourning, Miss Halbrook.'

Lucy thought the matron sounded anything but glad, but she murmured a response. Lady Preston followed her to a sofa, sat down beside her and proceeded to quiz her. The interrogation was subtle, but no less thorough. Remembering Ralph's instructions, Lucy kept her answers vague where they referred to her association with him, but she saw no need to prevaricate about her family. After all, it would take very little enquiry for anyone to discover that her father had died a poor man.

'So this is a very advantageous match for you,' concluded Lady Preston. 'You are very fortunate that Adversane is happy to take you without a settlement of any kind.'

Lucy was about to make an angry retort when she heard Caroline's cheerful voice at her shoulder.

'We think it is Ralph who is the fortunate one, ma'am, to have found a woman to make him happy. Lucy, my love, do come and try out the duet again with me....'

Caroline carried her off to the piano, saying as they went, 'Pray do not mind Lady Preston.'

'I do not. It must be very hard for her to see someone in her daughter's place.'

'It is a place she wants Charlotte to fill,' retorted Caroline. 'However, the child is far too young.'

'But she is very pretty, and she will be quite beautiful in a few years.'

Caroline's shrewd look, so like her brother's, rested upon Lucy for a moment.

'Ralph has been caught once by an empty-headed beauty. He will not let that happen again. This time I believe he has found real affection and I for one am very glad of it.'

Lucy felt the warm blush of embarrassment on her cheeks and was thankful that Caro had turned her attention to the piano. She wanted to tell them that it was all a pretence, that Ralph cared not one jot for her. However, she was not free to do so, and if she was honest she did not wish the pretence to end, for when it did she would have to leave Adversane, its owner and his family and she was beginning to realise how hard that would be.

The gentlemen joined them shortly after, Sir James leading the way. He was hardly inside the door when he addressed his wife in ringing accents.

'I say, my dear, Adversane tells me the Players will be performing here on Midsummer's Eve. Is that not good news? I am particularly fond of a good play.'

Ralph glanced around the room, watching to see how the others took the news. Adam was looking particularly solemn and went to sit with his wife. Lady Preston's lips thinned.

'Life must go on, I suppose,' she muttered.

'Indeed it must, ma'am,' agreed Harry in his cheerful way. 'The Ingleston Players lost a great deal of income from last year's cancellation.'

Charlotte looked up.

'Oh, are they are paid, then, for their trouble?'

Margaret nodded.

'Yes, they are local people who give up their time and Adversane rewards them handsomely for coming here. The tradition started in our grandfather's day. The library is turned into a theatre for the first part of the evening and all our neighbours are invited to attend the play. Ralph lays on a good supper for everyone, including the Players, and then afterwards the Players go back to Ingleston to enjoy the Midsummer's Eve celebrations and the rest of us dance in the white salon until the early hours.'

'I know.' Charlotte nodded, her blue eyes sparkling. 'It is indeed the most wonderful evening. Last time I was allowed to watch the play, although I did not understand it all.'

'Thank heavens for that,' murmured Caroline to Lucy,

sitting beside her at the piano. 'It was Vanbrugh's *The Provoked Wife*. Not at all suitable for a child of fifteen!'

'And this time you shall be allowed to dance as well, my sweet,' announced Lady Preston, 'It will be good practice for your come-out next year.'

'Unless she snabbles a husband before that, eh, Adversane?'

Ralph closed his lips firmly as Sir James dug an elbow into his ribs.

Charlotte giggled.

Singing and music filled the remainder of the evening, until the arrival of the tea tray. Finding herself momentarily alone, Lucy moved to a quiet corner of the room, from where she could observe the rest of the guests.

Mr Colne followed her.

'Am I disturbing you, Miss Halbrook?'

'By no means.'

'You were looking very pensive,' he said, pulling up a chair beside her. 'I hope you are not worrying about what we said earlier.'

'Not at all. I was thinking how sorry I shall be to leave all this.'

Harry's glance followed hers to where Ralph was standing with his brothers-in-law.

He said quietly, 'If it is any comfort to you, I think your presence here has done Ralph a great deal of good. He has been looking much happier of late.'

'That is not my doing, Mr Colne. It is because he has company.'

'Perhaps. It has been a difficult two years for him. When Helene died he blamed himself. He is not one to share his feelings. Rather, he shut himself away with his grief and his pain. It is good to see him going into society again.'

'And this…' she dropped her voice '…this charade—my pretending to be Ralph's fiancée. Are you sure you do not think it is…deceitful?'

The sombre look fled from Harry's eyes and he laughed.

'You have met his sisters and seen the way Sir James thrusts Charlotte into Ralph's path at every turn. They are all determined to see him wed again. How much worse would it be if you were not here?'

'And the fact that I look like Lady Adversane?'

He regarded her for a long moment.

'Try not to let that worry you.'

She leaned a little closer.

'But it *does*, Mr Colne! You see, Ralph insists that I wear identical gowns, that my hair is dressed the same as hers. I am very much afraid that he is grieving for his lost love—'

'Ralph never loved Helene, Miss Halbrook. That is a good part of the reason he feels so guilty about her death.' He smiled, and she found herself blushing, as if Harry Colne had discovered some secret. 'You need have no worries on that head. Now if you will excuse me, my wife is looking tired. I must take her home.'

She watched him walk away. Perhaps she should not have voiced her concerns, but she guessed that Harry Colne knew Ralph better than anyone. If he did not believe Ralph had been in love with Helene, then it was very likely to be true.

And Lucy was surprised how much that mattered to her.

The warm, sunny weather continued and Lucy realised she was seeing Adversane at its best. The atmosphere in the house was relaxed, with the visitors left to amuse themselves for most of the day. Sir James and Lady Preston preferred to remain at the house with Ariadne after breakfast each morning, while the rest of the party went out riding. Ralph rarely accompanied them, attending to business during the mornings so that he could be free to spend the afternoons and evenings with his guests.

On the second day Caroline suggested they should all go for a walk. Lady Preston declined, and insisted that Charlotte should remain indoors at least until the midday sun had lost some of its heat. It was therefore late afternoon when the party set off, by which time Ralph had finished his business and was free to join them. Lucy was not surprised when Ariadne decided to remain at home and keep Lady Preston company, and Sir James also declared that he would prefer to spend the afternoon in the library with a good book. The others, however, congregated in the Great Hall, eager to be on their way.

'Which way shall we go?' asked Caroline as they stepped out of the house.

'Oh, to Ingleston, if you please,' cried Charlotte. 'We drove through it on the way here, and there were such pretty shop windows that I should dearly like to browse there.'

'So far?' said Ralph. 'It is nearly three miles. Are you sure you wish to walk such a distance?'

Margaret brushed aside his concerns.

'Pho, what is three miles? We have plenty of time to be there and back before dinner. And you may treat us all to a glass of lemonade at Mrs Frobisher's when we reach the town.'

'We could take the route across Hobart's Bridge,' suggested Charlotte, pointing to the wicket gate. 'It must be a good deal shorter.'

'Past Druids Rock?' asked Margaret. 'Are you sure you want to go there, Charlotte?'

'Oh, yes,' she said blithely. 'I have not been there since Helene died, but it holds no terrors for me.' She giggled. 'Although I confess I should not like to go there at night. It is haunted.'

'Who told you that?' asked Adam, frowning. 'It is no such thing.'

'Oh, not by Helene,' said Charlotte quickly. 'No, it is by spirits.' She looked around, her blue eyes very wide. 'The servants told me. They say that on moonlit nights you can hear the tinkle of fairy laughter at Druids Rock.'

'That would be the packhorse bells,' said Ralph prosaically. 'The jaggers often cross the moors by the light of the moon.'

'You are a spoilsport, Brother.' Caroline laughed. 'Don't you know that ladies like nothing better than to be terrified by tales of hauntings and ghosts?'

'Not when one is talking of Druids Rock,' said Adam, repressively. 'It does have very tragic associations.'

'Perhaps we should walk somewhere else,' murmured Judith Cottingham, casting an anxious look up at Adam.

'No, no, if Miss Preston would like to go there we shall do so,' said Margaret, putting up her parasol. 'Come along, then, no dawdling!'

Ralph held out his arm to Lucy, saying with a smile, 'We have our orders, it would seem.'

'Do you mind?' she asked, taking his arm.

'Not in the least.'

'I think, upon reflection that I might remain here,' said Judith Cottingham, giving the group an apologetic smile. 'It is still very hot.'

'It will be cooler under the trees,' Margaret pointed

out, but Judith could not be persuaded and returned to the house.

'Well, that is very convenient,' declared Caroline, unabashed. 'Now we have an equal number of gentlemen and ladies!'

They all paired off, Ralph's sisters taking their husbands' arms while Ralph escorted Lucy and Adam looked after Charlotte Preston. The trees lining the old ride still provided some shade, and when they emerged on the far side, a gentle breeze was sufficiently cool to make walking very pleasant.

The walk downhill to the town was accomplished in good time and it was a merry party that entered Mrs Frobisher's store, where the grocer's wife had set aside a room with tables and chairs for weary shoppers to refresh themselves with tea or cups of hot chocolate in winter, and barley water or delicious lemonade during the hot summer months.

It did not take long to stroll up and down the High Street, the ladies looking in the shop windows and the gentlemen falling behind to talk amongst themselves, but by the time they set off again the afternoon was well advanced.

The old road twisted its way steeply upwards through the trees to emerge high above the valley, where the path levelled out and the going was much easier. Their route took them towards the afternoon sun and as they approached Druids Rock it towered over them, shadowed and menacing. The uphill walk had separated the little party. Margaret and Sir Timothy were marching well in advance, followed by Adam Cottingham, who had given his arm to Lucy, while Ralph followed a short distance behind with Charlotte Preston, and Caroline and Lord Wetherell straggled along at the rear. As Adam and Lucy made their way around the base of Druids Rock they heard Charlotte's youthful giggle behind them, followed quickly by Ralph's deep laugh.

Adam smothered an oath.

'How can he be so unconcerned?' he muttered in a strangled undervoice. 'I cannot—'

He broke off and Lucy turned to look at him, startled.

'Whatever is wrong, Mr Cottingham?'

'I beg your pardon, Miss Halbrook. Perhaps I should have kept silent, but it is unbearable. It is beyond anything that he should laugh here, where Lady Adversane died. How can he act so, knowing—?'

'Knowing what, Mr Cottingham?'

He pressed his lips together, but then, as if the words forced themselves out against his will, he hissed, 'Knowing that he is responsible for her death!'

'Oh, surely not!'

She glanced over her shoulder, but Ralph and Charlotte were too far behind to have overheard. Adam continued to speak in a low, angry voice.

'He was besotted with her, but she never loved him, never! And when his demands became too much she fled here to Druids Rock to escape him.'

'Please, Mr Cottingham, I do not think you should say anything more. Especially not to me.'

Lucy withdrew her arm and began to walk on a little faster.

'But don't you see?' Adam lengthened his stride to keep pace with her. 'You are precisely the person I should speak to. You have the look of her. I noticed it immediately. Do you not see what is happening, Miss Halbrook? He is turning you into his dead wife.'

'Nonsense,' said Lucy, flushed. 'There is some slight similarity, perhaps, but—'

'And he is making you in her image,' he persisted. 'You dress your hair the way she did. And your clothes— he chose them for you, did he not?'

They had dropped down to Hobart's Bridge and were momentarily out of sight of the rest of the party. Adam grabbed her hand, forcing her to stop.

He said urgently, 'Miss Halbrook, I believe you are in danger here. You should go. Leave Adversane, before it is too late.'

'Too late for what? I do not understand you, Mr Cottingham.'

But at that moment Ralph and Charlotte came into view.

'I cannot tell you here,' he muttered.

Lucy began to walk on.

'I do not believe there is anything to tell,' she said robustly. 'Mr Cottingham, you have allowed your imagination to run away with you.'

'Perhaps you are right, madam, but I am concerned for you. I would not like you to suffer Lady Adversane's fate.'

'That will not happen, sir. I am aware that some people think she killed herself because she was so unhappy, but such an action would not be in my nature.'

'Nor was it in hers!'

They were approaching the trees, where Margaret and her husband were waiting for the rest of the party to catch up. Lucy put her hand on his arm to stop him again.

'What are you trying to say, Mr Cottingham?' she demanded.

'I think,' muttered Adam with deadly emphasis, 'that Adversane deliberately drove her to it!'

Chapter Ten

The last few yards to where Margaret and Sir Timothy waited were barely sufficient for Lucy to recover from the horror of Mr Cottingham's words. She could not believe it. Ralph would not do such a thing. But could she be sure? Her own parents had kept from her the truth about their finances and she had never guessed. Even after her father's death Mama had said nothing, until the truth could be concealed no longer. And if Mama could hide things from her, how much easier, then, for a man she had known barely three weeks? Lucy moved away from Adam Cottingham and fixed herself with Margaret, engaging her in conversation as they walked back through the old ride and the park.

Lucy thought perhaps it was her disordered thoughts that made the remainder of the journey uncomfortably hot, but as they made their way across the gardens to the house she noticed the heavy black cloud bubbling up on the horizon.

'We shall have a storm soon, I think,' opined Margaret, following her glance. 'Good thing, too. Clear the air.'

'Well, I for one am ready for my dinner,' declared Lord Wetherell as they all made their way into the house. He took out his watch. 'And, by Jove, there is barely time to bathe and change. I hope that new-fangled range of yours can cope with supplying so much hot water in one go, Adversane?'

'Of course it can.' Sir Timothy laughed, clapping his host on the shoulder. 'Next thing we know he will have found a way to pump it up to the bedrooms, ain't that so, my boy?'

'I am working on it,' replied Ralph, smiling a little.

The party dispersed, and Lucy felt a hand on her arm.

'One moment.' Ralph detained her. 'You professed an interest in the orrery. Perhaps you would like to come into the library and see it now.'

She swallowed. She would much rather not be alone with Ralph at that moment, but short of running away she had no choice. She followed him to the library.

It was not a room she was familiar with. It was such a large, lofty chamber that until the house party it had been rarely used and she had come in here only to gaze at the thousands of books on display and to choose one of the more popular novels to read. Now she noted that there was a large terrestrial globe beside the desk, and Ralph pointed out to her the odd-shaped lamps positioned on shelves and side tables around the room.

'Argand lamps,' he told her. 'They burn oil, but in a way that makes them ten times as bright as any candle. Excellent for reading in the winter.'

When I will no longer be here.

In just over a week's time, the end of the month, she would be gone. Life at Adversane would go on as it always had done but she would not be there to share it. Lucy did not know why she found the thought so depressing.

Ralph led her to the far end of the room, where the

brass orrery stood in the bay window, gleaming in the light. The delicate brass arms stretched out from the circular base, each one carrying a miniature planet or an even smaller moon fashioned from ivory.

'It belonged to my father,' Ralph explained, coming to a halt before it. 'I have had it brought up to date to include Herschel's planet with its two moons, and the extra moons around Saturn. It has a fine clockwork mechanism.' He grinned. 'When my nephews are here they like nothing better than to wind it up and watch the planets spin around.'

He wound it up now, and Lucy watched, fascinated, as the various planets and moons circled the sun in a slow and stately dance.

'Why was Cottingham holding your hand at Hobart's Bridge?' Ralph asked. 'What was he saying to you?'

He was telling me that you are obsessed with your late wife and that you hounded her to her death.

Lucy kept her eyes on the spinning globes.

'Why, nothing. Our conversation became a little animated, that is all.'

He caught her wrist. 'Was he making love to you?'

'No! Nothing like that.'

'Then what?'

She should tell him what Adam had said and allow him to defend himself. She should watch his reaction and judge for herself if it was true, but suddenly Lucy was afraid. She did not want to learn the truth. She tore herself from his grasp, saying coldly, 'It was nothing that need concern you, my lord.'

'Lucy!'

She drew herself up and met his challenging gaze steadily.

'There is nothing in our contract to say I must report

to you every conversation I have, sir. That would be quite unacceptable to me.'

'Your reaction smacks of evasion.'

'And yours of jealousy,' she flashed.

His black brows drew together.

'I beg your pardon,' she said quietly. 'I am perfectly aware that it is nothing of the kind, but surely your logical mind must tell you that it is perfectly possible for a lady to engage in an innocent conversation with a gentleman?'

His scowl was put to flight and in its place she saw the gleam of humour in his eyes.

'So you would fight me with logic, would you?'

Sadness gripped her and she was suddenly close to tears. She said quietly, 'I would rather not fight you at all, my lord. Now, if you will excuse me, I must change my gown.'

Ralph watched her leave the room, curbing the urge to call her back, to demand she tell him what his cousin had said to her. He did not want to force her; he would much rather that she trusted him enough to confide everything. Yet how could he expect that when he would confide in no one?

He walked to the window, looking out across the gardens but seeing only Lucy's distressed face. He wished there was a way to carry out his plan without involving her. He admired her spirit, the dignified way she conducted herself. His sisters liked her, too; that was very clear. He could foresee a stormy time ahead, when Lucy left Adversane. His sisters had made it very plain that they considered Lucy the perfect match for him and would take it very ill when the engagement was terminated.

As would he.

The thought came as a shock. Ralph raked his hands

through his hair and exhaled slowly. When had Lucy Halbrook changed from being a mere pawn in his plans and become a person? One with so much more spirit than the dead wife he had hired her to impersonate.

He had married Helene because it was expected of him, because she was beautiful and desirable, but he had known from the start that his heart was untouched. She was so complaisant that he had thought she would make him a comfortable wife, but it had not taken him long to realise the truth, that it was most uncomfortable to be in a loveless marriage, especially to a woman with whom he shared no common interests. And Helene's truly sweet nature had become a constant barb of guilt. He could give her as much spending money as she desired, but he could not love her, any more than she could care for him. He had resigned himself to the fact that once she had provided him with an heir, they would live separate lives.

Yet, although he had not loved Helene, he considered it his duty to find out the truth about her death and for that he needed Lucy Halbrook. His own desires were secondary. He frowned. What of Lucy's desires? Despite her avowed dislike of him, Ralph was convinced she was not indifferent. When he had kissed her he had ignited a fire equal to his own. He had recognised it in her response, even if she would not acknowledge it.

Ralph squared his shoulders. Perhaps, when it was over and he knew the truth, he could tell Lucy, but would she want anything to do with him once she knew how he had used her? He doubted it, but it was too late to change course now. Much too late.

Lucy had no appetite for dinner, but it was impossible for her not to attend. There were no orders as to her attire, but then, she thought despondently, whatever she wore would be styled upon one of Helene's evening gowns. Ruthie had laid out a rose silk and she put it on, not even bothering to look in the mirror before she went downstairs.

In the drawing room Lucy did her best to avoid both Ralph and Adam Cottingham and was relieved to be sitting between Lord Preston and Sir Timothy when they went into the dining room. Not that either of the gentlemen she was avoiding seemed aware of her efforts. Adam sent her no anxious looks, made no attempt to continue their tête-à-tête. Lucy wondered if he had realised the imprudence of declaring his suspicions to Ralph's fiancée. Yet if that was the case, Lucy thought he should have tried to make her an apology. As for Ralph, apart from the occasional thoughtful glance in her direction he kept his distance and in such lively company the reserve between them went unnoticed.

After dinner she waited with the other ladies for the gentlemen to join them. To retire early would attract more comment than to sit quietly in the corner. The long windows were thrown wide, but even so there was no breeze to refresh the room and all the ladies seemed a little subdued as they fanned themselves and talked in desultory tones. Lucy stepped outside, watching the sunset and enjoying the slight breeze. She was still there when at last the gentlemen came in.

As the party rearranged itself, Ralph joined Lucy on the terrace.

'You are very quiet tonight. Is anything amiss?'

She shook her head, but he saw quite clearly that she was not her usual self. The sparkle was gone from her eyes and there was a slight droop to her mouth. Ralph longed to kiss away that troubled look, but he suspected he had put it there by questioning her about Adam Cottingham. Perhaps he should not have done so, but he had felt such a worm of jealousy in his soul when he had seen them together, a feeling so much stronger than anything he had ever felt for his wife.

He was about to try and coax Lucy into a smile when he became aware of the conversation going on in the room behind them. Lady Preston was talking with Judith Cottingham but her high voice carried easily to the terrace.

'It was quite understandable that Adversane should cancel the play last year.'

'Mourning, d'you see,' explained Sir James cheerfully. 'He was besotted with Helene, of course, but I'm glad to see he's over it now and back in the world again.'

Damn the man, thought Ralph. Preston had been drinking heavily at dinner, and was now talking far too loud and free.

'Aye, he's back,' Sir James continued, his words slurring a little. 'And this year's Midsummer festivities will be an ideal opportunity for Charlotte to become accustomed to society.'

Judith murmured something which drew a laugh from Sir James.

'Oh, no,' he said cheerfully. 'We won't force her into a marriage, Mrs Cottingham. Are you worried she might make a mull of it, like her sister? No fear of that. Helene was always highly strung, of course, lived on her nerves. There's no denying Adversane handled her very ill, but Charlotte won't be driven to such desperate measures as her sister. Made of much sterner stuff. In fact, if only she'd been a few years older she'd have made a much better bride for Adversane.'

Ralph turned, ready to put a stop to the conversation, but his sisters were before him. Margaret called for Sir

James to join her at the piano for a duet and Caroline swept everyone into a discussion of what the pair should sing. Glancing back at Lucy, he saw that she was staring at him, her face as white as the trim on her gown. He was almost overwhelmed with an urge to protect her. He wanted to gather her in his arms but with everyone watching them he had to content himself with taking her hand.

'I wish you had not heard that.'

'It is not the first time, but to hear Sir James utter it, and so coolly.'

'The magistrate recorded Helene's death as an accident.'

'Naturally, in deference to your standing, but that is not what everyone believes, is it?'

'No.'

He wanted to tell her what he thought had really happened that night, but what if he was proved wrong? Would those eyes now fixed so anxiously upon him fill with disgust and loathing to think he was merely trying to exonerate himself? When she pulled her hand free he made no attempt to stop her, even though it left him feeling bereft. Caroline came to the window.

'Lucy, Ralph, do come and join us. You must sing another duet.'

She took their arms, trying to move them inside, but Lucy held back.

'Not tonight, Caroline, if you please. I—I have a headache.'

'Oh, poor love.' His sister was all concern. 'It is this thundery weather. We will all feel better once there has been a storm.'

'Yes.' Lucy's eyes flickered over him once more, their

troubled look piercing his heart. 'Yes, yes, I think you are right.'

When she excused herself and left the room, Ralph wanted to follow her. He would abandon this charade, do anything to put the smile back in her eyes. Yet how could he? How could he allay her fears, offer her any happiness until he knew the truth himself? And for that he needed to go on with his plan.

The others were calling for him to join them, and he was their host, after all. He forced his thoughts away from Lucy Halbrook. He was paying her well for her part in this charade, there was no need for him to feel concerned for her welfare. But even as he joined his guests he knew that he was fooling himself. Lucy's happiness had somehow become the most important thing in his life.

Lucy passed a sleepless night, caused by the stuffiness of the room, she told herself, but she knew it had more to do with Adam's declaration as they walked back together from Ingleston. The thought that Adversane was still in love with his wife and wanted to recreate her presence made Lucy uneasy, but it was nothing to the revulsion she felt at the idea that he had deliberately caused his wife to end her own life. Lucy was convinced now that they had not been a happy couple but she could not believe Ralph had intended to be cruel. And yet...why did Helene run off to the Rock alone after the play?

She tossed and turned in her bed, Adam's accusation gnawing at her mind. After all, what did she know of Ralph? She had seen that hard, implacable look in his eyes, guessed he could be ruthless, when he chose, but at that point she sat up in bed, saying aloud to the night air, 'No. I *know* he would not do such a thing.'

Not deliberately, perhaps, but his harshness might easily overset a more gentle nature. Unfortunately that was all too easy to believe.

And as she lay down again, another thought, equally unwelcome, returned to haunt her. That he was still in love with Helene—so in love that he could not bear to let her memory go.

There was no storm that night and by the next morning the heat in the house was oppressive. Lucy rose, heavy eyed and irritable from lack of sleep. There were no orders from Ralph so she chose a fine muslin gown worn over a gossamer-thin petticoat.

Ruthie regarded her doubtfully.

'Well,' Lucy demanded, 'what is it? Why do you look at me in that way?'

'I never saw my mistress wearing such a gown.'

'Well, thank goodness for that!'

'There *was* a muslin like it in the linen press,' Ruthie continued. 'I remember seeing it when Miss Crimplesham and I packed up all my lady's things. She took them with her when she went back to be lady's maid to Miss Charlotte.'

'Well, at least there is something that won't remind him of her,' Lucy muttered to herself as she went off to breakfast.

With the threat of thunder in the air no one wanted to ride out that morning and the guests gave themselves up to less energetic pursuits. Lucy decided to try out her new paint box. She ran upstairs for an apron to protect her gown and took her things to the empty morning room, where the light was good. Byrne brought in the old easel Lord Adversane had found for her, and after suggesting diffidently that she should avoid setting it up on the master's treasured Aubusson carpet he retreated, and she was left in peace.

The view from the window was very fine, but there was a heaviness in the air that dulled the aspect so she reached for her sketchbook to find a suitable subject. Flicking through the pages, she found herself staring at the craggy likeness of Lord Adversane.

A wry smile tugged at her mouth. No watercolour could do justice to that harsh countenance; it needed the strong lines of pen and ink, or the heavy surety of oils. She moved on and soon found a small sketch she had made of a drift of cotton grass, the delicate tufts standing white against the dark boggy ground. Her hand went to her cheek, feeling again the soft downy touch of the fronds upon her skin. That was what she would paint.

Lucy worked quickly, but painting was not engrossing enough to keep her mind from wandering. Adam Cottingham's words kept coming back to her but each time she dismissed them. She was sure Ralph could not be so ruthless, even if he no longer cared for his wife.

How can you be so certain?

The question, once posed, had to be answered. She could not ignore it. Ralph's kindness to her, his wit, their shared moments—even when they disagreed violently— had given her more pleasure than anything she had ever known.

'I love him.'

She spoke the words aloud to the empty room.

Love. What did she know of that? This was nothing like the love she felt for her parents. Apart from the painful grieving when Papa died, that love had always been a comfort. There was nothing comfortable about her feelings for Ralph Cottingham, fifth Baron Adversane. She wanted to rip and tear at him, whether it was a difference of opinion or—a shiver ran through her—in the dreams that disturbed her rest. Then she would imagine him in her bed, her hands touching his naked body, her mouth covering his skin with kisses, tasting him.

She shifted restlessly. This was beyond her experience. It could not be right to feel such violent emotion for a man she had known but a few weeks. It was not sensible. It was not safe. The sooner she left Adversane and its difficult, disturbing master the better.

The door opened and she looked around quickly, expecting to see the object of her wicked thoughts coming in. Instead, it was Lady Preston. Lucy summoned up a smile.

'If you are looking for company I am afraid there is only me and my poor art here, ma'am.'

'It is you I wish to see, Miss Halbrook.'

Lucy put down her brush but before she could speak Lady Preston launched into an attack.

'You think to fill my daughter's shoes in this house, do you not, Miss Halbrook? I advise you to think again, and reflect upon what you are doing.'

'Lady Preston, I—'

'He has chosen you because of your likeness to Helene.'

'Really?' Lucy could think of nothing else to say, since she could not deny it.

Lady Preston's lip curled. 'Oh, you may have fooled Adversane, but you do not fool me. Very clever of you to style yourself upon my daughter. How did you do that? Talked to the servants, I suppose, and to her friends. And of course now you are at Adversane there is her portrait to guide you.

'Very clever, miss, but think carefully, before it is too late.' The matron came closer. 'He does not love you, my dear. It will all end in tears. You see, Charlotte promises to be as beautiful as her sister, and in a year or two, when she has matured, she will be her equal. Then what will you do? Adversane will not want *you*, a pale imitation, when he can have the real thing.'

'Lady Preston, if Lord Adversane wishes to marry me—'

'Oh, I am sure he does, at present, because you have bewitched him. He sees Helene every time he looks at you. But how long will that last, do you think? You are nothing like the glorious creature that was my daughter. And when he does see through the charade, sees the poor little dab of a creature he has married, what then?'

Lucy began to shake. Suddenly there was no pretence. Suddenly she felt she really was Ralph's fiancée. She called upon all her resolution to speak calmly.

'Perhaps we should allow Adversane to be the judge, ma'am.'

Lady Preston snorted.

'He is so in love with Helene he cannot see beyond the superficial likeness at present, but that will change. *You* cannot replace her, however much you try to imitate her. Do you think I have not realised? But you will not catch him with such wiles and stratagems. You are not Helene. You do not have her goodness, her sweetness of temper.'

'Perhaps not, but Ralph—'

'You dare to call him by his name? What have you to offer him? It was Helene he loved. He will tire of you, Miss Halbrook, and then what will you be? His wife in name, perhaps, but rejected, ignored.' Her lip curled. 'You have only to observe poor little Judith Cottingham. Do you wish to be like her, cowed and unhappy, pitied by everyone and desperate for the slightest attention from her husband? Better to go now, miss, while you at least have your dignity.'

The venom in the woman's eyes sparkled like knife-blades. Lucy had no defence. The knowledge that she had fallen headlong in love with Ralph had left her weak and confused. There had been a spark of hope, barely acknowledged, that Ralph might come to care for her. Now that was most effectively destroyed. It had never been very strong; more a faint, distant dream tucked away in her heart, but Lady Preston's words had sliced right to her core and cut it out, leaving her so raw that she felt the tears welling up.

Without a word, she ran from the room, her last glance showing that Lady Preston was wearing a satisfied smile. Lucy hoped to reach her room without seeing anyone, but as she crossed the Great Hall, Ralph was emerging from the entrance passage. He could not fail to see her distress but she did not stop when he called to her. Instead, she flew up the stairs. When she reached the Long Gallery he was merely yards behind her. If only she could reach the safety of her room!

He caught up with her even as she opened the door. Ruthie was pottering about in the room, but a curt word from Adversane sent her scurrying away. He closed the door behind the maid and turned to look at Lucy.

'Now, you will tell me what has overset you.'

His voice was as brisk as ever, but she knew him well enough to hear his concern. It brought forth from her another bout of tears. He gave her his handkerchief and waited in silence for her to speak.

'I beg your pardon. I am being very foolish. It was L-Lady Preston. She says you only want me because I look like Helene, which I know anyway, and since this is all a charade it makes no odds…'

She trailed off, her head bowed. Distant thunder rumbled in through the open window as Ralph came closer.

'You are wrong.' He removed the handkerchief from her restless fingers and dried her cheeks. 'This is no charade. Not any longer.'

He caught her chin and gently turned her face up towards him. He kissed her eyelids, his lips drying the remaining tears before his mouth moved over hers. Lucy melted into him. It felt so right to be in his arms, as if it was her natural home.

Suddenly, it did not matter if it was all a sham, if he thought he was making love to Helene. She wanted him. She would take whatever pleasure he offered her and hold the memory to comfort her through the empty years ahead.

His kiss deepened, and her body stirred in response. The thunder rolled again, but she did not know whether it was that or desire that made the very earth tremble. Her lips parted at his insistence and his tongue was plundering her mouth, drawing out an aching longing from her very core. She could feel its tug deep in her belly and between her thighs. With something like a growl he lifted her into his arms and carried her to the bed where he lay down with her, covering her face with kisses before his lips roved down to the hollow at the base of her throat. Her body was singing as his hands explored its contours. Her breasts ached to be free of the restraining gown so that he might caress them. She could feel him, hard and aroused, pressed against her, only a few thin layers of cloth between them.

She sighed and opened her eyes. She had slept in this bed for the past few weeks but now she saw it afresh. Everything looked different, brighter, the rich hangings, the elaborately carved posts—a sudden flash of lightning flooded the room and turned the folded silk above her head a deeper blue.

As blue as the eyes in the painting of Lady Adversane.

Quickly, Lucy shut out the thought. Thunder rolled again, like the distant grumble of angry gods. Ralph was kissing her breasts where they rose plump and soft above the edge of her gown. With one hand, he had pushed aside her skirts and was caressing her thigh. Her body responded, straining towards him. He would take her, she knew it. She wanted it as much as he.

But he is making love to his wife.

Lucy told herself again it did not matter—she was too hungry for his caresses to care. But even as her body yearned, ached for his touch, she knew it was not true. She did care. Very much. She struggled, her hands on his chest, trying to push him off.

'Ralph—no—'

Immediately he let her go and sat up.

'What is it? What is wrong?' His breathing was ragged, his eyes dark with passion. 'Tell me.'

Cold terror clutched at her heart. He would never forgive her for stopping him. She should not have let it go so far. With a sob, she scrambled off the bed and threw herself at the door. Even as the next rumble of thunder rolled through the house she was racing to the stairs.

She had to get out of the house, to get away. Lucy let herself out of the door and stepped out onto the drive. The sky was black and the first drops of rain were splashing down. A flicker of lightning illuminated the little wicket gate and she ran towards it, not stopping until she had reached the old ride, out of sight of the house.

She was crying in earnest now, for herself, for Ralph, for Helene. She had no thought other than to get away and she hurried on, walking and running by turns. The steady rain soaked her, mingling with the tears that would not stop. The very heavens seemed to be crying in sympathy.

Lucy barely saw Hobart's Bridge as she ran across it, great gasping sobs racking her body. She wanted Ralph more than she had ever wanted anything in the world before, but only if he wanted her. She would not be a substitute for his wife. The thought brought on more tears, this time for the man she had left behind. If his love for Helene was only a fraction of what she was feeling, how on earth did he bear it, day after day?

The violence of her grief could not last and when it began to abate she became conscious of her situation on the open moor, exposed to the elements. Her thin muslin gown was soaked through and the heavy rain was creating a thick grey mist that reverberated with the almost continuous roll of thunder. Lucy could see no more than a few yards in any direction and looked about her, wondering which way to go.

A solitary figure appeared out of the mist. Ralph.

Lightning flickered. She wanted to run, but what was the point? He was so close now there could be no escape. She waited for him to come up, flinching a little as the thunder crashed loudly overhead.

'The storm is getting closer,' he said urgently. 'We need to take shelter. The rocks are nearest.'

Lucy made no protest as he took her arm and hurried her towards Druids Rock. Rivulets of muddy water ran along the path and in some disconnected part of her mind she was aware that her muslin skirts were no longer cream but brown as high as the knee. Soon Ralph was leading her off the main path and up the narrow track to the rocks themselves. He pulled her through a small gap between two of the stones and into a small, dry cavity.

It was too low to stand and they knelt on the earth floor, staring out at the rain.

'We should be safe enough here.' Ralph shrugged himself out of his greatcoat and put it around Lucy's shoulders. 'These rocks have stood thus for thousands of years. They won't collapse upon us.' Lightning flashed outside, followed so quickly by the thunder that Lucy jumped. Immediately, Ralph's arm was around her. He said lightly, 'I said women go to pieces in an electrical storm. Is that why you ran away from me? Were you frightened?'

She bowed her head, too numbed to dissemble.

'Not by the thunder. I could not bear it, to be in your arms, knowing all the time you were thinking of your wife.'

'That is not why I kissed you.'

She managed a sad little smile.

'No. You wanted to comfort me. That was very kind, but—'

'Kind!' He gripped her shoulders and turned her towards him. 'By heaven, I was not being *kind*, Lucy. I have never been kind to you, more's the pity. I kissed you because I wanted to do so, because that is all I have wanted to do ever since I brought you to Adversane.'

His voice was harsh, and she peered through the gloom at him, trying to see his expression and understand what he was saying. He let her go, sitting back on his heels.

'It is true I hired you because of your resemblance to Helene, but I soon discovered that you are nothing like her. She never touched my heart as you do, Lucy. She was stunningly beautiful, yes, but there was nothing behind those blue eyes. At least, not for me.' He took one of her hands and stared down at it, saying quietly, 'I always believed I was not the kind to fall in love, but I was wrong. Since you have been in the house you have turned my world upside down. You question and challenge and stand up to me as an equal. You have invaded my head, Lucy Halbrook, but you have also touched me here.' He pulled her hand against his chest. 'That was why I want to kiss you, why I love you. Not because you are similar to Helene, but because you are *different.*'

Lucy could feel his heart thudding through the damp cloth of his waistcoat. She put her free hand on his shoulder, closed the distance between them and kissed him. She had intended it to be a gentle kiss, full of comfort and reassurance, but when their lips met the searing bolt that passed between them was as great as any electrical storm. She clung to him, almost swooning as his mouth worked over hers, his tongue flickering, caressing, calling up the now-familiar desire from deep in her core. There was no grace, no delicacy—just a passionate, urgent desire that drove them on. They began to tear off their wet clothing between a series of hot, breathless kisses.

Lucy's thin muslin gown was soaked through and had to be peeled away, leaving her body slick and wet. Ralph's greatcoat had slipped from her shoulders and once they had discarded their clothes he pulled Lucy down onto it. A shiver of delight ran through her when she felt his naked limbs pressed against her own and smelled the salty dampness of his skin. He wrapped her in his arms, covering her face and neck with kisses. When his hand began to caress her breast, she strained towards him. His hand slid away, and she felt his mouth on the hard nub he had aroused, sucking and teasing until she was moaning with the delightful torture of it. She dug her nails into his shoulders as he continued the delicious torment and when she pulled his head up so that she could kiss his lips again, his fingers continued their restless assault, moving down, stroking her thighs, caressing her so intimately that she arched, gasping against his mouth.

Ripples of delight were pulsing through her, growing ever stronger. Her body softened. She was opening like a flower, laying her soul bare to this man who could wreak such havoc with her senses. She was no longer in control; her body was responding to Ralph's demanding fingers as they stroked and circled and eased her to the very edge of ecstasy.

She cried out when he entered her, a tiny pain, followed by the slow building of pleasure again as he moved within her, slow steady strokes that had her crying out with delight. She had never felt such elation. Instinctively, she moved with him, matching his rhythm, the momentum carrying them higher and higher until at last they crested in a joyful union. The world shattered— Lucy heard Ralph shout, and she screamed, afraid that she was falling, only to feel herself held close, safely wrapped in his arms.

They lay together, bodies entwined, cocooned in a peace of their own making while the storm raged on outside. Ralph closed his eyes and breathed deeply, his body relaxed. He felt an immense satisfaction, but he was also somewhat stunned by the ferocity of their passion. Lucy had returned kiss for kiss, and if her lovemaking was a little inexpert it had been no less ardent and arousing. His sense of contentment deepened. She had much to learn, and he would enjoy teaching her. No doubt he, too, would learn a great deal in the process. She stirred and turned towards him, one arm slipping over his chest while her lips nibbled at his neck.

'Has the thunder been that loud all the time?' she murmured.

'Yes.'

'I did not notice.'

'Shall I take that as a compliment?'

She laughed softly, a low, delicious sound that stirred his desire.

'I hardly know,' she replied demurely. 'After all, I have no experience with which to compare what we have just done.'

Any remaining lethargy disappeared. He rolled over and pinned her beneath him.

'Then you should believe me when I tell you that was very good.'

'I should?' Even in the dim light he could see the mischief in her eyes. She moved slightly, and his body reacted immediately. He was tense and coiled like a spring again, ready for action. Her smile told him she was perfectly aware of the effect she was having, and she murmured provocatively, 'Perhaps you should show me again, my lord.'

Growling, Ralph stifled her laugh with a kiss. She responded eagerly, but this time there was no urgency to complete their union. He covered every part of her body with kisses. Her reactions delighted him, and she was eager to please him, too, exploring him with her hands and her mouth, learning quickly how to enslave him until he dragged her into his arms for another earth-shattering union that left them too exhausted to do anything other than sleep.

When Lucy awoke the rain had stopped. Sunlight gleamed at the entrance to their shelter and she could hear the faint song of a skylark somewhere over the moors. She stirred, and immediately Ralph's arm tightened around her.

'We must get back,' she murmured. 'We will be missed.'

Ralph rolled over and kissed her, then he eased himself up on one elbow.

'You are very beautiful,' he murmured.

She felt her whole body blushing under his gaze.

'So, too, are you.' She reached up and touched the hard contours of his chest, pushing her fingers through the smattering of crisp black hair. 'I have never seen a man's body before, save in paintings or sculpture. I think I would like to stay here and look at it for ever.'

'I would dearly like to indulge you, my love, but unfortunately you are right, we will be missed. I must get you back to Adversane. But don't worry.' He caught her hand and raised it to his lips. 'There will be plenty of opportunities for us to study each other in future.'

The thought made her shiver with pleasure. She sat up and reached for her clothes.

'They are so wet it will not be easy to dress,' she remarked. 'Will you help me?'

Putting the cold, wet material onto her body was neither easy nor pleasant, but at last she was dressed and while Ralph threw on his own clothes she tried vainly to tidy her hair. Then it was time to crawl out of their shelter.

The sun was blessedly hot and Lucy shook out the mud-splattered skirts, saying with dismay, 'I fear this gown is quite ruined. What will everyone think?'

'That we were caught in a thunderstorm,' said Ralph. 'They may of course guess at what occurred while we were sheltering, but if they do they will not think much about it. We are betrothed after all.' He took her hand. 'There can be no question of calling off the engagement now, Lucy.'

'Do you *want* to marry me, Ralph?'

His smile banished her doubts. He pulled her close and kissed her.

'Yes, I do. Very much.'

Another kiss set her heart singing. She clung to him for a moment, wondering how it was possible to be so happy.

With a reluctant sigh, Ralph lifted his head, trying to ignore the temptation of those soft lips and the green eyes that positively smouldered with passion. Not that she was trying to be seductive. He found her very innocence intoxicating. But it was a responsibility, too. He would take care of her.

Better than the care you took of Helene.

The thought was like a hammer blow to his conscience. Was he wrong to marry again? After Helene's death he had vowed never to do so, but his resolution had wavered and died when Lucy Halbrook swept into Adversane, turning his life upside down. But was she strong enough to stand up to him, or would he see her spirit crushed by his impatience? Dear heaven, he prayed he was not making a mistake!

Some of the pain it caused must have been displayed in his face, for he saw Lucy's look change to one of concern. Banishing his darker thoughts, he said with a smile, 'Let us get back before they send out a search party. Are you cold in those wet clothes? Would you like to wear my greatcoat?'

'Thank you, but, no. I am quite warm now and the sun will dry me a little as we walk.'

'Come along, then.'

He took her hand and with his greatcoat over his free arm they set off. When they reached the spot where he had come upon her she asked him how he had known where to find her.

'You left the wicket gate open. I saw it as soon as I looked outside. I would have found you sooner, only I thought you would be hiding somewhere in the house.' His frantic search of the dark, storm-filled house now seemed like part of another life. 'I did not think you would be so foolish as to go out of doors.'

'I wanted to get away from you and everyone. I thought you would be so angry that…that I had stopped you…'

The unease in her voice tore at his heart.

'Not so much angry as bemused,' he said, remembering that when she had pushed him away he had hoped—prayed—it had been the storm that had frightened her and not his passion. 'Then, when I realised you were heading for the moors I was afraid for you. Electrical storms can be very dangerous.'

'So you came after me.'

'Yes, although I had not planned to ravish you.' He squeezed her fingers. 'Do you regret it?'

She shook her head.

'Not at all.' She stopped. 'Unless you do—Ralph, you will tell me, won't you, if you decide you do not want to marry me?'

Looking down into her upturned face, he knew how much he wanted to marry her, but should he do so? Could he be a good husband? That little worm of doubt still gnawed at his conscience. He thrust the thought aside and pulled her close, giving in to the temptation to take just one more kiss.

'That will never happen,' he said. 'You are mine now, Lucy Halbrook, and I shall never let you go.'

Lucy's heart soared. She accompanied Ralph back through the old ride, her heart singing. However, when they reached the house grounds she found her apprehension growing.

'Ralph, is there a way we can slip into the house unnoticed? That door in the wall perhaps...'

'That leads to the kitchen gardens and unfortunately there will be servants everywhere at this time of the day. To creep in like a couple of thieves would give rise to the very worst sort of conjecture. No, my love, we must brave it out.'

My love.

The words gave her courage as he led her towards the main entrance.

Chapter Eleven

Byrne was waiting for them, his countenance even more wooden than usual.

'I have taken the liberty of sending water up to the rooms, my lord.'

Ralph resisted the temptation to put his hand up to his neck cloth as he saw the butler's eyes slide up to it, then on to Lucy's dishevelled appearance. He was relieved when Ariadne came bustling over.

'Oh, my heavens, I saw you coming across the lawn. Lucy, my dear, your gown—!'

'We were caught out in the storm,' Ralph explained. 'We took shelter at Druids Rock, but not before Miss Halbrook suffered a drenching. Perhaps, Cousin, you would be good enough to take her to her room?'

'Yes, yes, of course. Come along, my love.'

He said, as he accompanied them across the hall, 'Did anyone else observe our return?'

'No, I do not think so. Everyone is in the library or the drawing room. I had gone upstairs to fetch my book and saw you from the staircase landing.'

Lucy put a hand up to her wet hair.

'I must look quite frightful.'

Her voice shook a little and Ralph wanted to gather her in his arms again, but Ariadne was bustling around her like a mother hen.

'You will feel much better once we have found you some dry clothes.' She took Lucy's arm as they began to mount the stairs, sparing no more than an impatient look for Ralph.

'There is no need for you to tarry here, Adversane, I will look after Lucy. You should run on to your own room. The sooner you have changed the sooner you can look after your guests.'

Lucy watched him take the stairs two at a time. His short, dark hair was already dry. A change of clothes and no one would know he had been caught in the rain. For herself, she knew she would be going down to dinner with her curls still damp.

Mrs Dean accompanied her into the dressing room, where Ruthie was overseeing the filling of a hip-bath.

'We should put a little elderflower oil in the water. It is very good for aches and chills. I have some in my room.'

'Oh, would you fetch it, please, Ariadne? I am sure it will help.' Lucy gave the widow a tiny smile. 'Ruthie will look after me now.'

Having sent the widow bustling away, Lucy went back to her bedroom to undress. She assured Ruthie she could manage quite well on her own and ordered the maid to make sure the servants did not spill the bathwater.

'There, Miss, you looks quite respectable again.'

There was no guile in the maid's open countenance; she thought merely that her mistress had been caught in the heavy rainstorm which had quite ruined her gown. The thin muslin was muddy and too badly damaged to repair. It had been thrown away, bundled up with the undergarments that bore the tell-tale signs of Lucy's lost virginity. She was now ready to go down to dinner, dressed in green silk and the only evidence of her soaking was her damp hair.

She was a little apprehensive about entering the drawing room, and Caroline's cheerful greeting informed her that her escapade had not gone unnoticed.

'So, Lucy, my brother had to rescue you from the storm.'

Ariadne shook her head and murmured, 'So foolhardy to go out at all in such weather.'

'Miss Halbrook is not used to the sudden violence of our northern weather.' Ralph was holding out his hand to her and smiling. 'I hope her experience today will not give her a dislike of Adversane.'

Lucy read the message in his eyes and tried desperately not to blush. She risked sending him a message of her own.

'Quite the contrary, my lord.'

'Ralph,' he reminded her. He pulled her hand onto his arm and led her across to Ariadne. 'But you see, Cousin, she is looking even more radiant, so there's no harm done.'

'I sincerely hope not.'

The words were uttered so quietly that only Lucy heard them as she sat down beside Mrs Dean.

'But why did you go out at all?' asked Charlotte. 'Mama said you were painting in the morning room, only you were not there when I went to find you to tell you that we were going to play charades.'

'I wanted a little air,' Lucy replied. 'I did not realise I had wandered so far…'

Margaret chuckled. 'Giving Ralph the opportunity to play Sir Galahad.'

'And you took shelter at Druids Rock,' stated Adam.

'Yes.' Lucy knew he was watching her closely and hoped she sounded nonchalant.

'Remarkable place, Druids Rock,' added Sir James. 'I am glad the storm has passed, for I want to go there to see the dawn tomorrow.' He looked around, beaming. 'Summer solstice, you know. Perhaps some of you would like to join me?'

'With Midsummer's Eve looming?' Judith Cottingham shook her head. 'I for one will be resting and building up my strength for that.'

There was a general murmur of agreement and Ralph said, 'You are welcome to go, of course, Preston, but I doubt you will find anyone to accompany you.'

'Of course I would not expect *you* to go there, Adversane, but I am not unhopeful… Charlotte, my dear, what about you?'

His daughter wrinkled her pretty nose. 'Not I, Papa! I am not like Helene, slipping off to Druids Rock whenever she could get away. She must truly have thought it had magic powers, since she was always going there.'

Lucy felt the change immediately. There was a tension in the air and everyone was looking uncomfortable. Ralph was frowning and Lady Preston hissed at her daughter, who merely shrugged her shoulders.

'Why must I not mention her? After two years we should be able to talk of my sister without so much constraint. I thought that was why Lord Adversane had invited us here.'

'You are quite right, Miss Preston,' replied Ralph. 'The past is done, but I am afraid it still haunts some of us.'

Byrne came in to announce that dinner was ready and

Lucy was aware of a definite feeling of relief as they all made their way to the dining room. With only three days to go until Midsummer's Eve, the play was the natural topic of conversation once everyone was seated.

'What are they performing this year?' asked Caroline.

Ralph helped himself from a dish of chicken before him and did not look up as he answered.

'The Provoked Wife.'

'But that's—'

Sir Timothy's exclamation was cut short, Lucy suspected by a kick under the table from Caroline, who was sitting beside him.

'Yes,' said Ralph carefully. 'It is the same play they performed two years ago.'

'So everything is to be as it was before,' murmured Judith Cottingham.

'With one exception,' put in Lady Preston. She fixed her pale eyes upon Lucy. 'You have no Lady Adversane.'

'True, but I do have a fiancée,' Ralph replied coolly. 'I shall use the occasion to announce our formal betrothal.'

Ariadne's fork clattered onto her plate.

'That is not what was planned, Cousin.'

'Plans change.' Ralph was looking at Lucy, a little smile playing about the corners of his mouth. 'Well, my love? Would you object to it?'

Before she could reply, Adam brought his hand crashing down upon the table.

'Dash it all, Adversane, this is not the time or the place to ask such a question. You put Miss Halbrook in a most awkward position. If she has any objections do you think she would voice them here, in front of everyone?'

Lucy shook her head. 'Truly, I—'

Ralph put up his hand to silence her, his eyes solemn.

'Adam is quite right, my dear. You should consider well before giving me your answer.'

Lucy did not want to consider. She knew what she wanted, but Ralph's announcement had caused so much consternation that she dare not say so. Instead, she kept her peace and Lord Wetherell adroitly changed the subject.

No more was said of the engagement during dinner, but afterwards it seemed everyone had an opinion to share with Lucy. As the ladies made their way across to the drawing room, Lady Preston came alongside her.

'I advise you to think very carefully before you commit yourself to Lord Adversane's proposal, Miss Halbrook. Once the betrothal is made public there can be no going back.'

'I am aware of that, ma'am.'

'Are you?' Lady Preston put her hand on her arm and gave her a pitying smile. 'Are you truly ready to tie yourself to a man who can never love you?'

Lucy put up her chin. 'You are mistaken.'

Had Ralph not proved this very day how much he loved her? As if she were reading her thoughts, Lady Preston curled her lip.

'You are very young, my dear, and do not yet know the difference between a man's lust and true, lasting affection.'

Lucy responded with nothing more than a shake of her head as they entered the drawing room, but no sooner had she moved away from Lady Preston than Margaret and Caroline came up to her.

'Has her ladyship been trying to dissuade you, Lucy? Pay her no heed. She wants Adversane for her daughter.'

'I know that, Caro, but—'

Margaret patted her arm. 'If Ralph wants you, he will have you.'

'Meg's right,' added Caroline. 'Do you not yet know that my brother is not to be gainsaid?'

Their words did not give the reassurance Lucy wanted. She declined their invitation to join them at the piano, preferring to sit a little way apart and collect her thoughts. She was not allowed to do so for long.

'You are looking a little fatigued, Miss Halbrook.' Judith Cottingham sat down beside her. 'I am not at all surprised. I find Caroline and Margaret's company quite as exhausting as their brother's. They must always be on the go, always doing something. And so strong-willed, too.' She gave a little laugh. 'My husband says they have none of them any concern for anyone's feelings but their own.'

'I have not found that to be so,' said Lucy.

'Perhaps that is because you are naturally complaisant.'

'I do not think—'

Judith caught her arm, saying in an urgent undervoice, 'Have a care what you are about, Miss Halbrook. This is not a happy house. It is full of shadows and secrets.'

'Mayhap I can make it happier.'

'No. You look too much like Helene.'

'A little, perhaps, but—'

The grip on her arm became almost painful.

'You should not stay here,' Judith hissed. 'You should leave before he destroys you, too.'

Lucy drew back, startled. Mrs Cottingham put up her hand and shook her head, a frightened look on her face. 'Forgive me. Please, I beg you, forget that I said anything.'

She hurried away, leaving Lucy to stare after her. She had thought Judith Cottingham a meek, colourless little woman, so her sudden outburst had been all the more alarming. What did she mean? Was she warning her against Ralph? She looked around. If only he would come in. She needed the reassurance of his presence, but a glance at the clock told her not to expect the gentlemen for another half-hour at least.

Restlessly, she went over to the windows, throwing them open so that she could stroll out onto the terrace, but even there she was not alone for long.

'Such a lovely evening now, after the earlier rain.' Ariadne came to stand beside Lucy, looking out over the gardens. 'Ralph's decision to announce your engagement—does it have anything to do with your being caught out in the storm together today? My dear, I do not mean to pry, but I am anxious for you. This is a very long way from his original plan.'

Lucy hesitated, collecting her thoughts.

'I am aware how it must look to you, ma'am, but since I have been here, since I have become acquainted with Lord Adversane—'

'You have fallen in love with him?'

Lucy gave her a grateful smile. 'I have. I cannot tell you how much I—'

'Then pray do not,' exclaimed Ariadne, consternation shadowing her kind face. 'Oh, my dear Lucy, I would like nothing better, but...' She took her hands. 'Are you sure Ralph returns your affection? But of course you are. How could I doubt it?'

'You are not happy about it.'

'I cannot deny I am concerned, Lucy. You have known my cousin for such a short time, and you are so very young—'

'I am four-and-twenty, Ariadne.'

'Very well, you are not a child, but all the same, this

is so very sudden. Would it not be better to wait a little longer, just to be sure?'

Lucy pulled her hands free and gave a little cry of frustration.

'Oh, why is everyone so concerned that I do not know my own heart?'

She turned away, blinking back the hot tears that threatened to fall. After a moment Ariadne squeezed her arm.

'Oh, my dear, it is not *your* heart that I doubt.'

Lucy heard the older woman's sigh and then she was alone. The joy and happiness she had felt earlier had quite disappeared. Was everyone against her marrying Ralph? No, Caroline and Margaret were pleased for her, weren't they? What was it Margaret had said?

If Ralph wants you, he will have you.

There was nothing lover-like about that—it was more a statement of possession. As the threat of tears subsided, Lucy gazed out across the gardens, watching the shadows lengthen. This was Adversane land, as far as one could see. Ralph was offering to make her mistress of all this and more, but she knew it was not enough. She wanted none of it if she could not have his love, as well.

'So here you are.'

That deep, dear voice had her spinning round, reaching out for him. Without hesitating, Ralph took her in his arms. He kissed her, melting her doubts like snow in the sunlight.

'I would like to carry you upstairs right now.' He murmured the words against her skin as his lips nibbled her ear, making her shiver with delight. 'Yet I suppose we must be circumspect, at least while we have visitors at Adversane. It will not be easy for me to keep away from you.'

She put her hands against his chest and looked up at him.

'Do you truly wish to marry me, Ralph?'

His brows went up.

'What is this? What have my family been saying to you?

She dropped her eyes to his neck cloth, but the precision of those intricate folds only reminded her of how she had struggled to tear it off earlier. The thought brought the hot blood surging through her once more. He pulled her close again, murmuring between kisses.

'They all think we have been betrothed for the past year. Surely they cannot think it is too soon?'

'No, but Ariadne knows the truth and she is most concerned.'

'She will come round when she sees how I love you.'

'Do you, Ralph? Do you truly love me?'

He met her glance with a glinting smile. 'Can you doubt it?'

She shook her head. When he was so close, holding her like this, she did not doubt it at all.

'Then unless you have any objections we will announce our betrothal after the play, and then in a week or so I shall take you to London to inform your family. Would you wish to be married there, or shall we give my tenants the privilege of seeing you become my bride at the parish church in Adversane? It is your choice, although Hopkins will be most disappointed if he is not to perform the ceremony—'

'Stop, stop.' Laughing, she put a hand up to his lips. 'This is all too much, my—Ralph. We can decide upon such details later.'

He kissed her fingers. 'You are right. One thing at a time.' He raised his head, listening. 'And if I am not mistaken, Byrne has brought in the tea tray. I suppose we must go and join the others.'

After another swift kiss he took her inside. She knew her eyes were shining with pleasure and her happiness was not in the least dimmed by the arctic glare Lady Preston cast in her direction, nor by Judith Cottingham's frowning look.

She helped Mrs Dean to serve the tea, then took her own cup to a quiet corner, content to be alone with her own thoughts. However, she was soon joined by Adam Cottingham. She managed to greet him with a smile.

'You are to be congratulated,' he remarked, sitting down beside her. 'I do not know when I last saw Adversane so happy.'

Lucy looked across the room to where Ralph was talking with his brothers-in-law.

'Do you think that is because of me, Mr Cottingham?'

'Undoubtedly.'

'Then I, too, am content.'

Adam put his cup down, frowning. 'You should not be.' He directed a solemn look at her. 'I would beg you to have a care, Miss Halbrook.'

'You have said as much before, sir, but I believe you are mistaken.'

'You do not understand. I cannot speak here. Meet me at nine o'clock tomorrow morning. In the shrubbery, where we will not be overheard.'

She sat up very straight.

'I do not think that is wise, sir. I beg you will say what you have to here, now.'

He gave a quick shake of his head.

'I cannot, Adversane is watching us. But believe me when I say that you need to know this.' He rose. 'Tomorrow morning, Miss Halbrook.'

She watched him walk away and half expected Ralph to ask her what they had been talking of, but the party was breaking up. Adam collected his wife and retired, followed shortly by Caroline and Lord Wetherell. Lady Preston declared loudly that Charlotte needed to rest.

'The next few days are important if you are to look your best for Midsummer's Eve.' She turned to her husband. 'And you, sir, you will need some sleep if you are to walk to Druids Rock to see the sunrise.'

Sir James chuckled. 'Well, I did think I might sit in the library and read by the light of one of Adversane's new-fangled lamps. After all, it is hardly worth going to bed—the nights are so short.'

'By all means, if that is what you wish,' said Ralph mildly.

Lady Preston was adamant, however, and carried both her daughter and her husband away.

Sir Timothy grinned.

'We know who rules the roost in that household! If you do not object, Adversane, I shall step out onto the terrace to smoke a cigar before I retire.' He held out his hand to his wife. 'Are you coming, Meg?'

She went willingly, leaving only Lucy, Ralph and Ariadne in the drawing room. Mrs Dean rose, smothering a yawn.

'I shall go to bed, too,' she said. 'Shall you come with me, Lucy?'

Lucy began to follow her to the door, until Ralph detained her.

'You go on up, Cousin. I will escort Lucy upstairs in a moment.' Ralph added, when she hesitated. 'It is customary to allow engaged couples a little time alone.'

Ariadne's eyes narrowed.

'And that is a crow I meant to pick with you, Adversane. About your betrothal. When did—?'

'Yes, yes, but not tonight, it is far too late to explain

it all.' Ralph shepherded his cousin to the door. 'Good-night, Ariadne.'

When at last she had retired, he closed the door and stood for a moment with his back to it, regarding Lucy.

'I thought I should never get you to myself.'

He took her hand and pulled her down beside him on one of the sofas. Lucy made a half-hearted protest, reminding him that Sir Timothy and Lady Finch were still on the terrace.

'What of it?' he muttered. 'They will not come in for a while yet.'

He began nibbling her ear, causing such pleasurable sensations to course through her body that she forgot everything but the sheer pleasure of being in his arms. Her bones were liquefying, even before he moved his attention to her mouth. She returned his kiss, running her hands through his hair and turning her body into his, pressing against him as the familiar longing raged through her blood.

'Enough,' he muttered at last. 'Enough, or I shall have to take you all over again.'

Reluctantly, she let him pull her to her feet.

'I fear I must be sadly wanton,' she said, sighing, 'for there is nothing I would like more.'

'Not until I have made an honest woman of you.' He drew her into his arms, and they shared another long, lingering kiss. 'But, by heaven, I am tempted to purchase a special licence to do it!'

A gurgle of laughter escaped her as she relished her power over him. They went out of the drawing room and up the grand staircase hand in hand.

'I have business in Halifax tomorrow morning with Colne. Come with us,' he urged her. 'It should not take long, and the scenery is magnificent. You might bring your sketchpad.'

'I should love to come with you, but Mrs Sutton is bringing the scarlet gown.' She stopped. 'I could send her word not to come.'

Even in the dim light she saw the shadow cross his face.

'No, you need the gown for Midsummer's Eve, so you must see Mrs Sutton tomorrow. I shall take you to Halifax another time.'

They were on the stairs, and she stepped up onto the next tread so that her eyes were level with his.

'But why, Ralph? I have more than enough dresses—'

'But that is the one to wear for the play. There is something I must know.'

'If you are still in love with Helene, perhaps?'

The hard, distant look left him then. He cupped her face in his hands.

'No, I promise you it is not that.' Gently, he kissed her lips. 'I must ask you to trust me, just a little longer. Will you do that?'

'But I do not understand, Ralph. Why—?'

'I will explain everything on Midsummer's Day, I promise you.' He gazed deep into her eyes. 'Can you do that, Lucy? Can you trust me for just a little longer?'

'Of course, but—'

He put his fingers against her lips.

'No buts, my love. Trust me.'

He loves me, I am sure of it.

Lucy repeated the words to herself as Ruthie undressed her, but when she had blown out the candle and lay alone in the darkness, she questioned why, if she was to trust Ralph, he would not trust her with his reasons.

Unbidden, a memory came back to her. She was standing beside Mama on the pavement while the landlord piled their belongings around them.

'I don't understand, Mama. Why didn't you tell me?'

It was only then, while they waited for Uncle Edgeworth to send his carriage to collect them, that Mama had told her the truth. Only then that she had trusted her daughter enough to share the pain that she had endured during those final years, shielding Lucy, telling her Papa was away painting while in fact he was gambling and drinking himself into a pauper's grave.

Lucy turned her face to the pillow. Was it always to be thus, that those she loved most would not trust her?

The problem still nagged at her when she awoke the next day. She had arranged to go out with Caroline and Margaret after breakfast, and Ruthie had laid out her riding habit in readiness. As Lucy made her way downstairs she saw that it wanted but a few minutes to nine, the time Adam had suggested she meet him in the shrubbery. She had fully intended to stay away, certain that she did not want to hear what he had to say, but now instead of going to breakfast she made her way out to the gardens. Adam was Ralph's cousin; he had known him all his life. Perhaps talking to him might help her to understand why Ralph would not confide in her.

She found Adam waiting for her at the entrance to the shrubbery. As she approached, he held his arm out to her.

'Good morning, Miss Halbrook. It is such a lovely day no one will wonder at us strolling here, if we should be seen.'

After the briefest hesitation she stepped up beside him, placing her fingers on his sleeve.

'Sir James will have witnessed a beautiful sunrise this morning.'

It was all she could think of to say. Now she was here she could not bring herself to ask him about Ralph. That would be too disloyal.

'I am surprised he can go there, knowing it is where his daughter...where his daughter ended her life.'

Lucy said gently, 'But I understand it was also one of her favourite places.'

'Oh, yes.'

Adam said no more, and she looked at him. He was frowning, lost in his own thoughts, and she felt a flicker of impatience.

'Mr Cottingham, I—'

'You will be wondering what it is I wanted to say to you.' He interrupted her. 'I warned you to be on your guard, Miss Halbrook. My cousin is a passionate man.'

Lucy flushed.

'That is not a crime.'

'No, when it is under regulation. But...Adversane's temper is ungovernable.'

'I have seen no sign of it.'

'But how long have you known him? I mean *really* known him, not merely meeting him in company.'

She put up her chin.

'I think I know him quite well. He is a strong character, of course, but—'

'Strong! Oh, yes,' he said bitterly. 'Adversane must have his way in all things!' He fell silent, as if fighting with himself. At last he spoke again, his voice unsteady with suppressed anger. 'It was always thus. As heir to Adversane he was denied nothing—imagine what that did for a temper that was naturally autocratic. He grew up demanding that everyone bend to his will.'

'I do not believe that.'

'Oh, he hides it well, dressing up his demands as requests, but he will allow nothing to stand in his way.'

If Ralph wants you, he will have you.

Lucy tried to shut out Margaret's words.

'But he is well respected. I hear nothing but praise for him when I go out—'

'Hah! Money and power will buy you many friends, Miss Halbrook.'

'No, it is genuine, I am sure—'

But he was not listening to her.

'Ralph and Helene should never have married,' he said, scowling. 'She was an angel. Everyone says so. Everyone loved her. She was too good, too kind for that monster—'

Lucy pulled her arm away.

'Enough,' she said angrily. 'I will not have you talk of Adversane like that!'

She began to hurry away from him, but he followed her.

'He took Helene for his wife, frightened her with his passion and his harsh words, so much so that in the end she was desperate to get away from him. *That* is why she ran to Druids Rock on the night of the ball.'

'You cannot blame Ralph for her accident.'

'It was no accident.' Lucy stopped and he continued in a low voice, 'She went to Druids Rock to end everything, and it was because of my cousin.'

She shook her head and said again, 'You cannot blame Ralph.'

'Who else should I blame? He was her husband. He should have cherished her, loved her.'

'I am sure he did, in his way.' She looked up suddenly. 'But how do you know so much of this?'

'I?' he said, startled. 'Why, I am Adversane's cousin. I spent a great deal of time here. I observed him and his wife. Perhaps I saw too much.'

'I am not sure you should be telling me this, Mr Cottingham.'

'But I am concerned for you.'

'Thank you, but I can look after myself.' They had reached the entrance to the shrubbery, but as she went to leave he caught her arm.

'I am sure you can, ma'am, but you know he is trying to change you.' He came closer. 'She was beautiful, but when she did not live up to his ideal he drove her to her death. Now he is trying to mould you into her image!'

'No!' Lucy shook him off. 'Good day to you, Mr Cottingham.'

It was preposterous. Outrageous. She would not believe it. She had been a fool to listen to him. Lucy hurried into the house, glad that Adam did not follow her. Margaret and Caroline were already at breakfast with their husbands and they all looked up as she entered.

Margaret paused, her coffee cup halfway to her mouth.

'My dear, you are looking very pale. Are you unwell?'

Lucy stopped just inside the door.

'I hardly know.' She felt a little dazed.

'Missing Ralph, no doubt.'

Margaret frowned at her sister. 'Be quiet, Caro. Lucy, you do not look at all well. Let me take you to your room.'

Lucy waved her back into her seat.

'No, thank you, I can manage. But I will go and lie down.'

'Good idea,' agreed Sir Timothy. 'I think it is too hot for riding. In fact, I am trying to persuade the ladies not to go.'

'Pho, as if we should listen to you, Timothy! Meg and I will not melt because of a little sunshine...'

Lucy left them to their banter. She would stay quietly in her room for a while until she could organise her chaotic thoughts. Not that she believed a word that Adam Cottingham had said, but meeting with him had not helped her at all. It was her own fault, of course. She had encouraged him to be open with her and now she could hardly blame him for voicing his opinions. She entered her bedchamber and was surprised to see the dressing room door was open. Someone was moving around inside. Ruthie should have gone downstairs to her own breakfast by now. Lucy crossed the room, intent upon sending the maid away.

'Oh.' She stopped, frowning, when she found herself confronting not her maid, but a complete stranger.

Before her stood a thin, grey-haired woman, soberly dressed as befitted an upper servant. Lucy's brow cleared.

'Miss Crimplesham, isn't it?'

'Yes, ma'am.' The woman dipped a reluctant curtsey but made no attempt to leave. Her face was blotched, as if she had been crying.

Lucy said gently, 'I have no doubt you are very familiar with these rooms, but you are Miss Preston's dresser now, and she is in the guest wing.'

'It's all the same.'

Lucy frowned. 'I beg your pardon?'

'Nothing's changed.' Miss Crimplesham turned back to the gowns hanging on the pegs along one wall. She began to pull out the skirts, one after the other. 'All these dresses, all identical to those worn by my lady. The quality is not the same, of course—my lady always had her gowns made by the best modistes in Harrogate and London. And they are bigger, too. Slender as a reed was Miss

Helene. You've the look of her, but you're not as beautiful as my mistress. Lord Adversane always said she was the most beautiful woman he had ever known. She could have been so happy, if it hadn't been for that man.'

Lucy drew herself up.

'That is quite enough, Crimplesham. I think you should go now.'

She injected as much quiet firmness into her voice as she could, and was relieved when the dresser swept past her and out of the room. Alone at last, Lucy sank down upon her dressing stool. She was trembling and she wrapped her arms about herself. What did it all mean? Was there some sort of plot to turn her against Ralph?

She shook her head, putting her hands to her temples. No, she did not believe Miss Crimplesham was party to any conspiracy. The poor woman was merely disturbed by grief, but coming so soon after her encounter with Adam Cottingham, Lucy found herself wondering if she was wise to trust Ralph.

Perhaps he, too, was so grief-stricken that he wanted to recreate his lost love. That would explain why he had chosen her, why he insisted she wear gowns identical to those worn by his wife. Lucy did not want to believe it, but what other reason could there be?

'There must be another reason,' she told herself. 'There has to be.'

But no matter how much she thought about it, no other explanation presented itself.

Chapter Twelve

'Ooh, Miss, you look a picture!'

It did not need Ruthie's hushed exclamation to tell Lucy that she looked very well. She was standing before her mirror in the scarlet gown. The colour accentuated the creamy tones of her skin and set off her hair, which had been lightened to honey-blond by the recent sunshine.

'Indeed, madam, I do not think I have ever made a finer gown.' Mrs Sutton stood to one side, smiling with satisfaction as she regarded her handiwork. 'And it fits perfectly. No alterations are required, save to put up the hem.'

Lucy stared at herself in the long glass. If only she had not gone out to meet Adam that morning—and if she had not come back to find Miss Crimplesham in her room—she might have been able to overcome her doubts, but now the thought of wearing the gown filled her with unease.

She said suddenly, 'Would you mind waiting a moment? I would like to slip outside.'

Holding up her skirts, she went out to the Long Gallery and stood before the portrait of Helene. She was being foolish, she knew, but she was hoping there was some mistake, that the gown was not a perfect replica, but when she studied the painting it was clear the gown was exact to the last detail. Only the wearer was different, she thought sadly. A pale imitation of perfection.

'Helene!'

The tortured whisper made her swing around. Adam Cottingham was staring at her. After a moment he gave a start.

'Miss Halbrook, is that you? For a moment I—' He came closer, frowning. 'That gown, why—no, don't tell me,' he added bitterly. 'Adversane ordered it.'

'Yes.'

'He cannot make you wear it.' His face contorted with disgust. 'It is too monstrous! Tell me you will put it away.'

'I cannot do that, sir,' she said gently. 'I have agreed to wear it on Midsummer's Eve—'

'No, you cannot, you must not!' He grabbed her hand, saying urgently, 'Promise me you will wear something else. It is too dangerous!'

'Dangerous?'

She frowned, but he was already shaking his head and saying in an agitated voice, 'Forgive me, it is no business of mine.' He raised her hand to his lips. 'Seeing you there, suddenly I thought...' He cupped her face with his free hand and gazed at her, the sadness of the world in his eyes.

'Mr Cottingham,' she began, unnerved. 'Adam—'

'Forgive me,' he said again, before shaking his head and rushing away.

'Very touching.'

Ralph's voice, cold as ice, made her jump. He was standing at the far end of the gallery, and she guessed he had just come in. He was dressed for riding and still carried his crop in one gloved hand.

'Would you mind telling what you were doing here with Cottingham?' His tone was cutting, and the end of the riding crop tapped an angry tattoo against the side of one dusty top boot.

'Not at all,' she retorted. 'If you would ask me in a civilised manner!'

Ralph's jealous anger receded as quickly as it had come. By heaven, she looked magnificent, standing there in that red gown, her green eyes sparkling like fiery emeralds.

'I beg your pardon. I have this moment returned from Halifax. I was…surprised to see you here.' His eyes slid over her gown. He thought she had never looked better.

'Mrs Sutton is waiting in my chamber to finish the hem,' she explained. 'I just wanted to compare it to…' She tailed off, waving one hand vaguely in the direction of the portrait.

'And my cousin found you thus.'

'Yes. It was all very innocent.'

The image of Adam cupping her face flashed into his mind. He said curtly, 'For you, perhaps.'

'And what do you mean by that?'

'Ariadne tells me you were walking in the gardens with him this morning.'

'Yes, I took a walk before breakf—'

'I would rather you did not allow him to be alone with you.'

'Oh? Why?'

Ralph hesitated. Why indeed? Some instinct, a gut feeling, said Adam was a threat, but cold logic told him that could not be. After all, he had already ascertained that Adam was with his wife the night Helene died.

'Well, my lord?'

He was goaded into a retort.

'I should have thought that was obvious.'

Her brows went up.

'Can it be that you are jealous, my lord?'

Was that it? Was that the threat he feared, that Lucy might prefer his cousin? His mouth twisted into a wry smile.

'I think I am.'

He watched the stormy light in her eyes die away and a becoming blush mantled her cheeks. It was as much as he could do not to sweep her up and carry her off to his room. Instead, he contented himself with picking up her hand and placing a light kiss on her fingers. They trembled slightly beneath his touch.

'Ralph?' She was looking up at him, a faint question in her eyes. 'May I not wear another gown on Midsummer's Eve?'

'But you look truly lovely in that one, my dear.'

And perfect for his plans.

'But why is it so important to you that I wear this one?'

Tell her the truth, man!

He gripped his riding crop even tighter. The Adversane name, the family honour was at stake. Pride would not allow him to voice his suspicions without more proof.

'Please, Ralph, I would be happier in something else.'

How he wanted to please her, but he was so close now. She had to wear that gown if he was ever to know the truth. When it was all over he would tell her, even if it meant admitting he was wrong. But not yet. Not now.

'I need you to wear it,' he said at last. 'I need to prove something.'

'But you will not tell me what it is.'

'No.'

'Ralph—'

'By God, madam, must you question me at every turn? I cannot tell you. Not yet.' He dropped her hand. 'It was so much easier when you were merely an employee.'

Pain flickered in her eyes as his words lashed her, and he immediately regretted his rash utterance. She pulled herself up, almost trembling with a proud, stubborn anger that matched his own.

'Then that is what I shall be. I will wear this gown, since you insist upon it, but if you will not tell me why, if you cannot trust me, then I cannot marry you. I will fulfil the contract and then I will leave, as we originally agreed.'

Ralph stared at her, recognising a kindred spirit. She took his breath away. He was standing on the edge of a precipice and she was cutting the ground from beneath his feet. He needed to respond but could not find the words. Lucy met his hard gaze steadily. He only had to speak, to tell her. The moments crept by in a long, painful silence while he tried to formulate a sentence, a phrase, but nothing would come. At last, keeping her head high, she turned and walked away.

Lucy went back to her chamber. She fought back the tears, determined not to cry in front of Ruthie or Mrs Sutton and her assistant. She stood silently while they fussed around her, all of them too intent upon the beautiful robe to notice her wooden countenance or the brevity of her responses.

She had just stepped out of the gown when Adversane walked in unannounced. Ruthie gave a small shriek and quickly threw Lucy's wrap around her bare shoulders.

'Leave us,' he barked. 'I wish to talk to Miss Halbrook alone.'

Lucy gave him a haughty look.

'Mrs Sutton has yet to sew up the hem.'

'Then she may do so elsewhere. Go. Now!'

The dressmaker and her assistant snatched up their things and almost ran from the room, but the maid hovered beside Lucy, frightened but determined not to abandon her mistress.

Lucy touched her arm. 'It is all right, Ruthie, you may go. I will ring when I need you.' As the maid scuttled from the room, Lucy turned back to Ralph, saying coldly, 'What now, my lord, do you have some new demand for your employee?'

'You are angry with me, and rightly so. I have come to explain.'

There was no softening of his countenance or his tone, but Lucy did not expect that. The fact that he was here at all was more than she had dared to hope for.

'Very well.'

She glanced about her before perching herself on the dressing stool. The only other seat in the room was the small sofa at the end of the bed and she would not risk him sitting beside her. For a long time he stood in silence, looking down at her.

'I do not see her,' he said at last. 'When I look at you, I do not see Helene.'

'But I look like her.' Lucy shivered as she thought of Lady Preston's words. 'A pale imitation.'

'There is nothing pale about you. Harry saw it from the beginning. He said you had fire in you.'

'Mr Colne knows your plan?'

He nodded. 'I told him of it the night he brought Francesca to dinner. He had guessed something was amiss when he saw you in that blue gown and came to my study to challenge me.'

'I know.' Lucy nodded. 'I heard him.'

He sat down on the little sofa.

'Are you angry, that I told Harry the truth and not you?'

'He is your best friend. You should have told him from the outset.' Despite the weight on her spirits she felt a wry smile tugging at her mouth. 'I suspect you were too obstinate.'

'Too obstinate and too proud. It has taken an equally stubborn woman to make me see that I was wrong to keep all this to myself. Helene's character was frail, weak. Yours is much stronger. Where she was cold and fearful, you are warm and brave.' A faint smile lightened his countenance. 'Helene was a beautiful ninnyhammer. You are intelligent, and beautiful in a different way.'

'But you loved her.'

'No. I was dazzled at first, perhaps, and happy to have such a beautiful wife, but love? No. I never loved her, any more than she loved me.'

'That is very sad.'

'It is the way of most arranged marriages. I had resigned myself to it. I thought she had, too.'

Lucy gripped her hands tightly in her lap to stop herself from reaching out to comfort him. It was too soon.

'Perhaps you should tell me everything.'

'Perhaps I should.'

He sat forward and rested his elbows on his knees, hands clasped together and his eyes fixed upon the floor. Lucy forced herself to remain silent, waiting for him to begin.

'Three years ago I went to Harrogate looking for a wife. Helene Preston seemed an ideal choice. By birth she was a good match, her nature was sweet and of course she was stunningly beautiful. By the autumn we were married.

'It was not a love match, we both knew that, but her parents were eager for the alliance and Helene herself was not averse to it. And I—desired her. I thought that love would come later. If not love, then at least affection. I thought we could be comfortable together, despite the differences in our natures that very soon became apparent. We hid those differences well. To the outside world we were the perfect couple. We had separate interests, of course. Helene's were centred upon society. She wanted to see and be seen. Oh, she was accomplished—she had read the most fashionable authors, she could paint and draw and play the piano, but it was all done by rote, with little understanding.

'My interests bored her, as did the running of the estate and living at Adversane. I was equally bored by the life she wanted, the one we led for the first few months of our marriage, which was one long round of visits and house parties. Helene's beauty and impeccable manners made her universally admired. Everyone agreed I was a very fortunate man.'

'Everyone save you?'

'It was my choice. What right had I to complain? By the following spring, after a winter spent here, I realised how ill-suited we were. Helene's nature was timid. She disliked hunting, was terrified of the dogs and frightened of my horses—she was even frightened of me.' She saw his jaw clenching as he struggled with the memories. 'I hoped that would change, in time. I did my best to treat her gently. Sir James had told me she was highly strung, but it was more than that. She was unstable, like a skittish colt, shying away from my advances. I tried to be patient with her, I curbed my temper, never raised my voice, gave in to her every whim. By heaven, I showed her a good deal more tolerance than I have done anyone else.' He glanced up to look at Lucy. 'Certainly I treated her with more kindness than I have shown you! I thought we needed time to get to know one another, so I held back. I never forced my attentions upon her. We had our separate rooms and I allowed her to go her own way.' He added, as if to himself, 'Perhaps that was my mistake.'

With a hiss of exasperation, Ralph jumped to his feet, saying roughly, 'This is an unedifying tale. I should not be sullying your ears with it—'

She was at his side in an instant, catching his arm as he made for the door.

'No, please, do not go.'

'It was madness to involve you in my hare-brained scheme. The more I think of it the more nonsensical it seems to me now.' He took her hands, saying urgently, 'You should leave now, Lucy. I can never make you happy. It was wrong of me to think I could. Do not worry about the money—I shall pay you everything I promised, and more. You need never want for anything.'

Some part of her wanted to rip up at him, to accuse him of trying to buy her off, but she knew that wasn't the case. He was trying to protect her.

She said simply, 'But I do not want to leave.'

'You must. If I find I have destroyed one woman, I will not risk doing the same thing to you.'

'I do not believe you destroyed Helene.'

'That is because you do not know the whole—'

'Then tell me,' she said. 'Tell me and let me decide for myself.'

'You may hate me when you know everything.'

'That is a risk, certainly, but if you send me away now

my imagination will conjure up something far worse.'
Lucy took a breath, desperate to make him understand.
'All my life the people I have loved have tried to…to
protect me by keeping unpalatable truths hidden from
me. If you care for me at all, then pray do me the honour of trusting me with the truth. I am not so feeble that
it will break me.'

His mouth quirked at one side as if a smile was being
forced out of him.

'No, I think in some ways you are stronger than all
of us.'

He returned to the sofa, and she sat down beside him,
saying quietly, 'It does not seem to me that your marriage
was a very happy one.'

'As happy as many another couple, but I began to suspect that Helene had a lover. Men had always clustered
about her, attracted by her beauty, but she never showed
the slightest preference for any of them. However, that
last spring at Adversane, she changed. She was more nervous and on edge than ever, and she began avoiding my
company. Her manner was agitated and she would burst
into tears even more often than before. She had always
gone to Druids Rock with her father when he visited Adversane, but now she began to walk there almost daily.'

'You never went with her?'

'Occasionally, but it was very clear she did not want
my company. She often waited until I was occupied with
estate business to go off.' He paused. 'She always took
Crimplesham and despite my suspicions I never followed
her, never questioned her maid or had her watched. I did
not wish for her to think of me as her gaoler.'

'And you never spoke to her about your suspicions?'

'Only once, on the morning of Midsummer's Eve.'
He exhaled slowly. 'Helene had been pampered and cos-

setted all her life. Everyone adored her and it was rare indeed that she incurred anyone's disapproval, but her gentle nature could not withstand the least hint of criticism. However, I knew I could not let the situation go on.' His lips thinned to a bloodless line. 'I have told you, soft words are not my style. I tried, but I had to explain to her that I could not accept another man's bastard as my heir. She ran off in tears, whether from guilt, or remorse, or because she was innocent—to this day I have no idea, because by morning she was dead.'

Lucy bit her lip to prevent any exclamation of horror and after a few moments' silence Ralph continued.

'The matter was not mentioned again. Helene appeared happy enough at the play that night, but then, her serene smile never gave anything away. I hoped, foolishly, that she had resigned herself to life with me. After supper there was the usual dancing. I watched Helene closely but could see no sign of her favouring any one of her partners over the others. As soon as the guests had gone she retired. I offered to go with her, but she refused, saying she had a headache.' He shrugged. 'I had grown quite used to that. She did not want my company and I would not force it upon her. It was only the next morning I found out she had not gone to bed, when the maid Ruthie raised the alarm.'

He ran a hand across his eyes.

'I am haunted by the thought that I might be maligning Helene, that she was innocent and killed herself because of what I said to her. I know it is what my family think. Yet there is another explanation, although I have no proof.

'I cannot rid myself of the suspicion that she went off after the dancing to meet her lover.'

Lucy's hand crept to her mouth.

'Oh, good heavens.'

'I cannot prove it,' he said again. 'After we found her body I made endless enquiries of those who had been present, to see if any of them remembered Helene saying or doing anything that might explain why she went to Druids Rock, but no one could help me. I questioned Crimplesham, but she insisted her mistress was innocent and was outraged that I should even think such a thing. Yet still the suspicion remained and I determined to know the truth.' Ralph straightened. 'You see, it has been proven that recreating a scene or an event can spark a memory, so that was my plan. I took a small portrait of Helene to Mrs Killinghurst and asked her to find me someone who bore a resemblance to my wife. She found you.

'I brought you here, dressed you in the styles and colours my wife favoured and waited to see what happened. Adam's reaction convinced me that my plan would work. I thought if you appeared at the play dressed as Helene had been on that last fateful night, her lover would not be able to hide his reaction. And I should be watching.' His lip curled. 'Foolish, perhaps, but better to think she was meeting a lover at Druids Rock than that she went there to kill herself because of me.

'I told no one. I wanted no hint of scandal attached to Helene if my suspicions were unfounded. I had no wish to sully her good name or cause her family more distress. I wrote to Ariadne and asked her to come here as chaperone, telling her the same tale I told you.'

He sat back and raked his fingers through his hair. 'But why should you believe me? It sounds too fantastical, as if I am trying merely to shuffle off the blame for what happened.'

'But I do,' she said slowly. 'I do believe you.'

He shook his head.

'You want to believe me innocent, because you cannot bear to think that my temper caused the death of such a sweet, gentle creature.'

'No. I believe it because I know—I was informed—that Lady Adversane was going to leave you.'

Chapter Thirteen

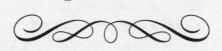

A heavy silence followed Lucy's words and she said quickly, 'Ruthie told me. She is a chatterbox, but she has given me her word that she kept the secret until now. She said she was appointed as lady's maid when your wife's dresser broke her arm.'

'Yes. That was why I assigned her to you, because I knew she could dress your hair in the same fashion.'

'I guessed as much, but it is not important now. Ruthie said Lady Adversane let it slip that she was planning to leave you. She then made Ruthie promise not to say a word about it.'

'Did she say why Helene was going?'

'Because…' Lucy faltered. 'Because she was so unhappy here.'

'So it comes back to me,' said Ralph bitterly.

'No! She would hardly have thrown herself from Druids Rock if she was planning to run away. It does not make sense.' She frowned, trying to recall her maid's exact words. 'Lady Adversane told Ruthie that when Crimplesham learned of the proposed flight she insisted on accompanying her. Don't you see, Ralph? Helene had already decided to run away before she even told her dresser. From all I have learned of your late wife I do not think she would contemplate going off alone.'

'She wouldn't!'

'No, it seems to me much more likely that someone had persuaded her, and that she went to Druids Rock that night to meet them.' She hesitated. 'Are you certain it would have been a guest?'

His lip curled. 'My wife was too conscious of her worth to dally with anyone beneath her own station. I questioned all my house guests, including my brothers-in-law. Logic told me I must eliminate everyone, however innocent I might think them. At one stage I seriously considered Helene might be in love with my cousin, for she was certainly on very good terms with him. You have seen for yourself that Cottingham has the happy knack of being able to put ladies at their ease. He flirts effortlessly, whereas I— Such frivolity is not a part of my nature.'

'That is no loss, to my mind,' she said softly.

He caught her hand and kissed it. 'Bless you for that.' He held it very tightly while he continued. 'But Adam cannot have been the one she was going to meet. Judith confirmed they were together all night, and in any case I saw them myself, going up to their room once the dancing had ended. The only other men I suspected are all neighbours—local gentlemen.' His mouth twisted. 'Everyone was asked if they could throw any light upon the matter, but by heaven, I have known all these men for years. I could scarcely accuse any one of them of being Helene's lover without very strong evidence.'

'Of course not. But you think, if I wear the gown, it will provide that evidence?'

'It might just stir up a memory or two that will lead me to the truth. Who knows, it might even reveal her lover, if there is one.'

'And if she *did* have a lover, do you think…?' She bit her lip. 'Do you think he killed her?'

'I don't know. All I am sure of is that I cannot bear the thought that I caused her death.'

'Then I will wear the gown.'

'No, Lucy, I cannot ask it of you. It is time I was honest with myself. I have been clutching at straws. Perhaps her death should be laid at my door. She was miserable living here at Adversane. She thought me hard and domineering.'

Lucy gripped his arm. 'No, no. You can be brusque, I admit, but I also know you are very kind. I will not believe you did anything to drive her to suicide.'

'I married her.'

'That was an arrangement between you and the Prestons,' said Lucy practically. 'You said yourself Helene was in favour of the marriage.'

'Yes, because she did not know then how difficult I can be.' He took her hand and laced his fingers through hers. 'Lucy, if I am wrong, if there is no lover, then I must face the fact that I killed my wife. If that is the case then you must leave here, and we must never see each other again. I will not risk ruining your life.'

'Ralph—'

'No.' He put a finger on her lips to silence her. 'My conscience would never allow it.'

She straightened, saying crisply, 'And my conscience will not allow you to punish yourself in this way, so we must do what we can to discover what really happened that night.'

Lucy lay in her bed, listening to the early morning birdsong flowing in through the open window. Midsummer's Eve, and there was still much to be done. She had thrown herself into the arrangements for the forthcoming festivities with an added zeal, following Ralph's disclosures. So much rested on the forthcoming event, her whole happiness was at stake. The library had been rearranged in readiness for the play, and dancing was to take place in the white salon, a large, richly decorated room on the ground floor. Lucy had happily donned one of her old gowns and worked alongside the servants to transform the salon into a ballroom. She worked hard, as eager as Ralph to discover the truth, knowing that if he thought himself to blame for Helene's death he would send her away and she would never see him again.

Ralph had been adamant about that, saying it would be a mistake, that he would not risk making her unhappy. Lucy had argued but he would not be moved. She could not help wondering if guilt was the only reason he had decided they should not be wed. Perhaps he had realised that he didn't love her. He had said he never loved Helene, but wouldn't any man say that to his future bride?

Her doubts would not quite go away, and they were enhanced by Adam Cottingham's behaviour. Since their encounter in the Long Gallery she had on several occasions found him watching her with an almost mournful intensity. From everything Ralph had told her, she knew Adam could not be Helene's lover, so he must truly believe that Ralph was in some way responsible for her death. She *had* to believe that he was wrong, just as Lady Preston was wrong when she thought Ralph was still in love with her daughter.

Lucy stirred restlessly. If only she could tell them why Ralph had brought her here, why she had agreed to wear the scarlet gown, but he had sworn her to secrecy. How she hated secrets!

She sat up and tugged at the bell-pull. She might as

well get up now and attend to the last-minute preparations. If all went well, they could soon know why Helene had gone to Druids Rock that fateful night. One way or another Lucy was determined to lay the ghost, so that she and Ralph could move on, free of the spectre of his dead wife.

An air of expectancy hung over the house. They had dined early so that they might all go off to change afterwards, in readiness for the forthcoming entertainment. When Ralph came to Lucy's door to escort her downstairs she rose quickly from her dressing stool to meet him as he entered her room.

Ralph was staring at her, a look she could not quite interpret in his eyes. When he did not speak she dismissed her maid before saying awkwardly, 'Well, my lord. Will I do?' She shook out the scarlet skirts. 'Ruthie has dressed my hair in an identical style to that of the portrait. The sun has made it much lighter, so I think the resemblance is now most striking.'

'It is indeed,' he muttered. 'No one could fail to see the likeness. Are you sure you wish to go through with this, Lucy? It will be an ordeal for you. There will be talk—'

She put up her chin.

'Let them talk. It may well jog a few memories.'

'I hope so.' He held out a small leather box. 'You will need these.' As he opened the lid she saw the flash and sparkle of precious stones. 'The Adversane diamonds.' He handed her the earrings, and when she had put them on he clipped the bracelet around her wrist. 'Now for the necklace.'

Ralph indicated that she should turn around, and she stood, head bowed a little, as he fastened the diamonds around her throat. His fingers were warm on her skin, and then she felt the unmistakable touch of his lips on the nape of her neck.

'My brave girl,' he murmured, putting his arms about her. 'Whatever happens tonight, I want you to know how much I love you.'

She turned to him, gripping his coat.

'If that is so, Ralph, then don't send me away. Whatever happens tonight, say you will marry me and let me help you to forget.'

His jaw hardened.

'No, we must wait and see. But heaven only knows how I will live without you.'

'You do not have to live without me, Ralph.' She reached up and cupped his face with her hands, drawing him down until she could kiss his lips. 'I believe in you, my darling. Whatever Helene did you cannot be held entirely responsible.'

'Not entirely, perhaps, but enough to make me blame myself for the rest of my life. I could not ask you to live with that.'

He drew her close and she leaned against him, closing her eyes. He would not change his mind, and she could only pray that they would learn something to ease the pain she knew he was suffering. But that could only happen if their plan worked. She stirred, and immediately he released her. Summoning up a smile, she took his arm.

'We must go downstairs, Ralph. Ruthie tells me the Ingleston Players are already setting up in the library and your guests will be arriving soon.'

'You are sure you wish to go through with this? They will all be agog to meet you, thinking you are my future bride.'

'And if your plan works that is exactly what I shall be.'

'But if it proves nothing—'

'Then I would still marry you,' she said with quiet vehemence. 'I would risk everything to be your wife!'

He stopped for one final, bruising kiss before he escorted her out of the room.

Lucy glided down the stairs beside Ralph, the scarlet gown billowing in a whisper of silken skirts. She could hear the faint echo of voices from the Great Hall, where everyone was gathering to greet the guests when they arrived.

Pulling Lucy's hand more firmly onto his arm, Ralph led her into the hall. The chatter and laughter stopped almost instantly. He heard Judith Cottingham's little moan of dismay and the gasps of surprise from his sisters. Lady Preston's countenance was impassive, save for a narrowing of her eyes. The gentlemen raised their quizzing glasses to regard Lucy and he even heard Sir Timothy mutter, 'Good Lord!' before giving a very unconvincing cough. Only Ariadne showed no surprise, but then, she had been present at the dressmaker's visits and knew what to expect.

Little Charlotte Preston was goggling at Lucy and she cried artlessly, 'Oh, my goodness, Mama, she looks exactly like Helene!'

'Nonsense,' snapped Lady Preston. Her eyes raked over Lucy and she leaned towards her daughter as if to speak confidentially, but her words still carried to everyone present. 'It is a similar gown, I grant you, but Miss Halbrook does not have Helene's figure, nor her elegance.' She turned away as if to demonstrate that Lucy was not worthy of her attention. Ralph felt his anger rising at this studied insult, but Ariadne was already drawing Lucy away from him, saying in her calm, unruffled way, 'Well, well, Lucy, you look delightful, my dear.

And Adversane has given you the diamonds to wear. How charming.'

The rest of the party had regained their composure, and Ralph watched as they crowded around Lucy, eager to compliment her and make up for Lady Preston's lack of manners. Lord Wetherell broke away and strolled over.

'For God's sake, Adversane,' he murmured. 'What hellish game are you playing here?'

Ralph gave the tiniest shake of his head.

'I'll tell you later. When my guests arrive, take note of how they react to Miss Halbrook, would you?'

'They may well be struck dumb, as Cottingham appears to be.'

Ralph's eyes shifted to his cousin and he frowned. Adam was staring at Lucy, a muscle working in his cheek. With a word to his brother-in-law, Ralph moved towards Adam until he was close enough to ask him what he thought of Miss Halbrook.

'Miss—?' Adam tore his eyes away from Lucy. He was very pale, but he recovered himself and gave a little laugh. 'By Gad, Cousin, for a moment I thought I was seeing a ghost. What in heaven's name are you trying to do, Ralph? Why have you dressed her thus?'

Ralph wondered if he should confide in his cousin, but after another, frowning look at Adam he decided against it. He said lightly, 'Scarlet is a favourite colour of mine.'

He glanced at Lucy. She looked nervous, and his heart ached for her. She was so brave, so determined to do this for him. She would be his saviour, he knew it.

I would risk everything to be your wife.

Her final words to him wrapped themselves around his heart, warming him, giving him hope. Suddenly he wanted to reach out to her, to show her how much he loved her. He raised his voice so that it would carry across the hall.

'Perhaps it would be a good time to tell you all that I shall be making Miss Halbrook my wife, just as soon as the banns can be called.' He saw Lucy's startled glance, then the tremulous smile and flush of pleasure that brightened her eyes. He held out his hand to her. 'I cannot begin to tell you how happy she makes me.'

Lucy approached, shaking her head at him.

'Why this change of heart?' she murmured as he pulled her close and kissed her fingers.

'My heart has not changed, only my head. If you are willing to take a chance with me, then I would be a fool to turn you away. I could not resist making the announcement. It was imperative that you know how I feel about you.' He added, as if to convince himself, 'It will not affect my plans. I have already ascertained that if Helene *did* have a lover the fellow is not anyone here.'

Ariadne came bustling up.

'The guests are arriving,' she declared, waving everyone into line. 'To your places, please. Lucy, you must stand with me. Come along, dear.'

Adam was scowling, and Ralph touched his arm.

'You are looking very grim, Cousin. Perhaps you had come to think of Adversane as yours?'

'What? Oh, no, no, nothing like that, I—'

The flush on Adam's cheeks gave the lie to his words, and Ralph regarded him with disdain. Adam had been his pensioner for years and had never made any attempt to rectify the situation.

'You need not worry,' murmured Ralph, as he moved away to greet the first of his guests. 'I shall not stop your allowance, even when I remarry.'

* * *

The guests were pouring in now. Ralph glanced at Lucy standing next to Ariadne. She looked adorable, the scarlet gown highlighting her flawless skin and dainty figure. There was a slight flush on her cheek and he knew she was nervous, steeling herself for the coming ordeal. He watched her as the guests moved along the line. She smiled and said everything that was necessary. As each gentleman was introduced to her Ralph registered their astonished looks, saw more than one frowning stare bent upon her, but could discern nothing more than a very natural surprise in anyone's reaction.

At last the introductions were over and everyone began to make their way into the library for the forthcoming entertainment. Ralph saw Lucy going in with Ariadne. He wished he could be at her side, but that was not possible, not yet.

'A quiet start to your evening,' murmured Harry, pausing beside him. 'No revelations as yet.'

'No, nothing. But perhaps the play will provoke a reaction,' agreed Ralph. 'I'd be obliged if you would watch for anyone taking more than a little interest in Lucy.'

'Of course. Francesca would prefer to sit at the back, in any case. In her present condition she might well have to slip away.' He hesitated. 'I hope you do not object—I told her of your plans for tonight. She knows it is in strictest confidence, of course, but I have always shared everything with my wife.'

Ralph was silent for a moment, thinking of the relief he had felt after he had told Lucy of his suspicions. He gripped Harry's arm and grinned.

'No, I do not object at all, my friend.'

Having ushered everyone into the library, Ralph took his seat at the front beside Lucy. He reached for her hand.

'Are you ready, my dear?'

'I am.' She smiled at him. 'I am quite looking forward to it. I have never seen *The Provoked Wife* before, although I believe it was very popular when Mr Garrick performed it.'

Ralph grimaced. 'In my opinion it is an unedifying piece, but it was the play they performed two years ago and I wanted everything to be as exact as possible.'

A drum roll announced the start of the performance, and silence enveloped the audience. Lucy watched the play unfold with growing disquiet. The portrayal of Sir John Brute as the drunken, buffoonish husband was nothing like Ralph, yet Lucy could imagine Helene's overwrought mind making the connection. She felt sick to her heart. Perhaps there had been no lover. Perhaps Helene had been driven to despair by her loveless marriage.

Lucy struggled through the first three acts and it was with relief that an interval was announced, and everyone repaired to the white salon for refreshments. She wanted to cling to Ralph's arm, but she knew he needed to circulate amongst his guests and he would want her to do the same, to try to stir their memories. She moved amongst the crowd, concealing her nerves behind a cheerful countenance, but her smile became genuine when she saw Mrs Dean approaching.

'Ariadne, pray stay with me a little while. I feel quite bereft of friends.'

'No, why should that be? I assure you everyone is delighted that Adversane has decided to marry again!' Ariadne patted her hand. 'I admit I was quite put out when

Ralph set it about that you were his fiancée. I was not at all in favour of spreading such a tale, since there was no truth in it, but now, of course, everything has changed. I am so happy for you both. I have no doubt that you will make Adversane a perfect wife.'

Heartened, Lucy said fervently, 'I do hope you are right, ma'am.'

With her spirits somewhat restored, Lucy moved on, but still the play haunted her. Had Helene's imagination turned Ralph into the monster Adam branded him? What if they proved nothing tonight, beyond the fact that Helene had taken her own life?

The thought was very daunting, because if that was so she knew Ralph would never forgive himself and she would not be able to help him. She felt the tension building into a headache and put a hand to her temple, moving towards the open windows, where the air was a little fresher.

'You look as if you might enjoy a little refreshment, Miss Halbrook.' She swung round to find Adam Cottingham beside her. 'I do not think you have yet sampled the famous Adversane punch, have you?' He held out one of the two glasses he was holding. 'Here you are. Do try it. It is made from a secret recipe that the family has used for generations.'

Lucy realised that she was indeed thirsty and she sipped gratefully at the dark liquid. It was a mixture of wine, brandy and herbs, although there was a faintly bitter after-taste that made her wrinkle her nose. Adam laughed.

'Do not worry, one grows accustomed to it. Drink it up, now, Lucy. It is just the thing to revive you for the remainder of the evening.'

She tried to laugh.

'With two more acts of *The Provoked Wife* to endure I think I shall need it.'

'Are you not enjoying the play?'

'The performances are very good,' she replied cautiously, 'but I do not find the subject matter—boorish husbands and unfaithful wives—entertaining.'

'Do you not? Helene did not like it, either. It was too much like her own situation.'

Lucy's heart sank. So she was right—it had precipitated the poor woman's flight. She put down her glass.

'If you will excuse me, I think I should find Ariadne. The heat and noise here are making me a little dizzy.'

'No need to bother Mrs Dean,' he said. 'Let me take you onto the terrace for a moment.'

Lucy glanced out through the open doors. It *would* be cooler, but it was almost dark now, just a glimmer of light showing on the western horizon. When she hesitated Adam took her arm.

'Come, there can be no harm in it. We need only step outside the door...'

Ralph was dog-tired. Sitting through that damned play was more harrowing than he had anticipated. He hoped it would be worth it. He glanced around the noisy, crowded room. Lucy should be easy to spot in that scarlet gown, but she was nowhere to be seen. He made his way back to the Great Hall where some of his guests had congregated. He spotted Judith Cottingham moving between the chattering groups. She was such a mouse-like, unsmiling little creature and he had never really warmed to her, but now, despite his preoccupation, he felt a twinge of sympathy. He doubted if her marriage to Adam was a happy one. There was an anxious crease on her brow and he reached out to touch her arm as she passed him.

'Is anything amiss, Cousin?'

She started.

'I was looking for Adam, my lord.'

Probably flirting with another man's wife.

He was shrugging off the bitter thought when he heard a giggle behind him and Charlotte Preston's childish voice assailed his ears.

'I certainly understand the play much better this year, Mama, but I cannot see what it is about it that made Helene cry so.'

His lips thinning, he was about to move Judith away when Lady Preston's response stopped him in his tracks.

'It wasn't the play, you silly girl,' she snapped. 'It was the scold I gave her beforehand. By heavens, I was never nearer to boxing her ears than that night!'

Ralph turned. Lady Preston had not seen him and would have walked on if he had not stepped into her path. She started, and he could tell by the dull flush on her cheeks that she had not meant him to hear her comment.

'And may I ask why you were scolding my wife, Lady Preston?'

Her cold eyes glittered angrily but her lips remained firmly shut.

'Oh, was that why you sent for Helene, Mama?' said Charlotte artlessly. 'We had all gone upstairs to change our gowns, do you remember, and I went to ask Crimplesham if she would put up my hair, only she could not because she said you had asked her to bring Helene to your room and Helene looked so guilty that I knew something must be wrong—'

Lady Preston waved a dismissive hand.

'Yes, yes, there is no need to go on!'

'Oh, I think there is every need to go on, Lady Preston,' said Ralph grimly, 'But not here.'

He took her arm and escorted her briskly out of the hall and into his study. He heard footsteps behind him and guessed Charlotte was following. Well, let her come. He was determined to get the truth from Lady Preston as soon as possible.

'Now, madam, you will explain, if you please, why you thought it necessary to admonish my wife.'

'I was saving your marriage!' When he said nothing she gave a huff of impatience. 'She was playing you false, Adversane. I am surprised you did not see it. I knew something was amiss the moment we arrived but Helene denied it. However, on Midsummer's Eve Crimplesham confessed the whole and I had her bring Helene to me. The foolish child was planning to leave you. She told me she had fallen in love and was going to run away. I soon put an end to that nonsense.'

'You never mentioned this after Helene's death,' said Ralph.

'There was no point. It could not change anything.'

'It might explain why she went out.'

'And would you want such a reason made public?' demanded Lady Preston.

'Why not?'

'She was meeting her *lover*, Adversane. She had been meeting him at Druid's Rock for months, although she assured me Crimplesham was always with her, and they had shared nothing more than a few stolen kisses. You will imagine my outrage, that any daughter of mine should—' She broke off, breathing deeply to control her anger. 'I convinced her that she must remain here and do her duty as your wife. She told me she had arranged to meet her lover later that night but I ordered her not to go. Let him cool his heels at Druids Rock.' She stopped again, her eyes snapping. 'She disobeyed me. That is what comes of your being too soft with her, Adversane. She would never have dared to do so before she was married. Crimplesham told me the next morning that Helene had come crying to her, saying she was determined to see him, to tell him it was over.'

'And who was this lover?'

'That is not important.' Lady Preston waved one hand dismissively and began to stalk back and forth across the room.

Ralph looked at her in disbelief.

'Not important, when you say she had fallen in love with this man?

'Love, hah! She told me how he had courted her, pursued her with his kind words and false promises. She said he would take her to London or Brighton, where there was an abundance of good company. It was I who pointed out to her that she would not be received by polite society in either of those places. She would be obliged to live abroad, an exile. But he had anticipated that, too, for she told me he would take her abroad, where the climate would suit her very well.

'By heaven, her infatuation was such that I believe she had lost the little wit she was born with! I scolded her mightily, I can tell you, and reminded her of her duty. Duty is all, my lord. She had a duty to you, as your wife. I told her that, since you do not appear to have done so.'

'And what of your duty to Helene? Did it not matter to you that by keeping quiet you might be shielding her murderer?'

'Not at all, as long as there was no breath of impropriety. To name him would result in the whole sorry business being dragged into the open and Helene's name besmirched.'

'And your good name means that much to you?'

'Of course it does. Think how poor Charlotte would suffer if her sister's *affaire* was known. And I was protecting your name, too, Adversane. I was determined to save us all from the scandal.'

'I would rather have had the scandal than your daughter's death, madam.'

She curled her lip.

'You may say that, but you would be singing a different tune if she had left you, and for your own cousin, too.'

'Cottingham!' Ralph's eyes narrowed. He said slowly, 'No, you are wrong. Adam was with his wife all night.'

There was a soft whimper and he looked around, surprised to see that it was not Charlotte standing behind him, but Judith Cottingham, her face ashen in the candlelight.

'Adam escorted you upstairs,' he said to her. 'I saw him. I remember saying goodnight to you both.'

Judith was shaking.

'He…he did not stay,' she whispered. 'He made me say he had been with me all night, but it was not true. No sooner had we reached our room than he slipped out again through the side hall.' She folded her arms across her narrow chest. 'I d-did not see him again until dawn.'

He turned back to Lady Preston, observing the defiance in her eyes.

'You knew,' he said slowly. 'You knew she was meeting him that night yet you said nothing?'

'She was dead,' she retorted. 'How she died was not important.' She had the grace to look a little embarrassed. 'Besides—it may well have been an accident.'

'It was.' An anguished whisper came from Judith. 'It *must* have been an accident.'

A cold hand was clutching at Ralph's chest as he made for the door.

'Let us hope for all our sakes you are right, madam.'

The play was about to recommence and the hall was emptying rapidly. Ralph saw Harry and beckoned him over. 'Have you seen Lucy?'

'She went into the white salon, but she's not there now.' Harry glanced into the library. 'And she has not returned to her seat.'

'We must find her,' Ralph told him urgently. 'Be a good fellow and look for her.' He caught Harry's arm. 'Discreetly, of course.'

Ralph's meaningful look was not lost upon his friend.

'Of course, leave it with me. She is probably in the cloakroom gossiping with your sisters.'

'Most likely,' replied Ralph, but without conviction. He added grimly, 'I need to find Cottingham, too.'

He saw the alarm in Colne's eyes.

'You think—'

'I don't know,' Ralph ground out.

Harry nodded.

'I'll check the house,' he said shortly. 'You had best see if anyone has driven off recently.'

Ralph left him and slipped out to the stables. The whole area was packed with horses and carriages belonging to his guests. He spotted his groom amongst a noisy group of stable hands gathered in one corner of the yard.

'All our horses are accounted for, my lord,' said Greg, in answer to Ralph's enquiry. 'And none of our carriages missing. Of course with so many people here tonight there's no knowing if any of them have gone out.'

The cold band around his heart squeezed harder. Ralph issued a few terse instructions before returning to the house. He found Harry waiting for him in the hall.

'Neither of them are in the house, Ralph, I am sure of that. Nor are they in the gardens.'

'Greg is even now checking with the man we posted at the main gate to see if any carriage has left that way.'

'Perhaps we should enlist Wetherell's help, and Sir Timothy—'

'No, not yet. I need to be sure I am not merely being fanciful.' He saw the butler crossing the hall and stopped him. 'Something has come up, Byrne, but I do not wish to spoil everyone's enjoyment. Tell the players to go on without us, will you?'

With a small bow Byrne moved off, and Ralph hurried to the door, saying over his shoulder, 'Come on, Harry, we'll go to the stables and wait for Greg to return.'

They had just reached the entrance to the stable yard when the groom came running up.

'No one has left by way of the gate, my lord.'

'Then where can they be?' muttered Harry. 'Surely they would have been seen if they had crossed the open park.'

Ralph frowned and slammed one clenched fist into his palm.

Think logically, man!

No, logic would not help him here. Cottingham would not be thinking reasonably...

'He has gone to Druids Rock!' Ralph grabbed Harry's arm. 'Adam could have taken Lucy out through the gardens and to the old ride with very little chance of being observed.' He began to run. 'Harry, inform my brothers-in-law of what has happened and ask them to cover our absence. Then you and Greg follow me!'

He dashed into the stable, issuing orders as he went. As soon as the bridle was fastened on Jupiter, Ralph did not wait for a saddle but hurled himself onto the horse's back and clattered out of the yard.

'Adam, we should go back.'

Lucy stumbled through the darkness. Her head was spinning, and she could not keep her balance. Adam had one hand around her waist, and although she knew she should protest she was afraid that she would collapse if he did not support her. Her head ached too much for her to think clearly, but surely they should not be quite so far from the house?

It seemed such a long time since she had stepped outside. Adam had suggested they walk around the gardens, assuring her that the fresh air and exercise would soon drive away her unaccustomed dizziness. She must be inebriated. The punch had been very strong and she was glad she had only drunk a little. In any case she could not go back indoors in such a state. Adam was right—she must walk it off.

She was dimly aware that they had strayed a long way from the formal gardens and the terrace. In the gathering gloom she did not recognise this area at all. Then Adam pulled her through a door set into a high brick wall and she could see the palings and the black shapes of trees in the distance.

'Why have we left the gardens?' She tried to tug herself out of his grasp. 'Adam, no more. Take me back now.'

The arm about her waist tightened and pulled her along.

'It is not much farther.'

She stumbled on beside him, but when they reached

the old ride a sense of danger broke through the fog in her brain.

'No!' She clung to the gate. 'No. Let me go.' Adam prised her fingers from the wood and dragged her roughly away. 'Help me! Someone, help!'

'There is no point in shouting,' he said. 'No one can hear you at this distance from the house.'

It was impossible to resist him. She felt so tired, all she wanted to do was to lie down and sleep, yet Adam would not let her rest. She struggled to put one foot before the other as he pulled her on through the evening twilight. However, by the time they reached Hobart's Bridge the exertion had cleared her mind a little.

'You drugged me,' she accused him. 'There was something in the punch.'

'It was necessary.'

His breathing was laboured. The heaviness was easing from her limbs, but she decided it would be safer if Adam did not know this, so she continued to sag against him.

'Why is it necessary?' she asked him. 'Why are you doing this?'

He gave a sob, but did not slacken his pace as he responded.

'You cannot live. You cannot be allowed to take her place.'

'Do you mean Lady Adversane?'

'Of course, who else? I cannot allow you to marry my cousin. I am very sorry. Ralph does not deserve you.'

She dug in her heels and tried to resist him.

'But he did not kill Helene.'

He whipped about.

'Yes, he did! He d-drove her to it.'

'No. He told me what happened——'

'And do you think he would tell you the truth? He

wants you to take her place. She never loved him, she loved me. *Me!* And I loved her, worshipped her.'

A chill of uncertainty made her shiver, but she pushed it aside, saying urgently, 'But this won't bring her back. Let me go, Adam. You do not really want to hurt me, do you?'

'No, of course not, but you are his punishment. I see that now. Adversane thinks he can find happiness with you, but why should he? If I cannot have Helene, then he cannot have *you.*'

Fear and the cool night air were combining to clear Lucy's mind. She realised they were heading for Druids Rock. A glance at Adam's contorted face made her shiver, for there could be no reasoning with him. She held back, making it necessary for him to half carry, half drag her along. It was slowing them down, and Lucy could only pray that it was using up his strength, too. Night was closing in but the rising moon was already giving off a faint light. If she ran away from him now there was no cover, nowhere to hide, but she must look for an opportunity to escape.

Ralph set Jupiter racing through the old ride at a gallop, but when the great horse stumbled he steadied the pace. He was riding bareback, and it would not help Lucy if he broke his neck getting to her. They crossed Hobart's Bridge and cantered on along the old track. He sat up, straining his eyes against the near darkness. The rising moon gave a little light, enough to show him the moors stretching away in every direction, desolate and empty. What if he was wrong? What if they had not come this way? He pushed aside his doubts and dug his heels into Jupiter's flanks, cantering around the ridge until Druids Rock was in sight, looming black against the night sky.

There was movement on the rock's sloping incline. He could see the outline of two figures struggling. Ralph slid to the ground and ran closer, crouching in the hope that they would not see him. Adam was slowly pulling Lucy up to the top but she was resisting him, talking, arguing. The steady wind was blowing his way, so they did not hear his approach. He dropped lower into the grass and moved a little closer, concealing himself behind the thick mounds of heather that grew all around. Lucy's voice floated to him on the breeze, calm, reasoning, no hint of panic.

'Adam, please. Helene would not want you to do this.'

'Adversane never loved her as I did. I wanted to make her happy—he only ever wanted to possess her, like some beautiful trophy. He never knew the real pain of her death. And now he wants to put you in her place. He thinks you can be another Helene, but I won't allow that. And this time he will feel it. When he sees your body smashed and broken he will suffer, just as I did two years ago.'

Ralph gritted his teeth. It was as much as he could do not to break from cover and race towards them, but the risk was too great. Adam was walking backwards up the slope and pulling Lucy after him. The moon was climbing higher now, and he would have a good view of anyone approaching. Ralph calculated the distance to the highest ridge. If Adam swept Lucy up in his arms he could be at the edge before Ralph could reach them. There was only one way to approach Adam without being seen: he must climb the steep face of Druids Rock. Ralph glanced again towards the couple. Lucy was still arguing, holding back, delaying the inevitable by precious moments. It might just work.

Keeping low, Ralph turned and hurried around to the

far side of the crag. Tearing off his coat, he looked up. The black rock towered over him, rising almost vertical to the sky. He had done this dozens of times as a boy, but not so much as a man, and never in the dark. The thought of Lucy being dragged inexorably closer to the precipitous drop sharpened his resolve. He put his hands against the rough stone and began to climb.

Lucy resisted with all her might, bracing her feet against each tiny ridge, but Adam forced her upwards inch by inch, stopping only when he had to reply to one of her questions. She kept asking them, using everything she could think of to slow him down. Far below in the valley she could see tiny pinpoints of red light in the darkness. The people of Ingleston were celebrating Midsummer with bonfires. She could even smell the wood smoke carried to her on the night air. In the town and at Adversane life was carrying on, and no one was aware of her plight. Ralph might not even have missed her yet. The thought made her feel terribly alone.

Concentrate, Lucy. Keep him talking.

'Tell me what you think occurred that night, Adam. Why do you hold Ralph responsible for Helene's death? He was not even here when it happened.'

'No, but he drove her to it. He wanted to possess her, and she would do anything to get away from him.'

Even through her fear, Lucy felt the stab of jealousy. Helene had been so beautiful, how could Ralph not love her, whatever he might say? Adam continued, unprompted.

'She knew it was a mistake soon after they were married. She was such an innocent. Her parents persuaded her to marry him for his money, you know. She thought he would take her to London, that they would live in society, but instead he brought her here, where he could have her all to himself. Oh, there are a few families in the neighbourhood, but Helene wanted parties and concerts every night. She needed to be admired, you see. She craved approbation. I could give her that. Ralph couldn't, it is not his way. He is too impatient, abrupt. I could see she was a delicate creature who needed to be nurtured. And I promised to take her abroad. The Italians would go wild for her fair beauty. I promised to love her and cherish her for the rest of her days.'

'But, Adam, you have a wife. What about Judith?'

He gave a wild, scornful laugh.

'An arranged marriage to a drab female no one else wanted. With Helene on my arm it would be different. Every man would envy me. And why not? Why should Cousin Ralph have everything? Let him keep Adversane and his fortune, but Helene—I wanted her. I *loved* her.'

His heart-wrenching cry tore into the night.

'I understand how you must feel—'

He interrupted her with a snarl.

'You understand nothing! She is dead, *dead*! And you are going to follow her.'

'No.'

Lucy struggled but to no avail. There was nothing she could do to prevent Adam dragging her the last few yards towards the brink and that sheer drop to certain death.

'Let her go, Adam.'

Lucy thought the deep, calm voice was in her imagination until Adam stopped. She looked past him and saw Ralph standing at the very edge of the rock, feet apart, the white sleeves of his shirt fluttering gently. Like wings, she thought dizzily. Her guardian angel.

'Never.' Adam's voice rose hysterically. 'Devil take you, Adversane. She will die, as Helene died.'

'No. I won't let you do this.'

Lucy forced herself to keep still. Adam might yet make a run for the edge, killing them both, perhaps even taking Ralph with them.

'I will stop you,' said Ralph. 'Look behind you. Colne and Greg are here, too. You cannot fight all three of us.'

Lucy glanced back. She had not heard the horses come up, but now she saw them quietly cropping the grass not far away while the two men stood at the edge of the slope, Harry Colne with a pistol in his hand. Ralph took a step nearer.

'It is over, Adam,' he said quietly. 'Let her go.'

'No!' Adam dragged Lucy hard against him. 'Why should you have everything? You think she will make you happy, another Helene to grace your house and your bed.'

Ralph was coming closer.

'Lucy is not Helene, Adam. I would not want her to be.'

'Helene is dead because of you—'

Even as Adam spat out the words Lucy felt his grip slacken a little and she wrenched herself free. Ralph reached out for her, drawing her close as Harry and Greg hurled themselves at Adam. He struggled against them, cursing, but he could not shake them off. He glared at Lucy, standing silent and trembling within the circle of Ralph's arms.

'Don't you see? He has turned you into the image of Helene. He is possessed, so much so he must replace her, even though he drove her to her death—'

The terrible logic of his words stabbed into Lucy like a dagger, making her sob. It made sense that Ralph was still in love with his wife, despite everything he had told her. She pushed her hands against his chest and stared up into his hard face, aghast. He met her eyes and gave the slightest shake of his head.

'Trust me, love. I have no secrets from you now.' His arms tightened about her and he said over her head, 'I did not love Helene, Adam, and I did not kill her. *You* did. You met her here on Midsummer's Eve. Judith has told us everything. Helene's walks here were nothing to do with nature or the druids, were they? It was not even to escape me. She came to meet you.'

'We had to meet somewhere. She could not take a carriage—the servants would have informed you, and she would not ride out alone. When I was staying at Adversane we only needed to slip out separately and meet up here. And when I was at Delphenden I would ride over and leave my horse in the woods, out of sight, while I walked up here. If anyone saw me it was easy enough to say I had business in Ingleston.' He laughed. 'We fooled you all. No one knew of our meetings.'

'Save your wife.'

Adam gave a dismissive shrug.

'Judith did not dare to speak out against me. She knew Helene was the love of my life, that nothing must come between us.'

'Oh, that is so cruel,' exclaimed Lucy.

'Judith does not need your pity. She was happy enough with the house and the children. Besides, what could she offer me, compared to my darling? Helene was too good, too kind, she did not want to hurt anyone, but at last I persuaded her that we could be happy abroad. They understand these arrangements on the Continent. But in the end she could not do it.' Adam raised his ravaged face to Ralph again. 'You tricked her, you warped her mind, hid your true nature behind a mask of kindness so that she believed she should stay with you.'

Lucy heard the barely controlled anger in Ralph's voice when he spoke again.

'So when she came to meet you, to tell you it was over, you killed her.'

'No, no. It was an accident. She slipped. It had been raining, do you remember, Cousin? The rock was wet. She came to tell me she would not leave you, that she would do her duty as your wife. Your wife!' His gaze shifted to Lucy and he said savagely, 'After all I did for her, the chances I took to meet her, to court her, I thought she loved me. I slipped away and came here to wait for her, but when she arrived it was to tell me she wouldn't leave. Adversane was a good man, she said. He was trying to make her happy, so she wanted to do her duty by him. Don't you see, Lucy? If he hadn't persuaded her to stay with him she wouldn't have refused me, we would not have quarrelled and she would not have slipped over the edge!'

Adam dropped his head in his hands as his tortured confession continued.

'I tried to reason with her, but she said she was going back. She refused to meet me again, save as your wife, Adversane. Even though it would break my heart. I tried to stop her, tried to kiss her, but she pushed me away, only she was standing too close to the edge, and lost her footing…' He fell to his knees and began to sob. 'I loved her. I have never loved anyone else. There isn't a day goes by that I don't wish I had died with her!'

Ralph stared down at him, his anger giving way to pity as he regarded the wretched figure crouched on the ground.

Harry pulled Adam to his feet.

'Come along, Cottingham,' he said. 'Let's get you back to the house.'

He and Greg began to lead Adam away. He walked quietly between them, his shoulders drooping, all resistance gone.

Ralph felt Lucy sag against him, and his arm around her tightened.

'What's this?' he muttered. 'You are not going to faint on me now?'

Her brave chuckle tore at his heart.

'No, indeed, but I am still feeling a little dizzy. He drugged me, you see, by putting something in the punch. Thankfully I did not drink it all.'

'My poor darling. Would you like to ride back? Jupiter has no saddle but there is Greg's horse, or Colne's.'

'No, thank you. I think I would be better walking it off, if you will help me.'

Lucy was grateful for Ralph's arm about her as they followed the others back to Adversane. As they walked Ralph recounted his meeting with Lady Preston.

'So you were in no way to blame,' said Lucy when he had finished.

'Except that my warning, coupled with her mother's scolding, drove Helene to tell Cottingham she would not run away with him.'

'From what Adam said it was your forbearance that persuaded her, Ralph. Helene recognised that you were trying to be kind to her.'

'She did.' He let out a long breath. 'We were not suited and I regret what happened, but I no longer hold myself responsible for her death. I shall try to do better by my next wife, I promise you.'

She stopped and turned to throw her arms about his neck.

'Oh, my darling, I know you will.'

He kissed her then, swift and hard, and her heart sang for the love conveyed in that one embrace.

The house was in sight, and they walked on in silence, following the others around to the side hall, where it was agreed they could more easily slip in unobserved. As they neared the house, Lucy was surprised to hear the scrape of fiddles coming from the open windows of the white salon.

'I thought the dancing would be ended by now,' she murmured.

Ralph took out his watch. 'No, we have not been away that long. Supper is over, but the dancing will continue for an hour or so yet.'

'Heavens,' she replied faintly. 'I thought it must be nearly dawn.'

'It will be by the time everyone departs.'

A figure ran across from the stables and Lucy recognised Robin. He tugged his forelock.

'Mr Greg said I was to keep an eye out for you,' he said, his astonished gaze fixed on Adam, standing passively between the groom and Harry Colne.

'Aye, well, take the horses back to the stable and keep your mouth shut,' ordered Greg.

The stable lad had just led the horses away when the side door opened and Judith Cottingham appeared.

'I was looking out for you.' She stepped back for them to enter, and Lucy noted how grey and drawn she was. She stared at her husband, then raised her anxious eyes to Ralph's face. 'Is it over?'

'Yes.' He nodded. 'He has told us what happened. It was an accident, as you thought. Helene slipped and fell.'

Judith sighed and closed her eyes for a moment, then she stepped up and took Adam's arm. He was gazing before him, his eyes not seeing anything. Lucy thought she had never seen such a broken man.

'Let me take him to our room,' said Judith. 'I will look after him now.'

'If you would rather not—' Ralph began, but she stopped him with a shake of her head.

'He is my husband,' she said simply.

She led him away, and Ralph turned to Greg.

'Find someone to help you stand guard on Cottingham's door. Make sure he does not leave his room again tonight, and assure Mrs Cottingham that she may call upon you should she require assistance.'

'Should we inform the magistrate?' asked Harry, as Greg went off.

Ralph looked at Lucy, who shook her head.

'Not on my account,' she said.

Ralph agreed. 'I shall make arrangements for him in the morning, but now we know the truth I do not think he is any longer a threat. However, I would like to keep tonight's little escapade quiet, if we can.'

'Then we must go back to join your guests,' declared Lucy.

'No,' Ralph objected, frowning. 'You should rest now.'

'I do not want to rest, and my continued absence might well give rise to conjecture.'

'Then I shall make some excuse for you—'

She put a hand against his mouth, saying with a smile, 'This is my adventure as much as yours, my lord. You shall not deny me my part in it.'

'We wouldn't dream of it, Miss Halbrook,' put in Harry before Ralph could respond. 'If Wetherell and Sir Timothy have done their work well, then it is possible we have not been missed.'

Ralph's eyes narrowed.

'Outmanoeuvred, by heaven!'

Harry laughed.

'Indeed, Adversane! I should admit defeat graciously if I were you. And *I* had best find Francesca and let her know that all is well.'

Ralph nodded. 'Very well, you go and do that now, Harry. Tell Wetherell and Finch that we are back, too, but pray keep this from my sisters if you can. I do not want them quizzing us about it just yet.'

As Harry went off, Ralph glanced down at Lucy's gown. The scarlet silk was torn and dirty from her ordeal.

'You cannot go into the ballroom like that, and if you change your gown people are bound to notice.'

She shrugged. 'They will, of course, but I shall tell them I spilled a glass of punch.' She added with a glimmer of a smile, 'Ruthie will help me and I am sure I can rely on her discretion. She has the makings of a very good lady's maid.' She saw the concern in his eyes and took his hands between her own, saying urgently, 'I want to do this, Ralph. For you. For us.'

She met his eyes steadily, trying to convey all that she felt for him. Gradually, she saw his hard glance soften to something much warmer.

'Very well.' He lifted her hand to his lips. 'Go, then. I will meet you in the ballroom.'

Chapter Fourteen

Twenty minutes later Lucy walked into the white salon, the scarlet gown replaced by midnight-blue. Ruthie had re-dressed her hair and even managed to fix the silver stars amongst her curls and they winked and sparkled in the candlelight. She looked magnificent.

Ralph felt a sudden tightness in his chest as she walked towards him. She was smiling, and he marvelled that she should look so calm and serene after all that had occurred. If anything, her green eyes glittered with an added brilliance. She positively glowed with happiness. Had there ever been a time when he had not loved her, this brave, intelligent girl who challenged him at every turn?

He took her hand and led her onto the dance floor, aware that those around them were smiling and nodding their approval. By this time formality had disappeared from the ballroom and the final dance was noisy and energetic. He watched Lucy closely, determined to whisk her away at the first signs of fatigue, but she skipped and twirled and smiled as if it was the first dance of the evening rather than the last. Ralph wanted to tell her, but whenever they came together he found himself merely smiling at her like a mooncalf.

At last the music ended, everyone applauded the small orchestra and the ballroom began to empty.

'I must take my leave of my guests,' he murmured to Lucy, reluctant to let her go. 'Come with me.'

'If you wish.'

Her smile lifted his heart. Caroline and Margaret were standing with their husbands by the door, and as he took Lucy past them Caroline put her hand on his arm.

'A pity you did not announce your betrothal to everyone after the play tonight, Brother. Meg and I were most disappointed.'

'I think Adversane had other things on his mind,' remarked Lord Wetherell.

'I cannot think what that might be,' she replied saucily, 'especially when the two of them have been smelling of April and May all evening. Why, when they were dancing they could not take their eyes off one another!'

With a laugh Ralph carried Lucy away. He sent a footman running for her shawl and draped it carefully about her shoulders before allowing her to stand by the open door to say goodbye as their guests filed out.

A rosy dawn was already lighting the eastern sky by the time the last guests took their leave. Lucy managed to stifle her yawn until the last carriage rolled away. Ralph put his arm around her.

'Tired, love?'

'A little,' she admitted.

'Too tired to walk with me? Ariadne and the family are waiting for us in the drawing room, but I want you to myself for a little while.'

'Oh, yes, and your brothers-in-law will have told them

everything by now! By all means let us stroll around the lawn. I would rather do that than answer their questions just yet.' She put her hand on his chest. 'But you must be exhausted. How *did* you manage to climb that cliff—and in the dark, too?'

He stopped and pulled her closer. 'It was easy, knowing you were waiting for me at the top.'

She closed her eyes as he kissed her, melting into him. When he stopped, she sighed and leaned her head against his chest. 'Oh, Ralph, it is quite horrible to think that Adam and Helene—'

'Then do not think of it. The Cottinghams will leave Adversane in the morning and it will be a very long time before they are allowed back again, I promise you.'

She raised her head, peering through the darkness to search his face. 'Are your ghosts laid to rest now?'

He nodded. 'Quite gone, my love.'

'Adam's revelations were very dreadful.'

'But not as bad as I feared.'

'Do you believe him, then? That it was an accident?'

Ralph nodded slowly. 'I do. I only wish he had confessed it all at the time.'

'Then we might never have met.'

'Oh, I think the Fates would have found a way.'

She smiled up at him

'Fates, my lord? I thought you only believed in reason and logic.'

With something like a growl, he pulled her closer.

'You have changed that, darling Lucy. Now I believe in love, too.'

* * * * *

LADY BENEATH
THE VEIL

To Sally, my best friend through good times and bad.

Chapter One

Those whom God has joined together let no one put asunder!'

The words boomed around the small church, echoing off the walls. The Honourable Gideon Albury grinned down at the heavily veiled figure at his side. Bless her, she was taking maidenly modesty to new heights!

Perhaps she thought it would inflame him, but she did that perfectly well without dressing as a nun. With her voluptuous body, golden curls and cornflower-blue eyes, she was a rare beauty. And that little trick she had of peeping up at him from under her lashes, those blue eyes promising the lush delights to come—his body hardened with anticipation. At last he would be able to enjoy those ample curves to the full!

Not that the little darling had flaunted her charms. She was, after all, a lady—the Earl of Martlesham's cousin, in fact. He would not else have contemplated marriage without his father's approval. Depraved as Lord Rotham might think him, he had not sunk so low that he would marry out of his sphere. But 'fore Gad, Gideon had never before seen such perfection in a gently bred young lady. She had allowed Gideon a glimpse of her pretty ankles, his hands had spanned that tiny waist and her plump, snow-white breast had been just crying out to be kissed. By heaven, just the thought of it made it difficult to concentrate on the marriage service. The register was produced. Gideon scrawled his own name carelessly and watched as his bride added her name to his. He guessed that damned veil was making it difficult for her to see because her hand shook a little as she held the pen. As a witness, Martlesham signed with a flourish and grinned.

'There—'tis done.'

'So it is.' Gideon smiled down at his new wife. 'I think we can dispense with this now.'

He reached for her veil, but she quickly put her gloved hand over his.

'Not yet,' she whispered.

He laughed.

'Be careful, my love, I shall begin to think I have married a little prude!'

He expected to hear her delicious, throaty laugh, but she was silent, merely putting her fingers on his arm as he escorted her to the door.

After the darkness of the stone building the spring sunshine was almost blinding when they stepped outside. He stopped and turned to her again.

'Now, Miss Propriety, let me kiss you… Good God!' He stepped back, his eyes widening with horror as he looked down into the face of a complete stranger.

Chapter Two

Dominique stood very still, staring up into the shocked face of her new husband. It was all there, everything she had expected: horror, revulsion, disgust. She had known how it must seem to him once the trick was revealed. He pushed his fingers through his auburn hair, disturbing the carefully arranged disorder, while behind them Max's cruel laugh rang out.

'Caught you there, Albury!'

'But I don't understand. Your cousin—'

'This *is* my cousin.'

Max chortled and Dominique's heart went out to the man standing before her. He looked stunned.

As well he might. Instead of the beautiful, voluptuous blonde he had courted for the past two months he was married to a diminutive brunette whom he had never seen before in his life.

'Is something amiss?' The vicar looked from one to the other before directing a vaguely worried look towards Max. 'Lord Martlesham?'

'No, no, nothing's wrong,' declared Max, still chuckling. 'The groom is struck dumb by the enormity of the occasion, that's all.' He began shepherding the guests away from the church. 'Come along, everyone, the carriages are waiting!'

'Just a moment!' The man beside her did not move, except to shake her hand from his arm. 'Where is Dominique?'

'Lord, Albury, have you not understood it yet? You have married her!' Max gave him a push. 'Come along, man, don't stand there gawping. Let us return to the Abbey.'

'Please.' Dominique forced her vocal cords to work. 'Come back to the Abbey and all this can be explained.'

Frowning, he grabbed her arm and set off for the gate with Dominique almost running to keep up with him. As was usual with weddings, the path was lined with well-wishers who showered them with rice as they hurried to the carriage. It was decorated with ribbons for the occasion, the Martlesham coat of arms displayed prominently on the door. Without ceremony her escort bundled Dominique into the carriage, climbed in after her and the door was slammed upon them. Max's grinning face appeared in the window.

'Now then, Gideon, try to contain your lust until after the wedding breakfast. The journey from here to the Abbey ain't long enough to tup a woman properly. I know, I've tried it!'

Dominique closed her eyes in mortification. The carriage began to move and the raucous laughter was left behind them.

'So, this was one of Max's little tricks.'

Dominique looked at Gideon. His voice was calm, but there was a dangerous glitter in his hazel eyes that made her think he might be about to commit murder. She swallowed.

'Yes.'

'And everyone at the Abbey was privy to the joke, except me.'

'You and…my mother.'

'Max told me she was too unwell to attend the ceremony.'

Dominique bowed her head.

'She does not know. *Maman* would never have agreed to such a scheme.'

'I take it the female I knew as Dominique was hired for the part?'

She nodded.

'An actress. Agnes Bennet.'

'And a damned good one. She fooled me into thinking she was a lady. Whereas you—' His lip curled. 'You may be Max's cousin, but no true lady would lend herself to this, this *joke*.'

His contempt flayed her. Given time, she could explain to him why she had agreed to Max's outrageous scheme, but they had already arrived at the Abbey. She waited in silence for the carriage to stop and a liveried footman to leap forwards and open the door. Her companion jumped out first and with exaggerated courtesy put out his hand to her.

'Well, madam, shall we go in to the wedding breakfast?'

Miserably, Dominique accompanied him into the house.

'Now, perhaps you will explain to me what the hell is going on.'

Gideon looked about him at the company assembled in the dining room. The servants had been dismissed and it was only the twenty or so guests who had comprised Lord Martlesham's house party for the past two months—with the exception of the blonde beauty, of course. The woman he had believed was Martlesham's cousin. She had been replaced by the poor little dab of a girl who was now his wife.

Everyone stood around, ignoring the festive elegance of the dining table, all gleaming silver and sparkling glass, set out in readiness for the wedding breakfast. His eyes raked the crowd, but no one would meet his gaze.

'It's a practical joke, old boy,' said Max, who was helping himself to a glass of brandy from the decanter on the sideboard.

'Not one that I appreciate!' Gideon retorted.

Max turned to him, still smiling.

'No? Strange, I thought you would, given what happened at Covent Garden last year.'

'Ah...' Gideon nodded slowly '...so that is it. You are paying me back for stealing the divine Diana from under your nose!'

The scene came back to him. He had been one of a dozen rowdy, drunken bucks crowding into the dressing rooms after the performance. Max was paying court to a pretty little opera dancer, but Gideon knew from her meaningful smiles and the invitation in her kohl-lined eyes that she would happily give herself to the highest bidder.

'Confound it, Albury, I had been working on that prime article for weeks, then just when I thought she was going to fall into my lap you offer her a *carte blanche*!'

Gideon felt his temper rising. There was a world of difference between competing for the favours of a light-skirt and trapping him into marriage!

'And because I bested you on that occasion you concocted this elaborate charade?'

'Why, yes, and I thought it rather neat, actually,' returned Max, sipping his brandy. 'I hired Agnes Bennet to play my cousin and you fell for her—quite besotted, in fact. All I had to do then was persuade you to propose. Of course, it helped that you were still smarting from the roasting your father gave you at Christmas and ripe for any mischief that would pay him back.'

Gideon could not deny it. He recalled that last, fraught meeting with his father. They had rowed royally. If he was honest, Gideon had already been a little tired of Max and his constant tricks and stratagems, but he did not like his father criticising his friends. He had lost his temper, declaring that he would do what he wanted with his life. He remembered storming out of the house, declaring, 'I will make friends with whom I like, do what I like, marry whom I like!'

How unwise he had been to relay the whole incident to Martlesham.

The earl continued, 'You knew that marrying any cousin of mine would anger your father. It helped, of course, that she was such a little beauty. A typical English rose.'

'Couldn't wait to get her into bed, eh?' cried one of Max's cronies, a buck-toothed fop called Williams.

Dear heaven, Gideon wondered why he had never noticed before just what a hideous smirk the fellow had! Max filled a second glass with brandy and handed it to him.

'Then, of course, you said you could never marry a Frenchie.'

'Well, what of that?' said Gideon, stiffening.

Max's smile grew.

'It so happens that my dear cousin here is most definitely French. Ain't that so, m'dear?'

The girl made no answer, save for a slight nod of the head. Gideon's eyes narrowed.

'Reynolds is an English name. And you told me Dominique was an old family tradition…'

'Now there I admit I misled you, my boy. The name *is* a family tradition, but it belongs to her French ancestors, not mine.' Max's hateful smile widened. 'My dear Gideon, you should have looked more closely at the register before you signed it. You would have seen then that her father's name was *Rainault*, not Reynolds. Jerome Rainault, a wine merchant from Montpellier. A full-blooded Frenchman, Albury, and a paid-up Girondin to boot.'

'What!'

Gideon was surprised out of the dispassionate hauteur he had assumed. Max's pale blue eyes gleamed with malicious triumph.

'Oh, yes,' he said softly. 'You swore that the French were all your enemies, did you not? It seemed poetic justice to marry you off to a Frenchwoman.'

More of Gideon's last, heated exchange with his father flashed into his head.

'Martlesham is a bad lot,' the viscount had said. 'You should choose your friends more carefully.'

He had been angered by his father's words, but now the truth of them stung him even more.

Williams guffawed loudly. 'What a good joke. You have been well and truly duped, Albury! You fell head over heels for Max's actress, didn't you? He made the switch this morning. He even had shoes made with a heel so that you didn't see that your new bride was shorter than the lovely Agnes.'

Williams pushed his silver-topped cane under the bridal skirts, but the girl whipped herself away from him, her cheeks aflame with embarrassment. The others sniggered and Gideon cursed silently. How had he ever found their childish humour amusing?

He said furiously, 'This goes beyond a joke, Martlesham. This time you are meddling with peoples' lives.'

Max shrugged.

'We all found it devilishly amusin', old fellow.' He held out the glass. 'Here. Admit we caught you fair and square. Then let us enjoy the wedding *déjeuner* and afterwards I'll summon the vicar and my lawyer from the village and we can arrange to have the marriage annulled. After all, there's witnesses enough to the fact that you have been tricked.'

Gideon took the brandy and sipped it. Everyone around him was grinning, save the bride. The heat had left her cheeks and she now stood beside him, pale and silent. This slight, dark figure could not be less like the bride he had been expecting. The enormity of his folly hit him. He had not consulted his father about the marriage—a petty revenge against his parent for daring to ring such a peal over him at that last meeting. He had not even notified his lawyer, knowing that Rogers would demand settlements should be drawn up. In his eagerness to secure his bride he had accepted Max's assurances that they could deal with all the usual formalities later. Now he knew why and a cold fury seized him.

He said slowly, 'Admit I was tricked and become a laughing stock? No, I don't think so.'

It gave him some satisfaction to see the smiles falter. Max frowned. His bride turned to stare at him. Gideon forced a smile to his lips.

'No,' he drawled. 'I have to marry sometime. Your cousin will do as well as anyone, Martlesham. The marriage stands.'

* * *

'No!'

Dominique gasped out the word. This was not the way it was meant to be. She looked imploringly to her cousin, but the earl's face was a mask.

'Come.' Gideon was holding his hand out to her. 'Let us sit down and enjoy our first meal as man and wife.'

His tone brooked no argument. Reluctantly she accompanied the stranger who was now her husband to the table. Only he was not a stranger to her. For the past two months she had watched him from the shadows as he laughed and danced and flirted with the woman chosen to impersonate her. How Dominique wished that she was more like the beautiful Agnes, with her deep, throaty laugh and bewitching smile. She had watched Gideon fall in love with the actress and realised that she would willingly exchange her dusky locks and green eyes for blonde curls and cornflower-blue eyes if Gideon would give her just one admiring glance. Max had not objected when he discovered Dominique had dressed herself as a servant so that she could watch the courtship. Indeed, he had enjoyed the added piquancy her masquerade gave to the proceedings and gradually she had found herself being drawn ever closer to Gideon Albury. He was different from the others, more thoughtful, and lacking the cruel humour that characterised so many of Max's friends. She had thought at first that his lean face was a little austere, but she had seen the way his smile warmed his eyes and she had learned to listen out for his voice, deep and rich as chocolate.

And she had fallen in love.

If someone had told her she would lose her heart to a man who didn't even know she existed she would have said it was impossible, but somehow, over the weeks of watching and listening she had come to believe there was more to this handsome young buck than his devil-may-care attitude. She had seen the brooding look that would steal into his countenance when he thought no one was attending and had caught the fleeting sadness that occasionally clouded his eyes. In her disguise it had been difficult to avoid the leering glances and wandering hands of Max's other guests, but Gideon had not ogled her, and if he noticed her at all it was with a careless kindness, a word of thanks when she presented him with his drink or a quiet rebuke when one of his friends tried to importune her.

He was a true gentleman, even if today there was only anger in his tone and a touch of steel in his hazel eyes when they rested on her. He despised her and, knowing the part she had played in this charade, she could not blame him. She knew how she would feel if someone played such a trick upon her, so why should she be disappointed that the bridegroom should now look at her with such contempt? She felt sick at heart, but it would do no good to repine. She had made a bargain with Max, and if he kept it then all this charade would have been worth it.

Dominique partook very little of the food served at her wedding breakfast and even less of the wine. On the surface Gideon appeared to be at his ease, smiling and joking with his companions, the perfect bridegroom. But when he called for a toast and turned to salute her his eyes were cold and hard, and a little frisson of fear shivered down her spine.

At last the meal was over, but not her torment. People

were getting up, congregating in little groups. Gideon tapped his glass and brought a hush to the assembly.

'Carstairs, I cannot tell you how grateful I am to you for putting Elmwood Lodge at our disposal.' He rose and put his hands on the back of Dominique's chair. 'Now, *wife*, it is time you changed into your travelling dress and we will be away.'

She cast another startled glance at Max, who merely shrugged. Silently she rose, but as she passed her cousin she hesitated. Surely he would intervene now. She said quietly, 'The joke is played, my lord. I have done my part, pray you, call an end to it.'

To her dismay Max merely took her hand and raised it to his lips.

'Let me be the first to congratulate you, *Mrs Albury*.'

She gripped his hand, angered and frightened by his mocking smile.

'And my mother? You promised.'

Those haughty eyebrows lifted a fraction higher.

'I gave you my word, did I not?' He leaned a little closer and murmured, 'Go along, my dear, do not keep your husband waiting.'

Her lip curled and she wanted to retort, but Gideon was approaching, so she whisked herself out of the room.

Dominique went up to her bedchamber, seething with anger and not only for Max. She had lent herself to this and could hardly complain now if things did not go as she had expected. It had seemed so simple when the earl had explained it to her: the trick would be played and upon discovery the lawyers would be summoned, the sham marriage annulled and everything would be put right. Only Gideon was not playing by the same rules as her cousin. He wanted to continue the farce a little longer, to save face, to turn the joke on to her cousin and probably to punish her for her impudence in duping him. She glanced in the mirror, her spirits falling even further. It was inconceivable that he would really want to keep her as his wife, but for now she had no choice but to prepare to drive away with him.

The only gown she had with her was the olive-green walking dress she had arrived in. It was not new, but the colour suited her, and with its mannish cut and the gold frogging it looked well enough for an earl's cousin. The embroidered lace veil would fill in the low neckline and keep the cold March wind at bay. She squared her shoulders. If Gideon Albury wanted to continue with this charade it would have to do.

To her consternation everyone was gathered in the hall, waiting for her. They all seemed determined to pretend that this was any normal going-away ceremony. Max ran up the final few stairs and gave her his arm as though he was about to give her away all over again.

'I have had the maids fill a trunk for you,' he murmured. 'Can't have you going off without a rag to your back.'

He led her up to Gideon, who stood rigid and implacable. Dominique glanced once at his face—it could have been chiselled from stone, so cold and impassive did he look. Concealing a shudder, she dropped her eyes to his exquisitely embroidered waistcoat. Perhaps he had ordered it especially for the wedding, to impress his bride. She felt even more ashamed of allowing herself to be a part of Max's cruel scheme.

With much cheering they were escorted to the waiting travelling carriage, where her trunk was being strapped on the roof. She felt a light touch on her shoulder as the carriage pulled away.

'Well, madam, are you not going to smile for your guests?'

She shrugged off his hand.

'How far do you intend to carry this joke, sir?'

'Joke?' His voice was icy. 'I do not know what you mean, madam. It was Martlesham who played the joke.'

'And you have repaid him. He was quite shocked when you said the marriage would stand.'

'Yes, his reaction was delightfully amusing.'

'You have had your fun, sir,' she said coolly. 'Now I pray you will abandon this charade.'

'Oh, it is no charade, madam. I am in deadly earnest.'

She stared at him, a cold hand clutching at her heart when she saw his implacable look.

'But—but you never meant to marry me. You cannot *want* me for your bride.'

'Why not? As I told Max, I have to marry sometime, and you are as good as any other wife.' His eyes swept over her, as if stripping her naked and she felt a hot blush spreading up through her body. She realised for the first time how fully she had put herself in this man's power. She summoned up every ounce of indignation to respond.

'That is outrageous!'

'Outrageous or not, madam, you should have considered every possibility before you gave yourself to this plan. You married me, for better or worse. There is no way back.'

Unsettled by the look of horror on his companion's face, Gideon closed his eyes and feigned sleep. He was still furious at being duped into marriage, but he had some sympathy with his bride. Knowing Max, he suspected that pressure had been put on the chit to comply. But she could have declared herself in church, if she had really objected to the whole thing. No, he would punish her just a little more.

He wondered what they would find when they eventually reached Elmwood Lodge. Carstairs had almost choked on his wine when Gideon had reminded him that he had offered it—obviously no one had expected the marriage to go beyond the wedding ceremony, so no arrangements had been made. While everyone had waited for the bride to change her gown a rider had been despatched to Elmwood on a fast horse to notify the servants that a bride and groom were on their way.

How soon after they arrived he would call a halt to this masquerade Gideon had not yet decided.

When the carriage turned into the gates of Elmwood Lodge sometime later it was immediately apparent that the news of their arrival had been received with enthusiasm. The open gates were decorated with ribbons and as they bowled up to the entrance an elderly couple appeared, the man hurriedly buttoning his livery. Gideon recognised Chiswick, the butler and man of all work, and the woman following him in her snowy apron and cap was his wife and housekeeper of the lodge.

'Oh, lord,' Gideon muttered as the door was wrenched open. 'We are properly for it now.'

'Welcome, sir, madam! We are delighted you have come to Elmwood Lodge.' Mrs Chiswick almost hustled her husband out of the way as she greeted them with an effusion of smiles. 'If you would care to come into the parlour, you will find cakes and wine set out there, and a roaring fire. If we'd had more notice then the rest of the rooms would be ready for you, too, but they may take a while yet, although I have sent for Alice from the village to come and help me.'

Gideon jumped down and turned back to help his bride to alight. She did so silently, looking pale and dazed. He pulled her hand on to his sleeve and followed the still-chattering housekeeper into the house. The large, panelled hall had been hastily decorated with boughs of evergreens and spring flowers. Gideon's heart sank: the couple were clearly overjoyed to be entertaining a pair of newlyweds. He felt the fingers on his arm tremble and absently put his hand up to give them a reassuring squeeze.

More early spring flowers adorned the wainscotted parlour where a cheerful fire burned in the hearth and refreshments were set out on the table. Gideon waited until his garrulous hostess paused for breath, then said firmly, 'Thank you, Mrs Chiswick. We will serve ourselves.'

'Very well, sir. And…' She turned to look out of the window. 'Do your servants follow you?'

'No, we are quite alone.'

'Ah, of course.'

Her understanding smile brought a flush to Gideon's cheek and he dared not look at his companion to see the effect upon her, but as soon as they were alone he said, 'I beg your pardon. When Max told me your servant was remaining at Martlesham to look after your mother I thought it best to leave my man behind, too. Now I see that it has given rise to the very worst sort of speculation.'

'Very natural speculation, given the circumstances.'

Her calm response relieved his mind of one worry: she was not going to fall into hysterics. Yet he should not have been surprised. She could have no proper feeling to have lent herself to this madness in the first place.

He retorted coldly, 'These *circumstances*, as you describe them, are very much your own fault.'

'I am well aware of that.'

She took off her hat and gloves and untied the strings of her cloak. When he put his hands on her shoulders to take it from her she tensed, but did not shrug him off. He was standing so close behind her that he could smell her perfume, a subtle hint of lily of the valley that made him want to drop his head closer still, perhaps even to bend and place a kiss upon the slender white neck exposed to his view.

Shocked at his reaction, he drew back. This woman was nothing to him—how could he even contemplate making love to her? But the idea lingered and it disturbed him.

Gideon threw her cloak over a chair with his own greatcoat, placing his hat and gloves next to hers on the small side table. His temper was cooling and he was all too aware of their predicament. Perhaps it was not too late to remedy that. He dashed out of the room. He found the butler crossing the hallway and called to him as he ran to the main door.

'Has the coach gone? Quickly, man!'

'Y-yes, sir! As soon as you was set down. We took off the baggage and they was away, wanting to get somewhere near home before nightfall, there being no moon tonight.'

Gideon yanked open the door and looked out at the empty drive.

'But that was only minutes ago. We must fetch it back. There must be a horse in the stables you can send after it.'

Startled, the butler shook his head.

'I'm afraid not, sir. There's only Bessie, the cob, but she pulls the carts and has never worn a saddle in her life. I suppose old Adam could harness her up to the gig...'

Staring into the gathering darkness, Gideon realised it would be impossible for them to call back the carriage now.

'How far is it to the nearest town, or even the nearest inn?'

The butler looked at him with astonishment and Gideon thought grimly how it must look, the bridegroom wanting to run away before his wedding night! However, the truth would be even more unpalatable, so he remained silent while the man pondered his question.

'There ain't an inn, sir,' he said at last. 'Not one as would suit you, at any rate. And it's all of seven miles to Swaffham, but you wouldn't be wanting to set out tonight, not without a moon.'

'No, of course not.' With a shake of his head Gideon stepped back from the entrance, leaving Chiswick to close the door while he made his way back to the parlour. He could hardly complain. After all, he himself had hired the post-chaise and his instructions had been quite clear: it would not be required again for two weeks. He had fully intended to enjoy his honeymoon with his bewitching bride. Now he was stranded in the middle of nowhere with a young woman he had never met before today. And a respectable young woman at that, despite her part in this charade. Damn Max and his practical jokes!

Chapter Three

Gideon returned to find the lady in question pacing up and down the parlour. He said as calmly as he could, 'It seems we are stuck here, at least until the morning.'

'Was that not your intention?'

Her glance scorched him and he frowned.

'No, I had not thought it out. I was angry.'

'And now?'

'Now I realise that it would have been better if we had remained at the Abbey.' He paused. 'We are in the devil of a coil.'

She sighed. 'I know.'

His eyes fell on the table.

'Shall we sit down?' He held a chair for her, thinking that they were like two cats, warily circling each other. When they were both seated he filled two glasses and pushed one towards her. 'Why did you agree to Max's outlandish scheme? You do not look like the sort to indulge in practical jokes of your own accord.'.

'No.' She put a small cake on to her plate and broke it into little pieces.

'Did he offer you money?'

'Something of that sort.'

'But you are his cousin.'

'An impoverished cousin. My mother brought me to England ten years ago, seeking refuge with her brother, the earl—Max's father. When Max inherited Martlesham he also inherited us. We have been living off charity ever since. A few months ago Max set us up in a cottage in Martlesham village.' Her fingers played with the crumbs on her plate. 'He promised... If I agreed to take part in his scheme, he would sign the property over to my mother and give her a pension for the rest of her life.'

'And for this you would marry a stranger.'

Her head came up at that. She said angrily, 'Do you know what it is like to be someone's pensioner? To know that everything you have, every penny you spend, comes from someone else?'

'As a matter of fact I do, since I am a younger son. For many years I was dependent upon an allowance from my father.'

Their eyes clashed for a moment, then her glance slid away and she continued quietly, 'Max promised it would only mean going through the ceremony. He said that once the trick was uncovered the marriage would be annulled.'

'The devil he did!' Gideon pushed back his chair and went to the window. The darkness outside showed only his scowling reflection. 'The servants must have known what was going on—that the woman I thought was Martlesham's cousin was an impostor.'

'Yes. Max threatened instant dismissal to anyone who did not go along with his deception.'

He turned back to face her.

'And your mother? Will Max explain everything to her?'

'I doubt it.' She bit her lip. 'Max tends to think only of those things that affect him.'

'But won't she worry about you?'

She looked down at her hands clasped in her lap.

'I wrote a note for her, telling her that I would be remaining at the Abbey for a few days.'

'And she will be content with that?'

Her head dipped even lower.

'*Maman* has her own concerns and will think nothing amiss.'

Gideon finished his wine and poured himself another glass. Dominique—he almost winced. He must get used to calling her that. The girl had hardly touched her wine and the cake lay crumbled on her plate. A tiny spark of sympathy touched him.

'Do not despair,' he told her. 'In the morning we will return to Martlesham and I will arrange for an annulment.'

'And until then?'

Her gaze was sceptical.

'We are not alone here. Mrs Chiswick is a respectable woman and, when we tell her there has been a mistake she will look after you until we can get you back to Martlesham.' He tried a reassuring smile. 'I think she can be relied upon to protect your honour.'

Dominique forced herself to meet his eyes, wondering at the change in tone. It was the first time Gideon Albury had done anything other than glower at her. Oh, he had smiled in the church, but then he had thought her someone else. Now he was smiling at *her*, plain little Dominique Rainault, and her heart began to thud with a breathless irregularity. Often in the preceding weeks she had dreamed of such a moment, but had never expected it, not after the scene outside the church that morning.

The revulsion she had seen in his face had quite chilled her and since then he had regarded her with nothing but repugnance. She was not prepared for the sudden charm, or the way it made her want to smile right back at him. Common sense urged her to be cautious. Despite the attraction she felt for him he was, after all, one of Max's cronies, one of that crowd of irresponsible young bucks who were more than happy to play cruel jokes upon one another. Just because he was the victim of this particular jape did not mean she could trust him.

There was a light scratching on the door, and the housekeeper peeped in.

'Beggin' your pardon sir, madam, but I was wondering if you would be wishing to change before dinner? The bedchamber's not prepared yet, but your trunks have been taken up to the dressing room and there is a good fire burning in there...'

Gideon shook his head.

'I will not change, but perhaps Mrs Albury would like to make use of it?'

'Yes, thank you, I would like to wash my face and hands.' Dominique made for the door, thankful for the opportunity to gather her thoughts. Unfortunately, the housekeeper was eager to talk as she escorted her up the stairs.

'I haven't had a chance to make up the bed, ma'am, for Alice hasn't come yet so I've only got Hannah, the scullery maid, to help me and I can't trust her to look after the kitchen, but I shall get around to that just as soon as I have finished cooking dinner. If only we'd had more notice, we would have been able to give you a welcome more suited to a new bride, but there, Mr

Carstairs has never been one to give us much warning.' The woman gave a wheezy laugh as she opened the door to the dressing room. 'I've no doubt he'll descend upon us one day with a bride of his own, and never a bit o' notice of that, either!'

Dominique knew this was her opportunity.

'Mrs Chiswick, could you have another bed made up for me, if you please, in a separate chamber?'

The housekeeper gave a fat chuckle as she went around the room lighting the candles.

'Lord bless you, dearie, you won't be needing that tonight.'

'But I shall. You see, this is all a mistake, I never intended—'

Dominique found her hands caught in a warm clasp.

'Now, now, my love, you ain't the first young bride to have last-minute nerves. Do you not know what to expect on your wedding night?'

'Well, yes, but that's not it...'

'Now don't you be worrying yourself, my dear, I've been with Mr Chiswick for nigh on thirty years and I can tell you that you have nought to worry about, especially with a kind young man like Mr Albury. He's always been a favourite here at Elmfield, more so than many of Mr Carstairs's friends, I can tell you. But there, it's not for me to criticise the master. Anyway I'm sure Mr Albury will take very good care of you. You just go and enjoy your dinner, and I've no doubt that once you and your man are tucked up warm and cosy in the bedroom next door you will enjoy yourself there, too!'

Dominique looked into that kindly, smiling face and knew she would have to tell the housekeeper that she and Mr Albury were not really man and wife and must have separate rooms. She took a deep breath.

'Thank you.'

The explanation withered before it even reached her tongue. The idea of confessing the truth—and her own collusion in the deception—even to this kind-hearted soul, was beyond her. She shrivelled at the very thought of it and allowed the housekeeper to withdraw without uttering another word.

Dominique berated herself soundly. She should have insisted Mrs Chiswick make up another bed for her and put a second bed in the room for herself. She removed the lace fichu and poured water into the basin to wash her face. Did she really expect Gideon Albury to keep away from her if she did not take such measures? She might think him charming, but what did she really know of him? Should one not judge a man by his company? He was friends with her cousin and Max was a cruel bully.

The heavy gold band on her finger touched her cheek, reminding her of her perilous situation. She was married. The register had been signed and she now belonged to the man sitting downstairs in that snug little parlour. The law of the land was quite specific: she was his property, to do with as he wished. A shiver ran through her.

The distant chiming of a clock caught her attention. She had dallied as long as she dared, but she could not remain in the dressing room forever. Picking up the bedroom candle, she snuffed the other lights and made her way out through the adjoining bedchamber. The large canopied bed loomed dark and menacing in the centre of the room, the hangings casting ominous shadows over the bare mattress. Dominique averted her gaze, looking instead around the room. A large linen press stood against one wall next to a bow-fronted chest of drawers, while under the window was a pretty little writing desk, still adorned with its accessories. As she passed the light glinted on the silver inkstand with its cut-glass inkwell, silver nib box and a fine ivory-handled letter opener.

Dominique stopped and set down the candlestick. She picked up the letter opener and slid it into her sleeve. The ivory handle pressed against the soft skin on the inside of her wrist, but the buttoned cuff disguised its slight bulge. She dropped her arm. The letter opener did not move, her tight-fitting sleeve holding it fast. Satisfied, she picked up her candle and continued on her way downstairs.

Gideon was waiting for her in the parlour, a fresh bottle of wine open on the table. He had loosened his neckcloth and was lounging in a chair by the table, one booted ankle resting on the other, but she thought he looked incredibly handsome, the candlelight accentuating the smooth planes of his face. Her eyes were drawn to the sensual curve of his lips and Dominique found herself wondering what he would taste like. The thought shocked her so much that she stopped just inside the door.

Perhaps he thought she was offended by his negligent attitude, for he rose to his feet and pulled out a chair for her. Silently she sank down on to it, aware of his hands on the chair back, his presence towering over her. She took a deep breath to steady herself, but instead found her senses filled with the sharp tang of soap and a musky scent. She had a strong desire to lean back against his fingers, to turn her head and press a kiss against them, inviting him to—

No! Good heavens, where did such wicked thoughts

come from? She sank her teeth into her lip, forcing herself to sit still.

'Well…' he refilled her glass and held it out to her '…did you explain our situation to Mrs Chiswick?'

'No.' His surprised stare would have made Dominique flush, if her cheeks had not already been burning with her own wayward thoughts. 'I thought perhaps you should do so.'

'Me?'

'Yes.' She took the glass, resisting the urge to slide her fingers over his. 'I thought if I broached the subject she might think you had coerced me into this marriage.'

'Instead of you tricking *me.*'

'I did not!' she retorted hotly. 'I was as much a victim as you. Well, almost.'

His lips tightened.

'Let us agree to blame Max for this sorry mess, shall we? He knew that someone with French blood would be the worst possible match for me.'

'Of course.' She recalled his reaction when Max had explained her parentage. 'Will you tell me why that should be?'

'Because—' He broke off as they were interrupted again, saying impatiently, 'Yes, Chiswick, what is it now?'

'Dinner is ready now, sir, if you is amenable.'

'Very well, we will be over directly.' As the butler withdrew he turned back to Dominique, 'We will continue this discussion later.'

He spoke harshly, but she detected a note of relief in his tone. Silently she rose and took his proffered arm as they crossed the hall to the dining room. Beneath her fingers she could feel his strength through the sleeve. He was tense, his anger barely contained. This courtesy was a veneer, a sham, and she felt as if she were walking beside a wild animal—one wrong word and he would pounce on her.

Chiswick served them, passing on his wife's apologies for the lack of dishes upon the table. Dominique was quick to reassure him that there was more than sufficient. Indeed, by the time she had tried the white soup, followed by the neck of mutton with turnips and carrots, a little of the carp and the macaroni pie she had no room for the fricassee of chicken or any of the small sweet tarts and the plum pudding that followed. Mrs Chiswick proved to be a good cook and the wines her husband provided to accompany the dishes were excellent. Dominique drank several glasses, partly to calm her nerves. She had never before dined alone with any man and she was all too conscious of the taciturn gentleman sitting at the far end of the table. She shivered, regretting that she had left her lace fichu in the dressing room. Not that she was really cold, just…nervous.

Conversation had been necessarily stilted and she was relieved when the meal was over and she could return to the parlour. She hesitated when Gideon followed her out of the room.

'Are you not remaining to drink your port, sir?'

'Chiswick shall bring me some brandy in the parlour. I do not like to drink alone.'

'I admit I have always thought it an odd custom, to remain in solitary state when there are no guests in the house. My cousin insists upon it at the Abbey, although he is rarely there without company.'

Dominique babbled on as Gideon escorted her back across the dark and echoing hall, but she could not help herself. It was nerves, she knew, but there was something else, an undercurrent of excitement at being alone with Gideon. It was a situation she had thought about—dreamed of—for weeks, only in her dreams he had been in her company out of choice, not necessity. She continued to chatter until they were both seated in the parlour. Chiswick deposited a little dish of sweetmeats at her elbow and placed a tray bearing decanters and glasses on the sideboard.

'Shall I send in the tea tray in an hour, madam?'

'No, let Mrs Chiswick bring it in now,' Gideon answered for her. He added, once they were alone, 'You can tell her when she comes in that you will require another bed to be made up.'

'Will not you—?'

He shook his head

'The running of a household is a woman's business, madam. 'Tis for you to order the staff.'

He got up to pour himself a glass of brandy while Dominique stared miserably into the fire. No matter how embarrassing, she must do this. The alternative was too dreadful to contemplate.

Gideon was still standing by the sideboard moments later when Mrs Chiswick bustled in.

'The tea tray, madam, as you requested. You must be very tired from your journey, ma'am, and you won't be wanting to prolong your evening.'

'Actually, Mrs Chiswick, I—'

'Alice and I are going upstairs to make the bed now. I've taken the liberty of heating a couple of bricks for the bed, too, seeing as how it hasn't been used for a while, but I don't suppose you will be wanting me or Chiswick to remove them, now will you?' The housekeeper gave a conspiratorial smile that made Dominique's face burn, which only made Mrs Chiswick smile more broadly. 'Bless you, my dear, no need to colour up so. You are on your honeymoon, after all! Now, the bed-chamber should be all ready for you in two shakes of a lamb's tail. Chiswick will leave your bedroom candles in the hall for you and we'll say goodnight now, so we don't bother you again. And we won't disturb you in the morning, either, 'til you ring for us. I doubt you'll be wanting to be up with the lark.'

With another knowing smile and a broad wink the housekeeper departed, leaving Dominique to stare at the closed door.

A strained silence enveloped them.

'By heaven, what a gabster,' remarked Gideon at last. 'Difficult to get a word in, I admit.' He sat down beside her on the sofa. 'I suppose I can always sleep here.' She turned to look at him, surprised. His lips twitched. 'We were neither of us brave enough to stem the flow, were we?'

Dominique's hands flew to her mouth, but could not stifle a nervous giggle. Gideon began to laugh, too, and soon they were both convulsed in mirth. It was several minutes before either of them could speak again.

'It is very like a farce one would see in Drury Lane,' Dominique hiccupped, searching for a handkerchief to mop her streaming eyes.

Gideon pulled out his own and, cupping her chin in one hand, turned her face towards him and gently wiped her cheeks.

'But if such a story was presented, one would say it was too far-fetched and could never happen.'

He was still grinning, but Dominique's urge to laugh died away. Carefully she disengaged herself.

'But it has happened.' His touch on her face had

been as gentle as a kiss and yet the skin still tingled. He was leaning back now against the sofa, relaxed and smiling. She thought again how handsome he was, with those finely chiselled features, the thick, auburn hair gleaming in the candlelight. If they had met in other circumstances... She stopped the thought immediately. He hated the French and there could be no denying her parentage, nor did she want to do so. She was proud of her father.

Gideon was on his feet, going back to the sideboard.

'You shouldn't be maudling your insides with tea. Let me get you some port.'

She looked towards the tea tray. He was right, she did not feel up to the careful ritual of making tea this evening. She was so nervous she feared she would drop one of the beautiful porcelain cups. When he held out a glass of dark, ruby-red liquid she accepted it with a murmur of thanks, holding it carefully between her hands. Perhaps it would put some spirit into her. She took a large gulp, swallowing half the contents in one go but thankfully Gideon did not see it, for he was busy pouring himself more brandy.

'We are in a pickle, my dear.' He sat down beside her again. 'I lost my temper and I apologise for it. If we had remained at Martlesham everything would have been so much simpler.'

'You were very angry, I understand that, and I beg your pardon for my part in it.'

The corners of his mouth lifted a little. He said ruefully, 'It is the red hair. When the angry mist descends I am not responsible for my actions.'

A smile of understanding tugged at her own mouth.

'My hair is not red, but I have a temper, too, at times.'

'Your Latin temperament, perhaps.'
'Yes.'

There was a shy smile in her green eyes, and Gideon was pleased to note the anxious frown no longer creased her brow. She looked so much better when her countenance was not strained and pinched with worry. A soft blush was mantling her cheek as she went to the sideboard to put down her empty glass. Gideon noted the way the walking dress clung to her figure, accentuating the slender waist, the sway of her hips. As she returned he could appreciate the curve and swell of her breasts rising from the bodice of her gown. She was no ripe beauty, but he would wager that beneath that mannish outfit was a rather delectable body. He remembered standing behind her earlier, breathing in her fragrance and felt a flicker of interest—of desire—stir his blood.

As if aware of his thoughts she chose to sit in the armchair beside the fire. Gideon cleared his throat.

'I believe there is a gig in the stables. When it is light I shall drive you to Swaffham, and from there we will hire a post-chaise to take us back to Martlesham.'

'Not the Abbey,' she said quickly. 'Will you please set me down in the village, at my mother's cottage?'

He shrugged. 'If you wish.' A sudden thud on the ceiling made them both look up. 'But first we have to get through this evening.'

The port had had its effect. Dominique knew now what she must do.

'I shall remain down here,' she announced, sitting very straight and upright in her chair. 'You may have the bedroom.'

'Nonsense. I have already said I shall sleep on the sofa.'

She put up her chin. 'I have made up my mind.'

'Then unmake it.'

His autocratic tone only strengthened her resolve.

'I will not.'

'I am not so unchivalrous as to condemn you to such discomfort.'

'I shall be perfectly comfortable. Besides, there are bolts on the parlour door, while the bedchamber boasted not even the flimsiest lock.'

Gideon sat up, frowning.

'Are you saying you do not trust me?'

'Yes, I am.'

He jumped up.

'Damn it all, when have I given you occasion to doubt me?'

Her brows went up.

'When you insisted we come here.'

The truth of her statement caught him on the raw and he swung away, striding over to the window.

'Do not be so damned obstinate, woman! I have said I will sleep on the sofa and I shall.'

His words appeared to have no effect.

'Impossible. It is far too short for you. Why, you must be six foot at least.'

'Six foot two,' he said absently. 'But that is not the point.'

'It is very much the point.' He heard the quiet rustle of skirts. 'You see, it is the perfect length for me.'

When he looked around she had stretched herself out on the sofa. Her gown fell in soft folds around her, accentuating the contours of her body, the swell of her breast and curve of her hip that only served to empha-sise the tiny waist. And how had he failed to notice the length of her legs? She stretched luxuriously and he had a glimpse of dainty ankles peeping from beneath the hem of her skirts. In any other situation he would have found the view enchanting, but—hell and confound it, she was mocking him!

'The bedroom has been prepared, madam and you *will* sleep in it.'

'And I tell you I shall not.'

He almost ground his teeth in frustration.

'I admit it was a mistake to come here.' He spoke carefully, reining in his anger. 'I was at fault, but you will agree the provocation was great.'

'Of course.'

'However, when all is said and done, I am a gentleman. I will not have it said that I enjoyed the comfort of a feather bed while you spent the night on a sofa!'

Dominique felt an unexpected frisson of excitement at his rough tone. He was rattled and clearly no longer in control of the situation. An exulting feeling of power swept through her. She put her hands behind her head and gazed up at him defiantly.

'But I am already in possession, so I do not see that you can do anything about it. I suggest you admit yourself beaten and retire in good order.'

She closed her eyes and forced herself to keep very still, feigning indifference. He would see she was not to be moved and would go away and leave her in peace. She expected to hear a hasty footstep and the door snapping closed behind him. Instead she heard something between a snarl and a growl and the next moment she was being hoisted none too gently off the sofa. Her eyes flew open and she gave a little scream as she experienced the novel sensation of being helpless in a man's arms. But not just any man, and along with her natural indignation she was aware of the urgent desire curling through her body. It frightened her, but she would fight it. She would show him she was no milk-and-water maid, to be treated so abominably.

'You said you were a gentleman,' she protested, struggling against his hold. In response his grip tightened, one arm pressing her against his chest while the other supported her knees, so that her frustrated kicks met nothing but air.

'I am, but you have tried my patience too far!'

'Put me down this instant!'

She tried to free her arms, but at that very moment he loosened his grip around her shoulders. Instinctively her hands went around his neck to save herself from falling. He looked down at her, a wicked glint in his hazel eyes.

'I thought you wanted me to let go?'

She was feeling extremely breathless and her heart was thudding so painfully against her ribs that he must feel it, since she was pressed against his hard chest, but she replied with as much dignity as she could muster.

'I do *not* wish to be dropped on my head.'

With a little grunt of satisfaction he settled her more comfortably before him. Her arms were still around his neck and she could not for the life of her release him. Dominique told herself this was solely for the purpose of supporting herself, should he drop her, but she could not deny the sensual pleasure of feeling the silk of his hair, where it curled between her fingers and the back of his collar. Shocked by the idea that part of her was enjoying Gideon's masterful behaviour, she gave a half-hearted kick. His arms tightened and her breathing became even more constricted.

'You are suffocating me,' she protested.

'Keep still, then.'

He crossed the room in three strides and somehow managed to open the door.

'Put me down!' she hissed at him as they crossed the empty hall. 'I can walk perfectly well.'

'And give you the opportunity to run straight back into the parlour? I think not.'

Silenced, Dominique marvelled at his strength as he took the stairs two at a time. He held her firmly with his arm around her back and his hand clasped about her ribs and she was achingly aware of how close his fingers were to her breast. She was filled with outrage—at herself, for her wanton feelings, but even more so at Gideon for his cavalier behaviour. How dare he manhandle her in this way!

As they reached the landing Chiswick appeared in the corridor. He stopped, his eyes almost popping out of his head.

'Don't just stand there gawping, man,' barked Gideon. 'Open the door for me!'

Speechless with anger and shock, Dominique watched the servant throw open the door to the bedchamber. The golden light of the fire and several candles greeted them. Gideon sailed through with his burden and the butler reached in to close the door behind them. As it clicked shut there was the unmistakable sound of a throaty chuckle. It was all that was needed to fan the spark of her anger into full flame. She began to kick and struggle violently.

'How dare you treat me like this!'

'If you behave like a fishwife, then I will treat you as one.'

'Fishwife! I merely asked you to leave me alone.'

With an oath he set her on her feet, but kept hold of her wrists.

'By Gad, woman, you are beyond reason! Do you not *want* to sleep in a comfortable bed tonight?'

'No! I was quite happy to sleep downstairs.'

'Well I was not! Damnation, madam, you are here now and here you will stay, whether you like it or not.'

'Oh, and who is going to make me?'

'I am, even if it means I have to stand guard outside your door all night.'

'Much good that will do you, since there is a door from the dressing room on to the landing.'

'Then I had best stay here where I can see you.'

He released her, but there was a challenging look in his eye. Dominique knew that if she made a bolt for the dressing-room door he would catch her. She threw up her head.

'I demand you let me go back downstairs.'

'Ho, demand, do you? What about those wifely vows you took, to honour and obey?'

'Worthless. Now will you let me go?'

'Never.'

He towered over her, sparking a tiny frisson of unease as she realised she was now in the very situation she had been trying to avoid. However, her temper was up and she was not daunted by his superior height and strength.

'I refuse to sleep in that bed.'

'That may be so, but you are not leaving this room again tonight.'

She took a step back, glaring up at him as she folded her arms across her chest. As she did so she felt the solid line of the letter opener against her left forearm. She pulled it out with a triumphant flourish.

'What the devil are you going to do with that?'

'Stab you with it, if you don't get out of my way.'

* * *

Gideon stared at her.

'Good God, madam, anyone would think I intended to ravish you, instead of offering you the most comfortable bed in the house.'

He wished he hadn't used the word *ravish*, it brought all sorts of unhelpful connotations to his mind as she stood before him, breasts heaving and eyes flashing fire. Her hair had come loose in the struggle and now fell in a dusky cloud to her shoulders. The desire he had felt earlier stirred again, only stronger. He reminded himself he was a gentleman and should retire now, before it was too late. But she was still defying him, brandishing the letter opener like a sword, and that was a challenge he could not resist.

'Step aside,' she ordered him. 'Let me return to the parlour.'

'The devil I will.'

'I—I will stab you if you get in my way.'

He threw his arms wide.

'Stab away.'

His taunt brought a blaze of anger to her eyes again and with a shriek she launched herself at him. He grabbed her wrist. The letter opener was not that sharp and he doubted it would do much damage, but she seemed intent upon attacking him and he was damned if he was going to allow that. She was surprisingly strong. He twisted her wrist and she dropped the weapon, but immediately she sank her teeth into his hand.

'Ouch! You little termagant!' He wrestled her backwards on to the bed, pinning her wrists above her head. '*Will* you stop fighting like a wildcat?'

She continued to struggle and he was obliged to use

the weight of his body to hold her down and prevent her flailing legs from kicking him.

'Let me go!'

'Not if you are going to scratch my eyes out. *Stop it!*' She ceased struggling and glared up at him, the gold braid on her bodice glinting with the rise and fall of her breast. 'That's better.'

He, too, was breathing heavily, but he recognised it was not just exertion. The feel of her body beneath him was exciting him almost beyond reason. He smiled and earned for his troubles a smouldering look that sent the blood pounding faster through his body. He was lying between her legs, crushing her skirts against the bed, and for one searing moment he imagined what it would be like if her thighs were pressed against his, skin on skin rather than separated by numerous layers of cloth.

'That reminds me.' His voice seemed very distant and slightly unsteady. 'I have not yet kissed the bride.'

He told himself he was teasing her, punishing her just a little more. She watched him from those huge eyes. Large and dark, unfathomable pools, dragging him down. His gaze moved to her mouth.

Better stop this now, before it gets out of hand.

Too late. The pink tip of her tongue flickered nervously across her lips and he could not resist lowering his head to capture her mouth. It was a swift, hard kiss and she trembled beneath him. Immediately he drew back.

Dominique took a quick, shuddering breath. That was the last straw. Her blood was up, she had been aware of a sharp exultation when she had flown at him with the paperknife in her hand and her heart was still pounding from the ensuing tussle. He had overpowered her, of course, but she was not beaten. She told herself she would never give in, even with his body pressing down upon hers she felt herself stronger, not weaker, as sensations she could not explain took control of her body. She felt alive, buzzing with energy, ready to fight him again. Then he had closed the distance between them, his mouth finding her parted lips and taking possession. Her body responded with a shudder of desire that shocked and startled her. A longing, a need she could not control was unleashed—she wanted him as she had never wanted anyone, or anything, before.

It was a shock to realise she would sell her soul to the devil for one night with Gideon Albury, and what did it matter? Her reputation was ruined, whatever happened, so why should she not have one glorious night to remember? He was easing himself away. In another moment he would be lost to her forever.

'I beg your pardon,' he muttered, releasing her hands. 'I should not—'

Gideon broke off in surprise as she reached up and clutched at his neckcloth. She pulled him close and began to kiss him, a little inexpertly, but with such eagerness that desire lanced through him. He was lost. It was as if someone had opened the floodgates and a torrent of passion poured forth, carrying all before it.

Clothes were hurriedly discarded, buttons torn off in their haste to disrobe and all the while they strove to continue those heady, desperate kisses that kept all coherent thought at bay. Gideon lifted her easily on to the cool silk covers of the bed and measured his naked length against her. She clung to him, eager for his touch, returning his embraces with a fervour that more than matched his own. She cried out as he entered her, but when he hesitated she pulled him to her, claiming his mouth, tangling her tongue with his and leaving him in no doubt that she wanted to continue the hot, passionate coupling that carried them on to a heady, exhilarating climax and left them both panting and exhausted.

Dominique woke up when the fire was dying down and the night air cooling her skin. She lifted one hand to her head, trying to make sense of where she was and what had happened. She remembered dining with Gideon, then arguing with him and finally, when he had laid hands on her—understandably, since she was trying to stab him—she had wanted nothing more than to cling on to him forever. It was as if she had been possessed, filled with desire that must be satisfied. She ran a hand over her body. It felt no different, yet everything had changed. She was no longer a virgin.

She tried to examine her feelings about that and about the naked man sleeping beside her. She felt numb. It was as if there was some great unhappy void ahead of her that she dare not face just yet. Perhaps in the morning she would be able to make sense of it all. For now her main concern was to get warm. She slid between the covers. The hot bricks so thoughtfully supplied were gone. They had fallen out on to the floor at some point, unnoticed, and the sheets were cold.

Her movements disturbed Gideon and he followed her under the covers, silently pulling her close. She could not deny the comfort of his warm limbs wrapped around her. Nothing mattered when she was in his arms. Tomorrow. She would think about it all tomorrow. She closed her eyes and, as she was drifting away into sleep, she felt his breath against her cheek, heard him whisper one word.

'Dominique.'

Chapter Four

The early morning sunshine was just peeping into the bedchamber when Dominique opened her eyes again. She was alone in the canopied bed. Soon she would have to get up and face the day—and Gideon—but for now she lay very still and allowed the memories to flood back. Perhaps she had been wrong to agree to her cousin's plan, but if it had secured her mother's independence then she could not regret it.

And her night of passion with Gideon? She would regret that, she was sure, but it had been inevitable. From the first moment she had peered through the thick wedding veil and seen him standing at the altar, tall and athletic, with the bars of sunlight from the windows striking red-gold sparks from his auburn hair, she was lost. Her heart had turned over and, oh, how she had wished that his smiles had really been for her and not for the person he thought her to be.

His anger, when he discovered the deception, had been monumental, but she could forgive that—as she would have forgiven him if he had taken her in anger, forced himself upon her. After all, what rights did she have now, as his wife? But she truly believed he had planned to protect her. If she had not been so obstinate, they might well have spent their wedding night in separate rooms, emerging chaste and unsullied this morning. But his autocratic behaviour had angered her and she had a temper equal to his own. Over the years she had learned to keep it in check, except in the most trying circumstances, and there could be no denying that yesterday had been extremely trying.

Once she had lost her temper there had been no way of regaining it again and when Gideon had kissed her she had reacted instinctively, taking her opportunity to possess him, if only for one night. She had given in to pure, wanton lust and now she must pay for it.

Dressing took some time. Clothing was scattered across the room—one stocking was dangling from the handle of the linen press and her garters had disappeared completely. She rummaged through the trunk that Max had supplied, but soon realised that her cousin's cruel sense of humour was present even here. The diaphanous nightwear and flimsy muslin gowns were more suited to a courtesan and had probably been left at Martlesham by one of Max's numerous lovers. She would have to wear her walking dress again.

However, she found in the trunk a clean chemise of the very finest snow-white linen and a pair of silk garters to replace her own embroidered ones. She considered cutting off the gold tassels from the garters, but in the end decided to leave them. After all, no one would see them under her skirts—unless Gideon wished to repeat last night's passionate encounter.

Oh, if only he would! A delicious curl of desire clenched her stomach and left an ache between her thighs as she remembered how it had felt to be in his arms, to have him love her.

Love. How could it be love? Gideon had no reason to think well of her. And for herself, she had watched him courting the actress, but had never spoken to him before yesterday. It could only be a savage, primitive animal attraction, acceptable in a man, but not at all the sort of thing that a respectable young lady would admit.

Dominique made her way downstairs. She found the housekeeper in the parlour, spreading a cloth over the little table.

'Good morning, Mrs Albury. I'm setting up breakfast for you here. Mr Albury thought you would prefer that to eating in the dining room, which can be draughty when the wind is in the east, as it is today.'

Dominique nodded absently and asked if she had seen Mr Albury.

'Aye, madam, he took himself off for a walk about an hour ago, it being such a fine morning. Would you like to break your fast now, madam, or will you wait for your husband to come back?'

'A little coffee now, if you please. I will take breakfast when my…husband returns.' She stumbled over the words, but she was glad to have a little longer to compose herself before meeting Gideon again.

She did not have long to wait. The thud of the front door, footsteps and the rumble of voices in the hall warned her of his arrival. She remained at the table, trying to look calm. He strode into the room, his greatcoat swinging open, his face alight with the effects of fresh air and exercise. He greeted her civilly, but she saw the sparkle fade from his eyes, replaced by a closed and shuttered look. She glanced away, trying not to feel hurt. She gestured to the table.

'There is coffee here, sir, and it is still warm, if you wish for it.'

'Thank you, yes. Mrs Chiswick is bringing in a fresh pot, but that might be some time.'

He threw his greatcoat over a chair and came to sit down. Dominique poured coffee into a cup and Gideon accepted it in silence. She wondered if she should say something and was relieved when the bustling entrance of Mrs Chiswick made speech unnecessary, at least for a while. They managed to get through breakfast with mere courtesies, but when the table had been cleared and they were alone again, the silence hung heavily between them.

'We need to talk,' Gideon said at last.

Dominique looked around her, seeking an escape from the suddenly oppressive room.

'It—it is such a lovely morning and I have not yet seen the gardens. Would you mind if we walked out-side?'

'Not at all.'

She picked up her cloak and they made their way to the shrubbery, where the high walls sheltered them from the biting east wind. They walked side by side, taking care they did not brush against each other. So different from last night, thought Dominique, when they could not touch each other enough. It had to be mentioned. She launched into speech.

'About what happened—'

'A mistake,' he interrupted her. 'And one I deeply regret. I apologise, madam, most humbly.'

She answered him firmly, 'I am as much to blame as you.'

'Perhaps, but the consequences for both of us are disastrous.' He paused. 'You realise the marriage cannot be annulled now.'

'Surely, if we return to Martlesham—'

He silenced her with an impatient wave of his hand.

'Do you think anyone would believe the marriage was not consummated? The servants would be questioned. Mrs Chiswick prepared the bridal chamber for us, her husband saw me carrying you up the stairs and I'd wager any money the maid will check the sheets!' He kicked a stone off the path. 'No, last night's folly is our undoing.'

Folly! That was how he saw the most wonderful experience of her life. Hot tears prickled at the back of Dominique's eyes, but she would not let them fall. She swallowed and clenched her jaw so that her voice did not tremble.

'What do you suggest?'

He looked up at the sky, the breath escaping between his teeth in a hiss.

'Divorce will be my father's suggestion. He abhors the French as much as I and will strongly oppose the connection. I believe he would even bear the ignominy of our family name being dragged through the courts.'

Dominique shivered. Was this to be her punishment, to have her wantonness publicly paraded?

'He could arrange the whole,' Gideon continued thoughtfully. 'But that would mean your taking a lover and I would have to sue him. A humiliating business for both of us, enduring shame for you. I will not countenance that.'

'Then what?' she asked. 'Separation? I can go back to Martlesham and live with my mother—'

He shook his head.

'No. Too many people know the circumstances of our marriage. It is unthinkable that they will all remain silent.'

'That is true,' she agreed, bitterly. 'Max has always delighted in bragging about his jokes.'

'And the chance to make me a laughing stock will prove irresistible.'

Dominique stopped.

'What shall we do, then?'

'Brazen it out.' He turned and looked down at her. 'We will continue with the marriage.'

She stared at him, her world tilting alarmingly.

'But…' She swallowed, struggling to push out the words. 'It will be a sham. You love someone else.'

That an actress would be even more unacceptable as the wife for the future Viscount Rotham did not concern Dominique, only that he loved the beautiful blonde. Gideon waved aside her objections.

'There are many such marriages in our world. It does not follow that it must be unhappy. We need only present a united front for a few months, perhaps a year or so, until the gossip has died down.'

'I have no dowry.'

He laughed, but there was no humour in it.

'Money is one thing the Alburys have in abundance.'

'Then your father will say we are even more ill matched.'

He shrugged. 'Father will come about, especially once you have provided a grandson to carry on the family name. And after that—if you want a lover you will not find me unreasonable, as long as you are discreet. That should not be a problem for you, since you grew up in France. These arrangements are understood there.'

Not in her world. Dominique thought of her mother,

still so very much in love with one man, after all these years.

'Well, madam, what say you?' Gideon asked her. 'Are you prepared to continue with this marriage?'

After the slightest hesitation she nodded.

'Yes. Yes, I am.'

After all, what choice did she have?

It was early evening by the time the post-chaise bowled into Martlesham village and drew up at a line of cottages. Gideon handed out his wife, then followed her through the nearest door. He was too tall to enter without stooping, but he was relieved when he entered the small sitting room off the narrow passage to find that the ceiling was considerably higher. The serving maid who had admitted them retired to the nether regions of the little house to fetch refreshments, bidding Dominique to go in and greet her mother. The maid had subjected Gideon to a frowning, silent stare before disappearing. He was well aware that she had been a party to the hoax and he had no doubt that she was agog to know how matters stood now. He gave a mental shrug. If his wife wanted to tell her, then he had no objection. In fact, it concerned him very little: he was about to make the acquaintance of his mama-in-law.

The little sitting room was comfortably if sparsely furnished. A couple of armchairs flanked the hearth, where a cheerful fire blazed and a small table stood by the window, its surface littered with papers. A silver inkstand rose from the centre of the chaos, like an island amid a turbulent sea and to one side sat a lady in a dark woollen gown with a tight-fitting jacket. She was hunched over the table, writing furiously, and did not appear to notice their entrance.

'*Maman?*'

Madame Rainault looked up. Gideon detected some likeness to his wife, but the lady's fair complexion and light eyes reminded him more of Martlesham, save that she had none of the earl's blustering arrogance. She wore a muslin cap over curls which were sprinkled with grey, and her eyes held a distracted look, as if her thoughts were elsewhere. She seemed to struggle to focus as she put down her pen and smiled.

'Dominique, my child. Are you back from the Abbey so soon? I had thought to have all these letters done before you returned.'

'*Maman*, I have something to tell you.' Gideon found himself pulled forwards by a small but insistent hand. 'This is Mr Albury, *Maman*. He—we...'

As the words tailed away he stepped forwards and picked up Madame Rainault's hand.

'*Enchanté, madame.*' As he bowed over the thin fingers he realised how long it was since he had spoken in French and he had to fight down the painful associations before he could summon up a smile. 'What your daughter is trying to say is that she has done me the honour of becoming my wife.'

Madame Rainault withdrew her hand and regarded him, bewildered.

'Your wife? But when, how?'

He felt a touch on his sleeve.

'Perhaps, sir, I should talk to my mother alone.'

'Yes, of course. I will go on to the Abbey. I need to arrange to have the rest of my luggage packed up and sent on to me.' He hesitated. 'Unless you wish to see your cousin?' He received a darkling look in answer and gave a wry smile. 'I thought not. I will be back as soon as I can.'

* * *

His arrival at Martlesham caused no little consternation. It was the dinner hour and Gideon told the butler not to disturb his master, but to send Runcorn up to his room immediately. It took very little time to explain the situation to his valet and give him his instructions.

Half an hour later he was ready to leave. He found Max waiting for him in the hall.

'Albury. Back from your honeymoon already? Is my cousin not with you?'

'I left her with her mother,' said Gideon, pulling on his gloves.

The doors to the dining room were open and the guests were beginning to wander out.

'Ah, tired of her already?' The earl grimaced. 'Can't say I'm surprised, she's too tight-laced and proper to please a man.'

Gideon was already furious with Max for the way he had cheated him. Now, when he heard the earl's insulting description of his young relative, Gideon was aware of a burning desire to knock the fellow's teeth out. But he had decided he would beat Max at his own game, so he concealed all signs of anger and merely raised his brows a fraction.

'Really? Are we talking about the same woman, Martlesham?' He noted the look of uncertainty in Max's face and smiled. 'We are going to London. I need to buy my wife a new wardrobe before I take her into Buckinghamshire.'

The uncertainty was replaced by amazement.

'You are taking her to Rotham?'

'Of course, that is her due.'

'B-but the viscount hates the French. He will refuse to acknowledge her.'

The thought had occurred to Gideon, but Max's shocked tones angered him and he responded with more than a touch of hauteur.

'He will be obliged to do so, since she is the wife of his heir.'

Williams came mincing forwards, quizzing glass raised.

'Now look here, Albury, we all know the marriage is a farce, it was never intended to go this far. Bring the gel back here and let Martlesham sort it all out—'

'But there is nothing to sort out,' replied Gideon, smiling again. 'I am exceedingly happy and I have you to thank for it, Max.' He patted the earl on the shoulder as he passed him. 'Now, if you will excuse me, I have to collect my wife. I have booked rooms at the Globe and we have an early start for town in the morning.'

'The Globe!' Williams dropped his quizzing glass. 'But that's devilishly…'

'Expensive, yes.' Gideon smiled. 'Only the best for Mrs Albury!'

He walked out, leaving them gaping and speechless behind him.

When he arrived back at the cottage, Lucy, the maid, accorded him a grudging curtsy and a slightly less-hostile look, from which he guessed that she had been apprised of the current situation. His wife he found in the sitting room with her mother. They were side by side in the armchairs, which had been drawn together. As Gideon entered the room Madame Rainault rose.

'Dominique has explained it all to me, Mr Albury, including my nephew's part in your marriage. It was a very wicked trick, sir, but I understand you intend to stand by my daughter. However, if you cannot be kind to her, then I pray you will leave her here with me.'

'*Maman*, you know that is impossible!'

'*Madame*, I give you my word that your daughter will receive all the kindness and consideration I can give her. As my wife she shall want for nothing.'

Madame Rainault's anxious eyes searched his face and at last, satisfied, she held out her hands.

'I believe you will do your best for her, sir, and I commend her to your care. Put on your cloak, Dominique, it is only a few miles to the Globe, but it is growing dark and there is no moon tonight.'

Mother and daughter exchanged kisses.

'*Maman*, I wish…'

'Go along, my love, I shall do very well here with Lucy to look after me. Besides, I have work to do. Now the new treaty with France is signed I am hopeful I shall begin to make progress. I have at last had word from one of my old friends and I am writing to him now, for news of your father. Lucy shall take it to the post office. She takes all my letters there now, instead of asking my nephew to frank them for me. I was never sure that he sent them on, you know…'

Madame Rainault was still talking as she waved them off. As his bride settled herself in the carriage, Gideon thought he saw the gleam of a tear on her cheek. He said, to distract her thoughts, 'What news of your father? I thought he was dead.'

She shook her head.

'He disappeared, soon after he sent us to England in ninety-three. He wanted to protect the king and queen, but the revolution had gone too far. Many moderate Girondins were executed, or imprisoned at that time.

When we lost touch, *Maman* began writing to everyone she could think of in France, trying to find out what had happened. She has been doing so ever since.'

'Ten years and you have heard nothing?'

'No. Max thinks Papa is dead, but my mother does not believe that.'

'And you?'

Her face was no more than a pale oval in the fading light, but he saw her chin go up.

'I never give up hope, sir.'

The Globe was a prestigious hostelry and the couple were made to feel their lack of servants and baggage, until Gideon's haughty manner and generous purse convinced the landlord that this wealthy viscount's son was merely eccentric. Gideon had sent a runner ahead of him to bespeak a suite of rooms, which included, as Dominique discovered as she explored their apartment, two bedrooms.

'It is de rigueur for married couples, so no one will think anything amiss,' explained Gideon. 'And I did not want to impose upon you.'

'You are very kind, sir.'

'Gideon,' he corrected her gently.

'Gideon.'

The lackeys had withdrawn and they were alone again, a situation that Dominique found disconcerting, despite their intimacy the previous night. Gideon came closer. His hand came up, as if to touch her cheek, then dropped away again.

'I want you to be comfortable,' he told her. 'Is there anything I can do, madam, that will help?'

She clasped her hands together.

'There is one thing, sir.'

'Yes?'

She raised her eyes to his.

'If—if you could call me Dominique.' Silence met her words and she hurried on, 'You never use my name—well, only once.' She blushed furiously at the memory. 'I do not think we can be c-comfortable if you continue to call me madam.'

She was looking down, and saw his hands clench into fists.

'That is one request I am afraid I cannot fulfil, my dear.'

'Oh.' She blinked to clear the tears that had suddenly sprung up. 'N-no doubt you think of Dominique as that b-beautiful actress.'

He did not contradict her. After a moment's tense silence he said, 'It is not only that. It is a French name.'

'And—and is that so very bad?' she asked him.

He hesitated, no longer than a heartbeat, but she noticed it.

'Yes, my dear. I'm afraid it is.'

He turned towards her, his face polite, smiling, but that shuttered look was in his eyes, telling her he was unreachable.

They retired to their separate rooms that night. Dominique did not sleep, but lay tense and still in the middle of the bed, listening. She convinced herself that she was dreading a soft knock at the door, but when it never came she realised just how disappointed she was. Yet what could she expect? Gideon had never wanted to marry her; he was in love with the actress who had taken her place. So much in love that now he could not even bring himself to use her name.

At breakfast the following morning Gideon was all consideration. He escorted her to her chair, poured her coffee and helped her to the freshest of the toasted muffins before sitting down to his own meal.

'You are right,' he declared. 'I cannot continue without a name for you.'

She bridled instantly.

'I have a perfectly good name, thank you.'

'You have indeed.' He smiled at her and she found her anger melting away. 'I have been thinking about it.'

'You have?'

Had he stayed awake to relive their night together, as she had done? The little flare of hope quickly died.

'Yes,' he continued. 'We could shorten it to Nicky. A pet name, if you like.'

'My grandfather, the old earl, used to call me that.'

'There we have it, then. I shall call you Nicky—but only with your permission, of course.'

She gave him a shy smile.

'I should like that, si—' She noted his sudden frown and corrected herself. 'I should like that, *Gideon*.'

By the time they reached London Dominique thought they were getting on famously. They laughed at the same things, shared a love of music and poetry, talked for hours, like true friends. But not lovers. Gideon was polite and considerate, but nothing more, and Dominique, afraid to risk the fragile bond between them, lay awake in her lonely bed and ached for him to come to her. It would not do, however, to admit such a longing, so she hid it behind a smile and accepted as much companionship as her husband was willing to give.

Chapter Five

Her new home was a neat house in Brook Street, which Gideon informed her belonged to his father.

'I do have a house of my own I inherited from my godmother, Lady Telford,' he told Dominique as he helped her out of the chaise. 'But it is a few miles out of town and so run down that I have never used it.'

'I think this would be more convenient for you,' remarked Dominique, looking up at the elegant facade. At that moment the door was thrown open and a liveried servant came out, beaming at them.

'Master Gideon, welcome home, sir!'

'Thank you. My dear, this is Judd, who has known me since I was a babe, which means he takes the greatest liberties.'

The old man chuckled in a fatherly way.

'Now then, Master Gideon, you don't want to be telling Mrs Albury such tales. Welcome to you, mistress. Mrs Wilkins is waiting inside and will show you over the house.'

'Perhaps she will begin by showing Mrs Albury to her bedchamber,' suggested Gideon, taking her arm and leading her into the narrow hall. 'We have had a long journey and I am sure my wife would like to rest before dinner.'

'Aye, of course, I will do that, Master Gideon.' A plump, rosy-cheeked woman in a black-stuff gown and snowy apron bustled forwards and dropped a curtsy. 'If Mrs Albury would like to come with me, there is hot water already on the washstands and I will send Kitty up to help you dress. She is only the second housemaid, but she's a good girl and has ambition to be a lady's maid, but if she don't suit we will send to the registry office for someone else.'

'I shall be delighted to see how she goes on,' said Dominique quickly.

'Very good, madam. Now, which of these trunks is yours, and we'll have them taken up immediately.'

'Only one.' They had brought only the trunk Max had sent with her to Elmwood and now Dominique met Gideon's eyes in a mute appeal.

'My wife is to have everything new, as befits a future viscountess,' he said coolly. 'She will manage with what is in the trunk and tomorrow we will set about replenishing her wardrobe.'

The housekeeper looked a little shocked.

'Very well, sir. If you would care to come with me, ma'am, I'll show you to your room and we'll unpack that single trunk of yours and see what there is for you to wear tonight…'

Taking a mental review of the items she had seen in the trunk, Dominique hastily declined the offer.

'You have more than enough to do, Mrs Wilkins,' she said. 'I am sure the maid you have found for me will be able to help.'

* * *

When Dominique came downstairs for dinner she was wearing one of the muslin gowns from the trunk Max had provided. The previous owner of the gown had been somewhat taller than Dominique, but Kitty had proved to be very useful with a needle and had soon taken up the hem. The unknown woman had also been more generously endowed and Dominique had had to cover the extremely low and rather loose décolletage by draping a fine muslin handkerchief across her shoulders, crossing the ends over her bosom and tying them behind her.

When she joined Gideon in the drawing room he raised his brows and she felt obliged to explain.

'I was delighted to leave off my travelling dress, but the trunk my cousin packed up for me was sadly lacking in suitable clothes. This is the most respectable of the gowns and even this required several petticoats beneath it before I was fit to be seen.'

Gideon raised his quizzing glass and surveyed her. His lips curved into a grin.

'Yes, I can see that.'

She fingered the skirts, chuckling.

'It is the finest quality, as is everything in the trunk, but most of it is highly improper. I think it must have been left behind by one of Max's less-respectable guests. He is forever filling the house with lightskirts and actresses— Oh!' She stopped, colouring painfully. 'I—I beg your pardon, I d-did not think...'

The cheerful camaraderie disappeared in an instant. Gideon's grin was replaced by a polite smile. He waved one hand, as if to dismiss her words, but Dominique knew she had erred.

* * *

Gideon saw her stricken look and wished he could say something to comfort her, but the words would not come. He had never been one for dissimulation. How could he tell her it did not matter that he had married the wrong bride when it *did* matter, when he regretted it so bitterly? The woman he had courted, the bride he had expected, was tall and fair and buxom, with blue, blue eyes and a smoky laugh full of sexual promise. Instead he found himself married to a diminutive brunette with a damnably obstinate streak. She was pretty enough, perhaps, if you liked thin women.

Here he stopped himself. She was petite, yes—the top of her head barely reached his chin—but she was not thin. He remembered their wedding night, when they had both allowed their pent-up emotions to run away with them. He recalled how well her small breast fitted into his hand, how her tiny waist contrasted with the full, rounded softness of her hips. Their lovemaking had been as hot and passionate as anything he had ever experienced and her untutored ardour had fuelled his desire. He hoped he had not hurt her. He had always expected to take his virgin bride gently, to go slowly and teach her the pleasures of the flesh.

Instead they had tumbled into a hedonistic, lust-filled coupling and he had risen at dawn bemused and mortified by his lack of control. He remembered glancing down at his sleeping bride, seeing her hair arrayed over the pillows in a dark cloud and feeling an unexpected tenderness for the innocent, fragile girl he had married. He had wanted to protect her—from the world, from himself. He had made a vow then, that he would conduct himself with proper restraint in future.

And there could be no going back. Having consummated their marriage, he must now commit himself to it and put aside all thoughts of the actress—what had Max called her? Agnes Bennet. Gideon doubted he had truly loved her, but he had been captivated by her beauty and she had shown him a flattering attention that had put all sensible thought to flight. No, it had not been love. Gideon recognised that it was his pride that was hurt most and the woman now sharing his life had colluded in the shameful trick. For that he could never forgive her. Of course, there was no reason why they should not be happy enough and have a comfortable, civilised existence together. Many couples entered into arranged marriages and rubbed along well enough, but it wasn't only her deceit—he could not ignore her French blood.

It was twelve years since his brother James had died at the hands of the French mob and the pain of that loss had never left Gideon. His father had trained him to take his place, to become his heir, but James had been everything Gideon was not, quiet and studious, but with a charm of manner that made him universally loved— not for him the rakehell existence of a young man on the town—and Gideon knew how unworthy he was to fill James's shoes.

Dinner was a strained affair. They were achingly polite to each other and by the time the covers were removed Dominique was glad to leave Gideon to enjoy his port in solitary state. She realised sadly that, however friendly he might seem, Gideon could not forgive her for her duplicitous actions. It had been a cruel trick and she should never have taken part, but when she had agreed to it she had been in turmoil. Blackmailed by her cousin and half in love with the man behind whose eyes she glimpsed a sadness that set him apart from the others, while at the same time detesting the man who would run with Max and his self-seeking, hedonistic crowd. However, standing beside him while Max gloatingly explained the deceit, the hurt and humiliation Gideon had suffered was quite clear to her, if to no one else.

Sitting alone now in the drawing room, she felt thoroughly ashamed and knew she should be grateful that he treated her with any kindness at all. Thoughts of their wedding night returned and she wrapped her arms about her, as if to hold the memory close. Desire had made her reckless and she had given in quite freely to the passion that had swept them up, but she knew—from what she had overheard from the gossiping servants and her own observations at Martlesham Abbey—that it was different for a man. Gideon's taking her that night had been no act of love, it had been simply lust, easily roused and as easily forgotten. She was not the woman he loved, merely a substitute.

Dominique wondered if she dared go to bed, but decided the proprieties must be observed and asked Mrs Wilkins to bring in the tea tray when the master joined her in the drawing room.

When Gideon came in she was relieved to see that the shuttered look was gone and he addressed her in a cheerful, friendly tone.

'I have been thinking, Nicky, I have not yet given you a wedding present. I shall take you to Rundell's and you shall choose something for yourself, but in the meantime I found this—my godmother's jewel case.' He held out a small leather box. 'Most of Godmama's jewellery is at the bank, but you might like these trinkets to be going on with.'

Dominique set the case on her lap and pushed up the clasp, her eyes widening as she opened the lid. The contents glittered in the candlelight. A profusion of gold and silver and coloured stones winked up at her.

'Th-thank you,' she murmured, bemused. She pushed her fingers gently into the tangle and lifted out a handful of the jewels, letting them fall back into the box in a sparkling cascade. 'They are beautiful, Gideon, *thank* you.'

'Some of the stones—perhaps all—will be paste,' Gideon explained, watching her. 'I noticed that you wear no jewellery, but I thought these trinkets might amuse you.'

'Amuse!' She gave a little laugh. 'They are much more than amusing. We brought very little to England, Papa disposed of everything to pay for the journey, including most of Mama's jewels.'

'No doubt she kept her most precious pieces to pass on to you?'

'They have all been sold now. The attempts to find information about Papa have cost her a great deal.'

'But surely Martlesham…?'

Dominique shook her head.

'While my uncle lived we were very comfortable, but once Max became earl he said he could no longer afford to fund Mama's search for my father. She sold her jewels, gave him everything she had to pay the bribes the French officials demanded for information, but it all came to nought. Max thinks Papa is dead and would do nothing more than frank Mama's letters.' She bit her lip. 'You have a penniless bride, Gideon.'

'Martlesham told me as much before the banns were called.'

Colour stained her cheeks, but she refused to look at him.

'But then you thought you were marrying someone else…'

An uncomfortable silence fell. Gideon felt a tug of sympathy and a keen desire to distract her from her unhappy thoughts.

'May I?' He reached down and pulled out a necklace gleaming with green fire. 'This would suit you, the stones are the colour of your eyes. I remember God-mama wearing it and there should be some ear-drops in there, too…'

'Yes, here they are.' She looked up. 'May I put them on now?'

'Of course.' He watched her, smiling at her enthusiasm as she carefully put the box down and went over to the mirror to fix the ear-drops in place. He followed her across the room. 'I was right, the colour does suit you. Let us add the necklace.'

She laughed. 'First I must remove the kerchief.' She reached around and began to fumble with the knot at the back.

'Here, let me.' Gideon untied the lacy ends and pulled it carefully away from her shoulders.

Without the concealing fichu it was apparent just how badly the dress fitted. Its original owner had obviously been of much more generous proportions than the waiflike creature who stood before him. Even with the drawstrings pulled tight the décolletage was extremely low, exposing the gentle swell of her bosom and more flesh than was becoming. Even as the thought entered his head he knew he was being unfair. Many ladies wore dresses as revealing as this, possibly even more so.

A glance in the mirror showed him that his wife was uncomfortable. One hand had come up to her breast, as if to protect herself from prying eyes and a faint blush mantled her cheeks. He smiled, wanting to reassure her as he carefully put the necklace around her throat. She tilted her head, lengthening the back of her neck, and as he brushed aside the dark curls his fingers grazed the delicate ridge of her spine. He wanted to place his lips there, then to trail a line of kisses across the soft whiteness of her shoulder, where the candlelight played upon the exposed skin. But she had trembled as he struggled with the catch. She was clearly frightened of him— why should she not be, since he had taken advantage of her innocence in such a way? Besides, to kiss her now would be the action of a lover and he could never be that.

He removed his hands and stepped back.

'There. You have a beautiful neck and the emeralds enhance it.'

She seemed to stand taller at his compliment and his breath caught in his throat when he met her eyes in the mirror. They twinkled with a shy smile that far surpassed the gleaming emeralds.

How long they would have remained there he did not know, for at that moment the housekeeper bustled in with the tea tray and the mood was broken. Nicky reached for her kerchief, but he held it away.

'No, you look very well like that, so there is no need to cover up again. Unless you are cold?'

'Not in the least, sir. There is a good fire in here, you see.'

'Indeed there is,' agreed Mrs Wilkins, setting the tray down on a small table. 'The mistress used to say this was the cosiest room in the house when the fire was burning.' She glanced back at the nervous housemaid following her into the room.' That's right, Jane, put that down here—it's the spirit kettle,' she explained as the maid set down the shining silver pot and its burner on a small square wooden stand beside the tea table. 'It hasn't been used since the mistress died, but I thought it should come out again, now we have a new mistress in the house.'

'How thoughtful of you, Mrs Wilkins.' As the servants bustled away Dominique returned to the table, throwing Gideon a look that was brim-full with mischief. 'Since Mrs Wilkins has gone to so much trouble you will have to take tea with me this evening, sir, even if you do consider it to be maudling your insides.'

He grinned, pleased to have their previous easy companionship restored. He took a seat on the opposite side of the hearth, where he could watch her. It was very restful, he thought, to be sitting at one's own fireplace with no need to go out for company or entertainment.

Dominique took great trouble brewing the tea. Gideon must have seen his mother do this a hundred times and she did not want to fall short of his expectations. And when she at last held out a cup to him, she had to try hard not to feel self-conscious in her low-cut gown. The emeralds, be they paste or real, rested heavily upon her neck and gave her a certain amount of reassurance. Gideon had given them to her and he was smiling now, so she was confident she was not offending him. She recalled the touch of his hands on her skin when he had fastened the necklace. It had caused such a leap of desire that she had found it difficult to keep still. If they had been sweethearts, she thought she would have turned and kissed him to thank him for his thoughtfulness, but they were strangers, thrown into marriage, so she must be careful not to put herself forwards.

* * *

'My sister Gwendoline is in town,' he said, settling back in his chair. 'I shall visit her tomorrow to explain our situation and ask her to take you shopping.'

Dominique almost dropped her cup.

'You—you will tell her about our marriage?'

'Of course. There is no point in hiding it. As soon as Max and his cronies return it will be all over town anyway.'

'I suppose you are right. But will she want to help me?'

'She is my sister and will want to dispel any gossip.'

Gideon replied with calm certainty, but Dominique was not so sure.

It was in a mood of trepidation that Dominique went downstairs to greet her visitor two days later.

She was immediately struck by the likeness between brother and sister, the same auburn hair and hazel eyes, but although Lady Ribblestone was tall she could not be described as lean. A gown of the finest cream displayed her ample figure beneath the holly-green pelisse that hung open from her shoulders, while a matching bonnet of the same dark green silk sat jauntily on her burnished curls.

'So you are Gideon's bride by mistake,' she said bluntly.

'Yes, Lady Ribblestone, I—'

'Oh, no formality, please, you must call me Gwen.' The lady came forwards and hugged her. 'And what shall I call you?'

'Dominique—that is, G-Gideon prefers to call me Nicky,' she said, emerging, startled, from the scented embrace.

'Now, why should he do that, when Dominique is such a pretty name?'

'I—it is French...'

'Ah, of course.' A shadow crossed Gwen's countenance, but she recovered quickly and gave another blinding smile. 'Gideon tells me you are seriously in need of clothes.' Dominique found herself being scrutinised from head to toe. 'Well, perhaps it is a little out of fashion, but it is not that bad.'

Dominique glanced down at her walking dress and gave a rueful smile.

'Perhaps not, but it is the *only* thing I have.'

'What? My dear girl, you must explain everything.'

And suddenly Dominique found herself on the sofa beside Lady Ribblestone, telling her about her sudden departure from Martlesham and the trunk Max had sent with her, full of improper garments. Immediately Gwendoline demanded to see them.

'I am sorry to say it, my dear,' she said as they made their way to Dominique's bedchamber, 'but I cannot like your cousin. If this whole sorry business has given Gideon a dislike of the earl's company then some good has come of it. And Gideon's marrying you, of course.'

'I am not sure he thinks of it that way,' replied Dominique, a little wistfully. She led Gwendoline into her room and pointed at the trunk. 'Everything is in there, save the muslin dress I wear in the evenings, which my maid has put in the linen press.'

Her sadness gave way to amusement as Lady Ribblestone began to pull out quantities of silk and lace, holding up the items for inspection before throwing them on to the bed. Gwen was not shocked or outraged by the see-through muslins, lacy undergarments or diaphanous nightgowns, she merely chuckled.

'Perhaps not *quite* suitable for you to wear in public,' she remarked, holding up a particularly sheer gown, 'but the lace negligee might be just the sort of thing Gideon would like.'

Dominique's face flamed.

'I d-don't think so.' She slumped against the edge of the bed, thinking of the chaste peck on the cheek he had given her the previous two evenings, before marching off to his own bedroom. 'Besides, all these clothes are far too big for me. They might even have been bought for the—the lady Gideon thought he would marry—'

'He told me she was an actress.'

'Yes.'

'Then you need not call her a lady,' Gwendoline corrected her, coming to sit beside her. 'Did you see her?'

'Yes, she is… She has a—a fuller figure.'

'And no doubt will run to fat as she gets older.'

Dominique giggled. 'Perhaps. But she is much taller than I am. She is very beautiful, too, and fair.'

'A big, blowsy woman, then,' said Gwendoline. 'Not at all the sort to suit Gideon. He is very chivalrous, you know, and will much prefer a wife he can cherish and protect. Once we have bought you a few gowns that are more becoming to your size and figure, I have no doubt he will find you irresistible.'

Dominique sighed.

'I doubt it. But it is not only that she was so very beautiful. He thought she—that is, he thought *I*—was English, but I am not. I am half French and I cannot alter that.'

'Ah.'

Dominique looked uncertainly at her new friend. 'Why does Gideon dislike the French so much?'

Gwendoline's smile disappeared.

'You do not know?'

'No. Will you tell me?'

Gwendoline hesitated, saying at last, 'Very well, but not until we have been shopping. My carriage has been standing at the door for far too long. We must leave now, if we are to get anything done today.' She jumped up. 'Come along, my dear, put on your bonnet, we are going out.'

To one who had lived very retired for the past ten years, a shopping trip with Lady Ribblestone was a revelation. Dominique soon lost count of the modistes, milliners, bazaars and warehouses they visited. Gwendoline sailed through the establishments, setting everyone running to do her bidding.

By the time they returned to Brook Street an alarming number of orders had been placed and an even more alarming number of packages and bandboxes filled the carriage.

'I think we have done very well for the first day,' remarked Gwendoline, reviewing their purchases.

'First day!' Dominique laughed. 'I do not think I have ever had so many new things in my life.'

'Well, you came to town with nothing,' reasoned Gwendoline. 'Tomorrow we shall order you a riding habit. I shall take you to Ribblestone's tailor, he makes all my habits. Unless you think Gideon would prefer you to use his own tailor…?'

'I think Gideon will say I have spent more than enough,' declared Dominique. 'Heaven knows how much all this will cost.'

Gwendoline shrugged.

'Gideon can afford it. Old Lady Telford left him everything, you know, and until now he has frittered it away on larks and sprees. It will be good for him to have some responsibilities.'

The word threw a cloud over Dominique's spirits.

'And I am a responsibility.' She sighed. 'Will you tell me now why Gideon did not want to marry a Frenchwoman?'

'The war, my dear, surely that is reason enough.'

'No, it is more than that,' said Dominique, a tiny crease furrowing her brow. 'He looked very shocked when he found out my father is French. He seemed quite, quite repulsed.' She fixed her eyes upon Gwendoline. 'Please tell me, then perhaps I can do something to alleviate the situation.' She added quickly, 'What is it, why do you look at me like that, as if you pity me? What is it I should know?'

Gwendoline hesitated.

'I think Gideon should tell you himself.'

'Please, Gwen.'

Her pleading look and the hand placed so insistently upon Lady Ribbleston's arm had its affect. She sighed and nodded.

'Very well. You see, our aunt—Papa's sister— married a Frenchman, the Duc du Chailly. They were guillotined during the Terror.'

'Oh, I am so very sorry!'

'She was also my godmother and I am named after her. We knew her as Tante Gwendoline and when we were children we spent many happy times with them in France, until the Revolution. It was quite devastating for the family when they died.'

'Oh, that is so very sad. And Max knows this?'

'Martlesham? Yes, of course. It was no secret and the executions were much talked of in town at the time.'

'Then how cruel of him to trick Gideon into marrying me!' declared Dominique angrily. She frowned. 'Max thought that as soon as the deceit was known Gideon would seek an annulment.'

'Yes, Gideon mentioned that.' Gwendoline added quietly, 'He also told me why that is not possible.'

Dominique bowed her head, her cheeks crimson.

'He could still divorce me.'

'Not Gideon,' said his sister decidedly. 'He is far too honourable to drag any woman through that.'

'Then we are man and wife, until death.' Dominique sighed. 'That sounds so bleak, but perhaps, given time...'

Lady Ribblestone reached out and covered her hands, saying quickly, 'You must not hope for too much, my dear.' She hesitated. 'I think it best if you know everything. Our older brother, James, died in France, too. At the hands of the Girondins.'

'And Papa was a Girondin.'

If there had been any light at the end of the long tunnel Dominique saw stretching before her, it was shut off in an instant. Beneath Gwendoline's warm clasp she gripped her hands together very tightly, hoping that small pain would stop her from crying.

'Tell me,' she said, her throat constricted.

'It was the winter of ninety-one. The Legislative Assembly had been appointed—young, fanatical antiroyalists hell-bent on destroying the old order. James went to France to try to help *tante* and the *duc*. Father had friends there, you see, contacts opposed to the new administration. He had arranged a meeting, but on that very night they were attacked and James was killed.'

'And the Legislative Assembly was Girondiste,' Dominique said in a whisper. 'Papa was against the violence. He wanted to end it, but who will believe that now?' She looked up, all hope gone. 'How can your brother bear to be married to me? Is it for revenge?'

'No, no. Gideon is an honourable man and he will take his marriage vows seriously.'

Dominique looked around her at the packages littering the carriage.

'What is the point of buying me all this? He can never love me.'

'Very few of us marry for love, my dear.'

'But I represent all that he abhors. And you are Gideon's sister—you have just as much cause to hate me—'

'Gideon does not hate you, my dear, I am sure of that, and nor do I. *You* are not responsible for what happened in the Terror. My godmother married the Duc du Chailly because he was a good, kind man, and before the war we met many such people in France.' Gwen turned and put her hands on Dominique's shoulders. 'You must look upon this as an arranged marriage. Not perhaps what you would have chosen, but you must make the best of it. Gideon has already decided to do so, that is why he asked me to take you under my wing.' She gave Dominique a little shake. 'You have to make a life for yourself, my dear. You are not an antidote, there is no reason why you and Gideon should not be happy together. With the right clothes and a little confidence I think we can pass you off quite creditably in society, and when Gideon sees other people taking notice of you, he will do so, too.'

Dominique looked at her. 'Do you really think so, Gwen?'

'I am certain of it. We will make you into such a beautiful, stylish wife that he cannot fail to be proud of you!'

Chapter Six

Dominique was not convinced by Gwendoline's brave talk, but they had reached their destination and there was no time to discuss anything more. Judd informed them the master was in the morning room and they went to find him.

'My dear Gideon,' declared Gwen, greeting him with a kiss. 'Have you been waiting in for us? How sweet of you. We are quite exhausted.'

'And is my credit similarly exhausted?' he asked, smiling slightly.

He invited Dominique to sit on the sofa and sat down beside her, once Gwen had dropped elegantly into an armchair.

'Lord, no. I had everything put to Ribblestone's account and he will sort it all out with you later.' Gwendoline paused while the wine and cakes were served. 'Now, Gideon,' she said at last, selecting a dainty confection from the selection on her plate. 'We have made a start in setting your wife up with clothes for the Season. I have been promised that the first of the gowns will be delivered here tomorrow. What about Court Dress? Are you presenting her at a drawing room?'

'Oh, I would rather not,' murmured Dominique in some alarm.

'Nonsense, your husband will be the next Viscount Rotham. You must be presented.'

'But not yet,' said Gideon. 'I think my father should meet Nicky first. This visit to town is merely an—er—informal one.'

'And when do you intend to go to Rotham?'

'All in good time.'

Gwen frowned. 'You cannot put off the meeting forever, Brother. Whatever was said in the heat of the moment Papa will not hold it against you, you know that. Your tempers are too similar for him not to understand. He is lonely, Gideon, and however harsh his words he does care for you, very much.'

'I do know that.' He rubbed a hand across his eyes. 'I shall go, but not yet, not yet.'

Dominique sipped her wine and listened to the conversation, aware of a tension between the brother and sister.

'Is it because of me?' she ventured. 'Will Lord Rotham be angry with you for marrying me?'

'Of course not—!'

Gideon put up his hand to stem his sister's denial.

'He will not be happy about it, but his wrath will be on my head, Nicky, not yours. I shall not take you to Rotham without his assurance that you will be received with the respect that is due to you.'

Respect! That sounded very bleak indeed. Dominique was relieved Gideon had no immediate plans to take her to Rotham. Perhaps once she had her own clothes she would feel more courageous. From all Gwen had told her she knew she would be a fool to cling on to any hope that Gideon would ever feel more for her than a mild friendship, but perhaps she could gain *his* respect. She resolved there and then never to embarrass him by any show of affection that he would have to rebuff. No, she would show him—and his father—that despite her French heritage she could be a model wife, a fitting consort for an English lord.

Dominique was soon on good terms with Mrs Wilkins and slipped naturally into her role as mistress of the house. She began to make little changes, such as ordering a fire to be kept burning in the morning room, and she asked Judd to remove some of the heavy silver from the dining table, so that she could at least see her husband when they dined together each evening. If Gideon noticed he said nothing, but she was heartened when he suggested a place should be laid for her at his right hand for dinner, rather than sitting so far apart, and she was quietly pleased when he began to seek her out for a glass of wine when he came in each afternoon, before going upstairs to change for dinner. For the first week she remained in the house, going out only with Lady Ribblestone on shopping trips, but by the end of Dominique's second week in Brook Street, Gwendoline declared that her sister-in-law was at last fit to be seen.

They were having breakfast and Lady Ribblestone suggested they should drive through the park at the fashionable hour.

'I should like to go out,' Dominique admitted, 'but Hyde Park—will it not be very crowded?'

'Oh, excessively,' replied Gwendoline cheerfully. 'The world and his wife will be there.'

'So many people?' exclaimed Dominique, dismayed. 'I am not sure I am ready—'

She broke off as Gideon came in.

'Now, what are you two plotting?' he said, smiling. 'Are you off to spend more money today?'

'Not at all,' retorted Gwen. 'I want Dominique to accompany me to the park. It promises to be a very fine afternoon and we could drive out in the barouche.'

He sat down at the table and poured himself a cup of coffee. Gwen watched him in surprise.

'This is a change, Brother,' she said, momentarily diverted. 'I thought you only drank ale at breakfast.'

He grinned. 'Bachelor fare, Sis. I am a married man now.'

'Then help me to persuade your wife to drive out with me. She has been cooped up in this house long enough.'

'I agree,' said Gideon, 'but I am not sure if riding with you in a stuffy barouche is how she should make her entrance into polite society.'

'There is nothing stuffy about Ribblestone's barouche,' retorted his sister, offended.

'Perhaps not, but I would rather drive Nicky in my curricle.'

It was the first time he had suggested they go out together and Dominique felt her cheeks going pink with pleasure.

'I cannot compete with that.' Gwen laughed and wagged her finger at Dominique. 'Accept immediately, my dear. I have never known my brother to take up a female in his curricle before!'

'Quite true, Gwen.' Gideon turned to Dominique, smiling. 'Well, madam, will you give me the honour of driving you out for your first introduction to the *ton*?'

Dominique was in a panic. What to wear to drive out with Gideon? Her new riding habit had not yet arrived, and although her new promenade dress was beautiful it had been bought for the warmer months. She even ran out into the street to test the weather. The sun was shining, but there was a chill wind blowing and she did not want to make her first public appearance wrapped up in a shawl. After much deliberation she decided she would wear her new pelisse of crimson silk, with a matching cap. Gwendoline had persuaded her to have it trimmed with fur and frogged *à la hussar*, prophesying correctly that the chilly days of spring were not yet at an end. She had also added that not everyone could wear such a strong colour, especially not a blowsy blonde.

At the appointed hour Dominique made her way downstairs to find Gideon waiting for her in the hall. He glanced up as he heard her step on the stairs, then turned for a second, longer look. She saw the surprise in his eyes, but there was admiration, too, and her heart gave a little skip. She was emboldened to ask him if she would do.

'You will do very well,' he said slowly. 'The colour suits you admirably.'

She was relieved and said with a smile, 'Remind me, then, to thank your sister for persuading me to buy it.'

A gleaming curricle waited at the door, two beautiful grey horses in harness and his groom at their heads.

'This is Sam, my tiger,' said Gideon, a laugh in his voice. 'And the reason he is looking so deuced savage is that we are not in the habit of driving females.'

'Not if they's gonna screech and frighten the 'osses,' muttered Sam, giving a reluctant tug of his forelock in Dominique's direction.

'Mind your tongue, man!'

'No, he is quite right,' replied Dominique, cutting

across her husband's sharp reply and smiling at the groom. 'I hope I know how to behave myself in an open carriage and *think* I can promise not to screech, unless of course we are about to be overturned.'

'He ain't likely to do that,' opined Sam. 'Top o' the trees is Mr Albury when it comes to driving.'

'Ah, then I understand why you are happy to stay in his employ,' she said as Gideon helped her into her seat. 'And since *you* have such confidence in Mr Albury's driving, I am more than happy to drive out with him.'

'I think you have made a conquest,' murmured Gideon as the groom jumped clear of the horses and waited to scramble up into the rumble seat. 'Sam was not at all happy when he discovered I had fallen into the parson's mousetrap.'

Dominique said nothing, but she was pleased to have come safely over another small hurdle.

The spring sunshine had brought everyone out of doors and the journey to the park gates was slow. Gideon kept his attention on negotiating the busy roads and Dominique had plenty of time to admire his skill as he inched the curricle through the traffic. If she expected to enjoy a quiet drive, she was disappointed. As soon as they entered the park gates she saw the crowds. Ladies with parasols, gentlemen with their canes, all parading up and down beside a procession of carriages and riders. Their progress was very slow, for it seemed everyone wanted to stop and be introduced to the new Mrs Albury. Gideon was a little concerned at first about how Nicky would react to all the attention, but he discovered his worries unfounded. She was a little shy, but her manners were perfectly good and she turned aside the more impertinent comments and questions with a quiet dignity.

'How did they know I was in London?' wondered Dominique when they moved on from yet another introduction.

'There will have been something in the society pages.'

Gideon said no more. He had deliberately ordered Judd not to bring the newspapers into breakfast each morning after he had seen the first sly reference.

The Hon. Mr A—has brought his new bride to town, but there are rumours that this is not the Bride he had been expecting, his intended having been replaced at the very altar by Another. The ceremony took place at the seat of that well-known trickster, the Earl of M—

Gideon recognised Max's hand behind that entry and he did not doubt there would be more, which was why he had been so keen that his wife should make her first appearance in his company. He knew speculation would be rife, but he had not expected quite so much interest. Why, the carriages were queuing up to speak to them.

'A new bride always attracts attention,' he remarked after a pause.

'Undoubtedly, but I fear my cousin has been at work to advertise our situation,' she said shrewdly.

Gideon heard the uncertainty in her voice and briefly put one hand over hers.

'I have no doubt he has.' *Damn Max.* 'Do not worry. If we present a united front the gossip will soon fade, dismissed as idle rumour.'

'Of course, but…'

He glanced down and saw the crease in her brow, the way she caught her bottom lip between her teeth. He said gently, 'What is the matter, Nicky?'

'Max and his friends are still at Martlesham. Would he really send word all the way to London, to make mischief for us?'

'You should know your cousin doesn't like to be crossed.'

'True, and you did rather take the wind out of his sails by not calling for an annulment. I'm afraid he will make more trouble for you, if he can.'

For him? Did she have no worries for herself? He shrugged, wanting to reassure her.

'What can he do? When people see that we are perfectly happy together then the rumours will soon die away.'

'I fear that will inconvenience you greatly.'

'Me?'

'Why, yes, if you must be seen everywhere with me, instead of enjoying your own life as you have been used to do.'

Gideon was startled at her matter-of-fact tone and rather alarmed, too. All her concern appeared to be for his well-being, while he had given very little thought to hers. He had been happy to leave his sister to look after Nicky, to provide her with the wardrobe she would need for her new life, but he knew most brides would consider him very neglectful. Not that Nicky wanted his attentions—she had been very reserved since their wedding night. True, she had seemed very willing then, but she had been an innocent and his passion must have frightened her as much as it had shocked him. It was not how he had expected to behave with his new wife.

It was one of the things his father had drummed

into him, that wives were fragile, delicate creatures and must be treated with great care and gentleness. Gideon had not visited her bed again and Nicky had shown no signs of wanting him to do so. He would need an heir, of course, but there was plenty of time for that when they were more comfortable together. Since they had arrived in London he had left her to settle in, seeing her only at breakfast and for dinner some evenings. He told himself it was for her sake, but there was something about his new wife that unsettled him, an unlooked-for attraction that stole up on him when he was too long in her company and he was determined not to take advantage of her again, but suddenly it all seemed incredibly selfish.

'I beg your pardon,' he said now, painfully aware of his shortcomings. 'I have been very busy, but you have every right to be angry with me for my lack of attention. Most new brides would be ringing a peal over their husbands for such behaviour.'

'But ours is a most irregular marriage. I do not expect you to—what is the term?—*live in my pocket.*' She shifted in her seat and looked up at him, her green eyes dark and earnest. 'I want to make you a good wife, Gideon.'

He did not know how to reply, but stared in silence at the serious little face framed by dark curls. No wonder the *ton* was so interested in his marriage. They had been in town for almost three weeks and this was the first time they had been seen out together. Well, he thought grimly, that would change. His friends would look for him in vain tonight. He would stay at home with his wife.

He did not realise he was still staring at her until he heard Sam's gruff voice, telling him to mind his horses. Nicky blushed and a shy twinkle appeared in her eyes.

'Yes, look to your driving, sir,' she admonished him, straightening in her seat. 'You are wandering all over the path.'

When Gideon informed Dominique at dinner that evening that he was not going out she could not conceal her surprise. It would be the first time he had spent the whole evening with her since the night they had arrived in Brook Street.

'Those who made your acquaintance in the park today will no doubt be sending you invitations very soon,' he told her, straightening the cutlery. 'This may be the last opportunity to enjoy a quiet evening together.'

When the meal was over Dominique left him to his port and went off to the drawing room. At first she nervously paced the floor, plumping cushions and straightening the ornaments, until she took herself to task for being so nervous. This was her home, too, and she should enjoy it. What would she really *like* to do? The beautiful pianoforte in the corner of the room gleamed enticingly, so she sat down and began to play. She was so lost in the music that she did not notice the time passing until she looked up and found Gideon standing by the door, watching her.

'Do go on,' he said, moving into the room and taking a seat by the fire.

Dominique continued until she had finished the Haydn sonata and, as the last notes died away, Gideon began to applaud.

'That was very good, Nicky. And to play without music, you are very accomplished.'

'Thank you, I have been practising here every day,

since I discovered this lovely instrument. I play the harp, too. My mother is very fond of music and insisted I should learn. When we came to England she badgered the earl into providing a tutor. The lessons continued until my uncle died three years ago.'

'And do you sing, too?'

'Yes, a little.'

'Then will you sing for me?'

A flush of pleasure tinged her cheeks.

'Of course. What would you like? An English folk song, perhaps?'

Receiving a nod of assent, she played an introduction, then added her voice, a little hesitant at first, but as the music took over she closed her eyes and sang with more confidence. It was a favourite of her mother's, a haunting love song about a young woman waiting for her lover to return. The thought of Mama, writing her endless letters, refusing to give up hope, gave an added piquancy to the song and when at last she had finished and opened her eyes again, for a moment she could not recall quite where she was.

'That was quite beautiful.' Gideon had moved closer. 'There is so much I do not know about you.'

His eyes were fixed upon her, dark and intense in the glow of the candles. A shiver ran down her spine and she felt desire curling deep inside her.

'We know so little about each other,' she said, trying not to think of the night they had spent together. He had seen her naked, explored her body in the most intimate way. Yet they were still strangers.

'Nicky—'

'I have asked Mrs Wilkins to bring in the tea tray,' she interrupted him hastily. 'And perhaps I should ring for Judd to build up the fire.'

He caught her hand as she walked by him and her fingers trembled in his grasp.

'You are afraid of me.'

She dared not look at him.

'Not afraid, no.'

'Then what is it?'

'You said it yourself. We do not know each other.'

'Then we must put that right.' His breath was warm upon her cheek. He must be bending, perhaps about to kiss the bare skin of her shoulder. If he did that she knew the slender rein she had over herself would snap, she would turn and throw herself at him again, and he would know what a wanton soul she had. She remembered the accusations against the late Queen of France: that she had been unable to control her lust. She had seen many such women at Martlesham since Max had become earl, not only actresses and whores, but also the wives of his so-called friends, all of them willing to share their favours. Her mother had kept her well away from those riotous gatherings, but she had heard Max's disparaging comments and knew the servants viewed them with contempt. Men despised such women and she was desperate that Gideon should not despise her any more than he did already.

She said with forced lightness, 'We can relate our histories over a dish of Bohea.'

'Yes, of course. And here is Judd now with the tea tray. Shall I light the spirit kettle?'

She uttered up a prayer of thanks at his friendly tone. This she could cope with, the ritual of making tea, sitting in separate chairs, their only contact the accidental touch of fingers when she handed him his cup. They conversed easily, but with a wary restraint, on guard lest any remark should cause offence or embarrassment.

'Your sister has invited me to her musical soirée on Thursday,' she said when he brought his cup to her for more tea. 'I would like to go, if you have no objection?'

'Of course not. May I come with you?' His brows snapped together. 'Now why should you look so surprised—would you rather I didn't?'

'G-Gwendoline thought you would not—she said I should not expect you to accompany me everywhere.'

'I think it might be expected that I would attend my own sister's soirée. That is, if you would like me to come with you.'

Dominique would like nothing better and wanted to say as much, but his next words stopped her.

'We are already agreed, are we not, that we must show the *ton* we are on the best of terms? You may be sure that someone will pass the word on to Martlesham.'

So that was it. They were to show Max that his little trick had failed. She forced herself to keep smiling.

'Quite.'

She made her excuses to retire as soon as she could after that, barely waiting for Gideon to kiss her fingers before pulling her hand away and hurrying off to her room. She heard Gideon's footsteps in the corridor some time later, but he did not even pause as he passed her door.

'Dominique, my dear, welcome to my little musical gathering. Ribblestone is at the House, but he will be back later to meet you.' Gwendoline bent to envelope her in a scented hug, the ostrich feathers in her turban quivering above her as she added in an excited whisper, 'I have never had such a crowd here before. Not one refusal to my invitations. This must be down to you, my love.'

'Don't put my wife to the blush before she is even through the door, Gwen.'

'Oh, tush, Dominique knows she is amongst friends here.' Gwendoline pulled Gideon to her and kissed his cheek. 'How are you, Brother? You are looking very fine this evening.'

Dominique thought so, too. Stealing another glance at her husband in his black coat and dazzlingly white linen, she thought he was easily the most handsome man in the room. His hair glinted with fiery red sparks in the candlelight, which also accentuated the strong angles of his lean face. He wore no jewellery save his heavy signet ring and a quizzing glass on a black-velvet ribbon around his neck, but the exquisite cut of his coat and artfully knotted cravat were the envy of many.

'My love, may I present to you…'

She found herself surrounded by gentlemen. Her instinct was to cling to her husband, but that would never do. She allowed him to make the introductions, accepted their compliments with a shy smile, but was relieved when, after a few moments' conversation, Gideon took her arm and guided her away.

'I can't have you falling into the clutches of those Lotharios tonight,' he murmured as he led her across the room.

'Are they all so bad, then?' She glanced back. 'They seemed perfectly respectable, save perhaps for Sir Desmond, who was whispering the most outrageous things to Gwen. The rest I thought were perfect gentlemen.'

'And so they are, as long as I am beside you, but leave them alone with a pretty woman—'

She felt her cheeks burn.

'Oh, do you mean that, Gideon, do you really think I am pretty?'

'As a picture,' he replied, lifting her gloved hand to his lips.

She knew it meant nothing, he performed the gesture with practised ease, as he had doubtless done hundreds of times before with other women, but she could not prevent her heart from beating just that little bit faster. Her body responded to his every look, every touch, but she had learned to hide it, so that she alone knew how much her skin tingled when he was close to her and how much she ached to feel his arms about her.

The gentlemen melted away, but the ladies were not so easy to escape. They clustered about the couple, trying to separate Dominique from her husband, ostensibly to sit with them for the forthcoming recital, but she guessed they really wanted to learn the circumstances of her marriage. She held tight to Gideon's arm and he turned aside every invitation, declaring with a laugh that he wanted to keep his wife to himself for this one evening.

When at length they sat down together she murmured her thanks to him and could not resist asking if he was merely staying by her for the sake of the gossip-mongers.

'Good God, no. I came here to be with you this evening. And besides, I want to know what you think. Many of my sister's guests have no musicality at all, and praise everyone to the skies, however dire the performance.'

He values my opinion!

Dominique sat up a little straighter. She had been apprehensive about the evening, but with Gideon beside her she began to relax and enjoy herself. They sat through some poor piano playing, and even worse poetry, but when they went in to supper Dominique could not agree with Gideon's remark that it was a wasted evening.

'I have made a number of new acquaintances and that will stand me in good stead in future. And,' she added, giving him a twinkling look, 'now I have heard the standard of music that is acceptable in town I shall not be afraid to play in public.'

'I am glad to hear that.' He grinned back at her. 'It has been particularly bad this evening. I shall have to have words with my sister.'

Later, however, when she brought her husband to their table, Gwendoline was unrepentant.

'They are friends, dear Brother, and desperate to perform. I get them over with first, so that we can all relax and enjoy the remainder of the evening.'

'Aye, that is why I am never here early,' agreed Lord Ribblestone in a grave tone that was decidedly at odds with the mischievous gleam in his eye. 'Gwen has too soft a heart when it comes to lame ducks and always likes to give them a chance to show their paces. You will learn, Mrs Albury, never to get to my wife's parties before suppertime.'

'*You* certainly do not,' retorted Gwen.

He smiled. 'Acquit me, my love. Tonight at least I would have come earlier, if matters had allowed.'

Gideon raised an eyebrow.

'Discussing the treaty, Anthony?'

Ribblestone's mouth twisted.

'This peace with France won't last the year.'

'Oh, I hope you are wrong there, my lord.' Dominique blushed at her impetuous words.

'My wife's father is French,' explained Gideon.

Lord Ribblestone's brows shot up.

'Is he, by Gad? But I thought—'

'Goodness, Anthony, if you took more notice of me and less of your dusty political papers, you would remember!' Gwendoline broke in hastily. 'I explained everything, so there is no need to go over it all again. Now, my lord, we still have any number of guests wishing to play for us tonight so you must help me get everyone back to the salon.' Gwendoline bore him away, giving Dominique a warm smile as she passed. 'I promise you the best players have yet to perform. I do not think you will be disappointed, my dear.'

Dominique tried to respond, but all she could think of was Lord Ribblestone's astonishment that Gideon should marry a Frenchwoman.

'My brother-in-law has many attributes, but tact is not one of them,' remarked Gideon. 'No wonder the government is in such disarray, if he is an example of their abilities.' He said gently, 'Your French connections are no secret in town, my dear, but I doubt anyone else will remark upon it.' He rose and held out his hand to her. 'Now, shall we gird our loins for more execrable music?'

She accompanied him back to the salon, but her new brother-in-law's shock had undermined her confidence. Everyone was watching her, wondering what could have persuaded Gideon to marry a penniless Frenchwoman without even beauty to recommend her. However, his continued presence at her side was reassuring, and since the musical offerings were indeed much improved she tried very hard to put her anxieties aside and enjoy herself. A particularly good duet between piano and harp had her clapping enthusiastically, as did a very funny ditty by Sir Desmond Arndale.

'Bravo,' cried Gwendoline, moving forwards to congratulate him. 'A splendid ending to our evening, sir. Now that everyone has performed—'

'Not quite everyone.' Sir Desmond interrupted her. 'Mrs Albury has yet to play.'

Dominique had been too busy applauding to take in his words until she found everyone looking at her.

'What? Oh, no—that is—'

'Come along, ma'am, I am sure everyone wants to hear you.' Sir Desmond was beaming and beckoning her forwards.

Gideon turned to her.

'I would like to hear you, very much, but if you wish I will tell them you would rather not.'

The kindly understanding in his eyes boosted her spirits. She squared her shoulders.

'No,' she said, smiling a little, 'I have been happy enough to listen to the others, it is only fair I take my turn.'

A smattering of applause went round the room as she rose and made her way to the pianoforte. Sir Desmond hovered around her, adjusting the candles and asking if he should search out any music for her from the pile of sheets on the table.

'Perhaps Mrs Albury will play us a *French* air,' sniggered someone from the audience.

Dominique affected not to hear, but she was heartened when Gideon responded with a laugh, 'Perhaps she will—whatever her choice I know it will be delightful. What is it to be, my dear?'

'A piece by Mr Mozart, I think,' she declared.

The 'Fantasia' was not long and not even particularly difficult. She had performed it many times for her mother and knew she could play it well, but her confidence wavered when she looked around the room and realised how many people were watching her. Then her gaze fell upon Gideon. He was smiling at her. Everyone else was forgotten. She would play for him and him alone.

As she struck the last confident chords she smiled, knowing she had done well. The applause was instant and the first 'brava' she heard was from Gideon. There were calls for an encore, but she shook her head, blushing, and would have joined Gideon, but Gwendoline carried her off to enjoy the praise and compliments of her guests.

'Gideon shall have you back in a while,' she told Dominique, sweeping her away. 'You must not allow him to monopolise you, my dear.'

'By Gad no,' declared Sir Desmond, accompanying them across the room. 'It's about time you gave the rest of us a share of your company, madam.'

When she glanced over her shoulder she saw Gideon smile and nod to her, before joining a group of gentlemen gathered about Lord Ribblestone, so she allowed Gwen to lead her to a lively little group who were enjoying a final glass of wine together before the carriages were called.

'I thought we should never get a word with you,' exclaimed Mrs Innis, a buxom matron swathed in mulberry silk. 'Albury has been guarding you all evening.'

'Not guarding,' Dominique protested with a smile. 'I enjoy his company.'

'La, madam, pray do not say such a thing!' cried Sir Desmond, throwing up his hands.

'At least not in front of Gideon,' added Gwen. 'It would make him horribly conceited, you know.'

'Yes,' declared Mrs Innis. 'A husband needs to be kept on his toes. 'You must not let him take you for granted.'

'You should set up a flirt,' whispered Gwendoline. 'As I have done.' She turned to Sir Desmond, who was hovering about her. 'My dear, will you be an angel and fetch me another glass of wine? I am quite parched this evening.'

As he lounged away Mrs Innis gave a fat chuckle.

'If only we were all fortunate enough to have such a devoted lap dog.'

'Desmond is very sweet,' agreed Gwen, smiling after his retreating form.

'But, does Lord Ribblestone not object?' enquired Dominique.

Gwen's smile slipped a little.

'I doubt he even notices.'

Mrs Innis tapped Dominique's arm with her closed fan.

'Lord bless you, Mrs Albury. A man don't want his wife to be forever clinging to his coat-tails, ain't that so, Lady Ribblestone?'

'No, indeed.' Gwen shook off her reverie and gave a bright smile. 'Pray do not look so shocked, dear sister. It is all the rage to have a cicisbeo, I assure you.'

'But I don't want a—a—'

'Not a case of what you *want*,' put in another lady, her eyes fixed rather wistfully upon a thin, bewhiskered gentleman on the far side of the room. 'Grayson only shows an interest in me if he thinks he has a rival.'

'Perhaps it is a little early for Mrs Albury to be setting up a flirt,' said Mrs Innis, considering. 'She is not yet married a month.'

'It is much too early,' Dominique replied emphatically. 'I mean to be an exemplary wife.'

'Very admirable, my dear, but you need to take care,' said the wistful woman. 'Nothing revolts a man more than an excessive display of affection from his spouse. Men are such contrary creatures, they are most attracted to the very thing they cannot have.'

And that would be the beautiful actress, thought Dominique, maintaining her smile with an effort.

'Very true, Lady Grayson,' averred Mrs Innis, the dyed ostrich feathers in her turban nodding vigorously. 'You must never appear too eager for his attentions—that way leads only to disaster.'

Dominique turned to Gwendoline, expecting her to say that was nonsense, but instead her sister-in-law nodded, saying slowly, 'You know, my dear, I think Gideon is very much like a dog with a bone. He may not want you at all, until someone else shows an interest.'

Dominique grimaced.

'I am not a piece of *meat*, Gwen.'

'No-o, but as his wife he may think he does not need to work for your affection.'

'Perhaps I should talk to him—'

'Fatal, my dear,' declared Gwen. 'You must keep Gideon at arm's length if you want to maintain his interest.'

'But surely—'

'Only a trollop would throw herself at a man,' stated Mrs Innis baldly, ignoring Dominique's attempt to speak. 'Give him your smiles, my dear, but never your sighs. Let him kiss you and make love to you, but never, *never* allow him to believe you care or it will be all over with you. He will be setting up his mistress and treating you like a bond slave. He will dominate and bully you until you are the unhappiest being in the world and he won't even *care*.'

'Who won't care?' demanded Sir Desmond, returning at that moment. 'If you are talking of Lady R, then I care very much.'

'Which just proves what we have been saying,' responded Gwendoline lightly. 'Men always want the one thing they cannot have.'

'What nonsense are you telling my wife?' demanded Gideon, coming up while they were all laughing.

'Merely a few home truths, Brother, regarding how best to remain happy.'

'My wife's happiness is, of course, my chief concern.' He made her a little bow and held out his arm. 'Our carriage awaits, ma'am. I think it is time we said goodnight.'

'I think that passed off very well,' he remarked as they drove home through the dark streets. 'And my sister introduced you to her friends?'

'Yes. Including Sir Desmond Arndale.' She drew a breath. 'Is…um…is he her lover?'

'I doubt it, but much of Anthony's time is taken up with government matters and Arndale is useful when Gwen needs an escort. A harmless fribble.'

'And is Lord Ribblestone jealous of him?'

'Lord, no.' He turned towards her. 'Why this sudden interest in Arndale?'

'I am curious to know how married women go on in London.'

'Many of them behave scandalously.' He leaned closer and reached out to cup her chin and turn her towards him. 'But I don't intend to allow *you* to behave like that, at least only with me.'

Her heart began to hammer as he kissed her and she raised her hand to touch his cheek, then pulled it back.

Men always want what they cannot have.

She must not show him how much she wanted him, yet surely he could hear her heart? She could hardly breathe it was thudding so heavily against her ribs. The carriage began to slow and he raised his head.

'We are home,' he murmured. 'Be ready for me tonight. I shall come to your room.'

If Dominique had thought waiting in the drawing room for Gideon to finish his port was nerve-racking, waiting for him to come to her bedchamber was almost unbearable. She allowed Kitty to dress her in one of the soft linen nightdresses she had chosen with Gwendoline, then dismissed her and sat on the edge of the bed with only the glow of the fire and a single candle to relieve the darkness. The trunk she had brought with her from Martlesham was just visible in the gloom and when a sudden flare of the candle flame glinted on its studded lid she went over and opened it, rifling through the contents to pull out a gossamer-thin creation. This is what the unseen and unknown Agnes Bennet would have worn, she thought. But Agnes knew exactly how to tease a man into submission—witness the way she had bewitched Gideon into offering her marriage.

Put it on, whispered the seductive voice in her head. *It will reveal your body and drive him to distraction.*

But Dominique knew her slender form could not compare with the voluptuous curves of Agnes Bennet. Gideon might be disgusted with her—worse, he might even laugh. Quickly she put the wispy confection away again. The trunk must be removed, it was a constant reminder of the woman Gideon had wanted for his bride.

She heard a soft noise somewhere in the quiet house and ran back to the bed. Straining her ears, she picked up the sound of footsteps getting closer and she clasped her hands together nervously.

Gideon had not entered this bedchamber since he was a child. It had been his mother's room and, apart from ordering that it was to be redecorated for his bride, he had not given it another thought—he realised a little ruefully that when he had issued those orders he had thought that his wife would spend most of her nights in his bed. But the woman he had envisaged sharing his life with was nothing like the woman he had married.

Something stirred within him when he saw the pale creature standing before the bed, her hair a dusky cloud around her shoulders. It was not the hot lust of their wedding night, more an urge to protect her, to make her happy.

'I…um…I hope this room is to your liking?'

'Yes, it is very comfortable, thank you.'

Silently he cursed his awkwardness. This was not a conversation for the bedroom. Why had he come here tonight? He recalled how beautifully she had played at Gwen's soirée, his pride in her performance, the possessiveness he had felt when the men had clustered round her. A spike of desire coursed through him and he tried again.

'You played like an angel tonight.' She smiled at that. Encouraged, he moved closer, holding out his hands. 'I did not know I had such an accomplished wife.'

Cautiously she reached out for him.

'I am glad that I pleased you, Gideon.'

'You do please me.' As he pulled her into his arms

he realised that he really meant it. 'You please me a great deal.'

She looked up at him, shyly accepting his kiss.

Gideon made love to her that night. Dominique returned his caresses but she kept her emotions in check and tried to respond as she thought a wife should, compliant and quietly accepting of his attentions. His lovemaking was gentle and restrained, as if he was afraid she might break beneath him, and although there was none of the hot heady passion of their first coupling, when it was over, Dominique found it immensely satisfying to have him lying with her, to hold him in her arms until he slipped from her bed to make the way back to his own room in the chill dark hours before dawn.

Chapter Seven

The following weeks were the happiest Dominique had ever known. Gideon bought her diamonds for her wedding gift and she wore them on almost every occasion. He took her driving in the park and escorted her everywhere, to balls, parties and breakfasts, introducing her to his friends and acquaintances. Whatever the news-sheets might say, he showed no signs of dissatisfaction with his bride, either in public or in private, when he came to her room at night. Dominique loved the special closeness of those nights and although he always returned to his own room before morning, when they met at breakfast, she thought his eyes had an added warmth when he greeted her.

As her confidence grew, Dominique began to make more changes to the Brook Street house. She ordered fresh flowers and arranged them in the hall and in the morning room, which had become her personal domain and where she was in the habit of entertaining her growing number of friends. The silent, tomblike atmosphere lifted, the servants looked happier and even Gideon remarked that the house felt much more like home. They were returning from a drive in the park when he said this and Dominique could not suppress a smile.

'Do you really think so? I am so pleased, because I was afraid you might not want me to change anything in your father's house.'

'You are mistress there,' he said, picking up her hand and kissing it. 'You may change whatever you wish.'

She felt the little bubble of happiness growing inside her. Gideon was more and more in the habit of such gestures and not only when they were in public. She was beginning to believe he genuinely cared for her. She wished she might respond in kind, but she could not forget Gwen's words of advice, that Gideon would find any such show of affection repellent. And Gwen was his sister, so she must know best.

When they reached Brook Street, Gideon helped her down and she felt his hand resting lightly on her back as he escorted her into the house. The butler opened the door to them, smiling broadly as he announced to Gideon that the delivery he had been waiting for had arrived.

'It has been set up, sir, just as you ordered.'

'Thank you, Judd.' Gideon relinquished his hat and gloves to the waiting footman, then put his hand under her elbow. 'Come, you should see this, too.'

He led her to the drawing room.

He said, as the butler closed the door quietly behind them, 'Well, what do you think?'

Dominique stared, blinked and stared again. Standing next to the piano was a golden harp and beside it a small stool covered with gold satin.

'Oh, Gideon,' she breathed, 'is it for me?'

'Of course. We have been in town for three months

now and it is something of an...er...anniversary present.'

She ran forwards and began to inspect it, running her fingers reverently over the strings.

'It is beautiful.'

'You said you used to play and I would like to hear you.'

'Yes, yes, once I have had time to practise a little.' She went back to him, unable to prevent herself from smiling. 'You are too generous to me, Gideon, thank you so much.'

Without thinking she threw her arms around his neck and kissed him full on the mouth.

'Oh! I beg your pardon.' She blushed and would have drawn back, but his arms slipped around her.

'Not at all. I must give you more presents, if that is the way you thank me.'

He was grinning down at her and suddenly all the careful restraint, the polite friendliness she had worked so hard to cultivate was forgotten. She could not speak for the heavy tattoo her heart was beating against her ribs and the sudden breathlessness that had overtaken her. She still had her arms about his neck and she could feel the silky softness of his hair against her fingers. The grin softened into a smile and the glint in his eyes heated her blood. She felt the tug of desire deep in her core and instinctively her body pressed against him.

Gideon's arms tightened as his body responded to the feel of her. It was the first time since their wedding night that she had taken the initiative and kissed him and he was surprised that her display of affection should please him so much. She felt so right in his arms and his sudden arousal was completed when he breathed in the scent of her, a mixture of summer flowers and an indefinable fragrance that he had come to recognise during those dark intimate nights as hers alone. The memory of her naked body heated his blood. He lowered his head to nibble at the tender lobe of her ear. She shuddered, but pressed even closer. A bolt of white-hot desire shot through him as he thought of the heights they might attain together.

'There is still an hour before we need change for dinner.' Dominique's very bones liquefied as his deep voice caressed her heightened senses. 'Would you like to—?'

A knock on the door interrupted them. As it opened Dominique quickly stepped out of his arms, but Gideon hung on to one hand, linking his fingers through hers. 'Yes, Judd, what is it?'

'The Earl of Martlesham, sir, wishing to know if you are at home.'

Gideon sighed. 'I suppose we must see him. Send him in.'

He cast a rueful look towards Dominique, who tried to hide her disappointment. Every fibre of her being screamed out that he should send her cousin to the devil, but the damage had been done, the magic of the moment was gone—perhaps Gideon had never felt it at all. The butler withdrew, to return a moment later and announce the earl in sonorous tones. Max came in, his fair features a little flushed from the heat of the day and his eyes going immediately to their linked hands.

Unhurriedly Gideon stepped forwards, saying calmly, 'Martlesham, good day to you. Have you come to see how we go on?'

Max returned Gideon's bow with a brief nod.

'Good day to you, Albury, Cousin. I thought I should call to let you know I was back in town.'

'How very good of you.'

Gideon's voice was heavy with sarcasm, which brought a dull angry flush to Max's face. Remembering her place as mistress of the house, Dominique invited him to sit down.

'Have you seen my mother?' she asked, when they had made themselves comfortable. 'Is she well?'

'Aye, as well as she ever will be. She came to see me just before I left Martlesham Abbey. Wanted me to use my influence to get her an audience with the Foreign Secretary. As if I had any! Told her she must look to you, Albury, for that sort of thing. As her son-in-law I have no doubt you would like nothing better than to seek out your new French relatives.'

The sneer in his voice was unmistakable. Dominique stiffened and opened her mouth to respond, but Gideon caught her eye and gave the slightest shake of his head.

'I shall of course do my best to assist Mrs Rainault,' he said evenly. 'Now we have signed the Treaty of Amiens I am sure there is a much greater chance of success.'

'Fustian,' Max retorted. 'Jerome Rainault's been dead these ten years. You of all people should know what savages the French are.'

Dominique flinched, but Gideon's smile did not falter. If anything, it grew as his eyes flickered in her direction.

'Not all of them.'

Max frowned, but after a moment he sat back in his chair, his brow clearing, and he addressed Dominique with at least a semblance of friendliness, 'So, how do you go on, Cousin? How do you like London?'

'Very much.' Dominique took her lead from Gideon and kept her tone light. 'I have made so many friends here. Everyone is very kind.'

'Well, perhaps they don't know—'

'Oh, everyone knows the circumstances of our marriage,' Gideon interrupted him, his voice dangerously quiet. 'The society columns of the news-sheets carried little else for weeks after we arrived. They were very well informed.'

A cruel smile curled Max's mouth.

'Were they, indeed? I wonder how that occurred.'

'Some malicious troublemaker,' replied Gideon. 'But their efforts were wasted. We have shown everyone that we are the epitome of domestic bliss. And you will be pleased to know my wife is becoming a firm favourite with all the hostesses. Ask anyone in town.' He smiled. 'But what are we thinking of? Perhaps you would like to take a glass of wine with us, to toast our felicity—'

'Thank you, no.' Max rose abruptly. 'I have an engagement to dine with friends.'

'Then Judd will show you out,' murmured Dominique, moving over to the bell pull. Max followed and took her hand.

'Accept my felicitations, Cousin. I am...pleased...to see you so comfortable.'

'Thank you.'

'And I have to thank you, too, Max,' said Gideon pleasantly. 'You have provided me with a perfect wife. Who could ever have thought things would work out so well?'

Without a word the earl gave another clipped bow and left the room.

Gideon smiled.

'I think we have done well, there, my sweet. Your dear cousin is not at all happy that his plans have misfired so spectacularly.'

She said slowly, 'We have made a fool of him, Gideon. He will not like that.'

'No, but he cannot alter it, so if he has any sense he will shrug and accept the situation.' Gideon glanced at the clock. 'I suppose we must change for dinner. We are engaged to join some card party tonight, are we not?'

'Yes, Lady Torrington's,' she said absently. 'Gideon— what you said, about helping *Maman*…would you mind if *I* tried to discover something about Papa? I was afraid to mention it before…'

He put his fingers under her chin.

'My dear, you should not be afraid to ask anything of me.'

His tone was light, but the warmth she had seen in his eyes earlier had disappeared.

'Are you angry with me, Gideon, because I want to find my father?' she challenged him. 'I cannot stop loving him, just because you have cause to hate all Girondins.'

His hand dropped.

'Who told you that?'

'Gwendoline. She—she told me about your aunt and uncle. And your brother.'

'Then you know my hatred is well founded.'

'But if you knew Papa—'

'I have no *wish* to know him,' he snapped. 'He was part of the regime which caused the death of three people very dear to me. That I can never forgive.'

'As you can never forgive me for being his daughter.'

There, she had said it. Dominique trembled at her own temerity. The colour drained from his face and his mouth became a thin line as he held back his anger. He turned away and walked to the fireplace where he stood with his back to her, staring down into the flames.

'I have tried to forget it, these past few weeks,' he said at last. 'But it is always there, a ghost between us.'

She walked up to him and put her hand on his shoulder.

'We have not fared so very badly, have we? We have to keep trying, Gideon. We have to make this work.'

'To prove Max was wrong? I am beginning to think that game is not worth the prize.'

'No, this is nothing to do with Max.' She ran her tongue over her dry lips and swallowed. She said, forcing the words out, 'I am carrying your child.'

He said nothing, but she felt a shudder run through him. She removed her hand and stepped back. The silence continued, unbroken, and at last, with a sigh, she turned and left the room.

Dominique fled to her bedchamber. Kitty was already there, waiting to help her change for dinner. She thought about dismissing her maid and indulging in a hearty bout of tears, but instead she fought down her unhappiness and allowed herself to be helped into the blue satin she had chosen to wear to Lady Torrington's card party.

Long after the door had closed Gideon remained staring down into the fire. So this was it, the last link in the chain that would bind him to his wife forever. A child. How ironic, that the heir to Rotham should have French blood in his veins, after all his family had suffered at the hands of that nation. It might be a girl, of course, but what did it matter? He would not cast off the mother of his child.

He raised his eyes to the mirror. It was as if the ghosts of his brother and his aunt were at his shoulders.

He waited, expecting to feel their disapprobation, but he felt…nothing. This baby was innocent of its history—as was his wife. He realised that he was in an impossible position: he could not turn his back on his marriage, any more than he could give up his inheritance. Nicky might not be the wife he had dreamed of, and he had never wanted to be his father's heir, but it was so. It was too late for regrets, he must move on and make what he could of his life.

There was a tangible lightening of the air around him, as if the shades of his brother and his aunt had disappeared.

Dominique was sitting at her dressing table while Kitty put the finishing touches to her hair when Gideon came in. Quietly she dismissed her maid, but remained in her seat, looking into the mirror as Gideon came to stand behind her.

'What you said. A baby. Are you—quite sure?'

She nodded. 'As sure as I can be.' She saw the dawning wonder and confusion on his countenance and turned to face him. He dropped on to one knee and took her hands.

'Then…perhaps you should be resting—do you want me to send our apologies to Lady Torrington?'

'No, no, there is no need for that.'

'Then, what shall we do? What do you *want* to do?'

His bewilderment dragged a shaky laugh from her.

'I want us to have dinner, Gideon, and to go to Torrington House. It is early days yet, no one need know that I am increasing.' She met his eyes. 'I want us to go on exactly as we are, Gideon.'

'Are you sure?'

'Yes, I am very sure.'

She did not have the courage to ask him not to avoid her bed and could only hope he understood her.

'Then I will go and change.'

'Please do.' She smiled. 'You will incur Cook's wrath if his dinner is spoiled because he has to wait for you.'

She turned back to her mirror, to pin up the last few curls.

'One more thing.' He stopped at the door. 'Of course you must do everything you can to find your father. You do not need to involve me—I will direct Rogers, the family lawyer, to come and see you.'

Even as she struggled to find the words to thank him, he was gone.

Gideon was more attentive than usual at dinner and towards the end of their evening at Torrington House, instead of going off to join his friends at White's and leaving his wife to make her own way home, he elected to accompany her back to Brook Street. When she remonstrated with him, declaring that she did not wish to curtail his pleasure, he replied with perfect sincerity that escorting her home *was* his pleasure.

They were in the hall, waiting for their carriage, and as he took his wife's cloak from the footman and gently placed it about her shoulders, Gideon reflected on the change that had come over him in the past few months. By heaven, he was becoming quite domesticated! His wife's soft voice brought him back to the present.

'I heard Mr Williams say you had been invited to Martlesham House.' There was a note of uncertainty in her voice.

Gideon gave her shoulders a little squeeze.

'I have no interest in associating with Max or his friends.' He escorted her to their waiting carriage and settled himself comfortably beside her before adding, 'I think I have outgrown such company.'

'I am glad. I fear Max has little regard for the feelings of others.'

'None at all, but it was not until he hoaxed me that I saw just how thoughtless he is.' He turned towards her, saying earnestly, 'I was careless, too. It was wrong of me to punish you for his trickery. I was a fool, Nicky, but I hope I have learned my lesson now.'

'Oh, Gideon—'

'I know this marriage is not what either of us wanted,' he rushed on, needing to explain, to make amends. 'But it will not be so bad, I promise you. I have no doubt we will rub along very well. And once the little matter of an heir is out of the way I shall not importune you with unreasonable demands.'

She had twisted in her seat and raised her hand, as if to touch his cheek, but now it fell again.

'Un-unreasonable?'

'Yes. I shall not expect you to submit to my… attentions.' He frowned. 'What is it, Nicky? Have I upset you?'

'No, no.' She shook her head quickly. 'I am merely tired, that is all.'

She drew back into the shadows of the carriage and they lapsed into silence. Gideon hoped she understood what he had been trying to say. He feared he had phrased it very badly, yet he could not bring himself to state it quite as baldly as his father had done. Gideon could still remember his father's words as they had lowered the wasted body of the viscountess into the family vault. 'So many years of pain, the stillborn babes, the illness—if I had taken a mistress for my lusts I would have spared your poor mother a great deal of suffering.'

His father had been at pains to impress upon him a husband's responsibilities: his wife would expect to give him a son, perhaps two, but childbearing was a perilous occupation and a gentleman would not overtax his wife's delicate body with his demands. That was twelve years ago. Gideon had been a mere boy of sixteen and devastated by the death of his kind, gentle mother. He had dreamed of joining the army, but his widowed father had insisted upon keeping him close, and when James had died two years later, Gideon's fate had been sealed. Not for him the glories of the battlefield. The title and the heavy responsibility of the estate and its people was his fate. Was it any wonder, then, that when the inheritance from his godmother had given him his independence he had rushed to town and proceeded to kick up every kind of spree and lark? That was when he had fallen in with Max's set and proceeded to prove to his new friends that he could drink, gamble and wench with the best of them. Or perhaps that should be the worst. His father clearly thought so.

When they reached Brook Street, Gideon suggested they should take wine together in the drawing room, but Nicky declined and with a brief goodnight she disappeared up the stairs. He watched her go and a shard of disappointment pierced him. She did not want his company, and, now she was carrying his child, she would not want him in her bed.

Invitations were flooding into Brook Street for balls, routs, riding parties and soirées and Dominique acknowledged that her sister-in-law was in no small measure responsible for her popularity.

'If you had not taken me in hand, I should not go on

half so well,' she said to Gwendoline when they sat together in the supper room during Lady Grayson's summer ball. 'You have shown me just how to go on here.'

'Nonsense, you would have come about,' replied Gwen, justifiably proud of her protégée.

The shy little sparrow, blown into town on the icy spring air, had been transformed into an exotic creature, dressing in hot, vibrant colours that made the most of her dusky curls and emerald-green eyes. Her liveliness and appealing manners charmed the hostesses, who considered her an asset to any gathering. She had also attracted the attention of a considerable number of gentlemen, but watching Dominique now, as Gideon led her on to the dance floor, Gwendoline concluded that her vivacious sister-in-law had eyes only for her husband.

Not that Dominique doted upon Gideon: on the contrary, she never clung to his arm and smiled complacently when he went off to the card room, or partnered another lady in the dance, but Gwendoline noticed those occasional, unguarded moments when Dominique's eyes would rest just a fraction too long upon her husband. She had seen that same look upon the faces of other young brides and it rarely survived the first year. After that they found other men to amuse and divert them. She sighed. As she had done in a vain attempt to pique Ribblestone's interest.

Dominique went down the dance with her husband, wishing the moment could go on forever. She knew no greater felicity than to stand up with Gideon. He was always most attentive when they were in public and she could pretend at such times that they were really the doting couple society thought them. It was a game they played, but this evening her confidence had been badly shaken, following an encounter with her cousin.

It was inevitable that they should meet Max occasionally, but they generally contented themselves with a brief nod in passing. However, this evening Max had sought her out. She thought he must have been waiting for his opportunity, because it was one of the rare occasions during the evening when she was standing alone. He asked her to dance with him and when she hesitated he gave a rueful smile.

'I suppose you think me too bad a person to partner you, but can we not put aside our animosity, just for half an hour? We are family, after all.'

'Very well, Cousin.' She took his hand and let him lead her on to the dance floor, well aware of the curious glances of those around them. The rumours might have died down, but the circumstances of her irregular marriage to Gideon were not yet forgotten. She held her head up and smiled at her partner. 'Perhaps this will show we are not at daggers drawn, my lord.'

It was a lively country dance and, by the end of it, the earl's countenance was more ruddy than ever and he was wheezing a little.

She went to move away, but he caught her hand.

'Not yet. I want to talk to you.'

'I do not think there is anything to talk about.'

He drew her towards the long windows which had been opened to allow in the balmy night air.

'Are you not interested to know what is going on at Martlesham?'

'My mother is a frequent correspondent. She tells me all I want to know.'

'Let us step out on to the terrace a moment—'

'No.' She stood her ground. 'I do not trust you, Max. You are wont to make trouble.'

He looked pained. 'I merely want to get a little air. Dancing is so exhausting.'

'You should dance more, Cousin, not less.' Her eyes fell on the bulging front of his waistcoat. 'The exercise would be beneficial.'

He scowled at that.

'Aye, you may mock me, madam, but I know this marriage of yours is not as it seems.'

'You know nothing. We are very happy together.' She added, a touch of relief in her voice, 'My husband is over there and he is looking for me. Do not detain me, Cousin, if you do not wish to anger him.'

He reached out and caught her arm as she went to walk away.

'Happy, are you?' he muttered, his lip curling. 'Well, enjoy it while you can, Cousin. As soon as he has got you with child, Albury will pack you off to Rotham so he can take up his old life again.'

With a great effort of will Dominique kept her hands from sliding protectively across her belly. It was two weeks since she had told Gideon about the baby and so far they had kept it a secret from everyone else. With a scorching look she pulled herself free and hurried away to join Gideon.

'I saw you with Martlesham,' he said as she came up. 'I hope he did not upset you?'

'No, he wanted to dance and I thought we should, to show the world there is no bad feeling between us.'

'And after?' He was watching her carefully. 'He tried to take you outside.'

She shrugged.

'He would make mischief if he could, but I am wise to him.'

'Perhaps I should warn him off—'

She put her hand on his arm.

'Please, Gideon, let it be. He is my cousin and I would rather we ignored him than quarrelled.'

'Perhaps you are right,' he said. 'After all, he has done his worst. He cannot hurt us now.'

Dominique allowed him to lead her away, but despite her smile and Gideon's assertion, the earl's warning remained with her.

Chapter Eight

Max's words were still in her head the next morning, when she stood naked before the mirror and placed her hands on her thickening body. Gideon had insisted she should see his doctor and she had just endured a lengthy examination, after which Dr Harris, a blunt, jovial man, confirmed what she already knew.

'Carry on with your life as before,' he said. 'I don't believe in ladies mollycoddling themselves just because they are increasing. You are a healthy young woman, exercise and fresh air will do you more good than lying on a daybed. Your body will tell you what you can and cannot do, but you should not need to make any changes just yet.'

She had no intention of making changes, but Gideon had already done so. He had not shared her bed since the day she had told him about the baby. She could only assume that he considered his duty done now, until she had given birth. Her hands moved over her belly: in a few months it would be swollen with their growing child.

A knock at the door interrupted her thoughts and she reached quickly for her dressing gown.

'Come in.'

Gideon entered. He was smiling.

'I have been talking to Harris. He agrees with your assessment that the child is due in December.'

'Are you pleased, Gideon?' she asked him shyly.

'Do you doubt it?' He came forwards and put his hands on her shoulders. 'I am delighted.'

'Then so, too, am I,' she said, smiling up at him.

He hesitated before lowering his head to kiss her. Tentatively she put her arms about him and felt his hands tighten on her shoulders. Her body tingled with anticipation as she felt his fingers close upon the wrap, as if he was about to push the thin silk from her shoulders and expose her nakedness. Her disappointment was searing when instead he gently put her away from him.

'Delighted,' he said again, smiling awkwardly down at her. 'I must go. I have work to do. How do you amuse yourself today?'

She turned away so that he should not see how his rejection had hurt her.

'I am going to Grosvenor Square to take tea with Gwendoline before we drive in the park.'

'Then we shall meet again at dinner.' He walked to the door.

'You haven't forgotten that we go to Knightson House tonight?'

He turned to look at her. 'You won't be too fatigued?'

'Of course not.' *But I would much rather stay here with you.*

She drew a breath, trying to frame her thoughts into words. 'But I would happily remain here, if you would rather not go?'

'No, no, you wish to go and I shall be delighted to escort you.' He smiled, gave a little bow and left her.

* * *

Dominique sank down on to the stool and stared into the mirror. Gideon was so polite, so distant. Not only did he avoid her room at night, but he rarely touched her now—the kiss he had just given her was a mere brushing of the lips. Her own had parted, but he had immediately drawn back, as if repulsed by the contact. Was Max right—did he want to go back to his bachelor existence? She wondered if she should tell him how much she missed his attentions, but she was afraid the admission would push him still further away. If the married ladies of her acquaintance were to be believed then a wife should keep her husband at a distance, never for one moment let him think *she* desired *him*. She must remain aloof, unattainable. Could that be true, when all her instincts told her the opposite?

Whenever she was with Gideon she wanted to put her arms about him, to touch him and kiss him. Such public displays were frowned upon. It might have been thirty years ago, but the Duchess of Devonshire's scandalous behaviour was still talked of—when, as a young bride, she had danced across the room to sit upon her husband's knee. If a duchess could not indulge in such forward behaviour, how much worse would it be for an ordinary lady, and one who was only half English? Gideon already had a deep hatred for the French, she must not give him even more cause to despise her. Sighing, she pushed herself up off the stool and went into the dressing room. She would talk to Gwendoline. When they were alone she would ask her again just what was and wasn't acceptable behaviour in a wife.

Dominique had lost no time in unburdening herself to her sister-in-law and had finished explaining her dilemma even before her teacup was empty. Lady Ribblestone was sympathetic.

'You are in love with Gideon.'

Dominique nodded miserably.

'Yes, I believe I am.'

'Oh, my poor girl.'

'I know,' murmured Dominique, trying not to cry. 'If Gideon knew of it, he would feel sorry for me and I do not think I could bear that.'

'Of course not.' Gwendoline sat for a moment, staring into space. 'Now, let us consider your problem. What is it you want from Gideon?'

'I suppose it is too much to hope that he might fall in love with me.' Seeing Gwen's doubtful look, she sighed. 'I know I cannot expect him to spend all his time with me, but I should like us to be…to remain friends.'

'Then you must make a life for yourself, show him you go on very well without him. A man does not like a miserable companion, but if he sees you are cheerful and content then he will be happy to spend time in your company.'

'Is that possible?'

'Oh, Lord, yes. It is the best one can hope for.' Gwendoline went quiet, as if contemplating what she had just said, but after a few moments she shook off her reverie. 'You could take a lover.'

'I do not want a lover,' retorted Dominique, her cheeks burning.

'No, perhaps that is for the best,' Gwen agreed with her. 'Gideon would be very likely to blame it on your French blood. However, it will do no harm if the gentlemen show a preference for *you*, my love, and they are already doing so. My efforts to turn you into a success seem to be working. Why, Lady Grayson told me how many gentlemen wanted to dance with you last night. But it is not just the gentlemen, every hostess in town is eager for your presence.'

'They are curious to see the bride Max foisted upon Gideon,' said Dominique bitterly.

'Those rumours are well and truly forgotten now, I assure you. They see you as the rich and fashionable Mrs Albury and, of course, as a future viscountess. Everyone is charmed by you and there is no better way to punish your mischievous cousin than to become society's darling.'

'I do not think I shall be going about in society for very much longer,' admitted Dominique. 'You see, I am…I am in an interesting state.'

'*Already*? Are you sure?'

Gwendoline's shocked response brought the colour flooding to Dominique's face again.

'Yes, but I would be grateful if you kept it to yourself, at least for a while.'

'Of course, my dear—but that is wonderful news. Does Gideon know?'

'Yes, I told him immediately.'

'And is he pleased?'

'I think so.'

'Well, that is a relief. I have no doubt he will want to take you to Rotham soon, to make you known to Papa. And you had best get used to standing up for yourself, for I doubt if Gideon will stay long with you there.'

Dominique felt her spirits sinking.

'That is what Max said. He s-said Gideon would be glad to be rid of me, so he could go back to his old life.'

'The Earl of Martlesham is an odious mischief-maker,' said Gwendoline frankly. 'Gideon's behaviour since he brought you to town cannot be faulted. He has been a model husband in public.'

'But only because he wants to show everyone that we are happily married. What if…what if he comes back to town and sets up a mistress?' stammered Dominique, voicing her deepest fear.

'That is a risk we all have to take,' said Gwendoline. She sighed. 'Not that Ribblestone has one, he is far too wedded to his politics. No, be advised by me—you must not show any tendency to cling to Gideon. And enjoy your remaining time in town as much as you can. Once you are immured in Buckinghamshire there is no telling when you will get away again. Heavens, is that the time? My coachman will be at the door any moment to take us to the park. And after that I shall drop you at Brook Street. You and Gideon are promised to attend the Knightsons' ball this evening, are you not? You must have plenty of time to change into another of those delectable gowns of yours. Everyone will be watching to see what new creation you will be wearing.'

Dominique laughed.

'There will be dozens of ladies there equally well dressed.'

'One or two, perhaps, but few can carry off the vibrant colours we have chosen for you. It makes you stand out in the crowd.'

'I am not sure I want to stand out, Gwen.'

'Of course you do. Gideon has already told me how proud he is of his fashionable wife.'

'Has he? Has he really?'

Gwen laughed and patted her hands.

'Yes, *really*, so let us not disappoint him!'

The Knightsons' midsummer ball was a crowded affair, but Dominique had so many acquaintances in town now that she was not overawed by the throng of people jostling to get into the ballroom. Her confidence was boosted by Gideon's compliments when they had arrived at Knightson House and she removed her cloak. She was wearing a new gown of green silk, a perfect match for the emeralds Gideon had given her on their first night in town, and she had piled her dark hair upon her head with just one glossy curl falling upon her bare shoulder.

'You continue to delight me, my dear,' he said, raising her hand to his lips.

She blushed at the compliment. He might well have spoken for the benefit of the other guests milling around them, but there was no mistaking the warmth in his eyes when he looked at her and she entered the ballroom with a smile on her lips and a song in her heart.

Her happiness continued when Gideon led her out for the first two dances and after that she was content for him to dance with his sister and other ladies of their acquaintance. Dominique herself was not short of partners, but by supper time she was eager to find her husband again. Her diminutive height proved a disadvantage as she pushed her way through the crowd, standing on tiptoe to try to see Gideon's tall figure. A slight jostling occurred and as she stepped back to avoid a cheerfully inebriated couple her heel came down upon someone's toe.

'Oh, I beg your pardon!' She swung around, an apologetic smile on her lips. The gentleman standing behind her was a stranger, but he was laughing.

'*C'est rien.* Madame…Albury, is it not?' He made her a bow. 'We have not been introduced, but in such circumstances…Raymond Lamotte, *madame*, *à votre service*. This is most fortunate. I have been wanting to talk to you.'

'To me?' She studied the young man before her. He was of average height and darkly handsome with his raven hair, cropped à la Brutus.

'*Mais oui, madame.* One could not help hearing the rumours…' He looked a little self-conscious. 'You are the daughter of a Frenchman, are you not?' Dominique was no longer concerned for the man's appearance. Seeing her intense look, he spread his hands. 'I fled from my beloved France several years ago. It broke my heart to do so, but…' he gave a shrug '…it is not the great country it once was.'

'N-no, indeed,' she murmured.

He glanced around.

'It is difficult to speak here, it is so crowded. Perhaps, could I beg the honour of escorting you to supper?'

It took Dominique only a moment to decide. Gideon was nowhere to be seen and this young man was watching her so hopefully.

'Of course, *monsieur.*'

The supper room was very busy, but her companion led her to a small table in one of the alcoves. An elegant supper was laid before her, but Dominique hardly noticed, for she was soon lost in reminiscences about France. Raymond Lamotte was eager to talk and she guessed that he was homesick, as she had been when she first came to England.

'Of course it was easier for me,' she told him. 'I was a child, just ten years old, and my English mother had tried to ensure that I was familiar with the ways of this country. For you, *monsieur*, it must have been so much more painful.'

'It was. I did not wish to quit France but what could I do? My friends were imprisoned, or worse. At first I was in favour of the revolution. The country needed to change, *mais oui*, but then came the Terror and the execution of the poor King and Queen—it was too much. The change was going too far.'

'That is exactly what Papa thought,' exclaimed Dominique. 'But his views were too moderate and no one wanted to listen.'

'So he brought you to England?' He raised his hand and signalled to the waiter to refill their glasses.

'No.' Dominique waited until they were alone again, pleased for the delay so that she could muster her thoughts. 'He arranged for Mama and me to come here while he remained in France.' She added quietly, 'We have not heard from him for ten years.'

'Ah, I see. *Je regrette*—'

She raised her hand, fending off his sympathy. Glancing up, she noticed with surprise that the supper room was almost empty.

'Oh, dear, how the time has flown,' she said. 'The dancing will begin again soon. Thank you, Monsieur Lamotte, I have enjoyed our conversation, but I must get back.'

'Of course, I shall escort you.' He rose and held out his arm to her. 'If you will permit, I should like to talk more with you. It is so refreshing to be able to speak freely about my country with someone who loves it as I do.'

She nodded, saying shyly, 'I should like that too, sir.'

'May I call upon you tomorrow morning?'

'No!' She stopped in alarm, imagining Gideon's anger if a Frenchman should arrive at his door. 'No, that is not possible.' She swallowed, aware of his disappointment. 'But perhaps…perhaps you will be walking in Green Park tomorrow, sir, at ten o'clock? It is a popular promenade.'

'And...will you be there, Madame Albury, at ten o'clock?'

'I will,' she declared, stifling her conscience. After all, there could be no harm in them meeting in public. 'I will be there.'

'Then so, too, shall I,' declared Monsieur Lamotte. They were entering the ballroom, where the musicians were already tuning up for the next set. He said, a laugh in his voice, 'I would ask you to dance with me, but I fear I have taken far too much of your time already and see several gentlemen giving me the angry look.'

She blushed and disclaimed, but did not seek to detain him. Even as she watched him walking away two young gentlemen came up, cheerfully vying with each other for the privilege of leading her out. Smiling, Dominique turned her thoughts away from Raymond Lamotte and gave herself up to the enjoyable task of choosing a dance partner.

'I am sorry I was not able to take you in to supper,' said Gideon as they rode home later that night. 'Anthony and I were caught up in a political discussion and I did not like to abandon him. I hope you found someone to look after you?'

'Yes, I did, thank you.'

Dominique struggled briefly with her conscience, wondering how she could explain to Gideon about Monsieur Lamotte, but even as she tried to frame her reply he took her hand, saying, 'That's good. I am glad you are finding your feet in town, Nicky.'

'Oh, yes,' she replied. 'I go on much more comfortably, now I know so many people.'

'Aye, I noticed you were never without a partner tonight.' He laughed. 'It will soon be that you will not have need of me to accompany you at all.'

She turned, looking at his dark shape beside her as she said earnestly, 'Oh, never say that, Gideon. I would not be half so comfortable if you were not with me.'

He laughed and raised her hand to his lips.

'Flatterer!'

Did he really think that, or was he perhaps looking forward to the day when he could leave her to fend for herself and return to his old bachelor ways? Dominique longed to ask him, but she kept silent, fearful of his answer.

Chapter Nine

Dominique met Raymond in Green Park the following morning. They spoke only briefly, but arranged to meet again the next day, and the next. Raymond was a charming companion. Not only were his recollections of France quite riveting, but he was also interested in her own childhood memories, and since she dared not mention her French connections to Gideon it was a relief to be able to talk about her family with someone who understood what she had been through. Soon she felt that they were firm friends.

However, they had very few acquaintances in common, so it was some weeks before they met again socially, at an evening party given by Lord and Lady Dortwood. Dominique spotted Raymond in the crowd, but although he acknowledged her with a faint nod the evening was well advanced before he came over to greet her.

'I thought you would never ask me to dance,' she said, when he led her out to join a new set.

'I was not sure you would wish to acknowledge me,' he murmured. 'I see you are with your husband.'

'Of course I will acknowledge you,' she said, feeling the heat burning her cheeks. 'I am not ashamed of knowing you!'

She danced on, unsettled by the realisation that she had not mentioned her friendship with Raymond to anyone. Their morning walks in Green Park had so far excited no comment since they had never met anyone with whom Dominique was acquainted. Now it occurred to her that others might consider such meetings to be clandestine. That would not do, at all.

When the dance ended she took Raymond's arm and firmly led him across the room to where Gideon was waiting. She performed the introduction and after a short exchange Raymond moved away. Gideon lifted his quizzing glass to watch him go.

'Where did you say you met him?'

'At the Knightsons' ball.' She frowned up at him. 'Really, Gideon, was it necessary to be so cold towards Monsieur Lamotte? You barely spoke half-a-dozen words to him.'

'I beg your pardon, my dear, but we have so little in common.'

'It was more than that. You were positively arctic!'

'I am certainly surprised by your friendship with the fellow.'

'You are offended, because he is French,' she declared hotly. 'Your hatred of the whole race is quite unreasonable.'

He did not reply and with a toss of her head she turned away.

'Nicky!' She stopped and he said quietly, 'I would rather you did not pursue your acquaintance with Monsieur Lamotte.'

She turned, her brows raised in haughty surprise.

'That is outrageous! You cannot dictate with whom I shall associate.'

'I was not aware I was dictating to you, my dear, merely making my wishes clear.'

'It is the same thing.'

'Not at all.'

'And if I refuse to comply?'

His eyes narrowed. He leaned closer so that his words were for her alone.

'Do not forget, madam, that you are my wife.'

Her head went up.

'But I am not your slave!'

With a swish of her skirts she flounced away from him.

How dare Gideon dictate to her! It was nothing but prejudice, because Raymond was French, and she was tired of it. She wished Gwendoline was here, but she was attending some tedious political dinner with Ribblestone. There was no one else present to whom she could pour out her anger and frustration, so she took herself off to the card room and proceeded to lose a large portion of her pin money.

However, by the time she left the card room her temper had cooled, so that when she saw her husband in the ballroom she went straight up to him, saying penitently, 'I beg your pardon, Gideon, I should not have ripped up at you so.' His brows went up, but the harshness left his face as he took her outstretched hand and she was emboldened to continue. 'I understand why you might not like Monsieur Lamotte, but he is a link with my childhood, the life I knew before we moved to England.' She clung to his fingers. 'Please do not ask me to give him up.'

He stared down at her, a look she could not interpret in his hazel eyes.

'Is he merely an acquaintance, Nicky, nothing more?'

'Of course. What else should he be?'

'And your morning meetings with him in Green Park?' When her eyes flew to his face he gave her a wry smile. 'You were seen, by Anthony. I told him it was nothing and the fact that you had your maid with you gives weight to my belief.'

'And it *is* nothing, Gideon, I give you my word.' She sighed. 'But I quite see how it must look, so I shall not meet him there again.'

'Thank you.' He squeezed her hand. 'I will not have the fellow call at Brook Street, but if you meet him at such parties as this and wish to dance with him, I will not object.'

A compromise. She was aware of how much ground he was giving.

'Very well, Gideon. Thank you.' She suddenly felt very tired. 'Do you think our hostess would object if I went home now?'

'No, of course not. I shall escort you. Go downstairs and collect your wrap while I give our excuses to Lady Dortwood.'

Dominique made her way to the hall, where a lackey was sent scurrying off to fetch her cloak.

'I fear your husband does not like me.'

Dominique whirled about to find Raymond Lamotte standing behind her.

She gave a sad little smile. 'It will be best if we discontinue our walks together, *monsieur*.'

He shook his head. 'Ah, that is a sadness, because I have something to discuss with you.'

'We will have to do so the next time we meet—'

'It concerns your father.' His words brought her eyes flying to his face. He continued, 'You told me you were trying to find him, so I have made the enquiries. I have friends in France who still have influence with the *Directoire*. They will know how to find the missing person. Some have been imprisoned for many years and it is not easy to gain information, but there is a man who knows how to do these things. He moves regularly between France and England, but secretly, so the less people who know of this the better. I have spoken to him about your father and he thinks we may be able to find him.'

She shook her head, hardly daring to hope. 'Then you must come to the house. Gideon could not object to that—'

'Oh, but I fear he would, *madame*. You have told me yourself he is not a friend to my country. He would think it a—how do you say it?—a ploy. *Non*, I would rather discuss this with you alone. I need information from you.'

'Anything,' she said eagerly.

'*Eh bien*, you must write down everything you remember of your father—where he lived, what he looked like, who his friends were. No little detail is too small. When you have done that, you must bring it to me at my lodgings and I will pass it on to my friend.'

'Yes, yes, I will, of course.'

'Good. I need the information by tomorrow evening. My contact is returning to France the following morning and he has promised to seek out news of your father.'

'Oh, oh, thank you.' She felt the hope bubbling up within her again. *Maman* would be so pleased when she told her! 'I shall begin writing it all up tonight and send it round—'

'No, you must bring it yourself. Can you be there at five o'clock? Then I can read it and if there are any things that are not clear, any questions, you will be there to answer them.'

'Yes, of course, I understand.'

'Good.' He gave her his direction, looking over his shoulder as the servant hurried up to them carrying her rose silk wrap over his arm. 'I must go now. Remember, my contact relies upon secrecy—if he is discovered, then all is lost.'

She nodded. 'You may trust me to tell no one.'

'Thank you, *madame*.' He smiled and pressed a final kiss upon her fingers. 'Until tomorrow, then. Five o'clock. Do not be late!'

He hurried away and Dominique absently fastened her cloak about her shoulders. *Maman* had been trying for years to find news of Papa without success. To have someone else searching, someone who knew the workings of the French government, surely they would have far more chance of finding out the truth? She had never quite given up hope, but it had lain dormant and now, suddenly, it was blossoming again. She could not wait to get back to Brook Street and write out everything she could remember about her father.

Gideon found his wife very distracted on the homeward journey. He wondered if she was regretting her promise to give up her walks with Raymond Lamotte. When Ribblestone had mentioned that he had seen Nicky walking with a French émigré in Green Park Gideon had shrugged it off. He guessed it was a chance meeting, and he quite understood why she had not mentioned the matter to him, but a casual remark to Kitty when he met her on the stairs two days later elicited the information that her mistress was in the habit of walking in the park every morning. And, yes, the French gentleman was always there.

Intrigued, but not yet alarmed, Gideon had asked Anthony to make discreet enquiries and found that the émigré was an impecunious young man from an obscure but perfectly respectable French family who had fled the Terror and was now living in bachelor lodgings in Cleveland Row. The worst that was known of the young man was that he frequented a gambling hell in King Street that Ribblestone himself favoured. However, Gideon knew that if his wife continued to meet with Lamotte it would only be a matter of time before the gossipmongers heard of it and began to speculate upon the nature of their acquaintance. Their liaison might be quite innocent, but it would not do and Gideon had known he would have to speak to Nicky about the matter.

However, he had been reluctant to do so—until he had seen Lamotte dancing with his wife. Then Gideon had been aware of a sharp stab of disapproval. He had watched Nicky dance with dozens of fellows since they had come to town and thought nothing of it—after all, he was a reasonable man—but Raymond Lamotte was a Frenchman and to see the handsome young dog paying such attentions to his wife had roused Gideon's temper. In fact, in any other circumstances he would have thought the emotion he felt when he saw them together was jealousy, but how could one feel that for a wife one did not love?

No, he did not love his wife, he thought as the carriage pulled up in Brook Street and he escorted her into the house. How could he? She was a constant reminder of the loss his family had suffered. He felt a tiny kick of guilt. Perhaps his disapproval this evening of her friendship with Lamotte had been a little severe. In an effort to make amends he invited her to join him in the drawing room. She gave a little start.

'Oh—no! That is, how kind of you, Gideon, but I—I am very tired. I think I will retire....'

He covered his disappointment with a smile.

'Of course, my dear, if that is what you wish.'

He raised her hand to his lips and her fingers trembled in his grasp. As he looked up he was surprised to find something in her green eyes that made his brows snap together. A wistfulness, a longing that touched a chord inside him and roused the desire for her that was never very far away. How long had it been since he had been in her bed?

'Perhaps you would like me to come up with you?'

Her recoil told him immediately how wrong he had been.

'Oh, I— If only... Not tonight, if you please, Gideon. I am nigh on dropping with fatigue.'

With a shy, apologetic smile she wished him goodnight and hurried away.

Gideon waited until she was out of sight before walking into the drawing room. It was perfectly reasonable for her to be tired. After all, she was increasing, although no one watching her lithe figure skipping around the dance floor this evening would have guessed it. She had looked quite animated, too, never more so than when she had been dancing with Lamotte. Quickly Gideon dismissed the thought. He glanced around him. It was the custom to keep this room in readiness every evening with a good fire and candles burning in their wall-brackets, but despite the room's cheerful aspect

Gideon found that he had no desire to drink alone, so he went up to bed. When he reached Nicky's room he stopped. A strip of light shone beneath the door, showing that she was still awake, but there was no sound from the room, and after a few seconds he went on to his own bedchamber, disturbed by a vague, niggling dissatisfaction.

At breakfast the next morning Nicky greeted him with her usual good humour and Gideon's day brightened immediately.

'You are not fatigued by last night's exertions?' he asked her as she poured coffee for him.

She gave him a sunny smile.

'Not in the least. You know Dr Harris said I could carry on very much as before.'

It was on the tip of his tongue to ask her if she thought that included her wifely duties in the bedchamber, but he was afraid to bring that haunted, frightened look back into her face, so instead he asked casually what she planned to do today.

'I have some letters to write, and after that I am taking Kitty to Grosvenor Square with me. Gwen's dresser is an excellent coiffeuse—'

'You are not going to cut it short?' He frowned, recalling the way her dusky curls cascaded over her shoulders, a perfect foil for the creamy whiteness of her skin.

He remembered her standing naked before him while he pulled the pins from her hair so that it fell in a dark curtain to the small of her back, almost resting on her gently rounded buttocks. He remembered pulling her towards him and tangling his hands in the thick skeins of silky hair, holding her fast while his tongue plundered her mouth.

His body responded immediately to the memory and he struggled to give his attention to her reply.

'Heavens, no. Kitty is merely going to learn a new way to put up my hair.'

'Ah, I see. And what do you do after that? I am busy this morning, but perhaps later you would like to drive out with me.' He grinned at her. 'We might go to the Park at the fashionable hour and show off your new hairstyle.'

A shadow crossed her face.

'Oh, I would enjoy that, only I... um... We are going to visit a new tea garden in Hampstead and I shall not be back until dinnertime.'

'Of course. Then we shall meet again at dinner.'

Gideon pushed his plate away and rose from the table. Why he should feel disappointed he did not know. The notion of driving out with his wife had only just occurred to him and was easily dismissed. However, after spending the morning poring over his accounts, he found the sun shining in through the study window was too tempting to ignore. It was not yet the fashionable hour for the promenade and Gideon decided he would exercise his greys in the Park before it became too crowded. He sent a message to the stable and ran upstairs to change into his riding coat and buckskins and to thrust his feet into his glossy top-boots.

By the time he came down again Sam was waiting at the door with the curricle. The greys were fresh and leaped into their collars as they set off, but as they swept through Grosvenor Square Gideon spotted his sister approaching in her open carriage. He waved to her coachman to stop, bringing his own team to a plunging halt when the carriages were alongside each other.

'Really, Gideon, we cannot hold up the traffic in this way, I shall be hounded out of the square!'

'I thought Nicky was with you,' he said, ignoring her laughing protest.

'She was, until half an hour ago.'

'Oh. Are you not going to Hampstead with her?' Gwen's brows rose.

'Hampstead? No, indeed. Why should she go to Hampstead?'

'There is a new tea garden, I believe.' Gwen's blank look made him frown and the horses jibbed as his hands tightened involuntarily on the reins. He said, 'She has her maid with her, I take it?'

'No, we sent Kitty home as soon as Dominique's hair was finished. Gideon, what—?'

He cut her short, not wishing to explain anything. With a hasty farewell he drove on. Plans for Hyde Park were abandoned. He considered driving to Hampstead, but something told him he would not find Nicky there. Instead he drove back to Brook Street, and with a curt order to Sam to walk the horses he went indoors to look for the maid.

He found her in Nicky's bedroom, mending a flounce, and asked her without preamble if she knew where her mistress would be.

Kitty jumped to her feet.

'I—I don't know, sir,' she stammered, dropping a wobbly curtsy. 'She sent me off from Lady Ribblestone's and said she'd be making her own way home later.'

'And she didn't say where she was going?'

'N-no, sir.'

'Are you sure?' Gideon bent his frowning gaze upon her. 'Think, girl!'

Kitty stared at him, wide-eyed as she screwed her apron nervously between her hands. Gideon drew a breath and forced himself to speak quietly, 'Did she give you no idea of where she might be going?'

The maid chewed her lip, frowning in concentration. At last she said, 'She—she did ask me where Cleveland Row might be.'

A cold hand clutched at Gideon's heart. Without a word he strode out of the room, thundered back down the stairs and out to his curricle. It did not take him long to find the lodging house, but the servant who opened the door told him that Lamotte was not at home.

'Has a lady called here for him?' demanded Gideon.

The servant looked blank and shook his head. Even a generous bribe could not elicit anything more than the information that *'monsewer'* had been out all day, but that he was expected back later, since he had sent out for a special dinner to be prepared and brought to his rooms that evening.

Gideon drove back to Brook Street, a mixture of fear and anxiety fermenting in his head. He tried to think logically. Perhaps he had misunderstood Nicky. She had many friends—it might well be that she was on a perfectly innocent outing. After all, she had said she would be home in time to join him for dinner. Gideon faced up to the fact that there was little he could do, save go home and wait for Nicky to turn up.

However, after he had dismissed his curricle and paced once through the empty house Gideon realised he could not be idle. He changed into his evening clothes, picked up his hat, gloves and cane and strode off to St James's Street. If he could find Lamotte, then his main worry about Nicky would be assuaged.

* * *

No one in any of the hells he visited had seen the young Frenchman that day. In growing desperation he made for the last one on his list, the narrow house in King Street that Anthony patronised.

Despite the early hour the rooms were quite full, the heavy curtains pulled across the windows and the room bathed in candlelight. Gideon recognised several of the players and was hailed merrily and invited to join them. He declined politely and continued to ask after Lamotte, but his enquiries drew nothing but blank looks. No one had seen him.

The Earl of Martlesham was presiding over the faro table in the final room and he looked up as Gideon came in.

'Albury, this is a new departure for you. Will you join us?'

'No, thank you,' he replied shortly. 'I am looking for Raymond Lamotte, do you know him?'

'Lamotte, Lamotte…' Max considered for a moment. 'No, I don't think I do.'

Two of the players glanced up and exchanged looks, their brows raised. Gideon said nothing and after a moment Max continued. 'What do you want with the fellow?'

'Ribblestone gave me a message for him,' he said casually. 'It doesn't matter.'

'As you will.' Max waved a hand. 'We are about to go in search of our dinner. Why not come along with us?'

'Thank you, no. I dine at home tonight.'

'With your lovely wife? Gad, sir, but the two of you are inseparable.'

Gideon misliked the smile that spread over the earl's face and his hand tightened on his cane. Did Max know something? How he would like to choke the truth out of him! Gideon left them to their play and went back out into the sunshine. He glanced at his watch. It was past six o'clock. Perhaps Nicky was home now and waiting for him.

And perhaps not.

He glanced up and down St James's Street, doubt and indecision crowding his mind. Now she was with child his wife might consider it safe to take a lover. His hand tightened on the head of his cane. By God, if that was the case she would soon learn her mistake! Eyes narrowed, his jaw tight with anger, Gideon strode off.

Dominique had never spent such a long afternoon. When she had left her sister-in-law there were still two hours until she was due at Cleveland Row. She wished she had asked Kitty to wait for her, but Monsieur Lamotte had told her to come alone and she was afraid that Kitty might not understand the need for total secrecy. She whiled away her time wandering in and out of the various shops in Bond Street. She was ill at ease on her own and found herself purchasing various items— gloves, ribbons and parasols, as well as a quite hideous bonnet in puce satin—all of which she ordered to be sent to Brook Street. At last she judged it time to make her way to Cleveland Row for her rendezvous.

She was admitted by a respectable-looking servant, who then directed her to Monsieur Lamotte's rooms on the first floor. Dominique knocked on the door and was a little relieved when the gentleman answered in person. She drew a folded paper from her reticule.

'This is all the information I have on my father.'

He held the door wide.

'Please, come in, madame.' Observing her hesitation,

he said gently, 'I will need to read this through and we can hardly discuss the contents here on the landing.'

'No, of course.'

She stepped across the threshold into the small, sparsely furnished room. An old-fashioned armchair and a sofa crowded the empty fireplace, a sideboard stood against one wall and a small table was placed beneath the window. A haphazard pile of newspapers and gentleman's magazines on one of the dining chairs suggested that the table had been hastily cleared.

Raymond closed the door.

'Pray, madame, let me take your coat. *Eh bien*, sit down, if you please, and be comfortable.'

Swallowing, she allowed him to remove her pelisse and guide her to the sofa, where she perched on the edge, her hands clasped nervously in her lap. Raymond dropped the paper on to the table and went to the sideboard, where he proceeded to pour wine into two glasses.

'No—not for me,' she said hastily. 'I cannot stay.'

'Just a glass, madame, that we may raise a toast to France.'

She took the glass from him and solemnly repeated the toast, but she was relieved that her companion then sat down at the table to read her document. She waited impatiently as he scrutinised every line, asking the occasional question, and making notes on the edge of the paper with a pencil. She glanced at the clock on the mantelpiece. It was nearly six. She must get back soon. A soft knock upon the door made her jump. Raymond answered it and after a muted conversation he stood back and a number of waiters came in, bearing trays.

'My dinner,' explained Raymond, smiling. 'I ordered

it earlier. I hope you do not mind if they set it up now, while I finish reading this?'

He threw himself into the armchair and continued to read. Dominique clasped her wine glass before her, wishing she had thought to wear a veil. She felt very out of place sitting there, while the servants marched in and out.

As soon as they were alone again she put down her glass and rose.

'Monsieur Lamotte, you have read every word now. I must go—'

'No, no, madame, not quite yet, if you please.' He was on his feet and standing between her and the door. 'I was hoping that you would do me the honour of dining with me.'

He reached out for her hand, but she snatched it away.

'Out of the question,' she declared. 'It would be most improper to dine alone with you.'

'But you are already here and alone,' he pointed out, coming closer.

'That is very different.'

'Is it?' He gave her his charming smile, but she was more alarmed than attracted.

Dominique retreated a few steps. She had placed herself in a most precarious situation. To visit a gentleman's lodgings, without even her maid in attendance, was the height of impropriety. Gideon would never forgive her, if he found out. She took a breath.

'Monsieur Lamotte, I think you misunderstand. You promised you could help me with news of my father.'

'And so I can, Madame Albury, but I would like you to show a little gratitude. Would dinner be such a trial?'

'Sir, it is impossible. Please stand aside and let me leave.'

His smile became predatory.

'Well, if you cannot dine with me, perhaps a little kiss—'

He lunged at her. Dominique whisked herself away, but not before his fingers caught the muslin fichu tucked decorously into the neck of her summer gown. It slipped from her shoulders as she retreated behind the sofa, anger blazing through her.

'How dare you?' She glared at him. 'I came here in good faith, monsieur. I thought as a fellow countryman I could trust you!'

'And so you can, madame.' He held out his arms. 'All I ask is a little kiss from you and I shall let you go.'

'Do you think I am a fool?' She snatched up the poker from the hearth. 'Stand away from the door, monsieur.'

He looked a little startled, but made no attempt to move out of her way. Dominique was enraged, but she was well aware that the Frenchman had the advantage of strength and size. She was debating what to do next when swift footsteps were heard on the stairs and a familiar voice sounded from the landing.

'No need to come with me, my man. I know the way.'

The door opened and with a smothered exclamation Raymond jumped aside, his eyes narrowing as Gideon appeared, his frame almost filling the doorway.

Dominique stared. To her amazement her husband merely smiled at her.

'My apologies, my dear, have I kept you waiting? I was delayed, don't you know, in Piccadilly.'

Chapter Ten

Gideon uttered the words cheerfully as he came in and closed the door behind him. He had entered the room with every nerve-end tingling, prepared for a brawl, but when he had opened the door to see his wife brandishing a poker to keep her would-be seducer at bay his worst fears were alleviated. In fact, he had a strong inclination to laugh.

'I think, my dear, you can dispense with the weapon now.'

She lowered the poker.

'How did you know where to find me?'

'A simple deduction.' He glanced at Lamotte, who was silently watching him, a guilty scowl darkening his countenance. 'What inducement did you use to entice my wife here?'

Nicky said quickly, 'He told me he could help me find my father.'

Gideon raised a brow. 'And can you, monsieur? I thought not,' he added drily as Lamotte shrugged. He picked up the fichu from the floor and handed it to Dominique. 'Here, madam. Put this on and your coat, too. I shall escort you home.'

She took the muslin scarf from him, but made no move to put it on. Instead she stood twisting it between her hands, her dark anxious gaze fixed on his face.

'B-but I have been seen here. The landlord and the waiters who brought in the dinner—'

'The landlord now believes you came here looking for me and as for the waiters, I think our friend here will be able to silence them.' He turned to Lamotte, placing the tip of his cane against the Frenchman's silk waistcoat. 'Let me make myself very clear,' he said icily. 'If the slightest hint of scandal attaches to my wife's being here, monsieur, then I shall take great pleasure in calling you out and despatching you. Do you understand me?'

Lamotte shook his head.

'Believe me, I never meant any harm to madame.'

'No.' Gideon's eyes narrowed. 'You were put up to this by another, were you not?' The flash of fear that crossed the Frenchman's face gave Gideon his answer. His lip curling, he gave the cane a little push, sending Lamotte staggering back.

Dominique had put on her pelisse and was now watching them. Gideon opened the door, saying loudly,

'I am very grateful to you, monsieur, for looking after my wife until I could join you. But we will not keep you any longer from your dinner. Adieu, sir!'

He flourished a bow and held out his hand to Dominique. She picked up a sheet of paper from one of the armchairs and stuffed it into her reticule before crossing the room to join him.

'It is the information about my father,' she said in response to his enquiring gaze. 'It will not be needed now.'

She bent a look of burning reproach upon Lamotte, who had the grace to hang his head.

'I beg your pardon, madame.'

Gideon took her arm.

'Come, my dear.'

He escorted her down the stairs and out into the street. As they walked away from the lodging house Dominique gave a little sob.

'I am so very sorry, Gideon. It was foolish of me to go there alone. I should have told you...'

'And why did you not?'

'B-because he said that success in finding out about Papa depended upon the utmost secrecy.'

Gideon looked down at her bowed head.

'But that is not all, is it? You thought I should refuse to sanction this line of enquiry.'

'Yes.' Her reply was so quiet he almost missed it. He sighed.

'Am I such an ogre, Nicky?'

'Oh, no, no!' She stopped and turned towards him. 'You are not an ogre at all, but your abhorrence of all things French—' She bit her lip. 'But in this case you were right to be suspicious of Monsieur Lamotte and— and I beg your pardon.'

He squeezed her hand.

'It was not totally your fault, Nicky.'

She was silent for a while, but as they walked out into St James's Street, she said slowly, 'You said someone else was behind this. Do you think it was my cousin?'

'I not only think it, my dear, I am sure of it.'

She gave an angry little growl.

'Ooh, of all the odious—' She stopped. 'There he is now, across the street with his cronies! And he has seen us. Let us confront him. I would like to scratch his eyes out!'

'I have a much better idea,' he said, catching her chin

between his thumb and finger. 'We will show him that his plan to cause trouble between us has not worked at all.'

He lowered his head and kissed her.

Dominique's heart stopped and she forgot all about being angry with Max. She forgot about everything, save the soaring pleasure that filled her whole being. Gideon was still holding her chin so she could not pull away, even if she had wanted to do so, which she did not. His lips were gentle, it was the lightest of kisses and she found herself standing on tiptoe to prolong the moment. When at last he raised his head he was smiling down at her, such a glint in his eyes that she wanted to reach up and pull him down so she could kiss him again.

'Is he still watching us?' he murmured.

'Who?' She ran her tongue round her lips, trying to drag her mind away from the distracting cleft in his chin and the seductive curve of his lips.

He laughed, settled her arm firmly in his and began to walk on.

'Your cousin is standing on the far pavement and staring at us as if he cannot believe his eyes. Look across, my dear, and smile while I tip my hat to him— like so. There, is that not more satisfying than, er, scratching his eyes out?'

Dominique chuckled even as she smiled and nodded at Max, who was glowering across the road at them.

'It is amusing to see him so dumbfounded,' she agreed, 'but I am so angry with him! He will be fortunate when we meet again if I do not box his ears!'

'What a violent creature you are,' marvelled Gideon, a laugh in his voice. 'I find you brandishing a poker at Lamotte and now you want to assault your cousin.'

'When I am in a passion I hardly know what I am about,' she confessed ruefully.

'No, you don't, do you?'

She looked up at that, a laughing question in her eyes, and found him watching her with such an arrested expression that her laughter died. Had she angered him, perhaps?

'Can you really forgive me for my foolishness today?' she asked him anxiously. 'I promise you I shall not keep anything from you again.'

The serious look disappeared and he smiled, flicking her cheek with one careless finger.

'Of course I forgive you,' he said lightly. 'Now let us hurry back to Brook Street. All this excitement has given me an appetite!'

It was almost an hour later when Gideon sat down to dinner with his wife, but despite his earlier protestations he only picked at the array of sumptuous dishes spread before him. His thoughts went back constantly to the events earlier that evening. Max's attempts to discredit his wife had angered him, but that was not the only reason for his distraction. He was shocked by the jealousy that had consumed him when he had suspected Nicky had taken a lover.

That had been superseded by fear for her safety when he realised Max's involvement, but more than anything he was confused by the overwhelming desire that had come over him when he had kissed her. It had been every bit as strong as on their wedding night. *Then* he had put it down to an excess of wine. Kissing his wife in broad daylight and in such a public place as St James's Street should not have had anything like the same effect, but the touch of her lips had shaken him to the very core. He had covered it well, of course, but then, when they were walking home and she had mentioned her passionate nature, the memory of her response to his lovemaking on that first, momentous night had hit him so forcibly that for a few moments he had not been able to speak and had only been aware of a strong desire to rush home and repeat the performance.

Since their night together at Elmwood he had tried to treat her as a wife should be treated. He visited her bed for the sole purpose of producing an heir, keeping all other feelings well under control and it shocked him, as they entered the shadowy portals of his Brook Street house to find that he wanted to pick her up and carry her to his room, to rip off her clothes and make love to her as violently, as passionately as on that first, tempestuous occasion.

It could not be, of course. Now she was carrying his child he had no excuse to make love to her. His father had told him to take a mistress, but Gideon knew now that he did not *want* a mistress, he wanted his wife.

He struggled through dinner, trying to converse, attempting to entertain Nicky with amusing anecdotes while all he could think of was the softness of her skin, the warmth of her limbs when they were wrapped around him. When she went off to the drawing room he lingered over his port, wondering if the excitement of the day would make her too tired to wait up for him, but as he reached the drawing-room door he heard the soft lilting strains of the harp.

He watched her from the doorway, marvelling at the concentration on her face, and when his eyes moved to her hands caressing the strings he found himself remembering how gently those same fingers touched his body. Gideon shifted uncomfortably. It would not do.

She was with child and as such would not welcome his advances. Indeed, he knew that such behaviour was downright dangerous. Father had made that quite clear. Looking across at the delicate little figure before him, Gideon knew he would not risk such a thing happening to Nicky.

Yet it took all his resolution to part from her that night and not to make his way through the dressing room to her bedchamber.

'I think we should go to Rotham,' Gideon announced at breakfast the next morning. 'It is time you met my father.'

Dominique continued pouring her coffee. It was not unexpected, but his next words caused her to heart to sink.

'You will remain there until the baby is born.'

'And will you stay, too?' she asked, trying to keep her voice casual.

'For a couple of weeks.'

So it had come. He had had enough of her—and how could she blame him, after her foolishness yesterday? There could be no arguing. Of course he would want the child to be born at Rotham, especially if it was a boy.

'When do we go?'

'In three weeks.'

'Gwen has invited us to join her in Brighton.'

'Impossible,' he said shortly.

She accepted this, but he must have observed her disappointment for he added in a kinder tone, 'Perhaps next year. Dr Harris is very good, but I should like you to have the services of my father's medical man, a very experienced doctor. He delivered both of my sister's children. Ribblestone's country seat, Fairlawns, is but five miles from Rotham and Gwen will vouch for him, I am sure. That is, have you told her that you are increasing?'

'Yes, but I swore her to secrecy.'

He gave a wry smile. 'Then I doubt it will remain a secret much longer.' He pushed back his chair. 'If you are in agreement, then I shall write to my father today and tell him we shall be at Rotham by the middle of July.'

What could she say? It was good of him to pretend she had a choice.

When Gwen heard that they were going to Rotham she screwed her face up in distaste. Dominique blinked away a rogue tear that threatened her eye.

'Gideon says I am to stay there until the baby is born.'

'Six months! You poor thing.' Gwen added quickly, 'I am sure he is thinking of your well-being, my love.'

'He says the doctor there is very good.'

'Oh, yes, indeed, you will like Dr Bolton, I am sure. Did Gideon tell you he delivered my babies? Perhaps if he had been our doctor when Mama was carrying that last child...'

'What happened?' asked Dominique.

Gwen sighed. 'When we were young Mama was never well. She was always enceinte, or recuperating after a miscarriage. She had six more children after Gideon, but they all died within hours. Not that she ever complained. I believe she loved my father passionately. But the last time she was brought to bed she did not recover. Papa was heartbroken. I did not understand at the time why he should blame himself, but now that I am married I understand that a man can be too…physical.' Gwen blushed.

'And when did she die?'

'Oh, it must be twelve years since. It was a bad time, we were all at Rotham, we all knew her suffering.'

'Poor lady,' murmured Dominique. 'Perhaps Gideon really is concerned for my health.'

'How can you think otherwise? You are still fretting over your cousin's words, is that it? You are worried Gideon wants to be a bachelor again. I do not think he has any such intention.'

'He did say he had outgrown Max and his circle,' said Dominique, hopefully.

'I am sure he has.' Gwen said slowly, 'Gideon's wildness in recent years was more a rebellion against Papa, I think. You see, after Mama died Father changed. I was engaged to Ribblestone at the time, so I never suffered too much from his melancholy, and James, too, was of age and spent most of his time in town, but poor Gideon—Papa tried to turn him into a pattern card. It became even worse when James was murdered in Paris, and then Tante Gwendoline and the *duc* were guillotined. Gideon remained at Rotham, Father said it was his duty, now he was the heir, but the constraint irked him a great deal. It was no wonder that when he inherited a small fortune he took the opportunity to escape to town. He spent recklessly and seemed intent on committing every folly imaginable…' She smiled. 'So you see, my love, marriage to you could well be the making of my brother!'

Dominique clung on to that small ray of hope as she prepared to leave London. It was not to be expected that her interesting condition would remain a secret, although Gwen had assured her sister-in-law that she had told only her closest friends. By July it was all over town and Dominique had to accustom herself to beaming smiles and knowing looks. She saw Raymond Lamotte occasionally, but afforded him no more than a distant bow. She was still very angry with Max, but thankfully the one time they met she had Gideon by her side.

They were attending a musical recital and she was coming out of the supper room on Gideon's arm when the earl appeared before them.

'Martlesham.'

As Gideon bowed she made her curtsy to the earl.

'Good evening, Albury. Cousin.' He held on to her fingers after kissing them. 'I understand I am to congratulate you.'

'Thank you, Max.' She withdrew her hand as she gave him a glittering smile. He responded with one equally false.

'It explains why you can do no wrong in your husband's eyes at present.'

Gideon gave a soft laugh.

'You are thinking of our embrace in St James's Street.' He pulled her hand on to his arm again and patted it. 'An outrageous display of affection in public, of course, but I could not help myself.'

'Could you not?' Max's lip curled. 'I thought it might be for my benefit.'

'Good Gad, no,' exclaimed Gideon, recoiling artistically. 'Whatever gave you that idea?'

'Oh, I don't know,' returned Max, considering. 'I think it was something Lamotte said to me.'

Dominique froze. A furious retort rose to her lips, but Gideon's hand was still covering hers and he gave it the slightest squeeze. She remained silent.

'Ah, yes, Monsieur Lamotte.' Gideon's voice was quiet, silky, but no less menacing. 'Odd that you should deny him one day and the next he is a friend.'

'I should say he is more of an acquaintance.'

'A charming young man,' said Gideon lightly. 'But French, you know. He is unfamiliar with the way we do things here, especially when it comes to husbands. They can be the most unaccountable creatures, you see.'

'Can they?'

Max sounded wary and, casting a quick glance at Gideon, Dominique thought that despite his pleasant tone his eyes had never been so menacing.

'Oh, yes,' he said softly. 'I did not realise it until I became one myself, but it seems now that if anyone should try to harm my wife, or even to upset her, then I should be obliged to wreak the most terrible vengeance. I just couldn't help myself.'

Despite the noise and chatter of the room, a dangerous silence hung around the two men. Dominique could feel the tension and remained still, not daring to do anything that might precipitate violence. At last Max gave her a tight smile.

'You are to be congratulated, Cousin, you have found yourself an admirable protector. I wish you joy of your bulldog.'

With a curt nod he stalked past them.

'Do you think he understood you?' she asked as they continued back to the music room.

'Oh, yes,' murmured Gideon. 'I think he understood me all too well. He will not bother us again.'

Recalling the fury in Max's eyes, Dominique could not be easy.

'Gideon—'

'Hush.' He held up his hand. 'We have given your

cousin quite enough time this evening. Let us instead listen to the music. This next soprano, I have been told, is quite matchless.'

Their last weeks in town were very busy. Dominique felt quite low when Gwen departed for Brighton, but she left Dominique a long list of things she considered necessary for a protracted stay in Buckinghamshire.

'Buy your loose gowns before you go, for there is but one dressmaker in the village, and although you will want to put some work her way you will need more gowns than she can provide. And make sure you buy some warm petticoats. Flannel ones, my love, because the corridors at Rotham can be icy in winter! Then you will need books,' Gwen continued, counting off the items on her fingers. 'I left one or two novels at Rotham, but I doubt my father will have anything new, and it is *such* a fuss to send to London every time one wants a diversion. If you wish to paint, then you should find everything you need in the old nursery.' She pulled a face. 'Poor Papa, he insisted we have the very best— tutors, materials, paints, charcoal and sketchpads—but I was a sad disappointment and not at all proficient at drawing or painting. Oh, and buy at least two pairs of stout boots, the lanes become prodigiously muddy...'

She went on for some time and when she had finished Dominique gave an uncertain laugh.

'You make Rotham sound like something from a Gothic novel, all gloomy shadows and empty, echoing halls.'

'Well, it is,' replied Gwen with alarming candour. 'Since Gideon escaped, Papa has rattled around in that great house all alone, with only an elderly neighbour to visit him.' Gwen noticed her sister-in-law's dismay and quickly assured her that Rotham was in no way as bleak as it sounded. 'The local families will be glad to welcome you, I am sure, and Ribblestone and I will be returning to Fairlawns in December, so we shall only be a few miles away.'

To Dominique, December sounded a very long time ahead, but she put aside her worries and threw herself into preparing to travel to her husband's family home.

Travelling in easy stages, they took two full days to reach Rotham. A baggage coach was hired to follow them, the roof piled high with trunks and Dominique's precious harp packed inside. Dominique rode in the elegant chaise sent up from Rotham for her comfort. Her only disappointment was that Gideon preferred to ride, but since this meant that Kitty could join her in the carriage she was not lonely on the journey, and when they stopped overnight at a prosperous coaching inn there was no lack of conversation with Gideon.

They dined in a private parlour served by the well-trained staff of the inn, who were efficient and unobtrusive. Even so, Dominique kept the conversation to innocuous subjects until at last the covers were removed and they were alone.

'Tell me about your father,' she said, putting her elbows on the table and resting her chin on her hands. Gideon looked nonplussed and she added with a smile, 'Are you very like him?'

'In looks, perhaps, but in temperament—my father is very reserved.'

She thought of the long silences she had endured with Gideon, but did not comment upon it and said instead, 'Is his health poor? Is that why he lives so quietly? Gwen told me,' she explained, when he raised his brows at her. 'She warned me that Lord Rotham rarely entertains.'

Gideon gave a crack of laughter.

'Rarely? He *never* entertains. However, that must change if you are living there. You must invite whom you please.' He was silent for a moment. 'You must not be frightened of my father, Nicky. He might appear cold, but his heart is very generous.'

'It will need to be,' she murmured. 'I bring no dowry.'

'You must not let that worry you.'

'But it does, Gideon.'

'I think Father will be too relieved to know I have settled down to worry about your lack of dowry. You see, he was sorely disappointed when I went off to make my own life in London.' He was silent while he poured himself another glass of wine. 'I did not behave well, I admit it. And once in town I fell in with your cousin and his friends. I am not proud of that time.'

After the suffocating discipline of Rotham, Max's mischievous merrymaking had seemed very attractive. Gideon had willingly participated in the pranks and jokes they played on each other and even on total strangers—boxing the Watch, stealing an old gentleman's wig, holding mock duels, bribing the coachman to let them take the reins of the stage and race it against one of their own carriages… It had all seemed like harmless fun at the time, but looking back he saw how childish it had been. When he stole that little lightskirt from under Max's nose it was inevitable that the earl would retaliate, but bullying his innocent little cousin into marriage—!

Glancing up, Gideon saw Nicky's anxious face and

he added quickly, 'That is no reflection upon you, Nicky. I could not want for a better wife.'

'But perhaps you could want a more beloved one.'

Gideon frowned.

'We will not discuss that, if you please. The actress Max employed to impersonate you would not have been acceptable to my family.'

Dominique met his eyes across the table, the wine making her brave.

'And am I any more acceptable?'

To her surprise the coldness in his gaze was replaced by something warmer, including a hint of laughter.

'With your grace and dignity and your indomitable spirit—yes, you are, my dear.'

She was inordinately pleased with his answer even though it made her blush rosily. At the same time she felt that strong tug of attraction to the man sitting opposite. His look seemed to burn right through her decorous gown and she could feel her body responding, the breasts tightening, pushing against the restricting material as she imagined his hands caressing her body. It had been weeks since he had touched her like that and she was filled with an indescribable ache to feel his arms around her. She longed to say so, but the words would not come. The silence stretched between them, becoming ever more uncomfortable.

'It—it has been a beautiful day,' she said at last, glancing out of the window. 'It seems a shame that we spent it travelling.'

'I at least had the benefit of riding. You were shut up in the chaise all day. Perhaps you would like to take a little stroll with me now and catch the last of the sun?'

'I would like that very much,' she said, reaching for her shawl.

* * *

The inn was situated on a busy street, but Gideon had noticed a lane to one side and once they had walked a few yards the noise and bustle were left behind. They strolled side by side in companionable silence. The lane was bounded on each side by large fields of ripening corn, gleaming and golden in the setting sun.

'How long will you stay at Rotham?' she asked him.

'Until you are established. I shall drive down to Brighton to see Gwen, then I shall go to Chalcots and see what is needed to make it habitable. I have been thinking we might set up home there.'

'That is your godmama's house, near Hampstead? I should so much like to see it.'

'And so you shall, once your confinement is over. Too much travelling will fatigue you and I would not risk your health.' His voice was kind, but Dominique's spirits sank. He did not want her with him.

'I shall write to you,' he continued. 'You shall have your say about the furnishings and the decoration.'

But from a distance.

'Thank you.' She could not keep the note of disappointment from her voice and Gideon's next words told her he had noticed.

'Believe me, it is best that you remain at Rotham, where Dr Bolton will be on hand if you need him.'

'But your father will not want me.'

'You are the mother of his grandchild, of course he will want you at Rotham.'

She nodded. Her first consideration now must be for her unborn child. She shivered.

'The sun has gone down. Shall we return to the inn?'

Her shawl had slipped to her elbows and as they

turned to make their way back to the inn she struggled to rearrange it.

'Here, let me.'

He pulled up the shawl and her spine tingled with the familiar touch as his hands rested on her shoulders.

Hold me, she begged him silently. *Kiss me.*

Gideon's hands stilled. He could feel the delicate bones of her shoulders through the thin folds of the shawl and the summer gown beneath. Her hair was caught up in a knot, but a few wisps curled darkly against the creamy skin at the back of her neck. He knew an impulse to place his lips there and taste her sweetness, but he feared that would lead him on to a more passionate exchange, so he quelled the desire rising in him and instead lifted the shawl a little higher.

'There, is that warmer?'

'Yes, thank you, Gideon.' She put her hand up over his, where it rested at the side of her neck, and turned to smile up at him.

It was as if someone had knocked the breath out of his body. When had she become such a beauty? Those green eyes with their lush fringing of dark lashes, the straight little nose and soft, full mouth—desire leaped inside him and the blood pounded through his veins. It was all he could do not to drag her roughly against him and ravish her here and now, in this secluded lane.

No! He reeled back. What was he thinking of? This was summer madness, the proximity of a pretty girl combined with the effects of the wine, a good dinner and the balmy summer evening. She had been trapped into marriage with him through very little fault of her own and she deserved more respect than that. In an effort to quell his desire he reminded himself that she was not the woman he had set his heart on, although it was strange that now, when he thought of the bewitching actress called Agnes Bennet, he could hardly recall her face.

Dominique saw Gideon's eyes darken, felt the jolt of mutual attraction, as if some invisible wire hooked them both, but the hot desire in his glance was quickly replaced by shock and he recoiled from her. She did her best to ignore the chill that filled her soul. She might be his wife, but she was not his love.

Hiding her own disappointment, she suggested they should go back to the inn and immediately turned her steps that way, head held high. This was her life now and she must be content.

Chapter Eleven

Dominique's image of Rotham as a sinister Gothic pile faded with her first view of the house. It was bathed in the golden glow of a summer's evening, a many-gabled Jacobean mansion built of red-brick and creamy stone and the windows of the three-storeyed house flashed a fiery welcome, reflecting the glorious sunset.

'Why, it is quite enchanting!' she exclaimed involuntarily.

'Is it?' Gideon leaned forwards to gaze at his old home. 'Yes, I suppose you might think so.'

As the coach pulled up at the front steps he leaped down, ready to hand out his bride. An elderly butler came out to meet them, bowing slightly as he announced that Lord Rotham awaited them in the drawing room.

'Thank you, Colne. I shall take Mrs Albury to him.'

Silently Dominique accompanied Gideon through the small stone porch into an ancient-screens passage. After the sunlight, the passage with its unpolished wooden panelling was very dark and she stopped to let her eyes grow accustomed to the gloom before stepping into the hall. The wainscoting here was equally dull, but the sun streamed in through the windows, the bars of sunlight full of golden dust motes. Swords, shields and antlers adorned the walls. The whole room had the feel of another era, but it looked sadly neglected.

'Is this room never used?' she asked.

'Rarely. When we had house parties everyone would gather here before going out for a day's hunting or riding and we used to hold a harvest supper here for the tenants and their families, but that stopped when my mother died.'

'And where is the drawing room?' she asked as they followed the butler out of the great hall and into another, inner hall.

'Upstairs,' he told her. 'All the principal rooms are on the upper floor.'

'Including the dining room?'

'Of course.'

'And the kitchens?'

'In the basement.'

'A twenty-minute walk, no doubt,' she murmured.

Gideon laughed.

'Exactly!'

They ascended the grand staircase to a wide landing. The house was built around a central courtyard and a series of windows allowed plenty of light into the upper rooms, which led one from the other. The drawing room was the first of these chambers to be entered.

Even to one used to the grandeur of Martlesham Abbey, the drawing room was impressive. Ornately carved panelling covered every wall and the patterns were repeated in the plaster moulding on the ceiling. An elaborate stone chimneypiece dominated the room, the Albury coat of arms emblazoned at the centre of the overmantel. Dominique took in the faded grandeur of the room and the heavy, old-fashioned furniture as Gideon led her forwards to meet her host.

Viscount Rotham had risen from a wooden armchair set on one side of the fireplace and now stood waiting to greet her. She dropped into a deep curtsy, but as she rose she looked up to study her father-in-law. The likeness between the viscount and his son was marked. Both were tall and lean, with the same finely sculpted lips and high cheekbones. Each had hazel eyes set beneath dark brows, but where Gideon wore his auburn hair unpowdered and just touching his collar, the viscount preferred the old style of a curled and powdered wig. He was dressed all in black, save for the narrow ruffles at his wrists and the linen at his neck.

'Welcome, madam,' he said politely. 'Pray sit down. I trust the journey was not too onerous for you?'

'Not at all, my lord. We made one stop overnight.'

'Just one?' Those dark brows rose and he bent his gaze upon Gideon. 'Was that wise, my son? Another night would have given your wife more respite from the rigours of the road—'

'But it was not at all necessary.' She knew an urge to turn and run as two pairs of hazel eyes turned towards her in surprise, but she held her ground. 'Your carriage is so well sprung, my lord, that the miles flew by. I am not at all fatigued, I assure you.'

She was rewarded by a smile from Gideon as he guided her to a sofa, the only padded seat in the room.

'Indeed, Father, we saw Dr Harris before we left town. He assured me that there was no danger in the journey.'

'Nevertheless, I have ordered dinner to be put back, to give you both time to rest...'

The exchanges continued, polite enough, a little

stilted, but not unfriendly. Dominique mentioned this to Gideon when he escorted her to their apartments on the top floor and he concurred.

'I am glad you were not intimidated,' he continued. 'Father's style is a little formal, but he is perfectly kind, I assure you.'

She had to remind herself of this fact when they went down to dinner. It was served in the dining room, another grandiose chamber beyond the drawing room. The long table in the centre was set with all the pomp and formality one could desire. Only Dominique did not desire it.

Conversation was almost non-existent, the food cold, and by the time Dominique returned to the empty drawing room while the gentlemen enjoyed their brandy she was beginning to long for the cosy comfort of Brook Street. Not one to repine, she spent the time alone tuning her harp, which had been set up in one corner of the room, where the big windows overlooked the gardens. She had completed her task and was gently strumming the strings when Gideon came in with his father.

'Since there is no pianoforte here we brought Nicky's harp with us.' Gideon explained in response to his father's look of surprise.

'Indeed?' The viscount's response was cool.

'I hope you do not object, my lord?' asked Dominique quickly.

'On the contrary. Gideon's mother was musical, but when Gwendoline married I had the pianoforte sent to Fairlawns. However, it will be pleasant to have music at Rotham once more.' He gave her a little bow. 'This house has been too long without a mistress, madam. I should be honoured if you would take on that role.'

'Th-thank you, my lord.'

Gideon touched her arm. 'Perhaps you will play for us now, Nicky.'

She complied, happy to avoid the long, awkward silences that had accompanied their dinner. No tea tray had been ordered. When the clock struck eleven she excused herself and retired. She and Gideon had been allocated adjoining rooms, with a connecting door, and she was not displeased when Gideon knocked and entered a short time later.

Dominique was sitting at her dressing table while Kitty unpinned her hair, but she dismissed her maid immediately. She was wearing only her nightgown and suddenly felt a little shy to be alone with her husband. To hide her embarrassment she kept her eyes on the mirror as she removed the last of the pins.

'I think that went off very well,' remarked Gideon, coming closer. 'Father was very complimentary about you.'

She was pleased, but could not resist asking him if all meals were taken in the dining room.

'When Father is alone he dines in his room and his man, Warner, takes him his breakfast, too. It is the custom here for all guests to break their fast in their room. Kitty will bring yours to you in the morning.'

The idea of sitting in bed with Gideon while he fed her tiny morsels of toast was very appealing—in fact, it sent a little shiver of excitement rippling through her—but that was something lovers might do and she and Gideon were not lovers. Instead, she knew she would be breaking her fast in a lonely state.

Dominique dragged the brush through her hair, sitting tense and upright. Gideon walked up behind her and held out his hand.

'May I?' Silently she handed him the hairbrush. He said quietly, 'I know everything is very new to you here, Nicky, but please be patient.' He began to brush her hair, one lock at a time, but she had the impression that his thoughts were elsewhere. He said at last, 'I have not been to Rotham since my quarrel with Father last December. For me to turn up now and with a wife whom I married without his knowledge or his blessing—'

Her tension melted as the rhythmic brushing had its effect.

'It is very hard for you both, I am sure.' She glanced up at his image in the mirror, but his eyes were fixed upon her hair. 'Does he know the truth about us?'

'Yes. I told him the whole at the outset—not that any blame attaches to *you*,' he said as she put her hands up to her burning cheeks. 'I explained to him that I was in a raging fury because Martlesham and that little actress tricked me into marriage. It was all the fault of my wretched temper, which he understands only too well.' He gave a small, twisted smile. 'He is more likely to pity you than blame you.'

'Which is as bad,' she exclaimed. 'I would not for the world have him feel sorry for me.'

Gideon looked at the reflection in the mirror, observing the anguish in those enormous eyes, the flushed cheeks. His skin still tingled from the feel of her lustrous dark hair between his fingers. Putting down the brush, he placed his hands on her shoulders.

'Was I wrong to marry you?' he asked suddenly. 'Was I wrong not to have the marriage annulled?'

Her chin went up.

'Yes. If you will not put the past behind you.'

With a jolt he realised he had not been thinking of the past, merely of the mischief he had done to Nicky by holding her to the marriage. She put one hand on her stomach as she continued.

'It is a little late to discuss this now.' Her tone was prosaic. 'You must do as I do and look forward.'

She gave a little toss of her head, sending her silky hair flowing over his hands. A few dark tresses rippled down over her breasts, outlined beneath the thin linen of her nightgown. Desire stirred again. Whether by design or accident she was leaning back towards him and he turned away before she noticed his arousal—more importantly before his need of her became too great to be denied and he carried her over to the bed and made love to her. He had to get away from her disturbing presence before he took advantage of her innocence. Before he put her at even more risk.

He crossed to the adjoining door and with a curt goodnight he left her.

For a long time Dominique did not move. She had seen that now-familiar look in his eyes, reflected in the glass. At times she could almost think he desired her.

Almost.

When she had sent her hair tumbling down her back it had not been by accident, she had hoped it might evoke a response. His hands had tightened on her shoulders even as the desire leaped in his eyes. He was standing so close behind her that she only had to lean back a little to press herself against him and she had begun to do just that, only to have him rapidly move away. She smiled a little sadly. There was surely an attraction between them. It was not love, but it was a start.

Stifling a sigh, she climbed into her lonely bed and pulled the covers over her. She would be a good wife and mother, she would make him proud of her and then, perhaps he might love her, just a little bit. Snuggling her cheek in her hand, she began to make her plans.

The first weeks at Rotham passed quickly enough. The viscount spent the greater part of each day locked in his study, reading or playing chess with Sir Edward Moorhouse, an elderly widower who lived nearby and called in occasionally. Gideon took his new wife to visit all the local families and the ladies in turn paid their visits to Rotham. When Dominique was not driving out or entertaining her visitors, she observed how the house was run and asked questions of Mrs Ellis, the housekeeper. At the end of the second week she made her first suggestion.

They were sitting in the drawing room after dinner, Dominique at her harp while Gideon and his father played backgammon. When it was time to retire she rose and walked to the door, but before she opened it she turned towards them.

'I have asked Colne to set up breakfast in the oak parlour tomorrow morning.' Gideon's brows rose, but she addressed the viscount, saying with a smile, 'My lord, on my first night here you told me I might act as mistress at Rotham, so I hope you do not object?'

'No, if you and Gideon wish to breakfast downstairs you are free to do so.'

Dominique knew Gideon would declare that he was quite happy taking breakfast in his room. Quelling her nerves, she met his frowning gaze with a smile.

'Thank you, my lord, that room is east-facing, ideal for the purpose, and so much easier for the staff than carrying trays up to the bedchambers. I hope you can be persuaded to join us there one morning.'

She whisked herself away and prepared slowly for

bed, half expecting Gideon to storm in and demand just
what she was thinking of, changing arrangements that
had stood at Rotham since time immemorial. However,
she heard his step passing her door, and the sounds of
him moving about in his own bedchamber, so she went
to bed. She would discover in the morning if she was
breakfasting alone.

'I decided I would not trouble Runcorn to bring
breakfast up to me when everything is set out down
here.'

Colne had just brought the coffee pot into the oak
parlour when Gideon appeared in the doorway. Dominique's welcoming smile was tinged with relief.

'Good morning, sir. There is everything you like—
cold meat, boiled eggs, hot rolls in the chafing dish and
even ale, should you want it.' She added, as Gideon sat
down at the table beside her and took a generous helping of ham, 'I shall continue to invite your father to
come downstairs to break his fast, too.'

'You will be disappointed,' he said, splitting a hot
roll and filling it with butter. 'My father is too set in his
ways. He dislikes company in the mornings.'

Dominique merely smiled, content to bide her time.

Soon her efforts were rewarded. She came downstairs one morning to find her father-in-law already at
the table. They greeted each other politely, and even
when Gideon joined them no reference was made to
this change in the viscount's habits.

Gideon was pleased to see his wife and his father
getting on so well. His conscience pricked him a little at the thought that he would soon be leaving Nicky

alone at Rotham and he was relieved that she was settling in. He told her so as they strolled in the gardens
a little later that day.

'You have made a great difference here,' he said. 'My
father mentioned it to me last night. The whole place is
brighter, somehow.'

'That is because the wainscoting has been polished
for the first time in years,' she retorted. 'It is surprising what a little beeswax can do.'

'You are much braver than I,' he replied. 'I should
have been afraid to mention it. Mrs Ellis is not one to
take criticism kindly.'

She chuckled. 'I won her over with a supply of French
barley and Jamaican pepper.'

Gideon stopped and looked down at her, his eyes
brimful of laughter.

'So that is why you had to go shopping again before
we left Brook Street. You were stocking up with bribes!'

'Not bribes...' she twinkled back at him '...merely
a few treats to ease my path—oh!'

She stopped.

'What is it? Nicky? Are you well?'

She looked up at him, a soft light shining in her eyes.

'Yes,' she breathed. 'I felt the baby move.' She took
his hand and placed it on her stomach. 'Wait.'

They stood for a moment, surrounded by sunlight
and birdsong.

'Yes! Yes, I felt it, too.' Gideon gave a delighted
laugh. 'My child.' He cupped her face in his hands and
kissed her gently. 'At last it feels real. Is that the first
time you have noticed it?'

'I suspected it before, but it was never so certain.'

'It is like a miracle.' He tucked her arm in his again

and they resumed their walk. 'I would like to feel my child kicking every day.'

'Then stay, at least a few more days.'

Seeing her shy, hopeful smile, Gideon was sorely tempted, but he glanced up at that moment and saw the viscount at the drawing-room window. A lonely figure gazing down at them, reminding him of the perils of loving one's wife too much.

'You would soon grow tired of my company,' he said lightly. 'Besides, I promised Gwen I would look in upon her at Brighton. Then I have to set work in motion at Chalcots, if it is to be ready for you and the baby.'

'Yes, of course.'

Was that a sigh in her voice? She had schooled her face into a smile and began to talk on other subjects. It was for the best, he told himself. Time away from Nicky would be a good idea. He was growing far too fond of her.

Dominique knew she had erred. Gideon had withdrawn from her as soon as she had asked him to stay, the moment she had shown a weakness, a desire to cling to him. Pride came to her aid and helped her to hide her disappointment. She was his wife, the mother of his child, but he could not love her and she must not expect it.

Dominique's sunny spirits had revived by the following morning and she stood at the door with the viscount to watch Gideon ride away. When they turned to go back into the house Lord Rotham held out his arm to her.

'How am I to entertain you, my dear? I would not have you suffering from ennui.'

'What with paying morning visits and receiving them, and the house to look after, I am well entertained, my lord.'

'You must not overtire yourself,' he said quickly.

She laughed as she preceded him into the house.

'I promise you I shall not do that. However, there *is* a little change I should like to propose.'

Those hazel eyes, so like Gideon's, held a wary smile. 'Well, madam?'

'I think we should dine in the breakfast room. With just the two of us it seems so silly to use the dining room. The servants have to carry everything twice as far and the table is so very long...'

She thought for a moment he was going to refuse, but after regarding her soberly for a moment he turned and made his way across to his study, saying over his shoulder, 'Whatever you think fit, my dear. Tell Colne to organise it.'

In an effort to keep herself from missing Gideon, Dominique threw herself into the running of the house. Her body was swelling and she was a little apprehensive, especially when she saw the viscount regarding her so anxiously, but she put her faith in Dr Bolton, who had told her she was perfectly healthy. Besides, there was far too much to do for her to take to her bed. She persuaded the viscount to allow the aged gardener to take on another boy, so that the shrubbery could be tidied up and the paths weeded. Inside the house she explored rooms that had been shut up for years, opening windows and ordering chimneys to be swept in readiness for the winter. She found trunks of material in the attics and used some of it to make cushions, which she scattered on the carved wooden chairs in the drawing room.

Gradually, as summer wore on, the old house came alive under her care, and such was her tact that the servants were happy to oblige her, polishing and dusting and cleaning the rooms until Mrs Ellis declared that the old house was looking almost as good as it had done when Lady Rotham was alive. She also confided to Colne that the master was looking better for the company.

'Aye,' returned the butler, 'he has even ordered the carriage tomorrow, to drive out with Mrs Albury. That will be the first time he has been further than the park for years, save to go to church on Sundays. Bringing the master out of himself, she is. She's proving herself to be a godsend, Mrs Ellis, even if Master Gideon was hoaxed into marrying her.'

The housekeeper wagged a finger at him, frowning.

'I hold no truck with that rumour and I'll thank you not to repeat it in front of the servants, Mr Colne.'

'As if I would,' he retorted, affronted. 'But 'tis what Warner told me Master Gideon had written to his father. Tricked, he was, by the lady's cousin, Lord Martlesham, and that wild set the young master used to run around with.'

'That's as may be, but Master Gideon is changed now, anyone can see that.' Mrs Ellis folded her arms, a satisfied twinkle in her kindly eyes. 'He and the new mistress is a match made in heaven, you mark my words.'

With a liveried coachman on the box and a footman standing up behind them, Dominique found her drive out with the viscount a much more stately excursion than when Gideon had taken her out in the phaeton, but she enjoyed it very much, as she told her father-in-law when he expressed his surprise at finding her in the drawing room after dinner that night.

'You have had a busy day, my dear. I would not have you tire yourself by sitting here with me late into the night.'

She laughed at that.

'A steady drive with you was a tonic, my lord, and not exhausting at all.'

'Nevertheless, I have sent a note to Dr Bolton to call tomorrow morning to see you.'

'I saw him two days ago and he declared me perfectly healthy.' Dominique bit her lip, then added in a milder tone, 'As I explained to Gideon several times, I always feel better for a little fresh air.'

'My son is anxious for your well-being.'

'A little too anxious,' she replied, smiling. 'Before we left London Dr Harris told him that we ladies should not be cosseted and encouraged to think ourselves ill—' She broke off, flushing, and added haltingly, 'I beg your pardon. I realise that not everyone is as fortunate in their health.'

'You are thinking of Gideon's mother.'

'Yes. I am very sorry if my condition brings back unhappy memories.'

'It does, but your presence at Rotham more than compensates for that.' He stared into the fire. 'It was my fault, you see.'

'My lord—'

'I loved her too much, and she—she could deny me nothing. I wore her out.'

He put a hand across his eyes. They were sitting together on the sofa before the fire and she touched his arm.

'Lord Rotham, I am sure—'

He shook his head.

'There is no excuse. She was delicate and I was too hot-headed, too passionate.' He put his weight on his stick to get up and walk to the hearth. 'I only realised what I had lost after she had died. But I made sure Gideon knew of it. I would not have him make the same mistake in his own marriage.'

Dominique thought of Gideon's letters. They were cheery, full of the entertainments and diversions he was enjoying. She could not believe he had gone away to avoid temptation.

'I think your case was very different,' she said candidly. 'You were very much in love with your wife.'

'Ah.' He rested one arm on the mantelshelf and gazed down into the empty fireplace. 'That is something else for which you should blame me, my dear. I am the reason Gideon plunged into marriage.

'When James was… After James died, I refused to let Gideon leave Rotham. He was my heir and I needed him to learn about the estate. He was a young man and needed to see more of the world, I should have understood that. When he inherited the Telford fortune it was only natural he should kick over the traces and go off to town. I live very retired here, but I have acquaintances in London and what I heard of Martlesham's set worried me deeply. Even then I could not see that it was my own doing—if only I had been less hard on the boy—!

'Last December, when Gideon came home, I could only criticise his way of life. Is it any wonder that he stormed off back to his friends?' He turned to look at Dominique, the sadness of the world in his eyes. 'It resulted in a marriage neither of you wanted and I beg your pardon, my dear.'

Dominique forced a smile.

'What is done cannot be undone, but I intend to be a good wife to Gideon.' She went over to him, reaching out to take his hands. 'My lord, I am not a delicate flower from the hothouse that wilts at the first chill breeze. My mother always told me I came of sturdy stock. I promise you if I am tired I shall rest, but otherwise let me do my duty here.'

He regarded her silently for a long, long moment, then nodded.

'Very well. I will send again to Bolton in the morning and tell him not to call. You must forgive me, my dear, I am an interfering old fool.'

With great daring she reached up and planted a kiss on his lean cheek.

'No, sir, you are my caring papa-in-law and I am very grateful for your interest in me.'

With that she said goodnight and went up to her room to reflect upon everything she had heard. It explained a great deal, but confirmed her worst fears.

'A marriage neither of you wanted.'

Well, she was not the first unloved bride, and she would not be the last, but she would make the best of her situation.

Chapter Twelve

Gideon was restless. In previous summers he had enjoyed making his way from one house party to another, but this year nothing pleased him. Even in Brighton with Gwen and Anthony his mind constantly wandered to Rotham.

He corresponded regularly with Nicky, but was a little disappointed that she did not appear to be missing him. At the end of August he made his excuses to leave Brighton and went to Chalcots. He had visited the house only once since he had inherited it—after all, the Brook Street house was much more convenient for when he was in town, but now he realised that this pretty little villa would make an ideal family home and he began to draw up plans for its refurbishment.

September slipped by as he threw himself into the work at Chalcots, exchanging letters with Nicky on colour schemes and plans for the gardens. With all the work he had put in hand the house was quite uninhabitable and he resided at Brook Street, but did not even consider going to the clubs, theatres and gambling dens that he had frequented as a bachelor. He spent his evenings writing to Nicky, or reading her letters.

He was sitting in his study, the cheerful fire there driving off the first chill of autumn, when he realised with a shock how much he missed her and, instead of picking up his pen, he gathered up all the drawings and swatches into a pile. He would take them to Rotham and discuss them with her in person. Tomorrow.

Once the decision had been made he was eager to get away and, after making sure that the builders and decorators knew exactly what was expected of them, he set off, arriving late in the afternoon, tired and dusty, to find the house in uproar. Servants scurried about, too absorbed to notice him. Intrigued, he left his horse in the stables and quickly ran into the house, but arriving in the great hall he stopped and stared in amazement at the scene of feverish activity. The gardener's boy was carrying in armfuls of plants and flowers while the maids were busy covering trestle tables with snowy cloths. And in the midst of it all, issuing directions, was Nicky. Her condition was very evident, but there was a bloom about her that he had not seen before. She looked…radiant.

At that moment she saw him and, after a quiet word to the housekeeper, she came towards him, hands held out. His heart lifted at the sight of her welcoming smile. He took her hands, pressing a kiss on to each in turn.

'What is this, madam?' he demanded with mock severity. 'I am away for a few weeks and return to find Rotham in chaos!'

She laughed.

'We are holding a harvest supper tonight. I am so glad you are here, you will be able to join us.'

'We have not celebrated the harvest here since Mama died.'

Long-buried memories returned as he watched the preparations and heard the snatches of song and laughter coming from the servants as they worked. That, too, was something he had not heard for many years.

He brought his gaze back to her face and grinned. 'How did you cajole my father into this?'

'I was reading *Robinson Crusoe* to him—'

'Wait!' He put up his hand. 'You were *reading* to Father?'

'Why, yes. It would be very monotonous if I could only entertain him with my music, so we play at backgammon or cards, and when the tea tray is brought in I read to him. I bought a number of my favourite works to bring with me. Lord Rotham enjoyed *The History of Sir Charles Grandison*, and Sterne's *Tristram Shandy* although I have not suggested I should read him Mrs Radcliffe's *The Mysteries of Udolpho*...'

'No, don't,' said Gideon, his mind reeling at this new vision of his father. 'I beg your pardon, I interrupted you.' He waved his hand towards the hall. 'You were telling me how all this came about.'

'Well, Defoe mentions sowing seeds and I merely *suggested* that he might like to hold a harvest supper.'

'And where is my father now?'

'In his study, keeping out of the way.' She tried to look serious and failed, going off into a peal of laughter.

Gideon found himself laughing, too, but he sobered quickly.

'I am surprised Father allows you to do so much. He was more anxious than I that you should not overtax yourself.'

'I am *not* overtaxing myself, Gideon. Your father and I agreed that I am the best person to know just what I can do.' He was not convinced, but she merely shook her head at him, her green eyes full of warm amusement. 'Pray do not be anxious for me, sir. My role here is merely to oversee matters. To prove it, I shall leave the rest to Mrs Ellis and take you away for some refreshment.'

As she led him upstairs to the drawing room, he noticed that the house no longer had a sad air of neglect. Fresh flowers adorned side tables, brass wall sconces gleamed and the grand staircase smelled of beeswax and lavender. The drawing room, too, was much more comfortable. Furniture had been moved into a less formal arrangement, curtains were thrown wide and the hard wooden chairs were covered in cushions.

His valet had also noticed the difference, as he told Gideon when he went upstairs to change.

'Warner tells me the viscount is like a new man. When Mrs Albury began changing things he thought there would be hell to pay, but it seems his lordship is content to let her have her way. And none of the staff have left, either, which was a worry, when the mistress began wanting this cleaned, and that moved, but, no, she's charmed 'em all, just like she did at Brook Street.'

'Yes, well...' Gideon buttoned his jacket, a slight frown creasing his brow '...I only hope she does not find it all too much for her.'

'Not Mrs Albury,' opined Runcorn confidently. 'She's as canny as she can hold together and knows what she is about.'

Gideon bent a searching look upon the valet.

'Do you think her scheming, then?'

Runcorn stepped back, a mixture of shock and outrage contorting his features.

'In no wise, sir! I hears nothing but good of the mistress from everyone who's met her. A proper lady she is, and no mistake.'

Gideon was relieved to know that Nicky was so well respected at Rotham, but he was still concerned that she was doing too much.

He found his opinion shared by the viscount. They were sitting together after the harvest supper, watching as the room was cleared for dancing.

Gideon's eyes were on Nicky as she left the minstrels' gallery after talking to the musicians. He heard his father murmur that she had been up since dawn and must be exhausted.

'She took a rest this afternoon,' said Gideon, 'but it was only a short one.' He jumped up to hold her seat for her when she returned to the top table. 'My father was just saying how tired you must be.'

'Not as tired as you,' she countered. 'You only arrived at Rotham today.'

The musicians struck up a lively tune and a number of couples took to the floor.

'You will not dance.' Her brows shot up and he added quickly, 'I beg your pardon, I do not mean to browbeat you, but I am concerned,'

She smiled. 'And I am grateful for it. You are right, this is far too energetic for me, but you must dance, Gideon. I believe it was always the custom for everyone to stand up together, was it not, my lord?'

'Aye, in the old days,' agreed the viscount, 'although I do not dance now.'

'Then your son must do the honours,' she declared, giving Gideon's hand a squeeze. 'Go along, sir, and do your duty.'

Smiling, Gideon went off to find partners for a succession of energetic country dances. The mood was very merry and the old rafters echoed with laughter and good cheer. When he returned to the top table Nicky pushed back her chair and rose.

'It looks such fun that I must join in.'

'Oh, no, you must not.'

'I have not worked so hard on this party to be denied.'

'Pray consider, madam, it would be most unwise,' put in the viscount, frowning.

Dominique pointed to a lady moving ponderously to join the new set that was forming.

'Mrs Plover is even more advanced than I.' She fixed her eyes upon Gideon. 'I am not so delicate that I must sit out every dance, sir. I may not be able to dance a fast jig, but I shall join in this more stately measure.' A mischievous smile lilted on her lips. 'Which is why I instructed the musicians to play something slower. Now, will you partner me?'

She saw the smouldering fire in Gideon's eyes and wondered if she had gone too far. The viscount laughed.

'Your wife is a very determined lady, Gideon.'

The anger was replaced by a reluctant gleam. And there was something else in the back of those hazel eyes that set her spirits soaring. Admiration.

'I am beginning to learn that, sir.' Grinning, Gideon took her hand and led her off to join the next set.

He felt a curious rush of pride at the spontaneous applause that greeted them. It was something of a surprise to find how well she had been accepted at Rotham. The servants called her 'the new mistress' and even his father had warmed to her, despite her French blood.

The harvest supper was hailed as a success, and although the servants were clearly stifling yawns as they served breakfast the next morning there was an air of gaiety about the house that Gideon had not known for years. Nicky was already downstairs and looking none the worse for her exertions and the viscount was positively jovial when he greeted his son.

'I thought I should be breaking my fast alone this morning,' Gideon remarked, smiling.

He noted the bloom on Nicky's cheeks. The thin, rather nervous girl he had married was gone, replaced by a cheerful, confident woman. He decided he liked the change. However, when the viscount suggested she should rest for the day, Gideon could only agree.

'You must think of the child you are carrying,' he told her, softening his words with a smile.

'But I had planned to take a carriage ride today with Lord Rotham,' she protested. 'It has become our custom—'

'Out of the question,' replied the viscount firmly. 'I would much rather you took a rest today.' He hesitated. 'I thought perhaps Gideon might ride out with me, to see the improvements that have been made to the estate.'

Dominique quickly perceived that she had been outmanoeuvred. The viscount was extending an olive branch to his son and he knew she would not do anything to prevent Gideon accepting this peace offering.

'Yes, of course, sir,' said Gideon. 'But I have the renovations at Chalcots to discuss with Nicky.'

Smiling, Dominique shook her head.

'We can do that later. I shall spend the morning attending to my correspondence.' She added shyly, 'But perhaps, Gideon, if the weather holds, you would take a turn in the garden with me when you come back?'

The alacrity of his assent was reassuring and she went off to write her letters. The windows of the morn-

ing room commanded a good view of the park, and she
happened to look up sometime later to see Gideon and
his father riding off together. They looked to be con-
versing and she hoped that this was the beginning of a
better understanding between father and son.

The pair did not return until late afternoon and
Gideon went immediately in search of his wife.

'If you still wish to stroll in the gardens, I am at your
command,' he told her. 'As long as you do not mind me
in all my dirt.'

'Not in the least.' She laughed at him and, taking his
arm, she accompanied him out to the shrubbery.

It was a beautiful afternoon with just enough breeze
to prevent the heat from being uncomfortable.

'The gardens look better than I remember,' remarked
Gideon.

'Your father gave permission for another appren-
tice gardener.'

He slanted a look down at her.

'At your suggestion? Of course it was, you have no
need to tell me.' He stopped and smiled at her. 'You
have made a great difference to this house, my dear. I
have much to thank you for.'

A stray curl fluttered across her face and Gideon
gently pushed the tendril behind her ear. His hand hovered for a moment, cupping her cheek, and she gazed
up at him, a shy smile in her eyes. He drew back immediately, alarmed at how quickly the slumbering desire deep inside him had awoken. He looked away and
they began to walk on.

'Father and I talked, when we rode out this morning,' he said. 'It is a long time since we did anything
together save quarrel.'

'I am glad. One should not be at odds with one's family.'

He heard the sadness in her voice and asked quickly, 'Have you had news of your father?'

She shook her head, frowning.

'No, it is not that. It is Max.'

'The earl? What has he been doing now?'

'It is rather what he did *not* do.' She bit her lip. 'When we lived at the Abbey Mama gave nearly all her letters to Max to frank, but since moving to the village she has been going to the posting office. The number of replies she receives now makes me think that my cousin was throwing her letters away.'

'It would be just like Martlesham to discard the letters and say nothing about it, if he thought Jerome Rainault was dead.' He patted her hand, keen to give her thoughts a happier turn. 'My father has suggested you should invite your mother to come here, at least until your confinement.' She stared at him and he added, 'Father knows how much pleasure Mrs Rainault's letters give you and thought you might feel happier with her close at hand.'

Relief shone in her eyes.

'Oh, I would. So…yes, yes, please. I shall write to her this very day. I did not like to ask the viscount—'

'Why not? You have shown no fear in persuading him to do so many other things.'

'Ah, but that was for Rotham.'

He stopped and gave her a quick hug.

'Dear Nicky, so brave about doing what you see as your duty, yet you would not ask for something for yourself.'

The weight of his arm on her shoulders, his body pressed close to her own, roused the now familiar desire inside her. The warmth in his gaze quickened her pulse, heating her blood. Their eyes were locked, saying so much more than could ever be put into words—but perhaps that was only her interpretation. Wishful thinking.

As if to prove her right, a sudden flush mounted Gideon's cheek. He looked away, cleared his throat and began to walk on again,

'Father is anxious for your well-being, my dear. If your mother's presence would be a comfort, then she must come to Rotham.'

'I would be v-very glad to have Mama with me,' she stammered, still shaken by the effect of his careless embrace. 'But I do not want to impose any extra guests upon your father.'

He chuckled. 'Rotham is big enough to accommodate a dozen guests and Father need not see any of them.'

'Then I will write immediately. In fact, I penned a note to her this very morning. I will open it and add a postscript. I know she will be happy to come and I will be delighted to see her.'

'Good. Tell her to come as soon as possible. I will feel happier if you have more company, especially as I shall be leaving for Brook Street tomorrow.'

He led her to the wooden bench set into an arbour at one side of the shrubbery and they sat down.

She said shyly, 'Must you go?'

'I'm afraid so, I have workmen waiting upon my return to Chalcots.' Work he had deliberately set up so that he could not be tempted to remain at Rotham, but Gideon now found he did not want to part from Nicky. 'I wish you could come with me—'

The words came out in a rush, as if he had spoken on impulse. They gave her some comfort, but she knew it was not practical and shook her head.

'I wish I could, but such a journey would be very tiring for me now and, knowing how anxious you and your father are for my health, it would be inadvisable.'

'Then I shall return again as soon as possible,' he told her. 'And I must set Judd to finding staff for us...'

'Mrs Ellis has a daughter who is looking for a position as housekeeper,' said Dominique, not looking at him. 'She has a sweetheart, Thomas, the first footman, who is very anxious to become a butler. They would make an ideal couple to look after Chalcots.'

'What if they should start breeding?'

Gideon took the opportunity to place his hand on the swell of her belly. The life she was carrying there never ceased to amaze him.

Dominique shrugged. 'We can always find extra help for a few months, if we need to. And you told me there is a cottage adjoining the stables at Chalcots. They might like to live there, even if it takes a little work to make it comfortable.'

'You have thought it all out. Very well, I will mention it to Mrs Ellis today. If the couple marry in the New Year, then they can run Chalcots for us.' He stood up and held out his hand for her. 'Come, it is nearly time for dinner and I must change—and I have yet to show you the plans I have drawn up for our new home.'

As Gideon made his way back to London he pondered on the change that had come over Rotham—and his father. He was surprised at the way the viscount had taken to Nicky—after all, his father had as little cause to like the French as Gideon and yet, not only had he welcomed his daughter-in-law, he had even suggested that her mother should join them at Rotham. Of course, it could be merely that he was anxious for the unborn child, which might well be heir to Rotham, but somehow Gideon did not think so. It was Nicky's doing. She had beguiled the viscount, just as she had beguiled him.

He thought back to their time in the gardens yesterday, the way his heart had stopped when he had looked down into her eyes. Not only his heart, but the whole world. He had wanted to catch her up in his arms and cover her face with kisses, to show her how much he...

His hands tightened on the reins, causing his horse to shy nervously. Madness even to think of it. She was the daughter of Jerome Rainault, a member of the hated Girondins who had murdered his brother. To feel anything for her would be to betray James.

Yet she was his wife and he could not deny he cared for her—as a friend, perhaps, and a companion, but it could not, must not ever be, more than that.

Chapter Thirteen

The first flakes of snow were falling from leaden skies when Gideon returned to Rotham. It was Christmas Eve and he had been fretting for days about the delays that had kept him in London. The baby—his baby—was due at any time and he was anxious to be with his wife. Since he had left her at the end of October their letters to each other had become even more frequent. When she wrote to tell him Gwen and Ribblestone were now at Fairlawns and that they visited almost every day, for the first time in his life he found himself envious of his sister.

At last the old house was before him, the windows glowing with candlelight as the short winter's day drew to a close. Leaving Sam to take the curricle to the stables, he jumped down and ran quickly indoors, only to stop in amazement when he reached the great hall. He placed his hands on his hips and gazed about him, a laugh trembling on his lips. After the harvest supper he should have expected something of this sort. The hall glowed with the golden light of the fire blazing in the huge stone fireplace. Swathes of greenery—holly, mistletoe and ivy—decorated the walls and trailed from the minstrels' gallery.

A discreet cough brought his attention to the butler, who was descending the stairs towards him.

'Well, Colne, it has been some years since we last saw the hall like this.'

'Quite so, sir. Mrs Albury was anxious to keep up the tradition.'

He grinned.

'Of course. Where is she, in the drawing room?'

'No, sir. She—'

He was interrupted by a shriek and Gideon saw his sister flying down the stairs towards him.

'Gideon! We did not expect you until tomorrow at the earliest.'

'I cancelled my appointments.' He caught her hands, saying urgently, 'Where is Nicky...the baby?'

Gwen nodded.

'She is in her room and Mrs Rainault is with her. Doctor Bolton has been called.'

Gideon felt a cold hand clutching at his insides.

'Something is wrong?'

'No, no, only it is her first time and that makes one anxious. Go up and see her, if you like, and then you can wait with Papa, who is so nervous he cannot sit still.'

'That is not surprising,' muttered Gideon, 'when you think of Mama—'

Gwen gave him a little shake.

'Dominique is *not* Mama, Gideon. Doctor Bolton has every expectation that all will be well.'

Gideon took the stairs two at a time as he ran up to Nicky's bedchamber, where he found her pacing the floor. Her dark hair tumbled over her shoulders and she was very pale, almost ethereal in her white nightgown, but she smiled when she saw him.

'I was praying you would be here.'

'So the baby is coming?'

She put her hands around her belly and nodded.

'Mama says it may be some time yet.'

He had not noticed Mrs Rainault, sitting by the fire with her embroidery in her lap, and he belatedly made a bow towards her. His first impressions had been of a rather absent-minded woman, pins falling from her hair and quite careless of her appearance, but since coming to Rotham she seemed to have become much more sensible and was now quietly devoted to her daughter's well-being. He was somewhat reassured by her calm tone when she addressed him.

'This first stage might go on for hours.'

'Then I shall stay and keep you company.'

Nicky took his hands. 'I would rather you dined with Lord Rotham. He is so anxious I fear he will not eat anything if he is alone.'

He pulled her into his arms and rested his head against her dusky curls. It felt so natural, so right, that he wondered why he had not done so more often.

'I am more anxious about you.'

'Thank you, but you need not be.' She relaxed against him and he could feel the hard swell of her belly pressing against him until she pushed herself free, saying with a little smile, 'Go now and look after your father. I have Mama here and the doctor is on his way. I shall do very well.'

It took some time to persuade him, but at last Gideon went off, promising to come back as soon as he had dined. He found Gwen and the viscount in the drawing room, sitting on each side of the fire. Lord Rotham looked up as he entered.

'Well?'

He said, as cheerfully as he could, 'I am told there

may be no news for hours, perhaps nothing until the morning. My wife is anxious that we should eat.'

'Of course you should,' said Gwen, rising and drawing on her gloves. 'You may be keeping this vigil all night and it will do you no good to go hungry.'

'You are not staying?'

'I must go back to Fairlawns.' Gideon's brows rose and she added in an airy tone, 'Not that Anthony will be anxious for me, of course, but he will want to know how things go on here. Send word as soon as there is news, or if you have need of me.' She kissed her father's cheek, adjured Gideon not to worry and sailed out just as Colne appeared to announce dinner.

They sat down at the table in the oak parlour, Gideon commenting that the chamber was so much more comfortable in the winter than the cavernous dining room.

'One of your wife's many suggestions.' The viscount gave a little smile. 'She has transformed Rotham, Gideon. She made me see how reclusive I had become.' He looked at his plate. 'I do not like to eat while she is...'

Gideon, too, was anxious, but he helped himself from the dishes before him and pushed one of them towards his father.

'Try a little chicken, sir. It could be a long night.'

With a shrug the viscount took a few slices on to his plate, but he ate sparingly.

'Childbirth is a dangerous time, my son. I cannot help but worry.'

'Doctor Bolton is a good man. He delivered Gwen's children quite safely.' Gideon tried to calm his own fears but Nicky was so small and delicate that it was not easy.

* * *

After dinner Gideon and his father retired to the drawing room. They were informed that Dr Bolton was even now with his patient, so there was nothing they could do but wait. They indulged in a half-hearted game of backgammon and were just setting up the board for another game when the doctor came in.

'Everything looks to be as it should,' he announced cheerfully, accepting a glass of brandy from Gideon. 'Mrs Albury would not have the month nurse here earlier, but I have brought her now. Mrs Moss is very experienced in these matters and Mrs Albury also has her mother to look after her. There is nothing for me to do at present, so I will call again in the morning.' He drained his glass and set it down. 'I suggest that you both get some sleep. The child will come in its own time.'

'May I see her?' asked Gideon.

The doctor shrugged.

'Of course, but do not expect a warm welcome—the birthing chamber is the women's domain.'

Gideon went immediately to his wife's room. She had been persuaded to lie down and, despite the nurse's less-than-friendly look, Nicky held her hand out to him.

'The pains come and go,' she told him. 'It is quite natural, isn't it, Mrs Moss?'

The nurse had retreated to a chair by the fire and was sucking contentedly on her pipe.

'Aye, lass, you've nothing to fret about, particularly with your mother and me to look after you.'

Gideon sat with Nicky until her eyelids began to droop. When he was sure she was asleep he returned to the drawing room, where he found his father sitting in his chair, his eyes on the dancing flames of the fire.

'Father, why do you not go to bed? You can do no good here.'

The viscount raised his eyes to meet Gideon's.

'Are you going to retire?'

'Er, no.'

'Then I shall keep the vigil with you, if I may?'

'Of course.' Gideon took the chair opposite. 'I shall be glad of your company.'

Nodding, the viscount rang for another bottle of brandy to help them through the long night.

'I did not anticipate I should approve your wife, Gideon, given her birth and the circumstances of your marriage, but I do. In fact, I have grown extremely fond of her. She has made herself indispensable here. Not that she ever puts herself forwards,' he added quickly. 'She behaves just as she ought and yet, one cannot ignore her.'

'No, indeed, sir.' A smile tugged at Gideon's mouth.

The viscount said quietly, 'I could not have chosen better for you.' He shrugged. 'So her father was French—are we to hold that against her? Your aunt fell in love with a Frenchman, after all.'

'And paid the price for it.' Gideon shifted uncomfortably. 'And my brother, too—'

Lord Rotham put up a hand.

'It is time we put that behind us. However, what I cannot forget is my wife's demise.' He said earnestly, 'Dominique may be strong, but too many babies will wear her out, Gideon. If you are prey to carnal lusts, then take a mistress, but for God's sake leave your wife alone, or risk losing her, as I lost your mother.'

They fell silent. It was not the first time the viscount had told Gideon that a surfeit of love had killed Lady

Rotham, that he had been unable to control his passion. Well, that would not be a problem in this case: Gideon did not love Nicky.

Even as the thought entered his head Gideon realised it was a lie. There had been plenty of passion on their wedding night, but since then he had tried to deny that he felt anything for his wife save animosity for her French connections. Now, however, as the clock ticked away the minutes and the night slid quietly and coldly into Christmas Day, he realised how much Nicky meant to him. He wondered what he would do if he lost her, if she died before he could tell her how much he loved her.

The cushions that Dominique had added to the drawing-room chairs made it possible for the two men to slumber fitfully until the grey light of a new winter's day filtered through the window. The fire had burned down and Gideon was becoming aware of the uncomfortable chill around his legs when the opening of the drawing-room door brought him fully awake with a jerk.

The butler stood in the doorway, clearly having difficulty in maintaining his impassive countenance.

'Yes, Colne, what is it?'

The elderly butler drew himself up and announced in a voice that shook slightly, 'Sir—my lord, Mrs Albury's maid has just come downstairs and told us that her mistress has been delivered of a healthy baby. A boy, my lord.'

'And Mrs Albury?' Gideon held his breath.

A smile split the old servant's face.

'She is well, sir.'

Without another word Gideon sprang out of his chair and raced up the stairs, reaching the landing just as Mrs

Moss appeared, her arms full of bedsheets. The woman grinned at him.

'You'll be wantin' to see yer new son, I'll be bound.'

'And my wife.'

'Aye, well, she's exhausted, but no doubt she'll be pleased to see you. We've just cleaned her up and the babe, so in you go.'

Quietly Gideon entered the room. Mrs Rainault was standing by the bed, a small snuffling bundle in her arms. She smiled.

'Come and meet your new son, sir.'

Gideon glanced at the red-faced scrap, but quickly turned his attention to the bed where Nicky lay back against the pillows, her eyes closed. He sat on the edge of the bed and reached for her hand. It was limp and cool in his grasp, but she gave his fingers a slight squeeze.

'We have a son, Gideon. Are you pleased?'

'Delighted.' He smiled down at her. 'But even more pleased that you are well, Dominique.'

Through the fog of exhaustion Dominique noted his use of her name—the first time since their wedding night. With a satisfied smile she slipped away into a deep sleep.

Dominique's insistence that old traditions should be revived made Christmas at Rotham more festive than any Gideon could remember since his childhood, but it was the birth of young Master Albury that gave the celebrations an added edge. Mother and baby continued to thrive under the watchful care of Mrs Rainault and the month nurse, and Lord Rotham ordered that Colne should treat the servants to a few bottles of his best claret to toast the health of his new grandson, James Jerome Albury.

With each day the viscount became more cheerful, never more so than on the first evening that Dominique was well enough to come downstairs for dinner. She took her place opposite her mother, while Gideon and his father sat at each end of the small table in the oak parlour. Conversation was desultory, until the covers were removed and Mrs Rainault announced that she should be thinking of returning to Martlesham.

'I have rather neglected my letter writing since being here with you,' she told Dominique, when she protested.

'Surely you can write your letters anywhere,' remarked the viscount.

'Why, yes, my lord, but I have taken advantage of your hospitality long enough.'

The viscount sat back and steepled his long fingers together.

'I wonder, ma'am, if you might consider moving to Rotham? I own a small house in the village that is empty at present.' He cleared his throat. 'I would like to help you in your efforts to find out what has happened to your husband—Gideon has told me of your quest, ma'am, and Lord Martlesham's—er—reluctance to help you.'

Dominique looked up. 'I believe he discarded Mama's letters, rather than frank them.'

The viscount frowned. 'That would not happen at Rotham, I assure you.'

'But we must not raise false hopes,' said Gideon quickly. 'Our lawyer in London has been looking into the case, but we have had no luck at all.'

'Rogers is a good man,' said the viscount. 'I am sure he has gone through all the official channels.'

'I believe so, my lord.' Dominique sighed.

'I, on the other hand,' he murmured, 'will go through rather more—unofficial channels.'

Dominique stared at the viscount. He was sipping his wine, that disturbing twinkle in his eyes.

'Would you do that for me, my lord? For Jerome?' Mrs Rainault gave a tiny shake of her head. 'I beg your pardon, but I know—that is, I am aware—that you have no cause to think kindly of any Girondin.'

'Dominique has told me your husband advocated moderation. I understand he gave up the chance to come to England with you because he wanted to save his king.'

'That is true, my lord, but we have heard nothing for so many years.'

He smiled. 'Let me see what *I* can do for you, Mrs Rainault.'

By the end of the evening it had all been arranged. Mrs Rainault would remain as the viscount's guest until her maid had returned from Martlesham with her belongings.

'I am amazed and so grateful for your father's kindness,' exclaimed Dominique, when Gideon escorted her upstairs later that evening. 'Especially when he has as little cause to like the French as—' She broke off, flushing.

'As I have,' he finished for her. 'I beg your pardon, Dominique. I treated you very badly when we first met.'

His use of her name again brought a flush of pleasure to her cheek.

'But the provocation was very great,' she admitted.

'True, but I should not have reacted as I did.' He stopped on the stairs and turned to her. 'Can you forgive me, my dear?'

Forgive him for marrying her? For making her fall in love with him?

'There is nothing to forgive.'

He kissed her hand.

'You are too good,' he told her, moving on. 'It is no wonder that my father wants to do all he can to help you and your mother.'

'Just to have someone supporting her has made *Maman* so very happy.'

'And what of you?' he asked her.

'I would just like to know the truth. It has been so long and we have heard nothing.'

He put his hand over hers where it rested on his arm.

'If anyone can find the truth it is my father. Although he has lived retired for the past decade, he is not without influence.' They had reached the door of her bedchamber and he stopped, leaning down to kiss her cheek. 'Sleep well, my dear.'

It was the end of March when Gideon took his wife and child to Chalcots. Thomas ran out to open the carriage door, puffing out his chest to show off his new butler's livery.

'Welcome, Mr Albury, ma'am.'

Silently Gideon jumped out and helped Dominique to alight, leaving Thomas to assist the maid who was following with the baby. Just when he thought he could wait no longer for her opinion of their new home, Dominique squeezed his arm.

'Oh, Gideon, it is lovely.'

He grinned and realised how anxious he had been for her to like the house.

'I hope I have followed all the suggestions you sent

me in your letters.' He took her hand. 'Come in out of the cold.'

'Everything is ready for you, sir,' said Thomas when they reached the hall. 'There is a good fire in the drawing room and Mrs Thomas has set out wine and cakes, too.'

'Perhaps you would prefer to rest first,' suggested Gideon as he lifted her travelling cloak from her shoulders and handed it to the waiting footman.

Dominique did not answer immediately, for she was issuing instructions to the maid to take Baby James upstairs. Then, tentatively, she took his hand.

'May we look around first? I am not in the least tired, I assure you. Now that I have a wet nurse to feed little James I no longer have to coddle myself so.'

'It is not only for our son that I wish you to look after yourself.'

Dominique's heart swelled with happiness at his words. She hoped, now they had a home of their own, that he might share her bed again and that his professed affection might blossom into love.

The house was everything Dominique had imagined. The reception rooms were light and elegant, the nursery perfect for a growing family. For *her* family. Word soon spread that the Alburys were at Chalcots and the invitations began to arrive, a trickle at first, but after Mrs Albury's Court presentation they became a flood. She was delighted that Gideon insisted upon accompanying her to all the balls, parties and receptions, especially when they met Max at so many of the assemblies.

'He is furious to see us so content,' remarked Gideon as they drove back to Chalcots after one particularly pleasant evening. He patted her hand. 'I cannot thank him enough for providing me with the perfect wife.'

'Am I?' murmured Dominique. 'Do you really think me so perfect?'

'Why, yes.' Gideon lifted her hand to his lips. 'I could not wish for a better.'

She said daringly, 'You do not d-demonstrate it.'

There was an infinitesimal pause before he said lightly, 'Faith, madam, I spend every day with you, is that not enough?'

No, I want you with me every night, too!

The words were loud enough in her head, but she could not bring herself to say them, afraid to see his warm looks turn to revulsion when she disclosed her wanton desire for him. She tried to convince herself Gideon was afraid for her, that he was trying to protect her, but when she looked in the mirror each morning a tiny demon in her head whispered that she was not the fair English rose he desired.

Dominique kept herself busy, dividing her time between the baby and the round of social calls that fell to her lot. There was no lack of visitors, but she was especially pleased to see her sister-in-law, who called often.

'I can never see enough of my little nephew,' Gwen explained as they enjoyed a glass of ratafia in the morning room after visiting the nursery. 'I sometimes wish that we had more than just the two boys.' She looked a little wistful, but the next moment the shadow was gone and she said brightly, 'And how do you like Chalcots? Is it not too far from all the amusements?'

'Oh, no, it is but a half-hour carriage ride to town and it is far better for the baby to be away from the dirt and smoke of London.'

Gwen's eyes lifted to the mantelpiece.

'I see you have an invitation to Grayson House to-night. Do say you will be there, Lady Grayson's soirées are always delightful.'

'Is Ribblestone going with you?'

Gwen avoided her eyes. 'Oh, he will be at the House,' she said airily. 'Cecil Hatfield is escorting me.'

'Really? I thought Sir Desmond Arndale—'

She was interrupted by Gwen's brittle laugh.

'Heavens, I have no particular gentleman friend. Goodness me, Dominique, that *would* set tongues wagging.'

Dominique was tempted to say that tongues already wagged, but she stayed silent.

'And talking of gentlemen,' Gwen continued, 'where is Gideon today?'

'He has gone to see Mr Rogers, to discuss business.'

'I must say I was pleased to see Gideon and Papa getting on so well at Christmas. I am glad they have put their differences behind them.'

'Yes, we shall be spending more time at Rotham in future, I think. Gideon is taking much more interest in the estate.'

'And so he should,' declared Gwen. 'It is his inheritance—oh, I know he has always felt a little awkward, stepping into his brother's shoes, but nothing can bring James back.'

'Your father has given him several commissions in town to carry out,' said Dominique. She added, unable to keep the slight quaver from her voice, 'Lord Rotham has also written to many of his old friends—in France and in England. Friends who may be able to help us find news of Papa.'

'My dear, that is wonderful,' cried Gwen, reaching out to take her hand.

'It is not just that we might at last find out the truth,' replied Dominique, wiping her eyes. 'It is that Lord Rotham and Gideon should be p-prepared to help.'

'Yes, that is quite extraordinary,' Gwen admitted. 'We were all devastated when James was killed, but Gideon took it very hard indeed. It was as much as we could do to prevent him posting off to France immediately to seek justice—not that there was any justice to be had, as we discovered when *Tante* and the *duc* were executed. Papa was even more determined that Gideon should remain at Rotham after that, and I think he would be there still, if his godmama's legacy had not given him a measure of independence. But poor Papa, I thought he would never recover from the blow of losing his son and his sister to the Terror. He has been a recluse ever since—until you came to Rotham, my dear. Such changes you have wrought there! I truly believe you have helped Gideon and my father to come to terms with the past. Anthony declares you have worked a miracle!'

Dominique accepted the tribute with a smile, but when she thought of lying alone in her bed every night, she knew there was one miracle it was beyond her power to work.

Chapter Fourteen

The Alburys set out in good time for Lady Grayson's soirée, their carriage bowling swiftly through the darkness.

'If you had known how long your business would take, you could have dined in town and met me there,' remarked Dominique.

Gideon pressed a kiss upon her fingers.

'But I prefer to dine at home with my wife.'

A little bolt of pleasure drove its way through Dominique and she leaned closer, hoping for a more intimate embrace. When it did not come she stifled her sigh and asked him in cheerful tones, 'And was your business in town successful?'

'I believe so. I delivered Father's letters and every one of the fellows declared they would do their best to help.' He squeezed her hand, adding gently, 'That is not to say it will be good news, Dominique.'

'No, Mama and I are both aware that Papa could be—that he might not be alive, but just to know the truth would help. We are very grateful, Gideon, to you and Lord Rotham.'

'Yes, well…' He cleared his throat and after an awkward pause he continued in a matter-of-fact tone, 'Rogers and I had a good meeting, too. We decided that the town house should be shut up for the present. I think if Father ever came to town he would prefer to stay with us. What do you think?'

'Lord Rotham would be very welcome at Chalcots, so I agree we do not need the Brook Street house,' she replied, gratified that he should ask her opinion. 'Perhaps it might be let out and the staff retained?'

'Yes, that is an idea. And a good one, too. I shall suggest it to Father when I write next.' He glanced out of the window. 'Ah, we are here. Come along, my dear.'

Grayson House was packed that evening. The hall and stairs were crowded with guests, the ladies' pale gowns a vivid contrast to the gentlemen's dark coats. Dominique took off her fur-lined cloak to display her own low-cut, high-waisted gown of ruby satin, the hem fringed with gold and worn over a white satin petticoat with tiny puff sleeves and a quantity of fine lace covering the low neckline. Now, as she prepared to accompany Gideon up the sweeping staircase, Dominique wondered if such a strong colour was a mistake, but at that moment Gwendoline appeared and put all her doubts to flight.

'My dear, you look positively dazzling in that gown! I knew we were right to put you in bold colours.' Regardless of the watching crowd, Gwen enveloped her in a scented hug, murmuring wickedly, 'And your figure is so much better since having little James. You are positively *voluptuous*, my dear!'

Dominique laughed and blushed at the same time, and when she emerged from Gwen's embrace she found Gideon smiling and holding out his arm to her.

'Time we met our hostess, don't you think?'

Happily she accompanied him up the sweeping staircase.

'I did not see the man escorting Gwen—' She looked back. 'Ah, there he is with her now...Mr Hatfield. Do you know him, Gideon?'

He glanced briefly down into the hall.

'Hatfield? Yes, I know him.'

She was quick to detect the note of reserve in his voice.

'You do not like him?'

'Not particularly. He is a crony of Martlesham's and a womaniser.'

'Oh. Then should Gwen—perhaps we should warn her.'

'My sister knows what she is about and is using Hatfield for her own purposes—I think she is trying to make Ribblestone jealous.'

Dominique looked again into the hall, where Gwendoline was now hanging on the arm of the rather louche figure that was Mr Cecil Hatfield.

'Will it work, do you think?'

Gideon shrugged. 'I have no idea. I have warned Gwen against pushing Anthony too far. He is an easygoing fellow, but he has his limits. As have I. Let me warn you, madam, that I should not tolerate you flirting with such a man.'

'Would you not?' She saw the dangerous gleam in his eyes and suddenly found it difficult to breathe. 'What—what would you do, Gideon?'

She waited, eyes wide with expectation. Would he knock him down? Challenge him to a duel? The intense look faded and Gideon laughed.

'I should lock you up,' he declared, pulling her up

the last few stairs to meet their hostess. 'Ah, Lady Grayson, good evening, ma'am...'

Dominique did not know whether to be flattered or outraged by his comment, but she put it behind her and set about enjoying herself. She was happy for Gideon to go off to the card room and leave her to join her many acquaintances.

It was some time later that she was momentarily alone and heard an unmistakable voice in her ear.

'So, Cousin, you have provided Albury with an heir. I congratulate you.'

She swung around to find the Earl of Martlesham at her shoulder. His insolent gaze swept over her.

'Marriage suits you, Cousin. You have blossomed. But then it is surprising what marriage to a wealthy man can do.'

'We are very happy, I assure you.'

'And how is my dear aunt?'

'Much better now that she is away from Martlesham,' retorted Dominique. 'You tricked her into thinking you were franking her mail.'

'What does that matter? By the time I became earl there had been no news of your father for years. Why should I humour a madwoman?' He leaned closer, hissing, 'And that is what she is, writing her interminable letters, hoping to find Rainault. Any sensible person would have given up long ago and accepted that he was *dead.*'

Hot rage flooded her and she glared at him before turning away with a shrug of indifference,

'It matters not. She is at Rotham now, where she is

respected and valued. Neither of us need concern ourselves with you again.'

He caught her wrist.

'So you think yourself safe now, do you, Mrs Albury? Well, just be careful that this idyllic world you
have created does not come crashing down about your
ears!'

With another fulminating look she wrenched herself free and stormed across the room towards Gwen,
who saw her approaching and immediately sent her
cicisbeo away.

'Whatever has upset you?' she murmured, linking
her arm through Dominique's and carrying her off to
the supper room. Gwen procured two glasses of wine
and a small table in one corner, where they could talk
undisturbed. Gwen listened while Dominique described
her encounter with Max.

'It was not so very bad,' ended Dominique, her anger
fading. 'He treated Mama abominably, but she is out
of his reach now. Yet still he is not satisfied. He cannot bear the thought that Gideon and I could be happy.'

'Then he must learn to live with it,' replied Gwendoline stoutly. 'No one who sees you and my brother
together could doubt your felicity.'

'And yet...' Dominique bowed her head. She leaned
across the table, lowering her voice. 'And yet—oh,
Gwen, he—he avoids my bed.'

'Oh, my poor girl.'

Dominique was obliged to blink away a tear.

'I th-think he still yearns for his actress—'

'No, no, this is my father's doing,' said Gwen. 'He
has convinced Gideon that—how would he phrase it?—
"carnal knowledge" of one's wife is detrimental to her
health.'

Dominique felt her face burning.

'But Dr Bolton sees no harm—'

Gwen squeezed her hand.

'You must remember that Gideon was a witness to Mama's protracted ill health and her early demise. That is a much stronger argument than any the good doctor can put forwards. Papa told Anthony the same thing— I had left the drawing room one evening, soon after we were married, and when I returned Father was giving his new son-in-law the benefit of his advice—*keep your lust for your mistress, my boy.*' Gwen added, a little wistfully, 'Not that Anthony had a mistress, apart from his politics.'

'So, am I not alone?' murmured Dominique, thinking of the poor French Queen and the salacious accusations against her. 'Am I not w-wicked to have such strong feelings?'

'Not wicked at all, love. But I have told you before— sometimes men need a little push to show them just what is under their nose. You should set up a flirt. There are any number of men here who would oblige you.'

'But I do not want a lover!'

'Not a *lover*, Dominique, merely someone to show you some attention and make Gideon realise how desirable you are.'

'There was such a person in town last year,' said Dominique miserably. 'A Frenchman. I nearly made the most terrible mistake, but Gideon f-found me just in time, only he was not the least bit jealous.'

'Well, that was last year. Gideon thinks a lot more of you now.' Gwen looked up. 'Hush now, he is coming.' She cast a mischievous glance at Dominique and beckoned to Gideon. 'So you have found us, Brother.

What do you think of your wife tonight? Is she not exquisitely *ravishable* in that red gown?'

'Gwendoline!' Dominique's protest was no more than an outraged squeak.

'Exquisite, certainly,' returned Gideon. He held out his hand. 'The singing is about to start, my dear, and I think you would enjoy it.'

'Yes, of course.' She rose with alacrity. 'Thank you, Gwen, for your advice.'

'And what advice would that be?' Gideon quizzed her as he bore Dominique away.

'She says I should make you jealous,' she offered, slanting a look up at him.

Gideon laughed.

'I am not the jealous type, so you would be wasting your time, my dear.'

No, thought Dominique as she accompanied Gideon to the music room. Jealousy argued a strong passion and, apart from their wedding night, so very long ago, Gideon had shown no passion for her at all.

By the time the singing had ended the evening was well advanced and Dominique was happy to agree when Gideon suggested they should go home. They sought out Lady Grayson to take their leave of her and found their hostess deep in conversation with Gwendoline.

'My dears, Lady Ribblestone has been telling me of the delightful burletta that is playing at the Theatre Royal,' said Lady Grayson, when they came up to her. 'What is it called, my dear?'

'*Midas,*' Gwen replied. 'We are all mad to see it, Gideon, and I am putting together a party for Friday night. Will you join us?'

Dominique held her breath, but Gwen met her eyes for a moment before she handed Gideon a leaflet, saying innocently, 'I obtained this playbill. You will see that the cast is quite unexceptionable.'

Gideon unfolded the paper and Dominique peeped across as he read it. She wondered whether he was relieved or disappointed to find that Agnes Bennet's name was not there.

'Why, yes, I suppose we might go,' he said at last. 'Will Ribblestone be there?'

Gwen replied with an elegant shrug, 'No doubt he will be at the House until all hours, so I shall not wait for him. But you must all come and dine in Grosvenor Square first. What do you say?'

'I should be delighted,' responded Lady Grayson. 'What about you, Mr Albury?'

'Very well, unless my wife has any objections?'

'No, sir, none.'

'Then it is settled,' cried Gwen, clapping her hands. 'We shall all go to Drury Lane on Friday!'

The idea of the theatre party occupied Dominique's thoughts all the way back to Chalcots. She was so lost in thought that when they reached the house and Gideon asked her if she wanted to take a glass of wine with him before retiring, he had to repeat his question.

'Oh, I am so sorry, Gideon, my thoughts were otherwhere.'

'And have been so ever since Gwen mentioned that comic opera.' He laughed and put his hand under her arm. 'Well, perhaps it is a little late. Let me escort you to your room, my dear.'

'I have never been to the theatre, you see,' she confided. 'We did have travelling players that called at

Martlesham when my uncle was alive. I thought their performances quite magical, but I was only a child then, of course. In recent years the only theatricals have taken place during private house parties and Mama deemed them unsuitable for me to attend.'

'Yes, I can believe it.'

His dry comment reminded her that he had probably been part of those same house parties and she said no more, anxious not to awaken unwelcome memories.

Gideon glanced down at the silent figure beside him as they made the short journey along the passage to her bedchamber. She had discarded her cloak and the ruby satin was almost black in the dim light of the wall candles, throwing into relief the white trimming of the décolletage and the creamy skin rising from it. She had filled out a little since having the baby and this gown showed her curvaceous figure to advantage.

When they stopped at her door he paused. He wanted to drop his head and kiss her neck, run his mouth along the fragile line of her collarbone until he reached that fascinating indentation at the base of her throat, to touch his lips to the little pulse that beat just beneath her ear. Desire burned within him—it was so long since he had lain with her, tasted the sweet fragrance of her skin, buried his face in her hair.

She was looking up at him now, her eyes inviting, trusting him. Mentally he drew back. She was too precious. He would not risk weakening her with another baby so soon.

It does not need to result in a child.

The thought flashed through his brain, but it was closely followed by his father's warning. A wife was a delicate creature, to be nurtured, protected. Not for them the carnal lusts of the body.

'Gideon?' She spoke softly, putting her hand up to his cheek. 'Gideon, will you not come in…?'

He reached up and caught her hand, planting a kiss in the palm.

'Not tonight, my dear.'

Dominique watched him stride away into the darkness. She was sure she had seen desire in his eyes, certain he had been moments away from sweeping her into his arms. She clasped her hands together. Oh, how she wanted him to carry her to the bed and cover her body with kisses! She went into her bedroom and looked at herself in the mirror. What had Gwen called her? Voluptuous. Yes, it was true and Gideon *had* been tempted, but not enough. Not enough.

In Drury Lane the crowds jostled outside the theatre and inside everything was colourful and noisy and chaotic. Dominique clung to Gideon's arm as they made their way through the press of bodies.

'Wasn't Cecil clever, to get us such an advantageous box?' declared Gwen, when they took their seats. 'No, truly,' she continued, when Mr Hatfield modestly demurred. 'I had thought there was no possibility of finding a ticket for this performance. I am sure we are all very grateful.'

Dominique agreed. They had dined at Grosvenor Square with Gwen and Lord and Lady Grayson and she had been a little apprehensive when Cecil Hatfield arrived, but since Gideon was perfectly polite to him she had soon relaxed. Their box commanded a good view of the stage and while they waited for the performance to begin she gazed around the auditorium, watching with interest as the audience poured in. Fashionable gentlemen and painted ladies jostled with apprentices in the pit, shadowy figures moved around in the upper gallery and the boxes were filling up, the lamplight sparkling and flashing off the jewels displayed by the ladies who were taking their seats. Max was standing at the front of a box opposite, but she ignored his exaggerated bow and took care not to look his way again, determined not to allow him to spoil her enjoyment of the evening.

The lights dimmed ready for the short farce that preceded the main event and Dominique gave herself up to the performance, applauding with enthusiasm when it ended. Lord Grayson took his wife off to spend the interval strolling in the foyer and Gideon slipped into the empty seat beside Dominique.

'Well, what do you think?'

'Oh, Gideon I am enjoying myself immensely,' she told him, reaching impulsively for his hand.

Gwendoline laughed. 'Then you have obviously been starved of entertainment, my dear! That was quite the poorest play I have seen in seasons. I am sure I have heard most of it a hundred times before.' She put her hand on Mr Hatfield's sleeve. 'What thought you, Cecil?'

'I, madam? Why, I saw very little of the farce, my attention was upon something quite different.'

He leaned closer to Gwen, laughing down at her in an intimate fashion that made Dominique uncomfortable. Her eyes quickly went to Gideon and she saw him frown.

He rose from his seat, saying curtly, 'Hatfield, perhaps you and I should—'

Whatever Gideon was going to suggest she would

never know, for at that moment the door of the box opened and the tall, lean figure of Lord Ribblestone appeared.

'Good evening. I hope I am not de trop?'

The way Gwen and Mr Hatfield jumped apart reminded Dominique forcibly of the farce she had just seen, but she did not find it in the least amusing.

'Anthony!' Gwen began to fan herself nervously. 'I—I did not expect—that is...'

'I left a message that I should conclude my business in time to escort you here, did I not, my love? I would you had waited for me.'

As Lord Ribblestone came further into the box, Mr Hatfield edged himself to the door and, muttering something about seeing an acquaintance in the pit, he disappeared. Recovering her composure, Gwen tossed her head.

'You are so notoriously unreliable, Anthony, I did not want to risk our being late and missing the farce. It is Dominique's first visit to the theatre, you see.'

'Ah, of course. Now I understand.' Lord Ribblestone smiled at Dominique, who fidgeted uncomfortably.

She was aware of the tension between Anthony and his wife and was relieved to feel Gideon's hand on her shoulder.

'My love, no visit to the theatre is complete without promenading through the foyer. It will be a crush, but it is something you should do, at least once.'

Gratefully she accompanied Gideon from the box.

'We are best out of the way,' he told her as he shut the door behind them. 'They can talk more freely if they are alone.'

'I do hope they will not fight.'

'I wish they would,' muttered Gideon as he led her away. 'Tony is far too complacent for my liking. He could put an end to Gwen's little flirtations, if he would.'

Dominique frowned.

'Perhaps he does not care for her.'

'Of course he does,' replied Gideon. 'He is as mad as fire, did you not see it?'

'I felt it,' she affirmed. 'But I thought I might be mistaken. And—and does Gwen care for him?'

'Aye. Why else would she set up all these flirts?'

'Perhaps she is lonely. After all, Lord Ribblestone is always busy with his politics.'

'Well, she needs to tell him. A little plain speaking would sort the matter out.'

Dominique was silent. She knew only too well how difficult it was to speak plainly about intimate matters with a man who hid himself behind a wall of politeness.

As Gideon had predicted, the foyer was crowded and with her diminutive height Dominique found the experience suffocating. It was almost impossible to see beyond the bodies immediately around her and she was about to ask Gideon to take her back when she saw Lord Martlesham's fair head approaching. Her grip on Gideon's arm tightened.

'It is my cousin. Must we meet him?'

But Gideon did not reply. He was staring at the dazzling beauty on Max's arm.

'Good evening, Cousin.' The earl bowed, smiling. 'You know Mrs Bennet, of course, Albury. Mrs Agnes Bennet?'

Chapter Fifteen

If Dominique had not been holding on to Gideon's arm she would have collapsed, for her knees suddenly felt very weak. She was at last face-to-face with the woman Gideon had expected to marry.

In those months leading up to the wedding Dominique had avoided the woman pretending to be Max's cousin, but now there was no escape and she forced herself to acknowledge every detail of the beauty who had stolen Gideon's heart. Agnes Bennet was tall, full-figured and as fair as Dominique was dark. Her golden curls clustered around her head and the whiteness of those smooth bare shoulders made Dominique very aware of the olive tint to her own skin. She hoped her face did not give her away, for Max was watching her carefully.

'Ah, I was forgetting,' he said smoothly, 'you did not meet Mrs Bennet, did you, Cousin?'

The actress laughed, a dark, smoky sound that Dominique thought was sinfully seductive.

'Of course I'm not really *Mrs* Bennet, as Mr Albury knows.' Her blue eyes were fixed upon Gideon. 'That is merely a convention for the stage—I am not married.'

Beneath the sleeve, Gideon's arm was hard as steel.

'I believe it is time we returned to our seats.' His voice was icy, and with barely a nod towards the earl he turned and walked away, Dominique almost running to keep up with him.

Damn Max, trying to stir up trouble!

Gideon fought to control his anger as he pushed his way back through the crowd. He should have expected something of the sort. He had spotted Max in the box on the far side of the auditorium, but in the dim light he had not recognised his companions.

'Gideon, please!'

Dominique's urgent entreaty pierced the red mist that enveloped him and he slowed.

'I beg your pardon.' She was looking up at him, her eyes dark with apprehension, and he muttered through clenched teeth, 'How dare he try to introduce that woman to you!'

'Max likes to make mischief. We should ignore him.'

'You are right, of course.' Gideon struggled for composure. 'Come, let us go back to the box. I hope Ribblestone has not murdered Gwen, or Hatfield...or both!'

She rewarded his attempt at levity with a strained smile. When they reached their box Hatfield was standing outside the door.

'Ah, glad you are back, Albury. Didn't like to go in on my own, don't you know.' He grimaced. 'Dashed awkward, Ribblestone turning up like that.'

Gideon raised his brows.

'Why should that be?' He added, with barely disguised menace, 'Unless you were intent upon some impropriety with my sister—'

'Oh, no, no, nothing like that. I am at Lady Ribblestone's service, of course. Pleasure to be her escort, but nothing more than that, I assure you!'

'Well don't act so damned guilty, then.' Gideon opened the door and stood back to let Dominique enter before him. He waved Hatfield in, but as the man passed he caught his arm.

'Just how did you secure this box at such short notice?'

Hatfield was watching Lord Ribblestone, trying to discern his mood, and he answered distractedly, 'Martlesham gave it to me. Said he had booked it months ago, but that now he was engaged to join another party.'

So Max had planned this. Gideon felt the slow burn of his anger as he took his seat for the main performance. From his seat he could see only Dominique's profile, but when Lady Grayson leaned to whisper something in her ear, the smile she gave in return was forced. The incident in the foyer was not forgotten.

The performance ended, but although Dominique applauded heartily she could not recall a single scene. Lord Grayson went off to his club and Lady Grayson, oblivious of the tensions in the box, reminded Gwen that they had planned to go on to the rout at Baverstock House.

'We shall be there in time for supper, is that not what you said, Mr Hatfield?' Lady Grayson fixed the gentleman with an enquiring gaze and he floundered hopelessly, unwilling to commit himself.

Lord Ribblestone took out his snuffbox.

'I have ordered the carriage to be waiting and I intend to return to Grosvenor Square.' He looked towards his wife. 'Will you come with me, madam?'

Dominique held her breath, willing Gwendoline to go home with her husband.

'But I am pledged to go to the rout,' said Gwen, tossing her head.

For a long moment no one stirred. The atmosphere was brittle as glass. Lord Ribblestone put away his snuffbox and Dominique thought she saw the veriest tightening of his mouth.

'As you will, my dear.'

He departed and Mr Hatfield gave an audible sigh of relief. Gwen did not look very happy with her victory and impulsively Dominique touched her arm.

'Let Gideon run after Anthony and tell him that you have changed your mind.'

'But I have not,' protested Gwendoline, shaking off her hand. 'La, that I should forgo a party of pleasure to sit at home! If you are ready, Lady Grayson, Mr Hatfield, let us be off to the rout.'

'Shall we go home, my dear?'

Gideon placed her cloak about her shoulders and Dominique immediately forgot Gwen's troubles as his hands lingered for a moment, their warmth seeping through the silk and into her skin. The meeting with Max and Agnes Bennet had dominated her thoughts since the interval. Gideon's face was a polite mask, but she had no doubt that he, too, was thinking of it. Dominique understood only too clearly why Gideon had wanted to marry the actress. She was everything that Dominique was not—tall, fair and beautiful—and no doubt well versed in the art of pleasing a man.

All through the comic opera Dominique had thought about her. As the musicians played she had heard that dark, smoky laugh, remembered the graceful beauty, the cerulean-blue eyes and painted lips curving into an alluring smile. It was useless to remind herself that she was Gideon's wife, the mother of his child. If his own father advocated taking a mistress, why should he not give in to the temptation?

In the darkness of their carriage as they drove back to Chalcots he reached for her hand.

'You are very quiet.'

'I am fatigued. It has been a long evening.'

'I hope you are not fretting about your cousin. Or Mrs Bennet.'

'No, of course not.' She was glad he could not see her face in the darkness. She added, unable to help herself, 'She is very beautiful.'

'Exquisite.' Her heart sank. 'But you have nothing to fear from her, Dominique. I have no intention of renewing that particular acquaintance.'

Fine words, but would he be able to resist, having seen her again? Only time would tell.

'Dominique?'

'Yes?'

'You do believe me, don't you?

'Yes. I believe you.'

'That is good.' He kissed her hand and squeezed it before letting it go so that he could put his arm about her. 'If there is anything troubling you, anything at all, you must tell me. Do you understand?'

She leaned against his shoulder, breathing in the familiar scent of him, the mixture of soap and clean linen and the faint spicy cologne he wore on his skin.

'I understand.'

But when they reached the house, he kissed her gently and left her at the bedroom door. As he always did.

* * *

Gideon found his wife very quiet the following morning and she did not greet him with her usual sunny smile. He poured himself a coffee and was debating whether to ask her what was the matter when the butler came in to tell him that the carriage had just returned from Brook Street.

'Ah, yes, thank you, Thomas.' Gideon put down his cup and addressed Dominique. 'Rogers told me yesterday that he has a tenant for my father's house, so I asked Mrs Wilkins to clear the rooms of all our personal effects and send them here. There should not be much, but perhaps you would like to tell the servants where you want everything stored?'

'Yes, of course.' She began to fold her napkin.

Gideon raised his brows.

'You do not need to dash off immediately, my dear. The luggage will wait.'

"No, I—um—I have finished here, thank you. I shall deal with it now.'

Gideon watched her go, a faint crease in his brow. There were dark circles beneath her eyes, but surely they were not caused by the events at the theatre, for he had reassured her that she had nothing to fear. Seeing Agnes on Max's arm had been a shock, but Gideon was surprised at how little he now felt for the woman. Perhaps Dominique was fretting over the baby. He decided he would visit the nursery when he had broken his fast, but when he got there Nurse assured him that Baby James was giving no cause for concern. He went off to his study, still frowning.

Was Gwen's behaviour causing Nicky to be anxious? There was no doubt that his sister was playing a dangerous game with her flirts and cicisbeos. Gideon did not believe she had taken a lover, but if she meant to make Ribblestone jealous by her actions then he feared she would find herself far off the mark. They were dining at Grosvenor Square that evening, so perhaps he would take the opportunity to drop a word of warning in Gwen's ear. Anthony was as easy-going as a man could be, but he would only stand her nonsense for so long. Gideon tried to think what he would do if Dominique were to tease him in the same way and was shocked at the anger that shot through him. He was obliged to push the idea away as he sat down at his desk and began to go through the post that Thomas had left there for him. If there was nothing urgent he would find Dominique and invite her to ride out with him. That might help to dispel whatever worries had driven the smile from her eyes.

The pile of letters was small: a few tradesmen's bills, a note from Rogers, confirming the arrangements for letting the house in Brook Street, and a small, sealed note that had been delivered by hand. He broke the seal and unfolded the paper, his jaw tightening as he read through the neatly written lines.

Dominique stood in the hall, looking at the boxes, bags and portmanteaux before her. She consigned them all to the attics, with the exception of the battered and corded trunk that Max had sent from Martlesham. Her eyes dwelled thoughtfully on the door to the oak parlour, where Gideon was finishing his breakfast, then with sudden decision she directed the servants to take the trunk to her bedchamber.

Mindful of the instructions in the letter, Gideon drove to Piccadilly and left Sam in charge of the curricle while he made his way on foot into Green Park.

He strode quickly to the area between the reservoir and the Lodge and as he approached, a cloaked figure turned and he found himself looking into the beautiful face of Agnes Bennet.

'We'd best walk on,' she murmured. 'It will look less suspicious if anyone should see us.'

There was a flatness to her vowels that he had not heard before. She was no longer trying to pretend she was a lady.

'You wanted to see me,' he said, falling into step beside her.

'Lord Martlesham ordered it.' She met his sceptical glance and looked away quickly. 'He threatened to break my arm if I did not do so. He wants me to make mischief between you and your wife.'

'And do you think you can?'

She shrugged. 'I don't even want to try. Making trouble between a man and his wife ain't my style. Martlesham played you both false last year when he contrived your marriage.' She paused. 'I wasn't easy about that, but if I hadn't done it he'd have found someone else. And he was paying me so very well it was impossible to refuse. I thought it would be a little harmless jollity—'

'Harmless!'

She flushed.

'I did not realise he meant to carry it through to a full marriage ceremony. When I heard—' She looked up at him. 'That was a cruel trick to play on you and on the young lady. I apologise.'

'Is that why you wanted to meet, to salve your conscience with an apology?' Gideon could not stop his lip curling in derision. 'Is that the important matter you wanted to discuss?'

'No! No, although I am glad of the opportunity to tell you I regret my part in the whole thing.'

'What, then?'

'I've information for you, about your wife's dowry.'

'My wife has no dowry. You yourself informed me of the fact when you were impersonating her.'

'That is what Martlesham told me and what he wants you to believe.'

'And now he wants you to tell me differently.'

'No.' She sighed. 'I had best explain. When Martlesham returned to town this spring he sought me out. He wanted to make me his mistress.' She gave a humourless little laugh. 'I am aware of my attractions, but I knew that was not the whole of it, because when I refused his advances he still took me to live with him—made it impossible to refuse him, if you want to know the truth. He believes you're still in love with me—no need to tell me that ain't true because I could see as much last night.' She paused and looked up at him, a sudden smile lighting her eyes. 'We enjoyed those weeks together last spring, didn't we? But it was never going to last, I knew that.'

Looking down into her face, she did not seem quite as bewitching as he remembered. She was still beautiful, but somehow the perfect features and intensely blue eyes failed to rouse any desire in Gideon. Her smile grew rueful, as if she could read his mind. With an expressive little shrug she continued.

'Max installed me in his London house, where he parades me in front of his friends as his mistress—he hasn't yet got me into his bed, but he will, in time.' She rubbed her arms and shuddered a little. Gideon had the impression that she was not at all happy with her current situation. 'He made me give up the stage and insists I remain in the house, even when he is out at some entertainment. The servants ignore me when they can, which suits me very well. I have spent my time exploring.' She looked up, her blue eyes cold as ice. 'I will tell you now, Gideon, that I do not like Martlesham. He is a cruel man.'

'Then why don't you leave him?'

'I intend to, but he is powerful, so I have to be careful. Whenever I am alone in his house I spend my time looking through his papers, trying to find something to give me a hold over him.'

'And have you succeeded?'

She shook her head.

'No. He is as careful as he is bad and most of his papers are in a strong-room. However, there is a locked drawer in his desk—he keeps the key, but it is a simple matter to open it.' She grinned. 'I knew a picklock once, and he showed me how to do it. At the back of the drawer I found some letters from France, from Jerome Rainault.'

'My wife's father,' said Gideon. 'But surely they are in French?'

Agnes nodded and allowed herself another smile. 'They are, but that language is something else I picked up in my career! The letters were written years ago, to Max's father. Monsieur Rainault consigns his wife and daughter to the earl's care, but he is also anxious that little Dominique should have a dowry. He transferred a large amount of money from a French bank to Coutts, in the Strand. Martlesham holds it in trust for Mrs Rainault and her daughter.'

'They certainly have no money now,' said Gideon, frowning.

'I know,' replied Agnes. 'The earl told me that Mrs Rainault and her daughter were his pensioners.'

'Then it is all spent.'

'That was my thought,' she said slowly. 'Until I saw a letter yesterday morning, from Coutts, concerning the Rainault funds. They have never been touched and Max wants them transferred to his own account.'

'The devil!' exclaimed Gideon. 'I must see these documents.'

'I thought that might be the case.'

'You did not bring them with you?'

'No, it was only after I saw you and your wife at the theatre last night that I decided to tell you, and I have not had a chance to get back into Max's study.'

'Why?' Gideon stopped and turned to face her. 'Why should you want to help me now?'

She spread her hands.

'I told you, I don't hold with the earl's trickery. I'm up for a bit of fun, but he carried it too far, making that poor chit marry you. And you don't need to tell me that he forced her into it, because I know his ways. And besides...' she wrapped her arms around herself again, as if for protection '...I should be glad to see his lordship get a taste of his own medicine.'

'Do you think you can still get those papers?'

'Yes. The earl will be out tomorrow morning, taking his boxing lesson. That will be my chance. He ordered me to see you—to entice you—so he will not be surprised if I want the carriage again.' She stopped and Gideon noticed that they had come full circle. 'Meet me here again tomorrow, at noon.'

He hesitated.

'You realise the risk, if Max should discover what you are about—'

She laughed. 'He won't. Don't you worry about me, dearie. I have funds. He doesn't know my real name, nor that I have a house of my own in Covent Garden that I rent out. I bought it with the money he gave me for my performance as his cousin. I shan't hang around once I have given you the papers. But first, I want to pay him back, just a little.'

With a nod she left him, hurrying away through the trees, never once stopping to look back.

Gideon drove back to Chalcots, barely noticing the route. If what Agnes said was true, then Dominique was not the penniless bride she thought herself and he knew how much it would please her to know that. It was a risk, of course. This could be one more elaborate plot by Martlesham to drive a wedge between them, but instinct told him Agnes was sincere.

Should he tell Dominique? He had promised her he would not renew his acquaintance with Agnes, but surely this was different. And it might all come to nought. As he deftly turned the curricle through the gates and bowled along the drive towards Chalcots he decided he would say nothing until he had the papers and knew them to be genuine. If they were, then Dominique would be delighted and he was beginning to realise just how much her happiness meant to him.

Dominique stood alone in her bedchamber and gazed at the open trunk. She remembered when she and Gwen had sorted through its contents, pulling out shifts and negligees, finely embroidered stockings and gowns of such sheer muslin they could be folded and packed into a pocket book. Highly improper, all of them. The sort of things a mistress might wear. She lifted out a filmy negligee. It was so fine that her hands were visible, even through two layers of muslin. In her mind's eye Dominique could see Agnes Bennet wearing such a gown, standing before Gideon, offering herself to him.

'No! No, she shan't have him.'

'Did you call me, ma'am?'

Dominique quickly dropped the gossamer-thin garment back into the trunk and was closing the lid as her maid came into the room. A shimmering gown rested across her arms.

'I was just looking out your green sarcenet, ma'am, for you to wear this evening, but if you would like something else…'

'I *would* like something else,' declared Dominique. 'Fetch me my ruby satin, if you please.' She glanced at the trunk. 'But before that, bring me a glass of ratafia—a large glass, I think.'

An hour later she went downstairs, a fur-lined cloak over one arm, her free hand gripping the bannister. Perhaps it had not been wise to have a second glass of liqueur, but the idea of seducing her husband was rather alarming, and she felt in need of a little sustenance.

A footman jumped to open the drawing-room door for her and as she entered she had to resist the urge to pull up her low décolletage. Gideon was standing by the sideboard, pouring himself a glass of wine, but the rustle of her skirts alerted him. He glanced up.

Dominique experienced no little satisfaction as his eyes widened and the hand pouring the wine shook, spilling a few drops on to the white tray cloth. Gideon cleared his throat and bent a searching look upon her.

'Is that a new gown?'

'No, sir. I wore it to the Graysons'.'

There was a fine pier glass fixed atop the walnut console table and Dominique stopped before it to consider her appearance. The last time she had donned this gown she had put on a demure white-satin petticoat with puff sleeves and a wide lace edging that had discreetly covered her bosom. Now she wore one of the shifts from the trunk. The effect was quite startling. Instead of tiny white sleeves covering her shoulders the muslin was so fine it was almost transparent and the delicate lace around the neck merely drew the eye to the low neckline and the deep valley between her breasts.

Gideon came to stand behind her and she met his eyes in the mirror.

'The colour suits you,' he said. 'And the way you have of dressing your hair.' He raised his hand to touch the solitary ringlet hanging down and as his fingers grazed her skin she drew in a sharp breath. His hand moved from the curl to her neck. 'Dominique—'

The soft knock on the door made them jump apart.

'Sir, madam. Your carriage is at the door.'

Dominique noted Gideon's blank look and it was a full minute before he could respond.

'Ahem, yes, of course.' Gideon drank down his wine, then picked up her cloak and placed it about her shoulders. 'I could almost wish we were not going out this evening.'

The quiet words sent a delicious thrill running down her spine. So far her plan was working admirably. She peeped up at him through her lashes.

'We need not stay for supper.'

Gideon was silent as he accompanied her to the door and a glance showed her that he was looking quite bemused. He said, when they were seated together in the coach, 'Has anything occurred today, my dear? A visitor, perhaps? You seem...different.'

'No, I have been at home alone all day.' She tucked her hand in his arm. 'That is why I am glad of your company tonight.'

Gideon said nothing, but he did not disengage himself and when they arrived in Grosvenor Square he helped her down and kept his hand firmly over hers as he accompanied her into the house. Lady Ribblestone's brows rose when she saw them, but a number of other guests had already arrived, so there was no opportunity to speak privately then or during dinner. It was not until the ladies retired that Gwen managed to draw Dominique aside.

'My dear, I have not seen that muslin on you before. It is outrageously revealing. What are you planning, you naughty puss?'

'I am fighting for my husband, Gwen.'

'If you are not careful, you will be fighting off everyone else's,' said Gwen frankly. She added, with the ghost of a sigh, 'Even Ribblestone could not take his eyes off you tonight.'

Dominique spread her fan.

'I have no interest in other men. I do not want to make my husband jealous, I just want him to notice me.'

'Well, you will, love, you mark my words,' retorted Gwen. 'Gideon must be made of stone if he doesn't realise that every man is looking at you tonight.'

If he had heard his sister's words, Gideon could have assured her that he was feeling anything but stonelike. The sight of Dominique in that red gown was teasing him to distraction. He found it difficult to converse and even when the ladies had retired he wondered what she was doing in the drawing room, if she was thinking of him. He had frequently found her looking at him during dinner, although every time their eyes met she would blush adorably and glance away. Damnation, he wanted her so badly he could hardly sit still! And he wasn't the only one to notice her. Every man in the room looked her way at some point—even old Mr Severn, who was seventy if he was a day, had raised his quizzing glass and positively ogled her.

And yet it could not be said that Dominique flaunted herself. She behaved with great modesty and charm all evening, but however frequently her eyes alighted on Gideon, he found it was not enough. He wanted to steal her away and keep her to himself.

Chapter Sixteen

'You wife is looking particularly well this evening,' remarked Anthony, when at last they made their way to the drawing room. 'Motherhood agrees with her.'

Gideon let his eyes rest upon his wife, who was sitting beside Gwen, laughing at something Lord Grayson was saying to her. Was this the same unhappy lady he had seen at breakfast? The sparkle in her eyes, the alluring tilt to her mouth, was captivating. Motherhood had certainly developed her figure, which looked truly delectable. The swell of her breasts rose from the low décolletage and the creamy tones of her skin were complemented by the vivid colour of her gown. But he could not forget the droop of her mouth this morning and her slightly sad, distracted air. A tiny worm of jealousy gnawed at him. He said suddenly, 'Do you think she has a lover?'

To his immense relief, Lord Ribblestone laughed.

'No, I do not. I believe this is all for you.' He clapped his hand on Gideon's shoulder. 'If Gwendoline tried such tactics with me, my friend, I should consider myself a very lucky man. I should certainly not be wasting my time chasing some lightskirt in Green Park.'

Gideon's head came up and Ribblestone nodded. 'I saw you there this morning. You know I often walk in the park when I need to think things out before a difficult cabinet meeting.'

'It was not—that is, it is not what it seems.'

'No?'

'As a matter of fact I was there to learn something to my wife's advantage.'

'I have heard some excuses in my time—'

'It is *not* an excuse,' Gideon muttered furiously. 'The woman has evidence that Martlesham is trying to defraud Dominique of her inheritance.'

'So Dominique knows of this meeting?'

'Well, no.'

'And are you going to tell her?'

'Yes, of course, eventually. I don't want to raise her hopes, in case it all proves a hum.'

For once there was no smile in Anthony's eyes as he regarded him.

'I think you are playing with fire,' he said at last. 'But then, that is the way with the Alburys. They have no notion of how fortunate they are in their partners.'

From the sofa on the far side of the room, Dominique and Gwendoline watched this exchange.

'If I am not mistaken, you are causing my brother considerable consternation this evening,' Gwendoline murmured. 'He does not know what to make of you.' She slanted a glance at Dominique. 'That is what you wanted, is it not?'

'I *think* so.'

Dominique clasped her hands tightly together in her lap. Gwen reached over and gave them a squeeze.

'Do not lose your nerve now, my dear. Gideon is quite besotted with you tonight.'

She went off to mingle with her other guests and Dominique was left alone with her thoughts, but not for long—Mr Severn was making his way towards her. With a sad want of manners Gideon slipped past him and sat down beside her. The old man stopped in his tracks, then turned and moved off, muttering. Dominique felt a smile bubbling up.

'You show scant respect for your elders, Gideon.'

'Would you prefer that elderly roué's company to mine?'

His voice wrapped about her, deep and rich as warm velvet, and the glow in his eyes sent a frisson of excitement through her. Dominique spread her fan and peeped at him over the top.

'It would be most unfashionable of me to agree, sir.'

'And who says we must be slaves to fashion?' He leaned closer. 'Shall we make our excuses now? I want to take you home.'

Her heart leaped at his words. It began to thud erratically against her ribs—surely he must hear it? She could feel the hot blush in her cheeks and kept her fan raised as she tried to answer demurely.

'It *is* a long drive to Chalcots.'

He turned to look at her, resting one arm along the back of the sofa. She could feel his fingers resting lightly on the nape of her neck, a gentle, sensual touch that bewitched her.

'If we stay to supper we shall be damnably late.'

Swallowing, she struggled to match his indifferent tone.

'G-Gwen promised us cards later. Are you sure you do not want to stay and play a hand?'

'There is only one hand I want to play tonight, my dear,' he murmured provocatively. 'Shall we go?'

She could only nod. Her eyes were fixed on his mouth, the finely sculpted lips which curved now into a smile so devastating she thought she might melt. The feeling intensified when he raised her hand to his lips.

'I shall go now and ask Anthony to order our carriage.'

'What excuse will you give him?'

She was suddenly anxious and was only partly relieved by Gideon's wicked grin.

'No excuse will be necessary.'

Gwen saw her husband on the landing and stepped out to join him. He was staring down into the empty hall, a little smile on his lips. She reached out and touched his arm.

'I cannot find Dominique or Gideon.'

'He has taken her home.'

'Really?' She clapped her hands in delight. 'She was looking particularly delightful tonight.'

'Ravishing.'

Her smile slipped a little.

'Yes. All the men were looking at her. Including you.'

He turned towards her, a look she could not interpret in his grey eyes.

'I am surprised you noticed, since you were busy flirting with Arndale.'

'Sir Desmond?' She fluttered her fan. 'I was not—'

'Don't lie to me, Gwen. I am growing weary of your games, my dear.'

'G-games, my lord?'

He caught the fan, his long fingers closing it up and pulling it from her hand.

'It has gone on long enough, madam, your flirtations and intrigues. I do not want to come home and learn that you are out at this party, or that rout. I need you here, supporting me, do I make myself clear?'

There was something implacable about Anthony's stern gaze that made Gwen's heart flip. She gave an uncertain little laugh.

'La, you are very masterful tonight, my lord. If I did not know better, I would think you were jealous.'

He did not smile.

'If you do not mend your ways, madam, you will discover just how masterful I can be.'

He held out the fan, and when she took it he turned on his heel and walked away.

'Oh, that was quite, quite terrible,' cried Dominiqiue, when she and Gideon were in their carriage and homeward bound. 'Everyone was smiling when we got up to leave! And, and—oh, heavens. They will think that we, that we—'

'And is that not the truth of it?' He caught her fingers and held them in a warm, sustaining clasp. 'I wanted you to myself, to make love to you.'

'Oh, Gideon.' She tried to make out his face in the near darkness. Whatever the outcome, she must be honest now. 'That is what I want, too.'

With a growl he pulled her into his arms, seeking her mouth, teasing her lips apart so that his tongue could plunder and explore. She responded instantly, aware that this was the first time since their wedding night, a full twelve months ago, that they had come together in passion, rather than the restrained couplings of the marriage bed.

He tugged at the strings of her cloak until it fell away

and his mouth moved to that sensitive spot below her ear, where the touch of his lips made her pulse leap alarmingly. He touched her jaw with light, butterfly kisses, continued down the slender column of her neck, his tongue flickering in the hollow at the base of her throat and making her moan softly. She leaned into him, her breasts hot and aching as they pushed against the restrictions of her gown. His hands smoothed over her shoulders, pushing aside the muslin sleeves and leaving her skin free for more kisses. Dominique reached out for him, fumbling with the buttons of his waistcoat and shirt. She slid her hand under the fine linen and caressed the smooth, hard frame of his chest.

The coach lurched over a particularly uneven section of the road and they were thrown apart. Dominique fell back into the corner while Gideon slipped to the carriage floor. She expected him to jump up, but instead he remained on his knees, gently pushing aside the whispering skirts. She caught her breath as his hands caressed the soft skin of her inner thigh. Where his fingers explored his mouth followed. He slid his hands under her bottom and pulled her towards him, holding her firm while he kissed her even more intimately, his mouth and tongue caressing her until she was crying out at the sheer, swooning pleasure of his touch. Time stopped. The rocking of the carriage merely enhanced the intolerable delight he was inflicting upon her, carrying her out of her body into the soaring, weightless heights of ecstasy.

When at last he ceased the relentless pleasuring she reached out for him, driving her fingers through his hair, tugging at the shoulders of his coat and pulling him up so she could kiss him. Excitement welled even further when she tasted herself on his lips. With a groan he held himself away from her and slid on to the bench.

'By God I cannot hold out much longer.' He quickly unfastened his breeches, pulling her on to his lap. 'Time for you to come to me.'

Eagerly she straddled him. He held her hips firmly and pushed himself into her slick heat. Dominique gasped, putting her hands on his shoulders to steady herself as he thrust again, and this time she was prepared. She pressed down on him, matching his movements, elated by his groans of pleasure as she rode him, exulting in the feel of his hard length inside her. She was almost out of control with the delicious torment, bucking and shuddering, but he held on to her, driving ever deeper into her until the final juddering thrust. She barely heard his shout of triumph for her own head was thrown back, her eyes closed as she tensed and shuddered and her consciousness exploded into a million stars.

Dominique collapsed against him and he held her close, his breathing ragged. Her whole body was glowing, like the hot coals of a fire after the first, hectic blaze has died down.

'Oh, heavens,' she murmured at last, her head on his chest where she could feel the hammering of his heart against her cheek. 'Have I behaved very wantonly? I do beg your pardon.'

His arms tightened.

'You have been quite delightful this evening, if a little surprising.'

Being in his arms was blissful, but she needed to explain so she pushed herself away into the corner.

'I w-wanted you to notice me. I have tried so hard to

be a good wife to you, but you never come to my bed any more. And I—I *miss* you.'

Gideon sat up and straightened his clothes.

'I have kept my distance because I do not want to harm you, Dominique,' he said quietly. 'I cannot forget what my mother went through.'

'Your mama had too many children too quickly.' She clasped her hands together. She had overcome her embarrassment to talk to the kindly doctor about it, now she must talk to her husband. 'I am very healthy, Gideon, Dr Bolton says so, and he also says we need not—need not refrain.' She added, her voice little more than a whisper, 'Unless you do not want me.'

With a shaky laugh he reached for her.

'After what we have just done you will know that is not the case.' He tilted up her chin and kissed her. 'I shall share your bed tonight, Dominique, and every night, if you will allow. And with a little care we can avoid making you with child again too often.' The coach slowed and turned. Gideon lifted his head. 'We are home, my dear.' He replaced her cloak on her shoulders and as the carriage came to a halt he jumped down on to the drive, turning back to hold out his hand to her. 'Shall we go in?'

'I am not sure I can walk,' she confessed as he helped her out of the carriage.

'Then I shall carry you, as I should have done when you first came here.' With that he swept her up into his arms, explaining to the astonished Thomas that Mrs Albury was feeling a little faint.

Dominique slipped her arms about his neck and buried her face in his shoulder as he carried her up the stairs, knowing that if the butler saw the glow on her cheeks it would give the lie to Gideon's words. Somehow he managed to open the door to her bedchamber and dismissed her startled maid.

'There. That will set the household ringing with conjecture! Now, can you stand? I want to look at you.'

He set her on her feet and pushed the cloak from her shoulders before running his hands down her arms and catching her hands. In the glow of candlelight the ruby gown was almost as dark as her glorious hair. A few glossy curls had escaped and now lay in wayward abandon against the creamy skin of her breasts. They were rising and falling rapidly and the fire in his loins began to burn again. He wanted to tell her how beautiful she was, how much he loved her, but when he looked into her eyes and saw the heat of desire in their emerald depths he lost the ability to speak. Silently he pulled her into his arms and kissed her.

Slowly he unlaced her bodice and with a soft sigh the ruby satin fell in a dark pool at her feet. She stood before him in her shift, a gossamer-thin layer that hid nothing, only enhanced the lines of her body and the beautifully rounded breasts, their pink roseate tips delectably visible. He reached out to take the pins from her hair, while she began to undress him.

They did not pause until every last stitch had been shed. They were standing before the fire and he held her away from him, drinking in the perfection of her body, golden in the firelight. She dropped her head, allowing the dark waterfall of her hair to shimmer over her body. Gently he pushed the dusky locks back over her shoulders, then put his fingers under her chin and tilted her face up to look at him.

'My wife,' he murmured and, unable to resist any longer, he swept her up and carried her to the bed.

* * *

When Dominique awoke she was alone. Sunlight filled the room and she stretched luxuriously, feeling the cool sheets against her skin. She had a new awareness of her body and she smiled, thinking it unsurprising, since Gideon had kissed every last inch of it at least twice during the night. When he had first taken her to the bed they had made love slowly and languorously, taking time to explore each other until desire swept them up and carried them to the final consummation. She had fallen asleep in his arms, only to wake at some point in the darkest hours to find they were making love again.

Dominique shivered a little at the delicious memory. She was thinking that she should get up and find her nightgown when the door opened and Gideon came in. He was fully dressed and, feeling suddenly shy, she pulled the blankets up to her chin.

'Good morning, wife!' He sat on the bed, smiling as he wrested the offending bedclothes from her hands to reveal her breasts. He lowered his head and kissed one rosy nub and then the other, sending little shock waves of excitement trembling through her. Reluctantly she pushed him away.

'What is this, tired of me already?' The warm glint in his eyes robbed his words of offence and she smiled back.

'Never,' she said, shyly reaching up to touch his face. 'It is just that your sister is coming to take me shopping this morning.'

'Ah, she will want to know what happened after we quit Grosvenor Square.' He laughed, catching her hand and pressing a kiss into the palm before sliding off the bed. 'Very well, I shall leave you to dress. What time is she coming? Will you break your fast with me before you go?'

'She promised to be here by ten o'clock so, yes, we can eat together first, if I hurry.'

'No need,' he said, walking to the door. 'Gwen was never one for timekeeping. Don't expect to see her until at least eleven!'

But in this instance Gideon was proved wrong, for the clock in the hall was chiming ten when Gwen swept into the breakfast room, the skirts of her bronze-velvet walking dress billowing around her and the ostrich plumes on her matching hat bouncing quite violently.

'No, don't get up, my dear, finish your coffee.' She put a hand briefly on Dominique's shoulder, then walked around the table to kiss Gideon, who had risen to meet her. 'Dear brother!' She shifted her searching gaze to Dominique. 'Well, what am I to make of your leaving my party so early last night?'

'My wife was fatigued,' offered Gideon, his mouth lifting with the beginnings of a smile.

'Indeed?' Gwen's eyes narrowed as she looked from one to the other, then she gave a little trill of laughter. 'Heavens, but you both look very guilty! You have no need, my dears, I do not need to quiz you, since there is such an air of happiness about you both.'

'So you are off to town this morning.' said Gideon, changing the subject. 'Where do you shop?'

'Bond Street, of course.'

'If you have time, perhaps you would call into Irwin's, on Oxford Street,' he suggested. 'He was fixing a new band on my best beaver hat and it should be ready.'

Gwen pulled a face, but Dominique said immediately, 'Of course we can call there, Gideon. It is not too far out of our way, is it, Gwen?'

Lady Ribblestone gave an elegant shrug.

'No-o, we can as well look in the shops there as anywhere else, I suppose. And afterwards I shall take Dominique to Grosvenor Square for a little refreshment before I send her back to you in time for dinner.'

'Excellent.' Dominique pushed back her chair. 'I will fetch my pelisse.'

As Dominique walked past her husband he caught her wrist. 'I have no objection to you spending whatever you need, my dear, as long as it includes at least one shift as outrageous as the one you wore last night.'

Gwen laughed, but Dominique's cheeks flamed and she almost ran out of the room, dragging Gwen with her.

Gideon drove the five miles or so into town at a steady pace, his mind as much on the events of the night as the forthcoming assignation. Dominique had surprised him yesterday. He stifled a laugh. She had said she deliberately set out to lure him and, by God, she had succeeded. From the moment he had seen her in that red gown, looking so delectable, he had been unable to think of anything else. He had even forgotten to warn his sister to cease her flirtatious behaviour or risk Anthony's wrath. Perhaps there would be time to speak to her when she brought Dominique back from her shopping trip. Dominique. He could even call her by her rightful name now. How wrong he had been to treat her like some fragile creature who would break at the slightest chill wind, when in fact she was flesh and blood, as passionate as he. All those months of restraint, of keeping his distance, of believing she was responding to him only out of duty.

He had thought that the passion they had shared on their wedding night had been a mistake, a heady mix of anger and nerves and wine. Since then he had done his duty, keeping his desires and his feelings buried deep, but it was a long time since he had thought of his wife as a burden, an inconvenience—his wife by mistake. When he had awoken this morning and found her asleep in his arms he had been overwhelmed by some deep, primitive emotion that he now recognised as a profound and all-consuming love. It had cost him something to leave her sleeping, when he had wanted to wake her and tell her of his revelation, but there would be time for that later. First he needed to meet Agnes, to look at those papers and see if they really did mean that Dominique and her mother were not penniless. He did not care a jot that his wife had no dowry, but he knew it mattered a great deal to Dominique and he valued her happiness and comfort far above his own.

He took out his watch: eleven-thirty. He was in good time. He skirted Hyde Park and entered Piccadilly from the west, knowing that Gwen and Dominique were unlikely to come so far out of their way, especially now they were collecting his hat for him from Oxford Street. As on the previous day he left Sam with the curricle and went off alone into Green Park. Several couples were strolling there, but the area of trees where he was to meet Agnes was deserted. He was beginning to wonder if something had occurred to prevent her coming when he saw her hurrying towards him, her grey cloak pulled close, despite the warmth of the late May sunshine.

'I beg your pardon, I was delayed.' She pulled a packet of papers from under her cloak. 'They are all there, including the letter from Coutts' Bank. I hope you can use them to serve the earl a bad turn. Give 'im a bloody nose from me, Gideon.'

'I shall do my best.' Gideon glanced at the papers. He would need to study them, but not here. 'Thank you, for these. What do you do now?'

'I ain't going back to the earl, that's for sure.' She folded her arms across her chest. 'That's why I was delayed. I sent my things off this morning and I mean to follow them.'

'Where do you go?'

She shook her head. 'Best you don't know, my dear. All I will say is that I am to catch the Holyhead mail.'

Gideon frowned. 'That sets off from the Bull and Mouth, doesn't it?'

'Aye, t'other end of Piccadilly. I left the earl's carriage waiting for me on the south side of the park. By the time they realises I ain't coming back I shall be long gone.'

'It is still dangerous,' said Gideon. 'If the earl discovers what you are about, he is bound to search the coaching inns.' He thought quickly. 'The next stop will be where, Islington?'

'Aye, the Peacock.'

'Then I'll drive you there. You will be safer out of town.'

'That's very kind of you.' She shot a glance up at him. 'Is it for old times' sake?'

He laughed.

'No, but when you tricked me into marriage it was the best thing that ever happened to me, so you deserve something for that! Come along. Let us get you away from here.'

Chapter Seventeen

Dominique spent the carriage ride into town warding off her sister-in-law's questions.

'This is most ungenerous of you,' protested Gwen, laughing. 'You arrive at my party last night, looking so ravishing that no man has eyes for anyone else, then you steal away with Gideon before the tea tray is brought in! What am I to think?'

'Whatever you wish,' replied Dominique twinkling. Then, relenting, she laughed and blushed. 'Oh, Gwen, it was *wonderful*. I really think he cares for me.'

'Did he say so?'

'Not in so many words, but I hope that will follow.'

'Yes, I hope so, too,' replied Gwen sincerely. 'He was certainly very loving towards you this morning.'

Dominique hesitated. 'Perhaps you should try the same thing with your husband.'

'I gave up trying to woo Anthony years ago. He is more interested in his politics than his wife. I have positively flaunted my flirts before him and he does not notice.' Gwen's mouth drooped and for a moment she looked very despondent, then she gave herself a little shake, and her generous smile reappeared. 'But this is dismal talk when we have shopping to do. Madame Sienna's first, I think, and then perhaps we should visit Bertram's warehouse and find something to make you another dashy dress!'

Dominique had been quite happy to go along with Gwen's plans, her head still full of Gideon and the night they had shared, but she was forced to put aside her beatific daydreams when they emerged from the modiste's shop.

'Oh, dear,' exclaimed Gwen, 'it is your cousin. Look, he has just emerged from Clifford Street. And he is coming this way.'

There was no avoiding him and, judging by the way his face lit up when he recognised her, Dominique knew he was going to stop and talk to her.

'There is no avoiding him now, I suppose,' muttered Gwen, linking her arm though Dominique's for support. When he raised his hat she said coolly, 'Lord Martlesham.'

'Lady Ribblestone, and my dear cousin.'

His oily greeting immediately put Dominique on the alert. She nodded silently, hoping he would stand aside to let them pass, but, no. He merely looked pained.

'So haughty, Dominique, after all I have done to promote your happiness.'

'To destroy it would be more accurate.'

'No, no, Cousin, your welfare has always been my first consideration. Does your husband know you are in town?'

Dominique raised her brows, saying coldly, 'Of course.'

'Perhaps he has arranged to meet you later.'

'No, he is at Chalcots.'

His smile grew.

'I think not.'

'You must allow Mrs Albury to know best, my lord,' put in Gwen. 'We left my brother taking breakfast.'

Max regarded them with such a knowing smile that Dominique longed to box his ears.

'I hate to disagree with you, ladies, but I think you will find—ah, no.' He stopped and sighed. 'If that is what you believe, then so be it.'

A cold hand clutched at Dominique's heart, but she replied stoutly, 'You can tell me nothing that will shake my faith in Gideon. I trust him implicitly.'

'You trust him implicitly,' he repeated slowly. 'What a good little wife you are to him, my dear. And how I pity you.'

'I do not need your pity. Now, if you will excuse us—'

'And if I should tell you that he is seeing Mrs Bennet?'

'Absurd!' exclaimed Gwen hotly.

Dominique clutched her arm, her legs suddenly very weak.

'You lie.' She glared up at Max.

The triumphant gleam in his eyes only deepened.

'He is meeting her in Green Park at noon.' He lifted his head as a distant church bell chimed the hour. 'Which is now. Why not come with me and we shall see who is right?'

Gwendoline said coldly, 'We do not need to go to the Green Park, my lord. My brother's integrity is beyond question.'

Dominique wanted to agree. She wanted to turn away from Max's tormenting, smiling face, but she could not.

'We will go with you,' she stated, her back very straight. 'But only to prove you wrong.'

Ignoring the earl's outstretched arm, she turned and marched along Bond Street until they reached Piccadilly.

'My dear, this is madness,' Gwen muttered, hurrying beside her. 'Let me take you home instead. I am sure…'

Her words trailed away as Dominique stopped, recognising the elegant curricle and pair trotting towards them at a smart pace.

'So Albury's integrity is beyond question, is it?' The earl's sneering voice only added to Dominique's misery.

She watched the curricle fly past, Gideon intent on negotiating the heavy traffic. At his side was a cloaked figure, the breeze making the voluminous hood billow out to display the unmistakable face of Agnes Bennet. Like a devil at her shoulder, she heard Max chuckle.

'Well, well. This has worked out even better than I expected. Cousin, I am so sorry for you.'

'But where are they going?' asked Gwen. 'Where can he be taking her, and in broad daylight?'

'I have no idea,' drawled Max. 'But it makes no odds to me. She has served her purpose well enough.'

'She has—' Gwen broke off, her indignation too great for her to speak for several moments. At last she said, in arctic tones, 'Pray excuse us, Lord Martlesham. I must take my sister-in-law away from here.'

'Of course, ma'am. If there is anything I can do…'

'You have done quite enough!'

Dominique was rooted to the ground, staring after the curricle. Gwen put her arm about her shoulders.

'Come, love, let me take you back to the carriage.'

Dominique tried to focus. Everything seemed very distant. She saw Max walking away, swinging his cane as if he had not a care in the world. And everyone else, too, was carrying on quite as normal.

'I shall take you back to Grosvenor Square,' said Gwen.

Dominique shook her head.

'No,' she managed, her throat so constricted that it was difficult to speak. 'No, I want to go to Chalcots, if you please.'

'Very well, love, if that is what you want.'

'Yes, yes, it is.' She struggled into the waiting carriage and collapsed into the corner, her world in ruins.

Gideon left Agnes at the Peacock Inn and made his way back to the city to the offices of Rogers & Mitchell. However, when he learned that Mr Rogers was gone out of town he drove to the newly refurbished offices of Coutts & Co in the Strand.

An hour later he was on his way home, well satisfied with the day's work and eager to share his news with Dominique. After last night he half expected her to be looking out for him and to come running out into his arms, but when he pulled up at the main door of Chalcots there was no sign of life. No matter, he would probably find her in the nursery. How her face would light up when he told her that she was heiress to a considerable fortune.

Thomas opened the door and Gideon greeted him with a grin.

'By Gad, you look as if you had lost sixpence and found a groat, Thomas. What is it, has Cook given notice?'

'No, sir.'

'Where is Mrs Albury?'

'She—she's gone, sir.'

'Gone? You mean she has not returned from town yet?'

'N-no, sir. I mean she has gone. Left.' Gideon paused in the act of stripping off his gloves and under his frowning gaze the butler stumbled on. 'Mrs Albury *did* come back, sir, with Lady Ribblestone, but she immediately left again, with her maid, and Nurse and Master James.'

'*What!*'

Gideon dashed up the stairs. Dominique's bedchamber was the first door he came to and he entered without knocking. The room was in a state of disarray, drawers and cupboards open and clothes scattered, as if someone had left in a hurry. He went quickly to the nursery, which was in very much the same state. He was still trying to take it all in when there was a discreet cough behind him and he turned to find his valet standing in the doorway.

'What has gone on here, Runcorn?'

'As to that I couldn't say, sir. Mrs Albury came in with Lady Ribblestone soon after one o'clock and set the household by the ears.'

'I can see that,' muttered Gideon, grimly surveying the empty nursery.

'From the little that I overheard,' continued the valet in a toneless voice, 'I believe they had met Lord Martlesham in Piccadilly...'

'The devil they did!' Suddenly it all made sense. Gideon swung round. 'Any idea where they were going?'

'I am afraid not, sir, but if it is any consolation, they all went off in Lady Ribblestone's carriage.'

Cursing his stupidity, Gideon went back down the stairs, barking orders as he went.

Lord Ribblestone looked up from the letter in his hand when Gideon was shown into his study.

'Is my wife here?'

Gideon wasted no time on pleasantries, but that did not seem to surprise his host.

'No, and neither is mine.' Anthony held out the paper. 'I have only just come in myself and this was waiting for me. It is very garbled, but it appears Gwen has taken Dominique to Rotham.'

'Thank God.'

Gideon sat down abruptly. Anthony walked over to a side table and filled two glasses from the decanter. He handed one to Gideon.

'Trouble?'

'Oh, yes.' Gideon passed his hand across his eyes and quickly explained the events of the past few hours.

'I hate to say I told you so,' murmured Anthony, when he had finished. 'But if you had told Dominique what you were about...'

'I know, but it is too late for that now.'

'Well, I suppose we must go after them.'

'We?'

Anthony's eyes narrowed.

'My wife has gone, too, you know.'

'Very well, but there is some business that needs attention first.'

'Where are we going?' asked Anthony, following him out of the room.

'To White's. I have a score to settle with Martlesham and I will need a second!'

* * *

Despite the early hour the club was busy and they found the earl at one of the card tables. He was surrounded by his cronies, including Carstairs and the foppish Williams. The earl was counting his winnings, but he glanced up as Gideon entered.

'Albury,' he called across the room. 'Have you come to escape your wife's wrath?'

'Not at all,' replied Gideon, stripping off his gloves.

Max cast a smirking glance at his cronies.

'Quite a shock for her, to see you driving through Piccadilly with the delectable Mrs Bennet at your side. After all, 'twas only a year ago you were intent upon making her your bride, eh?' A few stifled laughs were heard, but Gideon said nothing as he walked towards his quarry. Max was still chuckling as he rose from the table and stood before Gideon, his lip curled in a sneer. 'No doubt you have installed the whore in a little love nest of your own.'

'Don't judge everyone by your own standards, Max. Mrs Bennet is now safely out of *your* way, but she did send something for you.'

Without warning Gideon's fist came up and crashed into Max's face, sending him sprawling to the ground.

Uproar ensued. Everyone crowded around and there were some mutters of 'bad form!' but a gesture from Lord Ribblestone prevented anyone laying hands upon Gideon.

'By God, you will meet me for that!' Max scrambled to his feet, his face suffused with rage and one hand pressed to his bleeding nose.

'With pleasure,' retorted Gideon coldly. 'You planned to dupe my wife out of her rightful inheritance and *I* demand satisfaction for *that*. Hampstead Heath. Nine o'clock tonight.'

'Tonight!' The buck-toothed Williams raised his quizzing glass to stare at Gideon. 'Nay, sir, make it to-morrow, at dawn.'

'I have business that cannot wait,' said Gideon shortly. He fixed his eyes on Max. 'Nine o'clock, Martlesham. Be there, or be branded a rogue *and* a coward!'

The sun had set on a cloudless May day when Gideon drove on to Hampstead Heath. He stopped his curricle behind a closed carriage, from which a sober-looking gentleman in a bagwig was emerging, carrying a leather bag.

'So we have a surgeon on hand, in any event,' he remarked cheerfully.

'Are you sure this is wise?' murmured Ribblestone.

'No, but it is necessary. I should have done it a year ago, rather than forcing Dominique to go on with a marriage that was none of her choosing.' He looked up as he heard another carriage approaching. 'Here's Martlesham now, with Carstairs as his second. Let us finish this.'

Gideon talked to the doctor while Ribblestone conferred with Mr Carstairs. They inspected the duelling pistols—a pair provided by Anthony that Gideon had practised with on several occasions—then the combatants took their places. The light was fading fast and a cold wind had blown up. The white handkerchief fluttered and fell. Gideon's arm jerked up and he fired, seeing a simultaneous flash from the other gun. Martlesham collapsed with a yell and Gideon stood for a moment while his brain ascertained that he had taken no hurt himself. Tossing the pistol back to Ribblestone, he strode off towards the curricle.

'Very neatly expedited,' said Anthony, stowing the box containing the pistols beneath the seat and scrambling up. 'And he is not dead, so you needn't flee the country.'

Gideon set the team in motion, glancing back just once as they drove away. Max was being helped into his carriage by Carstairs and the doctor.

'I never intended to kill him. The bullet in his shoulder is nothing to the pain he will suffer tomorrow when the bank informs him that he no longer has any hope of touching Rainault's fortune. Dominique and her mother will soon have control of that.'

'And if he had hit you?'

Gideon gave a grim smile.

'Max has been drinking all day and in this light he had little chance of hitting a house, let alone a man.'

'What now?' asked Ribblestone as they hurtled through the gathering gloom.

'Back to Chalcots for a change of horses and supper, then off to Rotham.'

Anthony sat up. 'Tonight? But it's fifty miles!'

'What of it? The moon will be up and I know the road.'

'So you plan to arrive at the crack of dawn, unwashed and unshaven. That is sure to endear you to your wife.'

The jibe hit home.

'Very well, we will stop on the road for breakfast and a change of neckcloth. Will that suit you? Damn it all, man, do not expect me to wait until the morning to set out, for there is no possibility of my sleeping tonight.'

He glanced at Anthony. 'I want to see Dominique as soon as may be and put things right. What about you?'

What I want,' said Anthony, with unwonted savagery, 'is to wring Gwen's damned neck!'

The Ribblestone carriage arrived at Rotham shortly before ten o'clock, by the light of the rising moon. It had taken some time to pack up everything Dominique thought it necessary to take with them into Buckinghamshire and they had also broken their journey in order for little James to be fed in comfort, rather than in the jolting carriage. The viscount's household was thrown into a panic by the sudden arrival of the two ladies, together with the baby, his nurse and Mrs Albury's maid, but Lord Rotham took one look at Dominque's stricken countenance and immediately gave orders for rooms to be prepared with all haste. Then he carried Dominique and Gwendoline off to the drawing room, where the whole story came pouring out.

'I cannot believe this of Gideon.' Lord Rotham looked a question at Gwen, who shrugged, but it was Dominique who answered him.

'He t-told me, *assured* me, he had no intention of seeing her, after we met by chance at the theatre.' She pulled her damp handkerchief between her fingers. 'And then to discover him driving through town with her—'

The viscount shook his head.

'My son has many faults,' he said heavily, 'but I had not thought this of him.'

'I wanted to wait and see what Gideon had to say for himself,' put in Gwendoline, 'but Dominique was desperate to get away.'

'I c-could not stay in that house,' cried Dominique, jumping up. 'Not there, where we—where we...'

Her voice was suspended. She hid her face in her hands, feeling the hot tears leaking between her fingers. Gwen put an arm around her and gently eased her back on to the sofa.

'Hush now, love. You are overwrought, and tired, too, I shouldn't wonder.'

'Yes, of course. So foolish of me.' Dominique wiped her eyes. 'I beg your pardon. And yours, too, my lord, for descending upon you in this way, b-but I could not think where else to go.'

His smile was kindness itself.

'Where else should you go? You are my son's wife, the mother of his child. My grandson. You may remain here for as long as you wish.'

'And—and Gideon?'

'He will no doubt arrive here shortly, and when he does he may give his version of events. We may yet find there is a reasonable explanation.' Dominique shook her head and he continued, 'Well, let us wait and see what the morning brings. For now I suggest you should take a little supper and go to bed. I have also given orders for your old room to be prepared for you, Gwendoline. It is too late for you to be going to Fairlawns.'

'Thank you, Papa, but I do not want to burden you. Mrs Ellis mentioned another visitor—'

'Yes, Mr Rogers arrived earlier, but that need not concern you tonight.'

Gently but firmly he shepherded them into the care of the kindly housekeeper, who took them off to the oak parlour and plied them with hot soup and bread and butter. Dominique managed to force down a few mouthfuls before retiring to her room. Unhappiness wrapped itself around her like a cloak, but she was so bone-weary that thankfully, almost as soon as she slid between the warmed sheets, she was asleep.

Dominique awoke early the following morning, but was in no mood for company, so she spent an hour with little James before making her way downstairs to the breakfast room. Gwendoline and the viscount were already seated there, together with a gentleman in a brown wig and plain brown coat.

'Mr Rogers.' She greeted him as cheerfully as she could. 'I am very glad to see you, sir.'

'And I you, Mrs Albury,' he returned. 'Especially so, since my business with the viscount concerns you.'

Her worries were momentarily forgotten. 'You have news of my father?'

'Pray do not raise your hopes too high,' Lord Rotham warned her. 'We should discuss this in my study after breakfast.'

'Oh, please tell me now,' she begged him. 'I cannot bear for you to keep me in suspense—and I am sure there can be nothing that Gwendoline should not hear.' She laid a hand on her father-in-law's arm, saying again, 'Pray, my lord, tell me now. Any news will be welcome after all these years.'

'First let me pour you a little coffee,' said Gwen, suiting the action to the words. 'And take some bread and butter, Dominique. You may eat it while Mr Rogers talks.'

The lawyer dabbed at his dry lips with the napkin.

'Well, if Lord Rotham has no objection...?' The viscount signalled to him to continue and the lawyer twisted slightly in his chair to address Dominique. 'I have information about your father, madam, and because it is of such importance I thought it best to come in person to discuss it with Lord Rotham.'

'Monsieur Rainault is alive!' cried Gwen, clapping her hands.

'Exactly, Lady Ribblestone. That is, he was still alive at the time of the last communication,' amended Mr Rogers with typical lawyer's caution. He turned again to Dominique. 'As you know, Lord Rotham took an interest in this affair last year and he put me in touch with certain parties in France, relatives of his late brother-in-law, the Duc du Chailly. We have had to proceed very carefully. France is full of spies ready to expose anyone they think wishes to overturn the new order. However, with patience and perseverance we located your father. He was being held in a remote prison under a false name. We can only surmise that he assumed this identity in an effort to flee the country.'

'That explains why *Maman's* efforts to trace him failed,' said Dominique, adding darkly, 'Those that were not thwarted by my cousin.'

'Quite.' Mr Rogers nodded. 'My last communication from France arrived early Monday morning and I set off directly for Rotham. Our "friends" in France secured your father's release, madam, but even then it was not safe to make this information public. Your father's moderate views were well known and would not be popular with the present government. I was reluctant to apply for papers to bring your father from France as it would alert the authorities.'

'Yes, yes, I quite see that,' said Dominique eagerly. 'So what can we do?'

'We will smuggle him into England,' the viscount told her. 'I shall send a man to France to fetch him home to you.' He smiled. 'How we are to achieve that is best kept a secret. Mr Rogers and I will go away now to thrash out the details and leave you and Gwendoline to finish your breakfast.'

'Well,' declared Gwen, when the men had departed, 'that at least is good news for you, my dear.'

'I can hardly believe it, after all this time.' Dominique shook her head. 'I shall take little James into the village later to tell *Maman*. It will deflect her attention from my own situation.'

'Ah, yes.' Gwen paused, crumbling a piece of bread between her fingers while she chose her words. 'Perhaps Papa is right and Gideon has a good reason for what happened yesterday.'

Dominique put up her hands.

'Do you not think I have gone over and over it in my mind? He told me I had nothing to fear from Agnes Bennet. And then, at breakfast yesterday, do you remember how he asked where we would be shopping and could we call into Irwin's? Why did he not call in himself, if he was going into town? No, it was all a ploy to keep us from Piccadilly.'

'It is all the fault of your horrid cousin,' exclaimed Gwen, getting up from the table.

'Perhaps, but he could not *force* Gideon to meet with her, could he? And he certainly had no hand in Gideon's taking her up in his curricle.' Dominique drew a long, angry breath. 'I thought I could make him l-love me, but no. He might take his p-pleasure with me occasionally, but it is Agnes who owns his heart, and he can never forget that I am the p-penniless daughter of a F-Frenchman. And even if he could,' she said, angry colour returning to her cheeks, '*I* cannot forgive *him* for deceiving me!'

'So what will you say to him, when he comes?'

Dominique's spurt of temper died away.

'I really do not know,' she said despondently.

'Well, you had best think of something now,' said Gwen, looking out of the window. 'Gideon's curricle is at the door. And—oh, heavens, he has Anthony with him!'

Dominique had jumped up as soon as Gwen spoke and now she stood beside her sister-in-law, staring out through the leaded glass. Her throat dried. She had run away from Gideon, taken his child. How angry he would be about that. Her Gallic blood surged furiously through her veins. If anyone had a right to be angry it was she—after all, he had deceived her, lied to her, and that was unforgivable.

There was the low rumble of voices in the hall. She reached for Gwen's hand and together they turned to face the door.

Chapter Eighteen

Dominique flinched as Gideon strode in, Anthony close on his heels. Both men looked tired and grim, but fury blazed in their eyes. Gideon broke the silence.

'Well, ladies. This is a merry dance you have led us.' His voice was hard, his anger barely contained.

Dominique drew herself up.

'Hardly merry, sir. I did not come here out of choice, I assure you.' She stepped back, as if to hide behind Gwen, when Gideon made to approach. 'Lord Rotham says I need not speak to you unless I wish to do so.'

'By God, madam, you are my wife and you will—'

'Yes, I am your wife, sir,' she flashed, 'and you would do well to remember it!'

Turning on her heel, she dashed from the room.

'Dominique, stop.' Gideon ran after her. 'For heaven's sake, woman, hear me out—!'

As his voice died away Anthony shut the door and stood with his back pressed against it.

'So, you are teaching little Dominique your flighty ways.'

'I have taught her nothing, my lord.' Gwen watched him warily. There was something different about Anthony. A tension, like a predator, ready to spring. The anger still glowed in his eyes, but she noted also the dark shadows beneath. She said suddenly, 'Have you travelled all night?'

'How else do you think we managed to get here so quickly? And a curricle is *not* built for sleeping, I can assure you.'

'I suppose you expect me to come back to London with you.'

'Not immediately. You have not forgotten our last conversation, I hope?'

'Of course not, and I really did mean to support you. I appreciate how hard you have been working these past few weeks, what with the peace breaking down, and Bonaparte doing all he can to buy more time with his tricks and stratagems—but you must see that this was an emergency.'

'I see nothing of the sort. I told you I would stand for no more of your games, madam.'

'Flirtations, you called them,' she responded, trying to conceal her unease. 'This was not like that, I was helping my sister-in-law—'

'Yes, helping her to run away from her husband. It would have been better for everyone if you had encouraged her to have this out with Gideon at Chalcots.'

'La, I vow you are grown very censorious, my lord.' She tossed her head. 'I shall not stay—'

'You *will* stay, madam, until I have finished with you.'

She stepped back, eyes widening with apprehension. 'What are you going to do?'

'Something I should have done a long time ago.'

He turned the key in the lock and advanced towards her.

* * *

Dominique's headlong flight from the breakfast room caused the servants to jump aside to avoid a collision and she had reached the stairs before Gideon caught up with her.

'Dominique, listen to me!'

He grabbed her arm, but the fury blazing in her eyes when she turned to him made him release her again.

'Why should I listen to you, when all you tell me are lies?'

'No, believe me—'

'You told me you would not see Agnes Bennet and within *days* you were meeting her secretly. I *saw* you, Gideon, in Piccadilly.'

'Yes, but that was because she had news, about Max.' She waved her hand, dismissing him, and sped up the stairs so that he was obliged to run after her. '*Will* you listen to me, you hellcat? I did this for you!'

She had reached the landing, but his words made her turn, her lip curling in disbelief.

'Oh, yes, that is very likely! You met with the woman you love, the woman you wanted to wed, for *my* benefit!' She dashed her hand across her eyes. 'You should never have continued with the marriage, Gideon.'

'I had to, after what happened on our wedding night.'

Even as the words left his mouth Gideon realised his mistake. He saw the misery flash across her face and reached out for her.

'Dominique, I did not mean—'

She pushed him away.

'Oh, I know very well what you *mean*. You cannot forget that I am half French, can you? You abhor that part of me, even though you might desire my body. But that is how men are, is it not? They c-cannot resist the temptations of the flesh. Our marriage has never been anything more for you than a shackle, a yoke that you do not want.'

'No!'

'You were too honourable to put me away quietly.' She continued as if he had not spoken. 'But how I wish you *had* done so, for it would have been better than *this*!' She took a deep, steadying breath before saying icily, 'You need have no fear, sir. I know what is expected of me. You will want more children, of course, but pray give me a little time to become a-accustomed to your, your *diversions* before you demand that I resume my role as your wife.' She shuddered. 'And do not expect me to take any joy in it. You have killed that. I cannot love a man who thinks so little of me.'

Stunned, he remained rooted to the spot while she whisked herself away and into her room. He heard the key grate in the lock, and the heart-rending sound of her muffled sobs from the other side of the door.

Her last words lodged in his heart like a knife. He raised his arm to knock on the door, but realised the futility of it. Slowly he made his way back to the empty drawing room, where he sank down in a chair and stared blankly before him.

How long he remained there he had no idea, an hour, maybe two. He heard the door open and looked around as Gwendoline and Anthony entered, hand in hand. He scowled at his sister, who looked unaccountably cheerful. Gideon realised Anthony was regarding him and he raised his head, saying bitterly, 'You were right, Anthony. I should have told her I was meeting Mrs Bennet.'

'You explained to her the circumstances?' said Anthony, holding up a hand to silence Gwen's questions.

'I tried, but she will not listen. All she can see is that I broke my word. She thinks I see our marriage as a burden.'

'And is it?' asked Anthony quietly.

Gideon dropped his head in his hands

'At the beginning it was…difficult. But now—' He took a breath, facing the truth. 'Now, I cannot contemplate living without her.'

'Oh, Gideon—!'

Gwen's sympathetic utterance was cut short as the door opened again and the viscount came in. Lord Rotham nodded to his daughter and son-in-law and addressed Gideon.

'Ah, my boy. I was informed that you had arrived.'

'As you see, Father.' Gideon rose, nodding at the lawyer following his father into the room. 'Mr Rogers. I called at your offices yesterday, but you were already on your way here. Before you go back to town, I would be obliged if you would see Mrs Rainault and ask her to appoint you to act on her behalf, then you must call upon Coutts, the bankers in the Strand. They are holding a considerable sum of money for her, including a dowry for my wife.'

'A dowry!' declared Gwen. 'But why? How—?'

'Martlesham,' said Gideon shortly. 'Jerome Rainault sent letters to the old earl, instructing him to hold his fortune in trust for his family. Max was planning to keep it for himself.'

'Rogers will, of course, carry out your instructions, my son.' The viscount moved to his usual seat beside the fire. 'But first he has some news for *you*.'

* * *

So Jerome Rainault is alive,' said Gideon, when everything had been explained.

'We believe so,' said the lawyer. 'Lord Rotham hopes to get him to England very soon.'

'How?' asked Gideon, frowning. 'Bonaparte will not want to let him go.'

Lord Rotham nodded.

'You are right, it must be done carefully. I am sending a courier tonight.'

'I will go.' Gideon's announcement was met with silence.

'Out of the question,' said the viscount at last. 'It is far too dangerous.'

'Rainault is my father-in-law. Who else should go?'

'Anyone,' cried Gwen, her face pale. 'How can you even think of it, knowing what happened to James—?'

'Precisely *because* of what happened to James,' replied Gideon. 'My brother was heir to Rotham. *I* should have been the one to go to Paris all those years ago.'

'No,' said Lord Rotham. 'I ordered you both to remain in England. James disobeyed me.' He sighed. 'He was as stubborn and hot-headed as the rest of the Alburys, in his own way.'

Gideon met his father's eyes steadily. 'I have to do this, sir, if only to show my wife that I do not have an implacable hatred for all Frenchmen.'

'No, you cannot go.' Gwen jumped up from her seat and ran to Gideon. 'Think, my dear. You are heir to Rotham now.'

His mouth twisted into a wry smile.

'And *my* heir is presently sleeping in his crib upstairs, so the succession is safe.'

Gwen gave a little huff of impatience and turned to her husband.

'Ribblestone, pray tell him he must not do it.'

'I will,' said Anthony. 'Not for the reasons you have given, but because from today the difficulties of getting anyone in or out of France are increased a hundredfold.' He surveyed the company for a moment. 'It can make no odds if I tell you now, for you will learn of it in tomorrow's newspapers. We have today declared war on France.'

After a moment's horrified silence, Gideon shook his head.

'It makes no odds. I am still going.'

The argument raged on, but at length Gideon convinced them all that he would not be moved and suggested to his father they should discuss how it was to be done. Mr Rogers rose.

'My work is finished here, my lord, so if you will excuse me I shall visit Mrs Rainault and advise her of the news.'

Ribblestone took out his watch, 'And we can do no more good here, so we will go to Fairlawns.'

With a bow he ushered his wife to the door.

'Ribblestone!' Gideon's peremptory call stopped Anthony at the door. He looked back, brows raised. 'So you and m'sister have made it up. How did you do it?'

Ribblestone regarded him for a moment, a faint smile touching his lips.

'Well, if you want the truth—and begging your pardon, Lord Rotham—I gave her a damn good spanking!'

With that, and another slight bow, he went out and shut the door.

* * *

By the time Gideon accompanied his father into dinner their plans had been made. Only two places were set, Colne informing them that Mr Rogers had departed to catch the night mail and Mrs Albury had requested a tray to be sent up to her room. As soon as they were alone, Gideon explained about his meetings with Agnes Bennet.

'I should have told Dominique about it immediately, Father. It was a serious misjudgement.'

'We are both guilty of that where your wife is concerned,' replied Lord Rotham, sadly. 'Your mother was never strong and I should have taken better care of her, but my mistake was to persuade you that *all* ladies were so delicate. When you brought Dominique to Rotham, she quite stole my heart and I became morbidly anxious for her. If I have somehow caused this estrangement between you, then I am very sorry for it.'

Gideon listened in silence. It was the first time that his father had ever unbent enough to make an apology and he realised how much it had cost him. He looked up and met the old man's eyes.

'You are not at fault, Father. I have been a fool, but I shall do better in future, when I get back from France.'

If I get back.

The words hung between them, unspoken, but Gideon knew that they both silently acknowledged the risks.

They had not quite finished their port when Colne announced another visitor.

'I have shown him into the study, my lord, as you instructed.'

'My original courier,' explained the viscount as the

butler withdrew. 'He will accompany you as far as the coast, but after that you will travel alone until you meet up with your contact in Paris. How is your French?'

'A little rusty, but it will suffice. Come, let us get this over.'

An hour later Gideon went to his room to change for his journey. Once he was ready he walked to the connecting door that led to Dominique's bedchamber and after the briefest of knocks he walked in. She was standing before the fire, rocking the baby in her arms and crooning a lullaby.

Gideon glanced at the waiting servant. 'Please leave us.'

The nursemaid hesitated, glancing uncertainly at her mistress. Dominique handed her the baby.

'Take little James back to the nursery, if you please. I shall come to him later.'

Her tone was gentle, but as soon as they were alone she regarded Gideon with a stony glare, anger emanating from every rigid line of her body.

'What do you want?'

'To talk to you.'

'There is nothing to say.' She turned her back on him. 'Please leave me.'

'I *am* leaving. I am going away. Tonight.'

'Good.'

Her hands were clasped around the bedpost, as if to support herself. Gideon continued quietly, 'Agnes found proof that Max was holding your father's fortune. I wanted to make sure it was true, that I could secure the money for you and your mother before I told you. I was wrong to keep it from you. I beg your pardon for that.' There was no reaction, no movement at all from the silent figure before him. 'I am going to France, to find your father and bring him back. Perhaps that will prove to you that I don't hate you, or your French blood.' He stopped. He raised his eyes to the ceiling, exhaling slowly. 'No, it is more than that. My anger has been misdirected for years. I used it to disguise my hatred of myself. You see, my French was always better than my brother's. I might have survived.' He rubbed a hand across his eyes. 'There is not a day goes by that I do not wish I had disobeyed my father and gone to France instead of James. I thought Father's keeping me here was a punishment for allowing James to die—in fact, it was because he was afraid of losing me, too. I understand that now, because I finally know what it is to love someone so much that you cannot bear to contemplate life without them. Dominique, you say you cannot love me. I understand that. I promise you I shall never force my attentions upon you, if they are unwelcome. But I hope, when I return, that we may be able to salvage something from this mess.' He paused, his eyes fixed on her rigid, unyielding back. 'Will you not wish me God's speed?'

He waited, but when she made no move he turned on his heel and left the room.

Dominique heard the door click shut behind him. Her hands were clenched so tightly around the bedpost that the carvings cut into her skin. She had wanted to run to him, to cast herself on his chest and beg him to be careful, but her anger held her silent and immobile. She could hear his steps in the corridor, that firm, familiar stride, the *tap-tap* of his boots on the boards, gradually dying away to silence. With a sob she threw herself across the room and wrenched open the door.

'Gideon, wait!'

She flew along the passage and to the stairs. From the central stairwell she saw only the flapping edge of his greatcoat disappearing into the hall below. Desperately she sped down the remaining stairs. She could hear the rumble of voices and even as she reached the hall she heard the heavy thud of the door being closed.

'Colne, Colne, tell him to wait!' she called out as she ran. The butler opened the door again as she came up and she dashed past him and out on to the drive.

The moonlight showed her one figure already mounted, and Gideon with his foot in the stirrup. When he saw her he stepped away from the horse and without pausing she hurled herself at him.

'Oh, Gideon, I am so sorry, so sorry!' His arms closed around her and she cried into his shoulder. 'I was so j-jealous when I saw you with her and I quite lost my temper. Please don't go without saying you forgive me.'

He gave a shaky laugh.

'There is nothing to forgive, love.' He put his fingers under her chin and forced her to look up at him. With the moon overhead his face was in shadow, but she could discern the glint of his eyes and it tugged up that now familiar ache of desire deep in her belly. 'Wait for me.'

'Must you go?' she murmured between kisses.

'Yes. I have to do this. For you, for *Tante* and the *duc*. For James.'

'Not for my sake! Please, I could not bear to lose you now. And no one can blame you for obeying your father.'

'Only me. At the very least I should have gone with James—I can never forgive myself for letting him go to France alone.'

'Then your father might have lost both sons and I would never have known you.' She cupped his face between her hands and gazed up at him. 'I love you, Gideon. So very, very much. Promise me you will be careful.'

'Of course.' His grin flashed white in the moonlight. 'I have so much to live for.'

He gave her one last, lingering kiss before putting her from him and mounting up. As he and his companion cantered out of the gates, he raised his hand for a final salute.

Dominique stood on the drive and watched until the riders were out of sight, then she made her way slowly to the drawing room to join her father-in-law. When he saw her he went over to the sideboard and poured her a glass of Madeira.

'So you have made up your differences,' he said. 'I am glad.'

'It all seemed so petty, once he had told me where he is going.'

He held out the glass to her. 'Believe me, my dear, I would have stopped him if I could.'

'I know, my lord, but he is determined, even if it should prove dangerous.' Something in the old man's look alerted her and she sank down on a sofa, saying quickly, 'What is it, what should I know?'

'It *will* be dangerous, my dear. Extremely so, because we are now at war with France again.'

Chapter Nineteen

Days turned into weeks. Dominique busied herself around the house and looked after her baby. She scoured the newspapers every day, but the reports only made her more anxious. Bonaparte's fury at being forced into war before he was ready was manifesting itself in attacks and imprisonment of the English who had not managed to leave France in time. If that was the case for innocent travellers, how much worse would it be for Gideon, if he was caught?

Dominique took some comfort from the fact that Gwen and Anthony were now much closer—so much so that Ribbleston soon told Gwen of the duel Gideon had fought with Max and she promptly passed the news on. Dominique's worst fears—that Max should die and Gideon would then be wanted for murder—were soon eased when the social pages reported that the earl had retired to Martlesham Abbey amid rumours that he was seriously in debt. Dominique could only be thankful that she and her mother no longer lived under his aegis.

There was a small diversion at the end of May when she travelled to London with her mother to see Mr Rogers and go with him to Coutts' bank. The dowry her father had set aside for her was signed over and the remainder of the Rainault fortune was secured for her mother's use, but the knowledge that Gideon had made this possible only added to Dominique's unhappiness. She had not thanked him for his efforts and the fear deep in her heart was that now she would never have the chance to do so.

The atmosphere at Rotham became hushed, expectant, as if the house itself was waiting for news. Mrs Rainault spent so much time there with her daughter that the viscount suggested she should come and stay again until Gideon's return.

'And he will return,' he assured Dominique. 'The family has many friends in France, believe me.'

But as the summer wore on even the viscount's confidence wavered.

'I am sure that if it was not for our being here, and little James, Lord Rotham would return to his reclusive ways,' Dominique told her mother, when they were strolling in the walled garden one afternoon. The July sun was beating down, filling the still air with the scent of roses.

'He has told me how much you have changed his life,' said Mrs Rainault. 'Rotham had grown cold and silent before you came, but he says you brought it back to life—more than that, you restored his son to him.'

'And I am the reason he has gone away, perhaps forever.'

'You must not talk like that.' Mrs Rainault gave her arm a little shake. 'You must not give up hope, Dominique.'

'But it has been ten weeks. It feels like a lifetime. You have been waiting for news of Papa for ten years—

how, *Maman*? How have you lived with the pain, the uncertainty?'

Mrs Rainault smiled. 'With love, my dear. And faith. I always believed Jerome would come back to me, one day.'

Dominique felt hot tears pricking at her eyes. If only she could be so certain, but she was afraid that she had not earned such happiness.

'Oh, *Maman*, we have been so foolish, Gideon and I! We wasted so much time. If only—' She broke off, her head going up as she heard the faint scrunch of gravel. 'Is that a carriage?' She shook her head. 'No, no, it is the wind rustling the leaves on the trees. I vow, *Maman*, I am becoming quite a nervous being, jumping at shadows...'

But her mother was not listening. She was looking past Dominique towards the house, such a look of wonder on her face that Dominique found her breathing interrupted by the rapid thudding of her heart. Fearing disappointment, she forced her unwilling body to turn. The long windows leading into the house were thrown open and a tall man stood there, his thin frame slightly stooped. His white hair was brushed back from a pale brow and a pair of familiar dark eyes looked out from his gaunt face.

'P-Papa?'

With a stifled cry her mother ran forwards.

'Jerome? Oh, my love, is it really you?'

The old man stepped out on to the terrace, holding out his arms.

'Mais oui, ma chère.'

Whatever else had changed, his voice had not. It was firm and warm and brought a host of memories flooding back. Her mother was already in his arms, weeping softly into his shoulder. Dominique followed more slowly, not sure of her welcome. Over her mother's head Jerome smiled. He freed one hand and reached out for her.

'Dominique. Daughter.'

She took his hand and for the first time in many months allowed the tears to spill over.

'Welcome home, Papa.' She moved closer, hugging both her parents before stepping away. However much she wanted to be part of it she realised this was their time, two lovers reunited. Lord Rotham was standing in the doorway, his head bowed. He had one hand over his face and his shoulders shaking. His image was blurred by her tears, but she was filled with dread. She had managed to keep her fears buried deep, except in the dark reaches of the night when the demons would taunt her with the thought that Gideon would never return. Now those fears leaped free and she found herself comparing her mother's newfound happiness with her own bleak future.

But it was not only her unhappiness. She wiped away her tears and went to the viscount, laying a hand on his arm.

'Oh, my lord—' There was a movement in the shadowy room behind him and her heart stopped. 'G-Gideon?'

'Yes,' said the viscount, his voice a little unsteady. 'He is here. He is safe.'

He stepped aside and with a sob she flew across the room to the figure standing in the shadows. Gideon caught her in a fierce hug that lifted her off her feet. He was dusty from the road and smelled of dirt and horses, but she did not care, for when he sought her mouth and kissed her she lost herself in the taste and scent of her own dear husband.

When at last he released her she clung to him, burying her face in his shoulder.

'Oh, Gideon, I was so frightened you would not come back!'

His arms tightened.

'How could I not, when I knew you were waiting for me?' He put his fingers beneath her chin and tilted her face up towards him again. 'I dreamed of this moment every night.' He kissed her again, gently this time, his lips a soft caress. 'I cannot tell you how much I have missed you.'

'Let us go and sit down, I want to know everything.'

'Later,' he said, laughing. 'I am far too dirty to sully my father's furniture. Let us join the others in the garden.' He looked up at the silent figure standing by the open windows. 'My lord, will you come, too?'

'Thank you, no. I shall find Colne and tell him to delay dinner by at least an hour.' He held out his hand. 'I am glad to have you back, my son.'

'Thank you, Father. I am pleased to be here.' He clasped the proffered hand for a long moment, holding his father's eyes until the viscount gave a little nod and walked away.

Gideon kept his arm about Dominique as he led her out into the garden. Jerome and Mrs Rainault were some distance away, strolling through the roses, arms linked and their heads close together.

'They have a great deal to catch up on,' murmured Dominique, following his glance.

'As have we.'

Dominique held him even tighter.

'We read such terrifying reports—was it very dangerous?'

'A little, of course, but we had many people to help us, including some of the Duc du Chailly's family and friends.' He was silent for a moment and Dominique waited patiently for him to speak again. 'There are many good people in France, Dominique. I was wrong to harbour such hatred for so many years.'

She waved one hand at him.

'That is all in the past, my love. And I haven't yet thanked you, for thwarting Max's plans to take my father's fortune for his own.' She flushed and added quietly, 'Perhaps I should thank Mrs Bennet, too.'

'Yes, only I doubt you could find her. But I owe her quite a debt, too.'

'Oh?' Dominique stiffened as jealousy pricked her.

Gideon's arm tightened and she glanced up. He was smiling, his eyes boring into her, as if he could read her very thoughts.

He said, 'If she had not agreed to Max's plan in the first place I would never have married you and would never have known how happy a man could be.'

'Oh,' she said again, her jealousy melting away to be replaced by a tingling excitement deep in her core.

He leaned closer.

'You must come upstairs with me now. I cannot wait until tonight to make love to you.'

She blushed.

'I would like that, but what about Maman and Papa?'

'They will not miss us, and if they do, they will understand.'

Gently but firmly he led her back into the house. It was all they could do not to run through the rooms and up the stairs to his bedchamber, but as soon as they were inside all restraint disappeared. They came together eagerly, exchanging hot kisses even as they undressed one another, tearing off the layers until they could lie upon the bed together, skin against skin.

Dominique revelled in the kisses Gideon showered upon her body and she returned them with equal fervour. She cupped his proud erection in her hands, worshipped it with her mouth even as he gently parted her thighs to bestow upon her that most intimate of kisses. The sensations he aroused with his tongue and his mouth soon had her falling back upon the bed, surrendering to the delicious torment. She moaned softly, shivering as wave after wave of excitement rippled through her. His tongue played her, circling and lapping at her core. Her body arched as she felt the climax approaching. She was almost out of control, aching with pleasure, wanting him to stop and at the same time wanting him to carry her onwards.

She reached for him, her fingers clutching at the solid muscle of his shoulders as he slid his body over hers, claiming her mouth for a deep, penetrating kiss even as he thrust into her. Her body tightened about him and she cried out with the sheer joy of it. He moved carefully, stroking her, taking her with him to that final shuddering, shattering climax, a blinding explosion of thought and feeling as the world splintered and disintegrated, leaving them shocked, sated and exhausted.

Gideon wrapped himself around her and pulled her close.

'My wife.' His breath was warm on her ear as he murmured the words. 'My own.'

She twisted in his arms so that she could hold him.

'And I am no longer penniless,' she told him, gently pressing kisses on his eyes, his cheeks and down the length of his lean jaw. 'I have a dowry now, thanks to you.'

'So you have. I had forgotten.'

She stopped kissing him and he opened his eyes to find her regarding him solemnly.

'Does it not matter to you? Do you not want to use it? We could improve Chalcots, perhaps buy another property—'

He put his hand on her lips.

'Let us settle it upon our children. I feel sure there are more on the way. Besides,' he added, drawing her back into his arms, 'with you for my wife I am rich beyond my wildest dreams.'

* * * * *

Join Britain's BIGGEST Romance Book Club

50% OFF your first parcel

- **EXCLUSIVE** offers every month
- **FREE** delivery direct to your door
- **NEVER MISS** a title
- **EARN** Bonus Book points

Call Customer Services
0844 844 1358*
or visit
millsandboon.co.uk/subscriptions

CB3

MILLS & BOON®